FLARE OF PASSION

"Don't make fun of me, Nicholas. I daresay I do seem to you to be little more than a child but I assure you—"

"On the contrary, I don't think of you as a child at all," he said. I looked away from him, nervously pushing my tangled curls behind my ears. He went on, "In fact, it seems to me that it's you who have been trying to hide behind your innocence and inexperience."

"I don't know what you're talking about," I said in muffled tones, the color rising in my face. "And now, if you'd please excuse me, I'd like to go to bed."

"How refreshing to hear you say that. I'd very much like to go to bed, too." His gaze flickered over me and dropped to my bare leg.

There was a look in his eyes now that I could not mistake—an intensity, a smoldering.

Gathering my hair in his hands, he pulled my mouth to his . . .

THE HOUSE AT THUNDER COVE

MICHELE Y. THOMAS

ZEBRA BOOKS
KENSINGTON PUBLISHING CORP.

ZEBRA BOOKS

are published by

Kensington Publishing Corp.
475 Park Avenue South
New York, NY 10016

First printing: November 1987

Printed in the United States of America

For my parents

Where both deliberate, the love is slight:
Whoever loved, that loveth not at first sight?
                              Christopher Marlowe

Chapter One

I was seventeen when I left India, and I left it with no regrets. When the ship on which I had booked passage sailed away from the shore, I did not watch but remained below in my berth. India was a harsh country; my parents, dead of cholera, were proof of that. And although I had been born there and knew no other home, I had always felt somehow displaced, that I didn't belong, that I was merely filling up space like one of the painted idols in the Hindu temples.

I was not like my brilliant self-sacrificing parents, who were Congregationalist missionaries in the Bombay Presidency. I had tried to be their dutiful daughter but was much of the time a disappointment to them. I grew up in a simple ugly bungalow in the mission station, watching a strange glittering world which went on beyond those walls. It was a world I was never a part of just as I was not a part of the remote spiritual world my parents inhabited.

Not only did I sometimes feel strangely as though I did not belong in India, I also scarcely felt like my parents' child. I was not a brilliant student, not even particularly clever or scholarly in the way they were. Most certainly I was not possessed of the deeply religious fervor which guided everything they did. I said my prayers and asked God's blessing before we ate because those were things we did, not from any burning devotion to the Almighty. I was a dutiful daughter because there was no reason to be anything else.

Because my parents had no close friends, I had no other examples to follow. Consequently, I could not make friends easily. I was shy, tongue-tied, and ill at ease with people.

In the days following my mother's and father's horrible deaths, everything about India became ugly to me and I could think of nothing but departing that benighted land. The other missionaries—those who returned to the compound—were shocked at my decision to leave, and astounded that I meant to travel unaccompanied during the four-to-five-month journey to New England. I tried to silence their objections with my tentative statement that my parents had left money for exactly that purpose. When they asked where I was going, I answered with as much firmness as I could muster, "New Bedford." I tried to say it in the way that they would assume I had a definite goal, a place to go to, a refuge. In truth New Bedford, Massachusetts, was the first destination to which I could travel after Boston, which even I had enough sense to realize would be too large a city for a young girl with no connections.

New Bedford was also a port, an important one, for the nation's whaling trade but I had heard that it was still a small town. I thought that my chances of finding respectable employment would be better there than in some great city such as Boston. Also the little money I had would probably last longer; lodging in New Bedford was sure to be less costly.

No matter how I tried to keep the tremors from my voice when questioned about my plans, I believe I fooled no one. My parents' colleagues likely deduced that I had nowhere in particular to go and had selected New Bedford almost by closing my eyes and pointing to it on the globe. But they left me to myself, for they had the pieces of their own lives to put back together after the losses we had all suffered.

On a hot day in November I boarded the ship carrying spices and silks and other wares to New England. There were several passengers besides myself. I did not have enough money to book a private berth so I shared one with another lady, Miss Upton.

I took very little with me. The few clothes I owned, of course, and my lacquered wooden bangle box and brass swan. My parents' things I donated to the mission station to remain in the house for the next couple who would take their places.

Miss Upton was also departing ship at New Bedford, but she would be continuing her journey by stagecoach to her home in Albany, New York. She was very fond of traveling, and being possessed of an adequate income, she indulged in it frequently. She spent much time scribbling in her notebook about places she had visited, customs she had observed. She hoped someday to gather all her notes into a manuscript entitled *Reminiscences of an American Lady Travelling the World Alone* and have it published, always speaking of this goal in whispers as though by saying it aloud she might render it impossible to be realized. She had visited Egypt, where she had ridden a camel to the pyramids and then journeyed down the Nile, Rome, Florence — she was a great admirer of Italian art — Turkey, and the Greek Islands, before sailing to India. Her next trip, she confided to me excitedly, would be one to Australia.

"Spectacular scenery, I'm told, but aside from the wild Aborigines, there are few people there but convicts, you know. Still I believe my notes would be greatly enhanced by a visit to Australia."

Her lifestyle was enabled to be such as it was by her inheritance left her by her father, who had been a banker in Albany. She was somewhere in middle life but dressed surprisingly youthfully and colorfully. When she thought I did not see, her eyes would flicker over me with pity.

"You have the makings of a beauty," she told me one day, to my embarrassment. "Your skin's a bit sallow, of course, but after all those years in India whose would not be? I had to be quite careful of mine while traveling. And you're dreadfully thin. But that hair, those black curls — you shouldn't draw them back so severely — and blue eyes the color of sapphires. Yes, I'd say you might be quite spectacular someday given the right circumstances."

I was tempted to ask her to identify those particular circumstances. But I was not a product of my parents for nothing, and I knew it was not commendable to dwell on appearances or hanker after impossible goals.

I was miserably ill from time to time when the sea became rough. The storms terrified me, the ship rearing and plunging and rolling and pitching. I would lie on my bunk in frozen horror waiting for the ship to be sunk. But Miss Upton was intrepid at those times and her state of serene optimism comforted me.

One morning when our journey was more than half over, we were eating breakfast and she said to me, "Perhaps I can help you to find a post in New Bedford when we dock. I have an acquaintance there — the lady I'll be staying with before going by coach to Albany — and it may be that she will know of just the right position for you. She's a maiden lady like myself, but she knows all the New Bedford families. Yes, that is the solution. We'll go straight to Grace and ask her."

"Do you think she could help me?" I asked doubtfully. "That would be a blessing. I was expecting to advertise in the newspapers."

"This will be an entirely better way," she said firmly. "Leave it to me."

The anxiety which had troubled me these last weeks lightened considerably at her words. A period of almost heady relief had followed my departure on the ship, but lately I had been plagued with worries of how I would find a means to support myself. I knew nothing of the society and life-style to which I was going. Yet I had hesitated in discussing my doubts and concerns with Miss Upton lest my doing so be construed as an imposition on her good nature. So her suggestion, indeed, her insistence, that we could prevail on her friend to come up with the very thing was infinitely comforting. During the last third of the journey I had fewer headaches, and even the bouts of seasickness grew less frequent.

We docked in New Bedford on a cold March day, the

wind blowing off the water and cutting through my thin gown like icy knives. There was a great deal of activity on the wharves. Men of different nationalities were working to discharge cargo from the sleek ships or taking aboard the outfitting, their strange (to my ears) accents and tongues mingling with Yankee twang.

Miss Upton and I went ashore and waited while our luggage was loaded into a trap. "What are those barrels? There are so many of them stacked there on the dock," I observed.

"This is New Bedford, child," said Miss Upton. "What else are they but barrels of whale oil?"

We rode in the trap through the harbor area, past the ship's chandlery, past ropemakers' and coopers' shops. The buildings were narrow, some adjoining, some not, built of brick and wood. There were many sailors milling about and a few took off their caps to us. She pointed out several Greek Revival bank buildings that we passed.

"Enormous amounts of money pass through those doors, my dear, fortunes made from whale oil and spermacetti. New Bedford is a prosperous place. I'm certain you will have no difficulty finding work."

I was struck by the prosperity of the buildings also. There was a gray granite custom house and across from it was the large brick courthouse with brownstone facade. On our way up the hill we passed the lofty white Baptist church with a decorative, three-tiered steeple; no Christian church in Bombay had come close to it in size or style.

I turned back to look at the harbor. From here I could not tell which vessel had been ours — there were so many and such a fever of activity. The ships' masts made a forest of trees against the horizon.

We turned down a street of large gracious houses, some of stone, some of clapboard, some severe, some opulent. I had glimpses of what looked like well-laid-out gardens to the sides and rears of the houses, now bleak and brown in winter.

"County Street, my dear," said Miss Upton. "These are the homes of some of the owners of those ships you saw in

13

the harbor. Whaling ships, that is. A most hazardous occupation, whaling. I've never been fortunate enough to spot a whale but I'm told they are astounding in size and weight. Their tongues alone weigh as much as an elephant, think of it! And they can grow to one hundred feet in length. What a pity we did not spot one on our journey from India." I, on the other hand, was glad we had not.

The driver turned onto a street of more modest houses and I was relieved that Miss Upton's friend did not live in one of the grander residences. Those homes were such a far cry from anything in my experience that I trembled at the thought of entering one of them.

The trap stopped in front of a pretty yellow cottage with white trim and shutters—like frosting on a cake, I thought fancifully. "Ah, here we are," said Miss Upton.

"Is Miss Spooner expecting you?" I asked nervously.

"Well, I wrote that I would be passing through New Bedford in late winter, Miranda. Doubtless she expects me when she expects me."

"But she hardly expects you to bring another guest. Perhaps"—I bit my lip—"perhaps I should have gone straight to a boardinghouse while you spoke to her."

"Nonsense. No backing down now. When I take something in hand I see it through, and I am determined to do what I can to help you find a governessing position. And Grace will be only too glad to assist us. She's a Quaker, you know; there are many in New Bedford," as though this were of some significance to my plight.

We climbed down from the trap and I stood shivering in my light shawl.

"Come, child, chin up. Grace Spooner is not an ogress, I assure you, although she loves to be thought one. Depend upon it, she'll be the very person to help you."

The door of the cottage was opened by a maid in a mobcap and starched apron. She looked curiously at the two of us.

"Well, don't stand there gawking, my girl," said my benefactress. "Can't you see we are half frozen in this dreadful March wind? This child's not used to it at all.

We've come to see your mistress. I am Miss Upton."

We stepped into the hall, which was papered in a curious design of red and gray feathers. There was a dark varnished trim about the doors and a stairway just ahead, also varnished.

"Violet!" said a booming voice.

"Grace, dear, how do you do?"

The two women did not embrace and Miss Spooner, a large woman plainly but well dressed, said, shaking her head, "Still dressing as though you were half your age. I'd nearly given you up on coming. Thought you must have docked somewhere else, New York, perhaps." But she spoke absently, frowning at me.

"Oh no, I would never do that. I quite dislike New York, you know. This is Miss Miranda Cooke. Seventeen years old, an orphan of a missionary father who hailed from Massachusetts. We met on the boat, quite agreeably sharing quarters."

But why on earth did you bring her here, I could read in Miss Spooner's eyes. "Indeed. Well, come into the parlor by the fire, girl. You look nearly blue with cold. Not used to it, I expect. No meat on your bones either. No stamina, these modern girls."

"Poor Miranda suffered terribly from seasickness, Grace," said Miss Upton. "But you are right. She's much too wan and thin. India was not healthy for her, not healthy for anyone at the end. We're both lucky we escaped with our lives—cholera, you know. And she's had no bracing air or proper diet either, I imagine. You know the missionaries," she added in an undertone to Miss Spooner as I moved closer to the fire, "self-denial and all that."

"Hmmmph. I donate a generous amount every month to the mission fund, Violet, as do many others I know. Alice, bring us tea." The maid who had followed us into the parlor curtsied and withdrew.

"Well, with that in mind," replied Miss Upton, not in the least abashed, "here is an opportunity for you to do some related charity work." I winced, not looking at Miss

Spooner's rigid countenance, but Miss Upton continued sunnily, "Miranda is an orphan, as I've said. She's a teacher; she has taught little girls for several years in a mission school and now she has come to America to find a post as governess."

Grace Spooner looked sharply at me, her nearly black eyes hard and probing. I tried to look capable and older than my years, squeezing my hands together so they would not shake.

"You mean she left India with nowhere to go?" Miss Spooner said incredulously, drawing herself up. "Traveled all that way with no one to meet her or see to her?"

I colored hotly, feeling a fool, feeling useless and a terrible burden to my friend. Naturally Miss Spooner was astonished. I longed to rush from the room. But there was nowhere to go.

"That's precisely where I felt you could help us," said Miss Upton cajolingly, unmoved by Miss Spooner's disapproval and stiff bearing. "You know all the best New Bedford families. Surely one of them requires the services of a governess."

"Violet Upton, you're as naive as the day you were born. You'll never change. Don't you know how many girls there are like this one" — a jerk of her head at me — "that need positions like that? Governesses are a dime a dozen."

"But Grace, think. The daughter of a minister who was himself a graduate of Yale. How many other governesses can say that?"

Miss Spooner's opinion of this rejoinder was apparent in her indelicate snort, and at that moment the maid brought in the tea tray. I stood there by the fire, averting my face from my hostess in case she should read entreaty there — or worse still, hopeless misery. I gazed into the fire, wishing that a yawning hole would open up in the red Oriental carpet and swallow me.

"They say the Lord looks after fools and drunkards, but this is the first I've seen of it. Violet, you're an incurably foolish optimist. In any other situation — but that makes no never mind. As it happens I just may know of a family

16

who might hire the girl," she said grudgingly.

Miss Upton clapped her hands. "I was certain you would, Grace. What did I tell you, Miranda? Now let's each have a cup of tea and you can tell us all about them. Come over and sit down, child."

I came away from the fire and sat on the red velvet settee beside Miss Upton. Still I could not look at Miss Spooner. I feared she was assuming the worst about me, that I had played on Miss Upton's sympathies until she could do nothing but offer assistance. I took a gulp of tea and scorched my mouth.

"There is a family I know of," began Miss Spooner. "I say know *of* because I am not personally acquainted with them. They are not an old New Bedford family. But I happened to hear somewhere along the line that their last governess left them rather abruptly last week. It may well be that the position has not been filled. But beyond that suggestion I can do nothing."

"Of course you'll arrange an interview for Miranda," said Miss Upton cosily, still heedless of her friend's unrelenting manner. "What could be more ideal? Please tell us of the family."

Miss Spooner sighed heavily, her huge bosom rising and falling. "Captain Sears is a whaler. He owns a fine house on County Street and there are two children, I believe. The wife is rather frivolous but that needn't concern the girl. I'll see what I can do."

Miss Upton exclaimed ecstatically and I murmured grateful phrases. When we had finished tea — which was all it was, since Miss Spooner had not offered any cakes or sandwiches — the two ladies composed a letter concerning me to be brought around to Mrs. Sears. I felt even more awkward while they quizzed me in what subjects I was well versed, in what knowledge I possessed that I could pass on to children. Miss Spooner took pains with the letter, I had to acknowledge, making me sound as appealing an employee as possible, not, I was sure, out of any personal desire to help me but because she was one of those people who did their very best when undertaking a task, no matter how reluctantly.

This she confirmed after placing down the quill pen, folding the parchment, and sealing it with hot wax from a bayberry candle. "I hope this decides the matter, Violet, and we can be at peace once again. Really, it was too much of you to foist this girl on to me. Let's hope this is an end to it."

"Oh Grace, you do grumble so," said Miss Upton cheerfully. "Why don't you show us our room and Miranda can have a little rest before dinner? She needs a good rest if she is to meet her prospective employer in the morning."

Miss Spooner inclined her head and then rang for the maid. While the woman was clearing the tea things, Miss Spooner instructed her to take the note to the Sears home on County Street. Wearily I climbed the stairs behind Miss Upton, and when the door of our room had closed, I tried to thank her for all her kindness to me.

"There, there, my dear. Nothing to cry over, is there? I feel quite certain you will get the position. I feel as though fate directed our paths together for this purpose, that I should help a fellow female in what little way I can. Why else should we have shared a berth for our long journey if not that it was destined to be I who achieved for you a measure of future security?" This was stated in tones of such awe that I dried my face and regained my composure.

In a while Miss Upton returned to her friend's parlor while I lay down on the bed, pleading a headache. "You're not used to being on land yet, Miranda. That must be it. It takes some people a day or two to regain their land legs. You rest now and we'll let you know when dinner is served."

The guest room was an attractive one; if I had been in better spirits, I might have enjoyed myself. Yellow cabbage roses adorned the walls and there were white lace curtains at the windows. A tall mirror stood in a wooden frame at one end of the room. The only mirror we had had in Bombay was a tiny one of my mother's, which she had used to see if her hair was pinned up properly.

18

On impulse I got out of bed and went over to the mirror, looking for the first time at the full figure of myself. I wasn't impressed with what I saw. My gown looked even uglier from this view and I was surprised to see how short it looked—too short. I must have grown an inch while we were on the ship. My black stockings, darned several times, showed under my skirt and my shoes looked battered and shabby. As for my face, it was pinched and too thin and there were dark circles under my eyes. My curly black hair, subdued and drawn back at the nape of my neck, nonetheless frowsed out on either side of the center part. No wonder Miss Spooner had not felt disposed toward me. I looked scrawny, untidy, and altogether unprepossessing. How could I hope to find a respectable position in a good household? I stumbled back to the bed, now in the throes of a real headache. Closing my eyes, I eventually slept.

"Miranda, wake up. Dinner will soon be ready," a trilling voice was saying, and there was a touch on my shoulder. Opening my eyes, I looked up uncomprehendingly for a moment or so until everything fell into place. I was in the house of Miss Spooner in New Bedford with my friend from the ship.

"Yes, yes, of course," I said groggily, sitting up.

"Has your tiresome headache gone away?" Miss Upton asked solicitously.

I nodded. "I believe it has."

"Good. Why don't you tidy yourself up a bit and then join us downstairs? The dining room is to your left at the foot of the stairs."

"All right. Thank you, Miss Upton. I'll be right down. I'll try not to keep you and Miss Spooner waiting."

"Oh, we're making very merry over glasses of sherry wine. Take your time."

I took this as a tactful suggestion that my hair wanted brushing. My gown, stockings, and petticoats also needed washing and pressing, but there was no time for that now. Quickly I splashed cold water on my face from the ceramic basin and washed my hands. Then I undid the heavy knot

19

at my neck and brushed my hair. I did it up again, dabbed rather ineffectually at a small stain on the front of my gown with a wet cloth, and then went downstairs. I was feeling a bit better after my nap.

I looked into the dining room but the ladies had not yet gathered there so I went across the hall to the parlor. Miss Upton was reading aloud from a letter, a glass of sherry trembling in her other hand.

"Oh, Miranda, here you are. The most wonderful news! But no, I shall not be the bearer of the good tidings. I shall surrender that honor to Grace." She lifted her glass to Miss Spooner.

If I had hoped the sherry had had a thawing effect on Miss Spooner, I was disappointed. Her expression was as grim as ever. The only difference I noted was a bright spot of crimson in the middle of each cheek. Whether these were caused by the sherry or the announcement she was going to make, I didn't know. She drew herself up, her ponderous bosom swelling.

"Mrs. Amelia Sears has most graciously written that she will grant you an interview at eleven o'clock tomorrow morning. It appears that she has not yet engaged a governess for her two children. She writes that her knowledge of me and my position in this town allays any qualms she might have concerning your character and suitability." She said that last bit resentfully as though she were being forced to recommend a person whose character and suitability she was wholly ignorant of. Which was precisely the case.

"I'm deeply grateful, Miss Spooner. If I am fortunate enough to secure the position, I will always remember it was due to you and to Miss Upton."

She seemed somewhat mollified by my response and inclined her head like a despot acknowledging the efforts of a menial. "Well, now that that has been decided, let us go into dinner. I cannot bear to eat overdone beef, nor a cold roast."

Miss Upton hastily swallowed her last sip of sherry and jumped up. She clasped me about the waist and we

20

followed Miss Spooner across the hall and into the dining room.

And that is how the next morning found me walking with my two benefactresses down County Street to the home of the woman I hoped would be my employer. When I saw the house, I lost what little courage to which I had clung. It was one of the ones we had passed yesterday, a stately Greek Revival mansion, as large and grand as a temple, part stone, part mustard-colored clapboard, with a front circular drive, a second-story balcony supported by pillars, flanking porches, and a square cupola springing from the roof. To one side of the house was a garden and arbor, and an ornately wrought iron well decoration.

I must have made a sound which expressed my dismay and trepidation, but it was misinterpreted. "Yes, girl, a fine house. You're very fortunate."

"Oh Miranda, I'm so happy for you," sighed Miss Upton rapturously as though the house belonged to me and I was showing them about.

We walked across the gravel drive and up the steps of the flagged stone porch. Miss Spooner took the brass knocker in her large gloved hand and rapped it twice very loudly and decisively. I winced at the sounds.

A maid opened the door and waited politely while Miss Spooner told her that we had an appointment to see Mrs. Sears. "Please come in," she said, and stood by to take our wraps. Then she led us into a drawing room the like of which I had never dreamed.

Close to where I was standing was a tall cabinet of Oriental origin, intricately carved, inlaid with ivory snakes coiling up the sides to a pagoda-shaped top. There were emerald velvet curtains at the long windows tied back with gold tassels, and the same green fabric covered the medallion-back sofa, loveseats, and chairs. On a small, highly polished table a quantity of feathers were displayed in a glass case. There was a large painting over the jade marble mantel of a beautiful woman with fair hair and celestial blue eyes. In her hand was a fan with an elaborate scrimshaw handle.

"Amelia Sears," nodded Miss Spooner in the direction of the portrait. She looked about the room. "Handsome apartment," she said grudgingly. "These whaling people." Then she shrugged enigmatically.

Just then the woman of the portrait entered the room. She glided toward us in a satin gown which matched her eyes. She greeted Miss Spooner and nodded politely at Miss Upton. Then all three turned to me. I shrank into myself, conscious of the forlorn, unattractive appearance I must present.

"This is Miranda Cooke, Mrs. Sears, my friend from the long sea journey and, I have no doubt, the ideal governess for your children," trilled Miss Upton.

Mrs. Sears's eyes were doubtful. "She looks very young, Miss Upton."

"But she has been teaching children for several years, have you not, Miranda? Her parents were both teachers as we wrote you and it's in her blood."

"I began teaching Indian children when I was fourteen, Mrs. Sears. I do have a good deal of experience," I said in an effort to convince the both of us.

Her arched brows rose. "Well, teaching little heathens is quite different from teaching my Abigail and Charles. They are *sensitive* children and require a governess who understands them. We have not found an ideal one yet. Detestable women, all of them. And absurd. Perhaps you might be an improvement." The words "though I doubt it" hung in the air unspoken.

"I will endeavor to give satisfaction, ma'am," I said, holding my breath.

She studied me critically. "You must have new clothes, of course. My children's governess must be dressed suitably so as not to offend them. You will take them on walks about town in the afternoons and I wish you to do us credit. The cost of your gowns will naturally be deducted from your wages." She turned away. "Well, ladies, I have decided to engage her."

Miss Upton clasped her hands together. "Perfect! I just knew things would work out for the best. They generally do, you know. I could feel that this was meant to happen!"

Miss Spooner said nothing and Mrs. Sears continued as though Miss Upton had not spoken. "You may leave Miss Cooke here now. She can start her duties today. The last governess left us ten days ago and the children's routine has been severely disrupted. I trust you, Miss Cooke, will restore the equilibrium Miss Trask so carelessly disturbed."

"What ages are the children, Mrs. Sears?" I asked tentatively.

"Abigail is six and our boy, Charles, is eight. I trust you will like them very well, Miss Cooke. Everybody says they are enchanting children. My husband is fond of saying they take after me."

"Well, that's done, Violet, shall we go?" said Miss Spooner abruptly.

"Yes, I suppose that is all," said Miss Upton. "Miranda, my dear, good-bye and good luck. And do your best to please your new mistress." She gave me a swift hug.

I nodded, biting my lip. "Good-bye, Miss Upton, Miss Spooner, and my thanks to you both for all your kindness to me. I hope you get to Australia, Miss Upton."

The two ladies shook hands with Mrs. Sears before they were shown out by the maid. Miss Spooner had not looked once at me. I was loath to see Miss Upton leave and had to suppress an urge to call her back; she was my only friend in this terrifying new world. But I knew Miss Spooner was relieved to be rid of me.

"Well," began Amelia Sears, turning to me with a cold look, "I assume you have references aside from Miss Grace Spooner."

"Yes, ma'am. I have then right here. Two letters from colleagues of my father in Bombay." I fumbled clumsily with the packet of letters, untying the string and opening the contents. With hands that trembled a little, I handed them to her.

"Hmmm. Yes. These seem satisfactory. I am glad to see they are from two reverend gentlemen, as I want my children to be subjected to only the most proper of young women." She looked at me speculatively, her gaze taking in

23

my appearance again. I waited, frightened—would she decide that I was not the right sort of young woman after all? But my dowdy pale looks seemed to reassure her. She sat down on the loveseat, patting a golden ringlet complacently, and stated, "Let me say again that I hope you will be an improvement on the flock of governesses we have had at this house. I do not understand what is wrong with the general lot of your profession. It is very upsetting to the children to be given no example to follow from their governesses in fortitude and stability. You are very young, younger than any of them have been before. I trust that you, having lived in a primitive country, will not be spoiled and unduly proud like the rest."

"I will do my best, ma'am. I do not think I am spoiled."

"Well, as I said, you must have new gowns. Two should suffice for the rest of this season and then in warmer weather we will order a few more made. I will engage my seamstress to begin work immediately, this afternoon if possible. As for now you may go up to the schoolroom on the third floor. The children are there and you will want to get started taking over their care."

I nodded and stood waiting for her to lead the way.

"Well, Miss Cooke, what are you waiting for? The third floor, I said. The stairs are to the left once you leave this room."

I colored. "Oh, I'm sorry. I thought you would wish to go with me, to introduce me to the children as their new governess."

She raised her perfectly arched brows. "I assume your vast knowledge extends to counting the number of flights of stairs to reach the third floor. I rarely go to the schoolroom, Miss Cooke. That will be your domain and your responsibility. Once in a while I shall require you to bring Charles and Abigail down here if, say, we are entertaining. For now you are to go up and make yourself agreeable to them. Annie will be bringing their luncheon up soon. I shall, of course, instruct her to bring yours as well."

"Yes, ma'am, thank you," I said, and turning, went

from the room.

I went up two flights of stairs, and as I was halfway up the second, I heard noises—shouting, squeals, and the scraping of chairs against the floor. Following the sounds I turned to the right at the top of the stairs and went down the hallway to the schoolroom. This floor of the house was not like the luxurious two below it. The walls were painted, not papered, and there was a distinctive cheerless look and feel about it. Then I had to smile at myself—as if I had anything with which to compare it!

When I reached the schoolroom, I stood hesitating at the door. At first the children did not notice me. The boy was thumping a chair into the table, each time making a loud whack, while the little girl was tossing her rag dolls against one wall.

"Hello," I said.

They both stopped what they were doing. My unexpected appearance was enough to divert them but they did not welcome me in any way.

"Who are you?" the boy, Charles, asked imperiously. "Are you a new maid? Where's Annie?" He was a handsome lad, well dressed and with his mother's fair coloring and blue eyes. But the expression on his face was anything but cherubic. It was peevish, querulous with an overriding haughtiness that sat ill on his youthful features.

"I'm your new governess, Charles. My name is Miranda Cooke. Miss Cooke. Will you shake hands?" I held out my own and moved closer to him.

"You don't look like a governess. Did Mama engage you?"

"Yes, she did. Just now."

He ignored my hand and moved away. "I don't believe you. You look like a maid. Worse than a maid, like one of the Portuguese girls. Where have you come from?"

"All the way from India. Hello, Abigail." The little girl was regarding me with her finger in her mouth. She, too, was a pretty child with her long gold ringlets and wide blue eyes fringed with darker lashes. She did not answer me but kept her finger in her mouth.

Charles was annoyed to have lost my attention even for the moment. "Well, Abigail, don't you think she looks like a maid? What did you say your name was?"

"Miss Cooke."

"Why don't you go cook something then?" He laughed at his own cleverness and Abigail joined in, giggling behind her hand.

Just then a girl came in carrying a large tray with dishes of food, cutlery, and crockery. She was sniffling and crinkling up her red nose. The white apron tied round her gown did not disguise the fact that the gown was too large for her. Setting down the tray, she wiped her nose on her sleeve.

"Are you Annie? I'm Mir—Miss Cooke. Thank you for bringing up the lunch."

She looked surprised and nodded, sniffling again. "I heard Madam say you came from India."

I nodded.

"They have white, Christian people there then?"

"Some," I said, smiling.

"Cook says they burn widows there *alive*."

"That practice stopped years ago, Annie," I said quickly, seeing the alarm on Abigail's face.

Charles was morbidly fascinated. "Really *burn* people, like they used to do witches in Salem?"

"Yes, I'm afraid so—but that was long ago. Now let's see what Annie has brought for our lunch."

"Today's Wednesday so it's clam chowder," said Charles impatiently. "It's always the same. Tomorrow it'll be boiled mutton and Friday grilled fish."

"Monday we have stewed chicken and Tuesday roast beef," offered Abigail.

"What about Saturday and Sunday?" I asked, bemused.

"Cook's choice them days," said Annie. "Captain Sears, he likes everything regulated just so. Not that he and Madam eat the same things as the children."

"I hope I can do my job to his satisfaction."

"He's not at home now," said Annie with what seemed to be relief.

26

"No, Father's at sea, near New Zealand, harpooning sperm whales," said Charles proudly. "They throw the harpoons like this—and this—and then the whale pulls the boat until it dies and spins—like this—in a death flurry." He spun around in a narrow circle, grimacing. "Father will be back later this year with lots of oil and spermacetti. When I'm grown I'm going to be a whaler, too—whalers are the bravest, strongest men alive! They have to be because the whales are so huge and dangerous. They can sink into the sea and then rise up with their jaws wide open—like this—crushing the whaleboat in their teeth. Father says there's nothing like whaling, it's the greatest adventure. He's going to take me on a voyage someday. So I don't need a governess! My father will teach me everything he knows about whaling. I don't need you!"

Dismayed, I looked at Annie but her face was impassive. There was no help from that quarter. I bit my lip. "You know, Charles, to be a captain of a ship you must be able to read maps and charts and know how to use certain instruments to help you steer by. And to be able to use those you must have a knowledge of mathematics and geometry and astronomy. When you go on a voyage with your Father you will want to be able to impress him with all that you know, won't you?"

He frowned, mulling this over. "Well . . . but I don't *like* books."

"Neither do I," chimed in Abigail. "Only picture books."

"But when you read, your mind paints pictures just as though they were drawn there on the pages. Come now, Annie has served your chowder. Come and eat it before it gets cold."

Annie gave one last sniff and left the room, clumping down the hall to the stairs. Reluctantly Charles sat down and picked up his spoon but Abigail was already eating hers hungrily. I, too, ate quickly despite the fact that the soup was tepid and had little taste. Little clams, too, and few potatoes, just a milky broth. But I was hungry. I had scarcely been able to eat anything since docking yesterday,

27

so anxious was I about my future.

After lunch I suggested the children show me their rooms. "And you better show me mine, also. I forgot to ask Annie."

"Oh, yours is across from ours. It's plain, like you," stated Charles matter-of-factly.

"Then I'll feel right at home," I said lightly. "Abigail, why don't we have a look at your room first?"

"I don't want to. I won't take a nap!" she cried, stamping her foot. "Don't you try and make me!"

"Oh, you're much too big to take a nap. I just want to see your room."

Somewhat mollified, she took me by the hand and we went down the hall. "This is it."

I caught my breath. It was the sort of room I had longed for as a child, like the one I had seen in the picture book. Organdy tieback curtains at the windows, delicate furniture painted white with hearts cut out, striped wallpaper. "You're a lucky little girl. It's very pretty."

"See my doll collection in the glass cupboard? Father brought me those from his trips. He also gave me that doll bed." She pointed to an ivory cradle. "One of the sailors carved it from the whale's teeth."

"Come see my room! Come see my room!" shouted Charles, who had followed us. "I have a set of dominoes of scrimshaw and a model of Father's whaling bark, the *Sea Lion*. And I have an ivory ruler and a sled with ivory runners."

"A sled? For riding on snow?" I asked, delighted.

"Of course. What else is a sled for, riding on grass?" he asked scornfully.

"I've never seen snow, you see."

"Never seen snow! Why not?"

"There wasn't any in Bombay."

"You haven't seen much, have you? We have lots of it here. Maybe we'll have another snowfall before spring comes. I can make huge snowballs. Abigail and I throw them at people, don't we, Abigail? Remember that old Portugee woman—I hit her smack on the back and she

28

almost fell down. I bet I could do the same to you, Miss Cooke!"

"I'm sure you could; you sound positively lethal. Where was your governess when you were throwing snowballs?"

"Oh, Mama was giving her a good talking-to. She couldn't keep us quiet in church, silly woman."

"It was hardly her silliness that was to blame for your behavior at church."

"Yes, it was, Miss Know-it-all. I told her I'd be quiet if she gave me a quarter and she lied and said she didn't have it."

"Perhaps she didn't. And besides, that's a terrible thing to do—to have to be bribed to behave well in church."

"Mama pays her, doesn't she? So why shouldn't she give me something of her wages for being good?"

"Did it ever occur to you that she might need every quarter to live?" I asked sharply. But it would not do to lose my temper and give Charles the satisfaction of having shocked me.

He shrugged. "She must not have needed them that badly since she left soon after. We've made all our governesses leave, haven't we, Abigail? Or almost all of them. And we'll do the same to you. And then we'll get another and another and another!"

I tried to speak calmly and reasonably. "At that rate you won't learn much that will be of use to your father when he takes you to sea. Now I'd like to see the room which will be mine."

It was directly across the hall from Abigail's. A narrow bed with iron headboard, one curtainless window, a small oak chest of drawers. The children were right; it was as plain as I was. With a sinking heart I went over to the window, which looked out onto the carriage house. I had a position, yes, but what a position. A drudge to two mean spiteful children. And Mrs. Sears terrified me. Suddenly India seemed not the savage country it was but a warm comfortable place. I shivered in my thin gown. The room was not only dreary but very cold as it was at the back of the house facing the harbor, and a fire had not been lit in the grate.

I thought of Miss Upton. Could I rush back to her side, telling her I couldn't live here, begging her to help me to find another post? Of course not. She had done more than enough for me already. She had found me a place in a prosperous household; I was ungrateful to wish for anything else. Besides, she would soon be leaving to go back to Albany. I would never see her again. And most certainly I could not face that cold unyielding spinster, Miss Spooner, again. No, I had to see this through. There was no other alternative. If I was to live, I had to live here.

Chapter Two

That afternoon I studied the children's schoolbooks and tried to ascertain what material had been covered by my predecessors. Neither of them responded readily to my questions concerning their general course of study, and so I decided the next morning to give a little test on different subjects such as arithmetic and grammar to see how knowledgeable they were in those subjects. Then I would have a better idea where to begin my tutelage. It was important that I make the lessons as interesting as possible so they would pay closer attention. I learned that Abigail was fond of daydreaming, her mind wandering off while she sucked one finger. Charles was a better student — that is, he had a quick, natural intelligence — but he was lazy and inclined to interrupt our schooling, attempting to divert my attention toward himself rather than the subject at hand. They quarreled constantly, Charles bullying his sister and she in turn goading him and whining loudly.

I did not imagine that I would ever become truly fond of them as I had been of a few of my students in Bombay. They were very poorly behaved, used to having their way in all things and contemptuous of me and my efforts to instruct them. But I readily perceived that it was not wholly their fault — they were sorely neglected by their parents and had never been disciplined effectively. With their father away much of the time and their mother ignoring them (she had admitted to me she rarely came up to the schoolroom and they were rarely invited down-

31

stairs), and a frequent succession of governesses, how could it be otherwise? There was nothing for it but for me to do the best I could.

The first evening before supper the dressmaker came up to my room and measured me for my new gowns. She had to put her face right up to the tape measure in order to read the numbers.

"Do you make gowns for Mrs. Sears and the children's clothes, too?" I asked in an effort to make conversation.

Her narrow eyes opened wider. "That I don't. I make the servants' clothes. Me, sewing fashionable gowns! Ha! That's a good one!" She laughed without mirth, despising me for my ignorance, and I said no more. I wondered what my new gowns would look like.

"I'll have them for you by next week."

"Uh . . . what sort of . . ."

"The missus chose the materials herself," she answered with a slight smirk.

"Very well. Thank you," I said, attempting to sound dignified, but she had already turned and was going out the door.

When my new gowns arrived, I was not surprised to see that both were in a subdued color, one navy, one gray. They were without frills or furbelows but at least they were new and fit me adequately.

I had not seen Mrs. Sears to speak to since my interview. Sometimes I would glimpse her from one of the windows overlooking County Street as she climbed into her carriage, always beautifully groomed. I would wonder where she was going, to a luncheon party somewhere or a tea or perhaps to shop. I wondered whether she was lonely for her husband. If I were married, I should hate to be separated from my husband for such long periods of time — years, even. And she did not seek solace in her children's company.

The children were gradually becoming used to me and I to them. They always complained when I suggested we start lessons every morning but I knew it was essential to keep to a routine, to ignore their grumbling and insist we work. We did lessons all morning and then stopped for lunch. After lunch I insisted each go to his or her room to play or read quietly for an hour. This was my time to check their lessons, see how their work was progressing, and plan the next day's lessons.

In the midafternoons we took walks along County Street and the roads juxtaposed to it, but sometimes if the day was pleasant, we walked down the hill to the main part of town near the wharves.

There was an excitement down there which was contagious. So much activity, such crowds of people, sailors, both foreign and American roaming about, and artisans and craftsmen who supplied the needs of the ships. These were the shipsmiths, painters, ship's carpenters, coopers, caulkers, and ropemakers. They practiced their trades in the rows of narrow buildings sloping down the streets to the waterfront where one found banks, insurance offices, counting houses, customs offices, warehouses, and storehouses. On one corner there was a large brick candleworks building where the spermacetti was brought in casks from the ships and made into the superior candles used in fine households such as Captain Sears's. They were dripless and smokeless and burned twice as long, giving off a bright clean flame.

The children and I would watch the cooper at work as he drove the metal hoops around the staves of the barrels, which would then be rolled down to the ships' holds for storing flour, liquor, pickles, fish, water, tobacco, whale oil, and other things needed on the long voyages. The cooper also forged harpoons, lances, cutting spades, and mincing knives to be used on the whale carcasses.

Charles always wanted to stop in the shop which sold nautical instruments such as the chronometers, telescopes, barometers, sextants, and compasses. He would talk about how he would have his own someday when he was a ship's captain like his father. The sign in the shop read *navigation instruction, compasses adjusted,* and we would listen to the owner of the shop explaining how a sextant gave one an angle of a cellestial object, how the barometer predicted weather, how the chronometer determined the longitude of a ship's location at sea.

We would browse around in the chandlery, which advertised "canvas, cordage, charts, paints, oils, fishing gear, lanterns, ship's wheels, ropes, tar, turpentine, varnish, and other outfitting of all vessels."

My own favorite shop was that of the ship carver. Here a gentle old man carved, painted, and goldleafed figureheads of ships—those busthead or full-figure decorations at the bows of ships. These figures were often ladies with heads of golden or dark curls in old-fashioned flowing gowns.

"See this lady, my dear?" he asked me on one occasion, pointing to a yellow-haired damsel in a blue gown.

"Yes, she's a new one, isn't she?"

He nodded, his face pink and earnest. "See how her knee is coming forward, giving the look of movement."

"That's very clever."

"The drapery folds in her gown are like the waves peeling off the bow."

"I like the Indian one," said Charles, pointing to one with a full feather headdress and tomahawk. "I'd rather have an Indian than a lady anytime. Will you make me one when I have my own ship, Mr. Carr?"

"I certainly will, Master Sears. Just as I made the lovely lady for your father's ship, I'll make an Indian for you." It was a conversation they had frequently. "And you'll need goldleafed nameboards on both sides of the ship and maybe a golden eagle at the stern, eh? I'll make them all for you if I'm still able by then."

From the ship carver's shop we would go to the chemist's shop with the sign of a mortar and pestle above his door. The pharmacist made his own powders and pills and filled the bottles for the captains' medicine chests. His herbal remedies, stated on a sign on the wall, were "medicines of nature, invigorating remedies for nervousness, debility, consumption, insomnia, and lowness of spirits." But the children were only interested in the row of large glass jars containing assorted flavors of stick candy such

34

as licorice, spearmint, sassafras, peppermint, and cloves.

I enjoyed these leisurely promenades as much as the children. But the waterfront area was also home to various unsavories, and there were areas we carefully avoided as we avoided men such as the crimpers who recruited men to be sailors. I understood from the servants that the methods they chose were not always legal ones, that they employed force or drugs or other means to complete a ship's crew.

On Sundays we went to the Baptist Church, riding in the carriage with Amelia Sears. The children were usually delighted to be accompanying their mother on these days even though they whispered and wriggled restlessly in the pew. Mrs. Sears would conceal delicate yawns behind her gloved hand and nod to acquaintances. She spoke little to me except for a cursory instruction here and there, or an admonishment if the children had behaved particularly badly. Her eyes would pass over me as if she considered me too insignificant to acknowledge.

One day on the way to church Charles, who was in a bad temper, said belligerently, "I don't want to go to our church today. I want to go to a different one. Why can't we go to a different one, Mama?"

"Which church did you have in mind, Charles?" said Mrs. Sears, patting her ringlets beneath her straw poke bonnet.

"The Seamen's Bethel on Johnny Cake Hill. It's for seamen, isn't it? Well, Father's a seaman and so will I be someday."

"Your father is hardly what I would call a seaman, Charles. He is a sea *captain* and that is a very different thing, I assure you. The Bethel is for common sailors and not for people like us. Your father would be horrified at the notion of his wife and children hobnobbing with those rough men and being subjected to their low, odious attentions. We have our churches and the sailors have theirs and that is the way it should be."

Charles's lip was jutting out mutinously and I hastily intervened, saying, "Charles was telling me this week that Captain Sears is expected home soon, Mrs. Sears. That

35

must be welcome news."

She rose her arched eyebrows as though to say it was not my place to presume whether the news was welcome or not. She stated coldly, "Yes, I am looking forward to seeing my husband. And the children will enjoy having him about for a while."

"What is he going to bring us, Mama?" asked Abigail excitedly. "What is Father going to give me this time?"

"I have no idea, precious. But he always brings us fine things so I'm certain this time will be no exception."

"Will he have anything for Miss Cooke, Mama?" said Abigail.

I flushed, but before I could demur, Mrs. Sears said, "Hardly. He doesn't know Miss Cooke and wouldn't bring gifts to the servants anyway."

Charles frowned. "But he brought one for Miss Stacey, don't you remember? He brought her that silk scarf."

Amelia Sears's mouth tightened and there were two spots of color in her cheeks. "Charles, don't be foolish. You make it sound as though he brought that scarf particularly for Miss Stacey. That was not the case at all. He had some things he had brought back to be exchanged at Christmas as gifts to our friends. He merely offered her one of them. It was an impulsive gesture like those your father often makes."

But Charles, put out about going to church, was not daunted by her tone. "No, Mama, I remember. Papa came into the schoolroom and said he had presents for all of us. And Abigail said, 'Not Miss Stacey!' and he said, 'Yes, of course, for Miss Stacey. I bought this silk especially for her. It matches the green in her eyes.' "

"Enough, Charles! Your father is too generous for his own good. But to imagine he will have a gift for Miss Cooke is ridiculous."

"Yes, she's not as pretty as Miss Stacey," said Charles sagely.

Later that day I asked Charles about Miss Stacey. "Oh, she was our governess before Miss Trask. She was nice — she didn't care if we learned our lessons or not. But she left because Mama and Papa didn't like her anymore. I used to hear her crying at night. Papa was home then, don't you remember, Abigail? Mama got angry with her and said she had to go."

I felt a flicker of alarm though I wasn't certain why. After all, the children knew nothing of what had actually happened and I should not begin to read things into their confused observances. Miss Stacey had probably done something which had convinced Mrs. Sears she could not take proper care of the children. Something very irresponsible, most likely. It was foolish to speculate that perhaps the irresponsible thing she had done related somehow to Captain Sears. But at this point I began to dread his homecoming.

Charles and Abigail were what some referred to as "difficult children," what Amelia Sears referred to as "sensitive." In my care their manners did not much improve; I was not an effective governess, I suppose. Their schooling was not all I could have wished for either. Neither got a pleasure out of learning; they continued to regard each new aspect of education as a tedious chore to be opposed and loudly complained over. It was exhausting overriding their protests day after day, intervening in their arguments, calming Abigail's tearful squeals, stopping Charles's bullying, listening to their childish insults when they felt like lashing out at someone besides each other.

I had little time to myself. Once in a while, a rare while, their mother would take them on an outing such as a carriage ride in the country or a visit with a relative or friend. Then I would have a few blessed hours to spend as I liked. I spent them walking out-of-doors if the weather cooperated. I liked to watch the orderly confusion down by the waterfront, the ships being repaired and outfitted, the loading of hundreds of barrels into dark dank holds. There were always strong smells of fish and whale oil from the tryworks on decks but I didn't find them unpleasant, used as I was to the smells of India.

Once in a while, I witnessed a long-awaited ship sailing into the harbor. One particular day I stood near to families ready to greet those sons and husbands they hadn't seen in months or years. Watching them, I felt their joyful anticipation when they caught sight of a loved face on deck. And then would come the bliss of reunion, the happy tears, the excited cries, the embraces and kisses. I stood off to myself wanting to be a part of them, wanting to arouse that sort of love and emotion in someone.

It was cold that day; I huddled in my black cloak, shivering. The cold of that November day with the wind blowing sharply off the water carried with it the smell of salt — and the smell of loneliness. I felt the cold of being apart, of having no one, of being alone. The sky was the color of steel and looked as hard and inpenetrable; the water was a gray with no sheen in it and looked cruel, unrelenting.

The ship had sailed in, the crowds had cheered, the men from the banks and counting houses had come down to appraise, to inspect, and hopefully to congratulate. The wives and children had come to take the men back to their bosoms, to take what little time was given to them until the men sailed away on another voyage. I wanted to cry for them, for the infrequent spurts of family life they had, but instead I shed some tears for myself while watching. Because at least they had today in its glory along with the days ahead to cling together against the hardness, the coldness of life.

I thought of my parents but it was not only for them that I yearned. Had I come halfway round the world for this — to stand alone while others embraced, shared, lived? With a twinge of guilt and shame I felt I was a malcontent. Why could I not have been born with the ease of my parents for making any surroundings comfortable to them, for not always wishing for something else, never being content, always hoping for something even I couldn't name much less strive for? I had felt displaced in India. And yet in New Bedford I had no real place either. I was an onlooker of life here also.

At least these people who were taking such pleasure in each other, shaking hands, clapping backs, kissing, at least they knew where their happiness lay, even if it was theirs for only a short time. But surely they at times felt the way I did, the sailors that sat below for weeks on end without seeing a whale—didn't they yearn to be at home? And then once on shore—didn't a great many of them end up longing for the sea, the excitement of the chase with the largest creature on earth? Perhaps all these people here were like me—never content, always seeking, yearning for something beyond their reach, perhaps even something they were also unable to name. Turning from the noise and bustle I pushed my way through the crowd and began to walk up the hill to County Street.

Some weeks after that the master of the house returned. The day his ship was due to dock in New Bedford harbor Amelia Sears made a rare appearance in the schoolroom. The children welcomed her presence with enthusiasm not only because she looked lovely in a dark blue velvet gown but also because anything or anyone who caused an interruption in the day's lessons was eagerly greeted.

"Good morning, Miss Cooke," she said after giving each child a brief caress. "No, darling, don't pull at Mama's gown like that. You might tear it and I must look my best for your father."

"What will he bring us, Mama? I want a sword like they have in Japan!" cried Charles.

"Whatever would you do with a sword, Charles?"

"Run people through I didn't like, of course, what else?" And he proceeded to demonstrate this bloodthirsty pastime in the air and in Abigail's direction. "Ha! Abigail! I just got you!"

"You did not!"

"Yes, I did, you're spouting blood!"

Abigail began to cry and buried her head in the folds of her mother's gown.

"Abigail, Charles was only teasing. Now stop that at once—you'll get me all damp and wrinkled. Really, Miss Cooke, is this how you ordinarily keep order up here? Charles running around shouting and Abigail fussing so?"

I flushed. "I . . . I'm sorry, Mrs. Sears. The children are

39

restless and excited today because of their father's arrival. Charles, sit down at once please. Abigail, come over here by me. Your mother has something to say to you." I tried to speak with authority because I was conscious of her disapproval, of her distaste for Charles's boisterousness and Abigail's noisy weeping. She thinks I cannot keep order, I thought. And that is often the case.

"Very well, children. I just came to tell you that you may ride with me in the carriage to meet your father's ship this afternoon. I am to be notified by errand boy when it is sighted entering the harbor so we will leave then to ensure we are at the waterfront when it docks and your father comes ashore. Miss Cooke, you will not be needed. There is hardly room in the carriage for all five of us. And doubtless my husband will have certain parcels which shall take up room."

"What will mine be, Mama? What will mine be?" chimed both children as if on cue.

"When we return," continued Mrs. Sears as though she hadn't heard the children, "we will have tea in the drawing room. I shall send for you then. Be so good as to wear your best gown of the ones I have had made for you. My husband's homecoming is always something of a celebration."

I nodded, searching her face for a sign of the radiant happiness I had seen reflected in the faces of the people at the wharves, those who were also meeting loved ones. I saw none of it. She looked the same as she always did — beautiful, poised, and cold. I wondered whether she was in love with her husband. Perhaps she even preferred it this way, just seeing him for short visits in between long voyages. Perhaps that was the only way she survived. Perhaps in that way — not missing him — there was no heartache, no loneliness.

"Now Miss Cooke, I want you to see to it that the children are dressed in their best clothes also. We want to make Captain Sears proud of us when he comes ashore, don't we, children?"

She smiled slightly, doubtless picturing their arrival at

the waterfront in the carriage. She with the two golden-haired, blue-eyed children who were so like her. It would make a pretty, poignant scene, the rich, beautiful family reunited with their seafaring father. Only his image was vague to me as I didn't know what he looked like. And people would nod and smile at them, saying, "Look, it's Captain Sears come home. Isn't his wife lovely? Don't the children look adorable? What a pretty sight they make, don't they?" I was imagining it even as she was.

"Miss Cooke, I shall want the children ready to leave at a moment's notice this afternoon, is that understood?"

"Yes, Mrs. Sears. I'll have them dressed and ready to go. They'll just need to put their coats on."

She frowned. "Their coats, yes. But no bonnets or hats or mufflers, Miss Cooke. Those will muss their hair and obscure their faces. And make certain that Abigail's ringlets are in order."

"Yes, ma'am."

"Well, that's all for now. I will send Annie up when I have word about the *Sea Lion*." She twitched a velvet drape of her skirt and went from the room.

After that it was impossible to get the children to return to their lessons. Even ploys which I had used on other difficult occasions to reclaim their attention had no result. Charles kept rushing to the window which faced the harbor, searching for a glimpse of the three-masted ship. Abigail wandered about the room, picking up dolls and toys and discarding them in boredom. Finally in desperation I set up a puzzle they could do together and then it was time for luncheon. They ate little but at least it was a diversion. And then came the time to dress them for the short carriage ride down the sloping streets to the harbor. Annie dressed Abigail in her red velvet dress and I waited until Charles had put on his black velvet suit before I helped him tie his black silk scarf. Then more waiting. They were irritable and fidgety, so I thought a story might soothe and interest them. But all three of us were thankful when Annie returned a while later to say that the *Sea Lion* had been spotted and would soon be anchoring.

41

"Madam says the children must come down right away, miss."

"Yes, all right. Get Abigail's coat, Annie. Charles, put yours on. Hurry, your mother is waiting."

They rushed from the room and clambered down the stairs while I held my breath, afraid that one or both might stumble and fall. I peered over the bannister, watching as they descended the two flights of stairs and met their mother in the front hall. Then I heard the heavy door shut.

It was now time to get myself ready for tea in the parlor. I took off the navy gown I was wearing and put on the gray merino. How different it looked from Mrs. Sears's elegant gown and the children's clothes. It hadn't even a touch of lace to relieve its somberness. Going into Abigail's room I went over to her mirror and pulled the pins from my hair. It was easily disordered, the natural curliness hard to restrain. I brushed it and put it up again.

I was very nervous at the thought of meeting the children's father, at the thought of appearing in the drawing room. I had never been asked to do so before. Was I expected to converse? How would the children behave? I dreaded seeing that displeased look come over Amelia Sears's face, the look she directed at me when the children's antics irritated her. Suppose they misbehaved and Captain Sears decided that I was not a fit, capable governess? What would I do?

I pictured us down there together in the drawing room — the children excited, spilling their tea perhaps, or quarreling, vying for attention from their father. Some scene resulting. Amelia Sears's lips tightening, her eyebrows raising coolly, the captain, doubtless a stern man, giving me a hard look. "Is this how you teach our children to act in a drawing room, Miss Cooke?" And I would color, stammering something, casting pleading looks at my charges to stop their nonsense. And then the three of us being sent from the room in disgrace, the children angered and frustrated, my inability to cope with their tantrums. And then later, or on the following day, the summons to

42

Captain Sears's library. "We regret this decision, Miss Cooke, but you have shown yourself to be ineffectual in controlling the children and in teaching them proper conduct. You will leave today." And Mrs. Sears: "Well, I shall never listen to Grace Spooner again. After all, *she* has never had children; she knows nothing at all of what a governess should be! Really, Horace, how could I have been so foolish? Miss Cooke was raised in *India;* she knows nothing of polite society, of our ways. Charles and Abigail — they are not to blame — they are not *bad* children. It's only that they've been so unfortunate in their governnesses. The ones I have endured in this house, Horace!"

I was startled out of my musing by a knock at the door. "It's Annie, miss. The captain and Madam are back and are in the drawing room. Madam says for you to come right away for tea."

My heart hammering, I cast one more glance at Abigail's mirror. My reflection did not reassure me. I looked unpoised, dull, and insignificant. "Yes, Annie. I'm just coming." And I followed her out of the room and down the stairs. When I entered the drawing room, I was clasping and unclasping my hands, feeling their sticky clamminess even on this December day.

"Ah, here you are, Miss Cooke. We have been waiting." Mrs. Sears spoke as though it had taken me an unforgivable period of time to descend two flights of stairs. "Horace, this is Miss Miranda Cooke."

I stood there; was I expected to hold out my hand? It seemed that I was for his beefy one was extended and took mine. "How d'ya do, Miss Cooke?" His voice was booming, hearty. Probably from years spent barking orders at his crew. "Why, you're not more than a girl yourself."

"Welcome home, sir," was all I could think of to say.

I was surprised by his appearance. He didn't look at all what I imagined a sea captain to be. He was a big man, yes, with a fleshy face and rather prominent blue eyes but he was dressed in such finery that it seemed incongruous to his profession. A colorful silk waistcoat embroidered with birds, green trousers, purple coat, foaming layers of lace in his cravat—all this dandified attire didn't suit his portly build. He held a glass in one hand filled with amber-colored liquid and I could smell the liquor on his breath.

"Miss Cooke, look what Papa has brought me!" cried Abigail, holding up a delicate Oriental doll with a white face.

"That's very pretty."

"Look what I've got—a whale earbone!" Charles held up an ivory-colored twisting lump which curiously resembled a human face. "And my own brass speaking trumpet, just like the one Papa uses on the *Sea Lion*. Listen. Thar she blows!" He shouted into it and the sound was magnified, bouncing off the sides of the room.

"Very nice, Charles," I said weakly.

"That's enough, Charles. It's not for a drawing room. You may shout all you like later in the schoolroom or in your own room, of course," said Mrs. Sears. Yes, I thought. It would hardly matter if the noise drove *me* out of my senses.

"Give Miss Cooke a cup of tea, Amelia," said the captain jovially. "And she can tell me what she thinks of my two new paintings. Come here, Miss Cooke. I commissioned a local artist to do these watercolors for me." He gestured to two paintings displayed side by side on one wall.

One was of a whale lying upside down, its mouth open in agony, blood staining the blue water. Surrounding it were whaleboats, the men rowing or standing or cheering, the whaleship in the distance. It was revoltingly real, brutal. Until then I had not much thought about the coldbloodedness and savagery of whaling. But this whale, this beautiful, enormous creature—it was terrible.

The other one was even worse. It showed a whale, head above the water, holding a much smaller whale—doubtless its own child—in its mouth. The baby whale had been harpooned and a bloody wound showed in its side.

"The calf was sinking, you see," came Captain Sears's voice, "and the mother whale was holding it above water in an effort to save it. I've seen that happen myself. Of course we got the calf *and* its mother," he said with relish, "but others have lost whaleboats that way, when a mother is enraged after one of her own has been harpooned."

I moistened my lips and tried to swallow. "They look very real."

"Don't they? The artist was a whaleman. Now sit down and drink your tea."

The rest of the time I sat there, thankful to have something to do, to drink, to hold the cup and saucer. Amelia Sears was talking about the social events they would be attending while her husband was home. The children were munching on cookies and trying to get their father's attention.

"We used Temple's new toggle irons on this trip," the captain said a little while later. "They work better than the flued irons. When the whale is harpooned, the iron can't be pulled out of its blubber again. The beast can't get away and the death flurry comes much sooner because it's tired out from pulling the boat. Still, we lost one greenhand when he got entangled in the line—careless fool—and the fish suddenly went deep, drawing the rope out of the boat. The rope was cut so that boat and the rest of the men were saved but the one lad was dragged overboard, the line twisted round his legs, and that was the last we saw of him."

I could not but wonder whether the children should be listening to such harrowing descriptions, even relayed so casually, but neither seem to be affected. They were absorbed in their presents—Abigail with her doll and Charles with a small book he was reading, also a gift from his father. I could not read the title from where I was sitting but I saw the illustration of a whale on the cover.

"Do you know what a Nantucket sleigh ride is, Miss Cooke?" asked my employer, pouring another drink from the decanter in the tantalus.

I shook my head. "I've just recently seen snow for the first time, Captain Sears. Is it a ride down the hill on a toboggan?"

He laughed, delighted by my ignorance. "A Nantucket sleigh ride doesn't take place on snow, or on anything so ordinary as a toboggan, Miss Cooke. Its hills are the ocean; its sleigh the whaleboat. It comes after the whale has been struck and the beast takes off with the boat in tow. Waves rush past the boat, which climbs the crest of the wave and then shoots down headlong into the hollow between that wave and the next." He was demonstrating excitedly with his hands, his voice increasing in volume. All of a sudden I saw the resemblance to Charles.

"When can I have a Nantucket sleigh ride, Father?" cried Charles.

"When I take you on as one of my mates, my boy."

"And when will that be?" demanded the boy.

"When you are old enough, Charles, your father will take you with him," said his mother.

"But *when?* When will that be?" he asked, near to a frenzy.

"When you are eighteen, son. That's how old I was when I was one of the four mates. Those were the days, I tell you. Being a captain you don't see nearly as much action. The mates, the harpooner—they have the devil's own game, by God! But there's no life like it, Miss Cooke, no life like it at all. No braver men can be found than the New England whalers, eh, my dear?"

Amelia Sears smiled at her husband the way she smiled indulgently at Charles. Captain Sears's life was dedicated to playing games—highly dangerous, complex, skilled games, but games nonetheless. A man's game, not a boy's fantasy. Danger, adventure, thrills. But wasn't it just as courageous leaving one's own country, never to return, as my own father had done? As I had done myself, I realized. Yet I had never considered myself the least bit courageous.

"Miss Cooke . . . Miss *Cooke,*" Amelia Sears was saying. I looked up, startled. "The captain and I are going out tonight. We must get ready, so it's time the children were fed and put to bed."

Flushing, I said, "Yes, of course, ma'am. Come along, Abigail." She came to me willingly enough but when I motioned to Charles he said, "No! I don't want to go upstairs yet. It's your first night, Papa! I want to stay down here."

"Charles, go with Miss Cooke," said his mother. "You will most likely see your father tomorrow."

Charles's lip jutted out. He stood up but held his ground. "I don't want to go to the schoolroom. I'm sick of it up there. I want to stay with you, Papa!" His face was red.

"Miss Cooke will handle this," said Mrs. Sears, looking pointedly at me.

"Come, Charles, you heard what your mother said. You may see your father tomorrow. Come on, you can read me your new book."

"Yes, go on, my boy," the captain chimed in.

I took Charles's arm and had to nearly drag him across the floor. He was furious. Abigail saw this and began hollering, too. "I don't want to go upstairs! I don't want to!" I closed the drawing room door behind us and propelled them up the stairs.

As annoyed as I was by their behavior and the looks of disapproval Mrs. Sears had cast at me, I thought — why couldn't the children have stayed down a little longer? Their father's first night at home in two years and he was little more than a stranger to them. It was no wonder the children were the way they were.

The children were very difficult that night and I breathed a sigh of relief when at last they were both in bed and I could be alone. I went to the window of my room and looked out over the dark town. I heard the mournful fog horns — the day had been overcast — and the wind whipping up over the town from the water. I wondered how Miss Upton was and whether she was somewhere far off on another voyage; I had not heard from her since we had parted.

The next morning I asked Charles to read aloud to us from the book his father had given him. It was entitled *The Whale and the Perils of Whale-Fishery.*

"Dangerous as the whale-fishery is known to be, yet

47

great numbers of ships are sent out every year on this business. Where else should we procure oil for our lamps, and whale-bone for umbrellas, and for many other purposes?"

Charles went on to read about the bowhead whales inhabiting the Arctic waters, sought after for their baleen, a substance which took the place of teeth, "hanging from the upper jaw in long slat-like rows, acting like a strainer through which the whale expelled water from its mouth but trapping the plankton on which it feeds." Baleen was most valuable for corset stays — something Charles slyly, gleefully pointed out, knowing such garments were unmentionable — and umbrella whips and ribs. According to the book, hunting for bowhead whales was the most hazardous form of whaling since it took men to the "fields and mountains of ice where the threat of shipwrecks was very great and often occasioned the most dreadful suffering." I had no idea then what that was to mean to me.

When Charles had finally finished reading, I knew much more about whaling than I had ever wished to know. Abigail had sat drawing sketches in her copy book, ignoring Charles's glowing recitation. I considered that it was time for a total change of subject and set them to practicing their sums.

But something in Charles's book had caught my attention unwillingly and my mind quickly conjured up a scene which I had difficulty shaking. The scene of a ship caught between terrible icebergs, the sky an intense unimaginable cold of whiteness reflecting the ice. I had sailed the oceans myself and so the deep blue waters did not stir the terrible fear in me that those heartless "mountains and fields of ice" did.

Captain Sears remained at home for two or three months before he set sail again. He and his wife attended many parties during his stay and gave a few themselves which, naturally, neither Charles, Abigail, nor I attended. He made several visits to the schoolroom but did not stay long and seemed, on the occasions I saw him, restless and bored except when he could turn the conversation to whaling. I heard from Annie that he always got that way after he had been home a month or so, and Annie whispered to me that he and his wife argued with increasing regularity. It appeared neither could stand more than small doses of the other and so their marriage was a most successful one when they spent little time in each other's company. The captain would come home bearing gifts; his wife would be delighted with them and with him for a while until he was as anxious to leave as she was to have him go. He came up to the schoolroom on his last morning to bid farewell to the children but, truth to tell, they were not nearly as eager in their attentions toward him as they had been on his arrival. He nodded to me casually, disinterestedly, and then his heavy footsteps were heard on the stairs, eager, excited, boyish.

After his departure the household went back to its former ways—the mistress sleeping late, going out for luncheon or tea with other wives. We saw her no more than we had when the captain was at home. The servants were more lax, less strained, the children a little less fretful, less boisterous. Captain Sears had that effect on everyone. But he was gone for another long while and we resumed our routines.

Two years later when he returned, the course of my life was again altered radically. In those two years I wish I could say that I had become more resigned to teaching Charles and Abigail, that I liked them more, that I came to enjoy life in the Sears household. But that unfortunately was not the case. The children irritated me as much as they always had—their behavior and manners and reluctance to learn did not undergo a substantial difference and neither did my opinion of them. But we tolerated each other. I was not a stern taskmaster; indeed they were adept at diverting my attention from particularly dull lessons, at allotting them more play time, more time to spend on our promenades, more time spent doing things they wanted to do. These included making snowmen in the winter, having lessons in the garden in summer—any excuse to escape from the confines of the schoolroom and give themselves up to daydreams. We made frequent trips to places Charles insisted were educational, but only if one were obsessed with any and all facets of whaling. But because I indulged them from time to time, because I could not withstand constant fits of temper and quarreling, they did not always give me so terrible a time as they had done to several of my predecessors.

I did not dare let them in on my secret — that I was afraid of being let go, that they need not fear that I would resign my position as their governess. This I could not do, for where on earth would I go? If I had possessed more strength of character, more self-confidence, been less a victim of timidity — perhaps then I would have resigned and left New Bedford in search of some other position. But that I did not have the courage to do.

Some might say I deserved the fate of perpetual drudge to the Sears children because I made no move otherwise, took no pains to change my life. In my defense there would be little I could say except that here I had a certain measure of security, which I sorely needed. No other governess had lasted as long as I had; the mistress was satisfied on most accounts, as satisfied as a person of her nature could be; the master was nothing more than a visitor and did not interest himself unduly in the affairs of the household. So although there was much I disliked about my life, I saw no way to change it. Nor was I sorely tempted to try. And I did feel less a fish out of water than I had in India. I liked New Bedford; I liked the sea air and the bracing climate. I refused to look ahead.

I noticed from time to time glancing in Abigail's mirror that my appearance was improving. My hair was glossier, I thought, but even more tiresome as it was more difficult to keep confined at the nape of my neck. My skin also seemed different, less sallow, creamier, rosier. And I had filled out more; I wasn't the scrawny creature I had been when first coming to New Bedford.

I was now twenty years of age. I could not help but notice the glances I got from men around town, from sailors especially. But as Cook often said, sailors looked at all women and had evil thoughts always on their minds. So I could not be flattered by any attention I aroused in them. And certainly I had no occasion to meet any young men — Amelia Sears did not entertain gentlemen while her husband was away from home, and even if she had, I would not have been a guest. For a woman of twenty, I had no experience with men at all; in some circles I would have been considered past the first blush of youth, nearly past marriageable age. I was doomed to be like Miss Upton, I thought gloomily, except that I was not independently wealthy. No matter how my looks had improved, I was not deceived into believing I had anything to offer men. I had never been witty or clever; I owned nothing in the way of property; I numbered no men among my acquaintance except for the menservants and I had no means of meeting any in the future. I was no sparkling conversationalist; I did not think I had anything in the way of what people referred to as charm. In short, I could not attract a suitable man. I might have married a young missionary if I had remained in India, though even that possibility seemed highly unlikely as I was so disinterested in that sort of life. As a missionary's wife I would not have been much of an asset.

It was in early September that Captain Sears came back to New Bedford following yet another "greasy" voyage, which meant much whale oil and spermacetti had been acquired. But his ship had been expected weeks earlier and the servants had begun to whisper of wrecks and ill luck. The children were constantly asking when their father would return and I had to reassure them as best as I could. Amelia Sears's cool manner did not change, and I wondered at her apparent lack of anxiety.

When he did finally sail into New Bedford, the reason for his lateness was soon explained. The *Sea Lion* had been battered by a storm off Cape Hatteras, "the graveyard of the Atlantic," and had been lain up for repairs. Even when those repairs were made in the Pamlico Sound, it was evident that the bark would never be quite the same again — resheathing and retopping could not make it as good as new. Captain Sears would have to purchase another square-rigged vessel if he wished to continue his whaling expeditions, which naturally he did.

The children and their mother did not meet him at the waterfront as they had two years before. Instead he arrived unexpectedly one day but none the worse for his misfortune. He was again laden with gifts, and clumped up the stairs to the schoolroom, surprising us.

The children leapt up with whoops of excitement. "Papa! Papa! You finally came!"

He was again dressed in dandified clothes and was breathing heavily, his face red, after climbing the two flights of stairs.

"Good day, sir," I said. "This is a happy day indeed."

He looked at me then, an arm around both children. "Miss Cooke, is it?"

"Of course it's Miss Cooke, Papa!" cried Charles. "Who did you think she was? Don't you remember her?"

"Not looking quite this way," he said, and took my hand in his beefy one. "Why, Miss Cooke, your hand is cold."

I pulled mine from his moist grasp. He smiled then and I thought it was an unpleasant smile. His warm gaze raked over me until I felt distinctly uncomfortable and began to blush.

"Tell us about the voyage, Papa! Why were you so late arriving?"

"We sailed into a fierce storm, Charles, one of the worst I've ever seen. We had to tie ourselves to chairs, to the masts, so we wouldn't be swept overboard. Your father wondered whether this journey would have been his last."

"Oh Papa, don't say that!"

"Would you have minded, eh, Abigail? How pretty you've grown. Like Miss Cooke, eh?"

"Of course I should have minded, Papa."

"And you, Miss Cooke? Would you have minded?" Again the warm gaze, the intimate tone of voice.

"It's good to see you home safely, sir," I answered coolly, stiltedly. I wished he would go away.

"Well, children," he said. "I've come to tell you you're to

52

go with your mother and me on an outing this afternoon. We're to take tea with your grandmother in Fall River. It's been a time since you've seen her and she wrote your mother asking to see all of us when I returned. So Miss Cooke may have a free afternoon, after she sees that you are both ready to go. What do you think of that, eh?"

I was thankful. I had not had an afternoon off in what seemed like a long while. Also, I was eager to be relieved of the company of the sea captain. While the children chatted excitedly, he smiled again at me.

"And, Miss Cooke, we're having a guest coming to spend the next couple of days with us. My wife and I would like you to bring the children and join us in the drawing room tomorrow night. Now that I'm home, I'd like to see your pretty face — and those of the children — as much as I can."

My face was red with confusion. I had never had a man speak so to me and I did not like it, not from him. "I'll have the children dressed by — what time, sir?"

"Half past one, your mistress said."

"Do you have any presents for us, Papa?" cried Abigail.

"I do, and you shall see them when we are off in the carriage. Get on with your lessons and mind your pretty governess," he said heartily, and left the room.

"I don't see any pretty governess around here," said Charles, glancing about the room.

"Very amusing. But let's get back to work. It will be time for luncheon soon and then you've both got to get ready to go to Fall River."

When they had gone, I debated over how to spend the next few hours. They would not be back until six or later so I had the afternoon ahead of me. It was a mild day, balmy after the close mugginess of the last few weeks, so I decided to go for a walk and perhaps take refreshment in an inn afterward.

I walked down Williams Street past the white Baptist Church we attended on Sundays and just then I was reminded of the small Quaker chapel on Johnny Cake Hill, the Seamen's Bethel, which had been built for the sailors to worship in as they were not allowed in the more stately, grander churches of the town. I had never been inside but I had passed it many times, a simple unassuming white structure with an octagonal steeple from which sprung a weathervane of a whaling ship. I would walk there now and have a look inside. In a way it reminded me of the simple wooden chapels the missionaries had built in Bombay.

I walked down the hill, enjoying the fresh air, the day's mellow goldenness. After some thought I had reached the conclusion that Captain Sears was a flirt but I had no reason to be afraid of him. He was the sort of man who ogled women and payed them compliments. But I would give him no encouragement and surely he would realize that his attentions did not amuse me and he would turn them elsewhere. Besides, he would be off to sea later this fall—at least I did not have to beware of him all year round.

Thus reassured I turned right at the foot of the hill, deeply breathing the salty air, and walked the remaining blocks to the Bethel.

Chapter Three

It was very quiet inside the Seamen's Bethel. The interior was stark and austere, the pews low-backed with the barest of armrests. The pulpit was on the street side of the chapel, and so when I entered the pews were facing me.

There was a man sitting in one of the pews at the back of the church. I could not see his face as it was bent forward and partly shielded by one of his hands. I did not wish to disturb him as he seemed troubled, and so I went across to the opposite side of the small church to read the marble tablets on the wall. They were memorials to different individuals lost at sea. There was one to a captain who had been carried overboard by a line fastened to a whale, and another to a man who had died from wounds suffered in a shark attack.

There were mournful verses in memoriam to dead loved ones:

Far from home and scenes of Friendship,
And from those who loved thee well;
Suddenly by death arrested,
Where the foaming billows swell.
Long will we thy memory cherish,
Though life's fondest hopes are o'er;
Love and friendship never perish,

Though we see thy form no more.

An overwhelming sadness came over me as I read those lines, as I recalled the giddy relief which infected the crowds when a longed-for ship came in—when those on shore were certain their loved ones had been spared death once again. But there were always those sailors who were not spared.

"Whales are not the only victims," I thought. And then I went red with mortification when I realized I had spoken those words aloud. What a fool I was, talking to myself.

I glanced around at the man sitting down, hoping he hadn't noticed my presence, hoping he hadn't caught my heedless words. But he had looked up and he was gazing at me intently as though I had meant to speak to him. I tried to look away but found I could not; his gaze held me transfixed and I stood stupidly, returning look for look.

His thick hair was as black as my own, or nearly so, and his face was tanned with a slightly weathered look. He was frowning, black brows drawn together over wintry gray eyes. Gray eyes that were bleak . . . lost. Now why did I think that?

"I beg your pardon," he began, his voice deep and resonant, "but were you speaking to me?"

"Oh . . . no . . . no," I stammered idiotically, feeling my face as hot as fire in the cool room. "I was only . . . that is . . . these verses, they are all so sad, don't you think?" Fool, I thought, he probably hasn't even read them. And what a trite thing to say. Of course they were sad; they were memorials.

He nodded, rising. He was tall and very broad, dressed all in black except for the crisp white neckcloth at his throat. I wondered idly what he was doing in the Bethel as he was obviously a gentleman and not a common sailor. There was a curious scar the shape of a new moon above his jawline.

"I'm sorry," I continued foolishly, "I believe I disturbed you." Then I thought, No, I shouldn't have said that, I shouldn't have let on that I noticed his troubled mood.

I turned to go but he spoke again. "You said, 'Whales are not the only victims.' "

I said nothing, more and more uncomfortable under his scrutiny. Why did he keep looking like that, as though we shared some secret?

Then he seemed to re-collect himself, and his face took on a hard look. "What are you doing here?" he asked almost roughly. "Do you have a sweetheart at sea you've come to pray for?" He seemed annoyed, angry even. I could only look at him, slightly dazed, shaking my head.

"A husband, then? Though you look too young for that—and too ethereal."

"I'm not at all . . . I mean, I haven't any husband. Or sweetheart." I sounded defensive, which was ridiculous, but I couldn't help it. It was the way he had been staring at me, still intently, but in an accusing way. I took two steps backward because he had left the pew and was coming toward me.

"That's a pity. Or is it?" Now his eyes were no longer bleak or annoyed. He looked amused at my obvious unease.

"I . . . I don't know what you mean, sir."

He smiled, showing even white teeth. "I only mean that you're much too pretty not to have someone who is fond of you. Or perhaps it's as I first thought, that you're not real. Perhaps you're an angel sent down to comfort me. I didn't hear you come in—did you just appear in the Bethel, an unearthly creature in answer to a prayer?"

I fancied he was making fun of me and I did not like it. Though he *had* looked in need of comfort—but certainly none I could give. "I'll bid you good afternoon, sir. Again, I'm sorry for disturbing you," I said stiffly.

He laid a hand on my arm. "Don't go. Forgive me for offending you."

I smiled a little then, moving my arm away. "I thought it was I who had annoyed you by my presence."

"Is this how annoyed you think I am?" he asked swiftly, a trace of bitterness in his voice. And before I knew what he was about, he had pulled me into his arms and was kissing me hard on the lips. I gasped in total disbelief and alarm but instead of releasing me he only began to kiss me deeper, embarking on an intimate exploration of my mouth.

I began to push frantically at him, struggling to be free of his tight warm embrace. I was horrified at what he was doing—and in a chapel, no less, a public place where anyone might come in. Finally his grip lessened, his mouth released mine, and we stood there shakily surveying one another.

"Not so unearthly," he said, and his voice sounded different, hoarse, his words slurred, his breathing uneven.

Without a word I turned and hurried through the door, where I collided with another man. Not lifting my hot face to his, I ignored his apology and rushed outside and away to the safety of the Sears mansion on County Street. As I passed people I averted my gaze, confident they could tell what had just occurred, certain that it was written all over my face. Licking my lips, I tasted blood.

When I reached the house, I was relieved to find that the family had not returned in my absence, and I was startled to see by the grandfather clock in the hall that little more than an hour had passed since I had left the house. It seemed like hours ago, a lifetime even while the tall dark man and I had gazed at one another, spoken, kissed. I gave a little moan and went up the stairs to my room, where I splashed cold water on my face. The blood had dried on my lips but they felt bruised, violated.

Thank heaven there had been no witness to that scene, I thought. I will never go into that place again, or anywhere near it. And most of it, I never wanted to see that dreadful man again.

I remembered the hard intimate feel of his body, the way his mouth had taken savage possession of mine, his dark intent gaze. How had he dared take such a liberty with me? What had I done to encourage such an action? I thought back over what had happened before he took me in his arms—why had I stared at him for so long? Why

58

hadn't I left the Bethel before I did? Had I looked as though I wanted him to kiss me? What exactly did one look like when one conveyed she wanted to be kissed?

First he had implied that I was little more than a girl, then he had crushed me to him like any wanton woman. An angel, he had called me. And then, "Not so unearthly." Did that mean he thought I had enjoyed his embrace?

I covered my face with my hands. If the Sears were to get wind of this affair, I would be instantly dismissed. It made my head spin to think how narrow had been my escape—if that man who had entered as I was fleeing had come in a little sooner, he would have witnessed the scene. Not that he would have necessarily connected me with the Sears household, but even so I would have been sick with anxiety that somehow the word would get back to my employers. At least I was spared that. And this morning I had been afraid of Captain Sears!

I touched my tender lips, wondering at the outrageous behavior of the black-haired stranger. Perhaps he had been drunk. Drunken men often acted wildly, strangely. But there had been no telltale taste of liquor in his mouth. I blushed again. No, he had not been drunk. Perhaps he was mad. Yet he had not looked or sounded mad, deranged. Why, then, had he acted that way? Surely he had not *wanted* to kiss me, a simple girl dressed primly, a girl who had stammered and blushed. Perhaps that was why. Perhaps his kiss had been an experiment in kissing an unappealing, struggling girl. Suddenly I was unaccountably depressed. Tears sprang to my eyes but I brushed them angrily aside. There was no reason to cry, certainly. I had just to forget that the episode had ever occurred. I had no idea then how impossible that would prove.

The Sears were later than expected in returning so I had plenty of time to collect myself. I ate a solitary dinner in my room and tried to concentrate on the children's lesson plans. When I heard footsteps on the stairs, I went out on the landing.

Captain Sears was with the children. "Here is our Miss Cooke," he said when he saw me. "If I had had a pretty

59

governess when I was a boy, I wouldn't have minded at all learning my lessons." This was accompanied with an arch look which I did my best to ignore, saying, "You both look exhausted. Did you have a good time at your grandmother's?"

"Charles was naughty," said Abigail smugly. "He broke Grandmother's pitcher."

"You stepped on her cat's tail! On purpose. I watched you do it."

"Did not!"

"Did so!"

"I did not!"

"Then why did the cat scratch you? Look at her arm, Miss Cooke. She got a sorry scratch and bled on Mama's gown. Wasn't Mama angry!"

"She was not. And it's a mean, nasty cat anyway!"

"All right, children. That's enough. Go to your rooms. Miss Cooke will come tuck you in when you're ready for bed."

"I don't need to be tucked in!" cried Charles indignantly.

I turned to follow Abigail to help her off with her dress, but the captain said, "High-spirited children, aren't they? I like 'em that way. Don't break their spirits, Miss Cooke."

"I won't, sir," I said stiffly.

" 'Course it's different on a ship. Can't have the men too independent, they won't work as a team. Got to use the whip on those that get out of hand."

He was leaning close to me. He smelled strongly of liquor and tobacco and some sort of sweet cologne. He was repellent, his plump lips moist, his beefy hands clutched together. I pitied the men who sailed under him; he was the sort, I could tell, who would derive satisfaction from punishing others, from making certain they got what he believed they deserved even if their suffering was terrible. I hated him.

"Good night, sir. I must see to the children."

He straightened and tapped his cane to the floor. I had not noticed it until then. It had an ivory handle which had been carved — yes, that was actually what it was, I thought,

60

aghast — into the shape of a woman's leg. When he grasped the handle, it was a thigh he was grasping. How utterly revolting.

"Are you glad to see me back, eh? Thought I was a goner, did you?" In the dim light of the hallway his eyes held a glint I did not trust.

"I am pleased for the children's sakes, sir. Being an orphan myself I know how sad it is when children lose one or both parents."

It was the wrong thing to have said. He leaned down again and grasped one of my hands in his. "An orphan, are you? Poor little thing. Like I said before, you're not that much older than the children yourself. I'll have to look after you properly."

"Miss Cooke, are you coming in? I can't unfasten my dress," came Abigail's wail. Captain Sears dropped my hand abruptly and I turned away in relief. I went into Abigail's room and was glad to hear him descending the stairs. With difficulty I tried to suppress the fear he aroused in me.

But surely I was in no danger. I slept across the hall from his children, on the floor above that of his wife. I was not alone in his house at his mercy. And besides, was I perhaps reading a little too much into his attitude in the light of what had happened today? Not all men were threats to my virtue, I thought with a shaky laugh. I was acting as if everyone who saw me had an immediate desire to compromise me. How absurd. How conceited, too. Tomorrow after a good night's sleep I would be myself again. These fancies would disappear. Captain Sears would be nothing more than a man concerned about one of his servants who did a tolerable job, and I would never see that tall dark man again.

Late the next morning I was summoned to Amelia Sears's bedroom. I went downstairs, my nerves in a flutter. I had tried to put Captain Sears's familiar manner out of my mind and had succeeded somewhat. But now I was in a sudden panic. Could Mrs. Sears have noticed something? Was I to be admonished or worse? Had he said something

61

to her about me which had offended her?

I pictured myself standing before her and her accusing me . . . of what? "It has come to my notice, Miss Cooke, that you have been putting yourself forward to the Captain. He is developing an interest in you which I do not like." No, she wouldn't say that. It would be more like, "Your duties are confined to the teaching of my children, Miss Cooke. It is not your place to keep my husband standing in the hall talking so that you can avoid your responsibilities." And I would stand there in dismay and say nothing, my tongue useless in my defense.

When I knocked on her door, her voice answered in its usual cool tones, "Come in." Surely she would have a sharper tone if she were angry with me?

She was propped against layers of plump pillows while she entwined one long golden ringlet around her finger. She did not look either angry or irritated. She was wearing a pale blue silk dressing gown which looked as though it came from the Orient.

"You asked to see me, Mrs. Sears?" I said.

"Yes, Miss Cooke. My husband tells me we are to have a visitor tonight, a person from whom Captain Sears may purchase a whaling bark. I want you to see that the children are dressed suitably and brought down to the drawing room at precisely six o'clock to meet this Captain Blaize. Naturally they will not dine with us, but my husband wishes that they be present for a short time. Captain Blaize is, I understand, from the outreaches of Maine and thus scarcely a gentleman, but Captain Sears wants his children with us this evening."

"Very well, ma'am. I will bring Charles and Abigail down at six," I answered, hoping that they would behave nicely or it was I who would be faulted. The notion that Captain Sears had requested his children's presence just as an excuse to have me there I tossed aside as too ludicrous for contemplation.

"That's all then, Miss Cooke. I have a great deal to do today to prepare for our guest as he will also be staying the night. Remember, I want you to see that the children show themselves in a good light. Their conduct yesterday at their grandmother's left much to be desired. I employ you not only to instruct them but to instill in them proper social behavior."

I colored. "Yes, Mrs. Sears." Thus dismissing me, she rang the silver bell on her bedside table.

Why did we have to make an appearance in the drawing room tonight, I thought miserably. I feared the children would end up misbehaving in some way and I would be blamed. I was smarting from her critical words but I knew she was right. After the two years that I had been employed here, the children were still rude, selfish, and willful. And they doubtless always would be since their parents either spoiled them shamelessly or took no interest in them. I was used to the children's petty ways but in front of company, in a formal setting, they could not be expected to be seen and not heard — or not offend. The visit to their grandmother's had shown that. But all this was beside the point. We were to come down to the drawing room tonight. Hopefully it would be for a brief period. Hopefully the children would not be diverted into arguing or creating some sort of scene.

As I climbed the flight of stairs to the schoolroom, I heard shouting and wails. And had doubts about my last thought.

Abigail was jumping up and down in an effort to reach her Oriental doll, which Charles was holding above his head. Angry tears poured down her cheeks as she pulled at her brother's arms. Without a word I wrested the doll from him and handed it to her. Her sobs quieted and Charles said, "Oh, Abigail, you're such a baby. I only wanted to look at her hair."

"You wanted to pull her hair out!"

"Listen to me, both of you. Do you remember your father telling you yesterday that a visitor is coming today, a man your father may purchase a whaling ship from? Well, your parents want you to come down to the drawing room this evening to meet this Captain Blaize. You must put on your best clothes and your best manners to make them

63

proud of you."

"I'll bet that Captain Blaize doesn't catch as many whales as Papa does!" said Charles.

"Well, I wouldn't know about that. But please don't say anything of that nature when you meet him! Your mother and father want you to be polite and make a good impression." Which was doubtless too much to ask. But Captain Sears had claimed he liked his children high-spirited. They certainly were that.

Our lunch was even more poorly prepared than usual that day but I wasn't hungry. Evidently the cook's efforts were going into the dinner for the guest. No matter what Mrs. Sears had said, he had to be an important person. Again I hoped fervently that the children could be persuaded to behave.

After lunch we read from the McGuffey reader while Charles also fiddled with his toy soldiers and Abigail drew pictures in her copybook. At one point I looked up in time to see Charles lean across to write something in Abigail's book. His sister wrenched it away, knocking over her inkwell. She jumped up, squealing, as the blue liquid washed over the table and sloshed on her pinafore, dress, shoes, and stockings. Charles laughed until she threw what remained in the inkwell at him. Amid both their horrified, angry cries I rang for Annie and stripped off their stained clothing.

"Well, I hope you are both satisfied now," I said disgustedly. "These clothes are ruined, and I know that dress was a favorite of yours, Abigail. However, you have so many I daresay it doesn't matter. Oh Annie, the children have had an accident with the ink. We'll have to give each of them a bath. You take Miss Abigail and I'll do Master Charles." I wished they could have been *cold* baths.

Today of all days, I thought helplessly. Abigail's hair would have to be washed—Charles had smeared his inky fingers in it. And I doubted whether there would be sufficient time for it to dry and be curled with the irons before we were expected in the drawing room. Amelia Sears would not like it if her daughter's hair was not

64

properly arranged in ringlets like her own. There would be no more lessons today; that much was certain. Annie and I would have to take the remainder of the afternoon to get the children ready.

Soon the tubs were filled with warm water. Charles, outraged, insisted he could bathe himself, but this time I ignored him and scrubbed roughly at his face and neck where the ink had spattered. Cries from Abigail's room announced she was having her hair washed and none too gently. Annie was rather clumsy and did not have a deft touch, but I was too infuriated with both children to care. A little later they were wrapped in towels before the schoolroom fire while I gathered their clothes for tonight, and Annie was sent to make their cocoa.

While they were drinking it in a more subdued mood than they had demonstrated earlier in the day, I took that opportunity to get dressed myself. I changed from my gray gown to the navy one. For Christmas the year before the children had given me a white linen collar with cut-lace work, carefully selected by their mother, I was sure, as something suitable for a governess. Still, it was pretty and softened the severe lines of the gown.

When I was ready, Annie helped me dress the two children and afterward I stood by, apprehensively surveying them. Abigail's hair had, unfortunately, not dried sufficiently for me to curl it and now it hung straight down her back. I had tied a blue ribbon in it, though, and she looked quite charming in her navy blue velvet dress with its satin sash and pleated bodice. Charles also wore navy blue, a jaunty sailor suit which he was now complaining was too boyish for him.

"Your mother ordered it made for you, Charles, and requested that you wear it tonight. You look very handsome, I assure you."

"Charles is a baby! Charles is a baby!" chanted Abigail gleefully after he had put the idea into her head, and before I could stop him, he reached across and pulled hard on her hair.

"Stop crying, Abigail—you shouldn't have been teasing

65

Charles. And as for you, my lad, how many times have I told you you're not to hit your sister or pull her hair?"

"I'll show her I'm no baby," said Charles darkly. "I don't care what you say."

"Dry your eyes, Abigail. Your face is all pink. It's time to go downstairs. This is very important, both of you. When you enter the drawing room, wait to be introduced to Captain Blaize. Then, when you are, Charles, you shake hands and say, 'How do you do, sir?' and Abigail, you give a little curtsy. Then sit down quietly and do not speak again unless you are spoken to. Do not interrupt your parents or their guest. And no arguing with each other, do you understand?"

Just then the clock in the hall below began to strike the hour. "There, it's time. Now remember what I've said. Oh Abigail, your hair ribbon has come undone. Here, let me tie it again. All right, you both look quite presentable. Let's go down."

I was dreading seeing Captain Sears again, even in the company of others. This afternoon we had been so busy that I had had no time to worry over his manner toward me, but now that I was to come face to face with him again, I was in a panic. I would sit in the corner tonight and then do everything I could to avoid him until he left on his next voyage.

"Come in, come in," boomed Captain Sears's voice in answer to my hesitant knock. I opened the door and the three of us went inside.

"These, Captain Blaize, are my dearest children," Amelia Sears was saying, but then her voice became a meaningless jumble of sounds and the familiar room an alien, dangerous place. For the man who had risen at our entrance was the man from the Seamen's Bethel and the expression on his face was as shocked as my own. I could not breathe; I could not think or speak. He looked away, shaking Charles's hand; Charles was muttering something; Abigail was leaning against her mother's chair, refusing to curtsy; but all these things I scarcely registered. I felt as though I had been snatched up by a fierce gale and then

66

dropped as abruptly.

My face was hot and I pressed my hand to it. I thought of the man's hard mouth on mine and I felt they could all read my thoughts, that they knew what had occurred between this stranger and myself.

"Miss Cooke, may I present Captain Nicholas Blaize?" Captain Sears said jovially. He did not appear to notice anything strange.

"How do you do, Miss Cooke?" said the man in the deep voice I remembered. The room was quite warm and stuffy for a September evening; Amelia Sears did not open the windows very often. I nodded to Captain Blaize, not trusting myself to speak.

"Abigail, your hair," began Mrs. Sears, annoyed. "Miss Cooke, why is the child's hair damp?"

"I'm sorry, Mrs. Sears," I said, turning to her almost in relief. "There was a slight accident this afternoon and it was necessary to wash her hair."

"Really, Miss Cooke, what do I employ you for if not to prevent such accidents?"

I bit my lip, humiliated beyond belief in front of them all.

"A very pretty little girl," said Captain Blaize, smiling at Mrs. Sears, who was immediately mollified and gave him a coy look.

"Takes after her mother, don't she?" said Captain Sears. He looked in my direction; hastily I looked away.

Captain Blaize was again in black. I found myself staring at his shiny black boots, unable to look anywhere else with ease.

"A glass of Madeira, Miss Cooke?" came Captain Sears's voice.

"I beg your pardon? Oh no, no thank you." And I moved to sit down in the far corner of the room.

"I hardly think it appropriate for you to offer Miss Cooke wine, Horace. After all, don't you recall the trouble we had with the children's governess of some years ago? She *drank,* Captain Blaize, quite shockingly. Such a terrible example for the children."

"Terrible," repeated Captain Blaize, cocking a sardonic eyebrow at Captain Sears, who, it was apparent, had already had a number of glasses of wine. Then he looked across the room at me, a slight smile on his face, but I leaned further back into the shadows.

"Been to New Bedford before, Blaize?" inquired his host.

"Occasionally," Captain Blaize answered coolly. "I own a shipyard. We've been building vessels for your whalers for years."

"Ah, that explains why you've such a fine bark yourself. Despite the damage it suffered in the Arctic. You did the repairs yourself, eh? Wouldn't try Arctic whaling myself — too risky for even my liking, and too cold."

Captain Blaize's face had tightened as he spoke; the small scar whitened in his dark face. He said nothing but this did not deter Captain Sears, who continued to compare the types of whaling, stressing the superiority of the sperm whale trade over all the others. Captain Blaize remained silent and reached for his second glass of Madeira.

Apparently my employer had decided in favor of Captain Blaize's vessel; I found myself hoping that Captain Sears had had to pay handsomely for it. Captain Blaize, whatever he was, did not look a pigeon for the plucking.

Charles was bored with the adult conversation. He was fingering several of the ivory chess pieces which were set up on a small game table. Abigail sat at her mother's feet and had one finger in her mouth. I tried to attract her attention, motioning that she put both hands in her lap, but she ignored me.

"Captain Blaize," said Mrs. Sears, patting Abigail's head, "tell us about your home in Maine. My husband tells me you own a huge island."

"I own most of a rather small island, madam. Thunder Island is about twelve miles off the coast of Maine."

"Twelve miles! I declare I'd grow quite vaporish at the thought of being so far away from solid ground." She spoke as if an island were not solid ground at all but some sort of mud flat in which one would sink. Captain Blaize did not attempt to enlighten her as to the solidity of his island.

"Of course," she continued in the same arch, animated tones, "I'm certain it's very beautiful in a wild sort of way. Tell me, Captain Blaize, would I like it?" And she cocked her head to one side making her diamond earbobs shimmer.

"You are perfect for your setting, Mrs. Sears," replied her guest rather ironically, but she seemed to regard this as a compliment, waving her ivory fan in front of her face. Glancing around the cluttered, overdone room, I questioned whether it had indeed been a compliment or not.

"Are there other people on Thunder Island?" Amelia Sears went on.

"I assure you I don't live like Robinson Crusoe, Mrs. Sears. Besides my family, there is a village of people at one end of the island."

"I think Amelia is trying to find out whether you're married, Blaize," said Captain Sears, grinning.

"Oh, Horace," protested Mrs. Sears, again taking refuge behind her fan. I had never seen her in this coy flirtatious light and for some reason her manner increased the embarrassment I had been feeling.

"I've not been so fortunate, madam," said Captain Blaize coolly as though he meant just the opposite.

"Why ever not?" she asked, opening her eyes wide. "Don't they have beautiful women in Maine?"

He looked from her to me, his gaze full and pensive on my face. "Not as beautiful as the ladies here, certainly."

"Oh Captain Blaize, spare my blushes," I heard Amelia Sears say, her voice coming from a great distance.

"What sights have you seen around New Bedford?" asked Captain Sears. "We're proud of our town."

Captain Blaize's mouth quirked. "Well, I stopped at the Seamen's Bethel yesterday afternoon," came his unbelievable answer.

Oh God, I thought, was he actually going to admit he had met me there? I shut my eyes, waiting, hating him, hating them all.

"Why ever would you go there, Captain Blaize? That hardly seems the place for a man like you," said Amelia Sears, startled.

"Why not? I was under the impression it was for any seafaring man or family."

"Well, yes, but surely for common sailors, not sea *captains*. Just a lowly meeting house, really. Of course, it improves the waterfront area, which used to be quite dreadful, teeming with all sort of unmentionable places and people. They had to have somewhere respectable to go, didn't they? I mean, they could hardly be permitted in *our* churches. Think of the effect such low people would have on ladies and children!"

"Think of the effect that such ladies and children would have on them," was the sardonic answer.

"Oh, you mean it might elevate them to be in our company? What an original thought. How wise you are," she said, fluttering her eyelashes.

"Actually the company yesterday afternoon at the Bethel was no lower than you'd find in your own drawing room," Captain Blaize continued with an underlying tone of amusement in his voice.

"Indeed," said Mrs. Sears, not knowing how to take this.

I waited for the torment to be over, for him to tell them that he had met their children's governess there. The Bethel was surely a place Mrs. Sears would not wish me to visit and for once she was right, although she couldn't know the real reason why. It was not a common sailor that had taken liberties with me. But when he said nothing more, I realized he had been teasing me; he had got a perverse pleasure out of reminding me of our meeting. I was trembling with anger. When would the children and I be excused? Perhaps I could invent something, a headache, perhaps? But no, that would only call attention to myself and that I didn't want.

There was a sudden crash which interrupted my thoughts. The game table had flown over and the chessboard was sliding to the floor, scattering pieces helter-skelter. Charles, embarrassed by his clumsiness, made matters worse by deliberately kicking a few of the pieces. They flew in all directions, one striking Captain Blaize's black boot.

"Charles!" cried Mrs. Sears in dismay, and then looked over at me. Quickly I was up and going across the room but Captain Blaize was before me. He set up the table and retrieved the board, which had landed with a thud on the Oriental carpet. Then both of us were down on our knees gathering up the pieces. The whole thing was so characteristic of what commonly went on in this house that I had an absurd desire to giggle.

"Captain Blaize, it's very good of you but you don't have to do that. Miss Cooke is quite capable," said Amelia Sears.

"I daresay she is capable of repairing any damage caused by your children, madam," he said.

She laughed uncertainly. I retrieved the last pawn and set it on the board and then Captain Blaize took my hand and helped me to my feet. With heightened color I moved back to my chair.

"I think it's time you took the children upstairs, Miss Cooke," said Mrs. Sears. I suppose she was anxious to get them from the room before another fracas occurred.

"No, I don't want to go upstairs yet, Mama. I want to stay down here," cried Abigail.

"Now, my dearest, it's time for bed. I'll send Annie up with a treat for you. How would you like that?" she asked coaxingly.

"No!" she cried. I went across the room to her and reached for her hand but she eluded me in her most ungracious manner. She began to cry with frustration.

Amelia Sears stared at her as though she had never seen her before and I was going to take her arm forcibly when Captain Sears picked up his daughter, who, by now, was in the full throes of a tantrum. He carried her across the room to the door.

"Say good night to Captain Blaize, Charles, and come

with Miss Cooke and me," he said.

I glanced over to where he stood holding the sobbing Abigail and then looked back at Charles and Captain Blaize. In spite of his help with Abigail, I did not want him accompanying us to the schoolroom. I did not want to be alone with him except for the children. But there was nothing I could do, I realized with sick dismay.

"Goodnight, s — sir, ma'am," I said weakly. Mrs. Sears gave a cold nod. Captain Blaize was frowning and his sharp glance moved to Captain Sears. I turned and followed my employer from the room, Charles in my wake.

Abigail's sobs quieted as we ascended the stairs and her father said, "You were a very naughty girl downstairs, Abigail."

"I don't care, Papa," she said brokenly, "I wanted to stay there with you and Mama. I don't want to have to go upstairs with Miss Cooke. We're always with her and never with you and Mama!"

"Now, Abbie, that's scarcely complimentary to your governess. You will hurt Miss Cooke's feelings and then I'll have two crying girls on my hands. Perhaps tomorrow I'll take you and Charles and Miss Cooke, of course, on an outing somewhere. Perhaps to see the new ship I've bought from Captain Blaize. Would you like that?"

Abigail nodded.

"Well then, dry your eyes. Your nose is as pink as a rabbit's. Would you enjoy a look at my new bark, Miss Cooke?" And again there was that fleshy face close to mine and that certain look in his eyes.

I could hardly tell him that I wanted nothing less than to be in his company, even for a short while. So I just smiled faintly, thinking that at the last minute I could plead a headache.

"Charles, take your sister in the schoolroom," said Captain Sears. "I can see that Annie has left a tray of milk and cookies for you." Hastily I followed the two children into the room before he could detain me on some pretext. He stood in the doorway while the children sat at the table and I made myself busy by picking up toys, folding

72

papers, stacking books. Anything to keep from looking at him, from having to talk politely to him.

"Poor Miss Cooke, she works so hard, doesn't she?" he went on. "She has her hands full looking after the two of you."

"Why shouldn't she work hard?" demanded Charles. "She's paid to, like the rest of the servants."

"Oh, I wouldn't call Miss Cooke a servant," said Captain Sears heartily.

It was belittling the way they were talking about me as though I weren't in the room. Why didn't he just leave and allow me to put the children to bed?

But it seemed he was. "All right, I must get back to our guest. Your mama will be wanting to serve dinner soon. Good night, Charles. Good night, Abigail."

"Good night," they chimed absently, their good humor restored.

"Good night, Miss Cooke," said Captain Sears across the room to me.

"Good night, sir," I answered, refusing to meet his eyes.

When he had gone, I sat down in relief, thankful that the long evening was over. At least I shouldn't have to see Captain Blaize again. Since Captain Sears had decided to purchase his vessel, surely he had no more business here. He would doubtless leave on the morrow. But just then I had a sudden sharp feeling of regret, of something missed, something just touched but not realized, grasped but not fully known, like a glimpse of something so lovely it brought tears to your eyes before it was whisked away. And the odd thing was, I realized, I was not frightened of Captain Blaize in the same way I was of Captain Sears. That seemed foolish considering it was Captain Blaize who had kissed me. But somehow now I was sure that he had kissed me in spite of himself without intent to hurt or frighten me, not cold-bloodedly for a perverse pleasure as Captain Sears might have done in similar circumstances. I had to be very careful these weeks while my employer was at home, careful to stay with the children as much as possible and not take solitary walks. Even a poor govern-

73

ess, it was now obvious, was not safe in his house. I recalled what Charles had said about one of their former governesses, Miss Stacey, to whom Captain Sears had brought a present from his travels, the one who had been dismissed. Had the poor woman been forced to succumb to his advances or had she actually been in love with him and believed him to be in love with her? Had she been dismissed because she had become tiresome to him or because Mrs. Sears had suspected something? Either way, it was his fault entirely. Yes, I had to be very careful.

After the children were in bed, I went to my room and changed into my dressing gown. I took the pins from my hair and shook out the thick curls. The room was chilly; Annie had been too busy to light the fire and I had not bothered to myself. I opened a book of poetry, trying to soothe my mind for sleep. But I could not concentrate. I kept seeing Captain Blaize across the drawing room, in the chapel. I wondered whether Horace or Amelia Sears had noticed anything unusual in our meeting tonight. But they had not acted as though they were aware of any undercurrents in the room. They were both so self-absorbed that they did not commonly notice feelings that others might be experiencing.

I wondered what Captain Blaize thought of me, if he chanced to think of me at all. Assuredly he could not have admired me tonight; I had shown myself to be a very poor governess, unable to instill grace or graciousness in the children. Mrs. Sears would hold me accountable for the children's actions tonight. She had been very embarrassed by Charles when he had kicked the pieces of the chess set and by Abigail when she had begun to cry. Mrs. Sears would be very angry with me indeed. Tomorrow was certain to be difficult, I thought miserably. I lay down on the bed for a long while before eventually falling asleep.

When hours later a knock came at the door, I thought it was in my head, in some vague dream, but when it was softly repeated, I struggled up, rubbing my eyes. Abigail sometimes woke in the night and wanted a drink of water, or to climb in bed with me if she was frightened. Draping

74

my dressing gown around my shoulders, I put my hand on the knob. But then I remembered that I had locked the door. And I remembered why.

"Who was it?" I asked softly.

"It's Horace, Miranda. Open the door. I must speak with you."

Captain Sears! "What do you want, sir? Is Mrs. Sears ill? It's very late." I held my breath.

"Open your door, my dear. The children will wake up if you keep me standing out here. Open up, there's a good girl."

If I kept him standing out there! "Whatever it is, can't it wait until morning?"

"Open the door or I'll break off the lock," came his voice, no longer wheedling, but threatening, sinister. I was terrified; I had not been mistaken in my assessment of his character. He was a lecher who meant to force his attentions on me.

"If you break the lock, you will wake the children, and they'll wake Mrs. Sears," I countered desperately. "That won't please you."

"If that happens, I'll tell her it was *you* who invited me here, Miss Cooke. Now open the door!"

"She won't believe that!"

"Why not? She's believed it before. If you don't open the door, I'll see to it that either way you lose your position here."

I covered my face with my hands. It was hopeless; I had no choice but to let him in. If I didn't, he would contrive some ugly way to have me dismissed and then I would be without a reference, without a post, no money, no future. Oh God, I thought wretchedly, why didn't I just die of cholera too? Why on earth was I spared just to be reduced to this? I was shaking uncontrollably but somehow I managed to draw back the bolt.

The door opened quickly and there stood Captain Sears holding a candle in his unsteady grip. He wore a red velvet dressing gown, which was open to reveal his barrellike chest. His face was slack, the flesh loose, his eyes bloodshot.

"Now that's a good girl. I came to tell you, my dear, that I don't hold you to blame for the way the children acted this evening. Now Amelia, she's another story, but I think I can bring her round. I'll have a talk with her tomorrow when she's had a chance to calm down, after that fellow Blaize has gone. I'm certain I can promise you that you won't hear another word about it. I'll tell her I spoke to you myself, man of the house and all that, eh?"

I forced myself to take a deep breath and speak calmly. "That's very generous of you, Captain Sears. I, too, am sorry that the children did not behave better, but they don't have much practice in sitting quietly in drawing rooms. But now it's very late and I have to get back to bed." I tried to push the door shut but he laid a heavy arm across it.

"Now don't be unkind," he said. "You just said I was generous. Why don't you be a little generous? You don't want to lose your place here, do you? You're a very tempting little piece, so fresh, so innocent and timid and skittish as a colt. When I saw you the last time, you were pale and thin as a starved cat. But being here agrees with you, m'dear. And it's agreeable for me as well. I like to think of you here in my house, looking after my children."

"And the other governess you sent packing? Did you also like to think of her here, looking after your children?" I did not care what I said to him. What did it matter? I would lose my post here at any rate.

That sobered him a trifle; he started and his eyes narrowed. "Let's just say I can make things very pleasant for you here — or very unpleasant. You see, Miss Cooke, the choice is yours."

He walked farther in the room, setting down the candle. I moved backward until I felt the back of my knees touch the bed. "If you don't get out of here I'll scream! I don't care what you have done to me — I'll scream if you come near me. Please, for God's sake, Captain Sears, go away!"

But he had grabbed me, encircling my waist with one hand and fondling my breast with the other. Then as I

76

opened my mouth to scream, he clamped his thick lips on mine. Tears of horror scalded my eyes as I struggled to push him away but he only forced me down on the bed, hurting me, squeezing me, until I could scarcely breathe. The foul breath of him was suffocating. His mouth forced mine to open, his hands were tearing the bodice of my nightgown. I wanted to scream and scream but only succeeded in making ineffectual little sounds no one could have heard. I wished with all my heart that I could faint and thus escape him, at least consciously.

Suddenly Captain Sears's shoulders were wrenched back and the odious pressure of his body was gone. I opened my eyes to see Captain Blaize releasing him; his eyes were flashing, the scar standing out pale in his dark cheek.

"What the hell, Blaize?" said Captain Sears thickly. "Just havin' a bit of fun, you know."

Captain Blaize put his clenched fists behind his back. "It didn't look like the lady was having much fun, Sears. Seducing your children's prim governess! Can't you find a more willing victim? I thought better of you!" His voice was mild, ironic even. If I hadn't caught the look of rage transforming his handsome features, I'd have thought he were slightly amused by what he had interrupted.

Captain Sears was a large man but Captain Blaize was taller. He was still dressed in evening clothes. His expression was scornful as he surveyed his host, who could not help but look ridiculous in his elaborate dressing gown, his hair mussed, his mouth slack.

Sobbing, I sat up and clutched the torn bodice of my nightgown together. Captain Sears gave Captain Blaize an ugly glare, then he shrugged. "I suppose I can at that," he said. "Don't know what I saw in her anyway." And taking his candle, he lurched from the room. We were silent while we listened to his unsteady progress down the stairs. Then, far off, a door opened and closed. And we were alone.

"I was hoping he'd fall and break his bloody neck. I was tempted to throw him down the stairs myself but I am, after all, a guest in his house and the resulting fray wouldn't have done either of us any good."

"No, you wouldn't have sold your bark," I said. I was not looking at him. I was sitting in bed, my knees tucked under my chin, my legs under the bedclothes.

"That wasn't what I meant," Captain Blaize said, amused. Then, in a different tone, "Don't cry anymore, Miss Cooke. You are quite safe now, I assure you." He sat down on the bed.

I flashed him a look then and inched farther away from him.

He smiled. "I know you are not convinced of that after our first meeting, but it's true. I won't touch you. Here, put on your dressing gown." He handed it to me. "Does your door have a lock on it? Yes, I see there's a bolt. Well, bolt it tonight after I leave and don't open it until the servants are stirring in the morning."

He hardly needed to tell me that, I thought angrily. I knew I should be thanking him for coming to my aid but the words refused to come. I wished he would leave. I wanted to be able to fling my arms about my pillow and cry with abandon to release the emotions which had been raging inside me. I was not thinking about tomorrow, not yet.

"How did you know to come up here?" I asked softly.

He frowned. "I saw your face earlier tonight when Sears was going to carry the little girl to the schoolroom. You had such a look of wild fear, like a trapped animal waiting to be tortured. I had noticed he couldn't take his eyes off you in the drawing room and I didn't like the way he was looking at you. I wondered whether he had a scheme like this in mind—it's very common for the master of a house to force his attentions on his female servants. So I decided to stay awake to see if you needed any assistance. My room is across from theirs so I knew I'd hear him if he stole out. I listened for a long while but eventually fell asleep in the chair. When I awoke, I opened my door and thought I heard voices upstairs. I came to investigate. I'm sorry I fell asleep for even that short while, Miss Cooke. If I hadn't, I could have spared you his attentions altogether."

"I'm just grateful you came in time," I said faintly. "And

78

now please don't think me rude if I ask you to leave. I want to be alone."

He leaned over and flicked a tear from my cheek with his finger. I jerked back, away from him, and brushed the tears aside myself. He looked as though he wanted to say something more but I looked down and began to smooth out the damp sheet. He stood up.

"Good night, Miss Cooke," he said quietly. "I'm glad I could have been of service." I nodded, still avoiding his gaze, and he walked to the door. "I didn't think I'd ever see you again, after yesterday." And I heard the door close behind him.

Chapter Four

In the morning I was awakened abruptly by Abigail pounding on my door. I realized I had overslept and got out of bed to unlock the door.

"Miss Cooke, why did you lock your door?" she demanded crossly.

Until that moment I had not thought of the events of last night or the reason why I had had to slide the bolt aside. But illumination poured into my head, scorching me with its dreadful memories. "Oh, I had a bad nightmare and felt better locking my door."

She frowned. "But you always tell us that nightmares are not real, that they cannot hurt you."

"Yes, that's true. Abigail, but I still felt better locking my door. Come on, let's get you dressed before Annie brings up your breakfast. Is Charles awake?"

She nodded, a finger in her mouth. We went into her room and I found her shoes, stockings, petticoats, and dress. I helped her into them and brushed her hair. It amazed me that I could chat with her and do the things automatically that I had done for hundreds of mornings while in another part of my mind I cowered and wondered what on earth I was going to do, how things could possibly go on as they had been after the devastating events of the night. The master of the house had taken from me what little dignity and pride I possessed, and he had tried his best to rob me of even more. How could I stay in this house seeing him, seeing his wife, taking care of his children all the while remembering the sickening way his fleshy lips had clamped on mine, the way his hands had groped my bare skin, the horrible smell and feel of him, remembering with horror that I was as helpless as a caged animal, as Captain Blaize had said.

I was grateful for the timely intervention of Captain Blaize but he may have only forestalled an inevitable event. Captain Sears might try again to molest me, this time with no interference to thwart his desire. Or even if he did not, he would still hold it to my account that a guest in his house had come upon him in so unadmirable and compromising situation. He would not forgive either Captain Blaize or myself for the fool he had been made to look. Idly I wondered whether he would go back on his plan to buy Captain Blaize's bark. That would be blamed on me also, both men losing out on a financial deal. Both would have cause to resent me.

"Ouch! You're hurting me—you pulled my hair!"

"I'm sorry, Abigail." I set down the brush, fighting a desire to burst into tears. What should I do, I wondered as we went into the schoolroom where Annie had just set down steaming bowls of porridge. Charles was there before us, spooning brown sugar on his cereal.

"Is that Captain Blaize still here, Annie?" asked Charles without much curiosity.

"Yes, Master Charles. He was up very early this morning. Jane saw him leave the house when she was sweeping the hearth in the drawing room. He didn't want no breakfast, he said."

"Perhaps he's left for good then." I tried to speak lightly but I felt my face grow warm.

"Oh no, I don't think so, miss. He left all his things in his room. Just gone for a walk, I reckon. Jane said his face was as black as the devil's. It's another fine day."

I smiled at her and nodded. Another fine day. In heaven's name, what was I going to do?

"Don't you want your porridge, miss?"

"No, thank you, Annie. Just tea this morning."

"And you didn't eat your supper last night either. You better be careful, miss, or you'll start looking the way you used to when you came here."

I wish I did, I thought glumly. Captain Sears had not

81

given me a second glance then.

"Not feelin' well, are you, miss?" pursued Annie, and the children both turned to look at me. "Don't look like you slept too good."

"I'm fine, just not hungry." Why didn't they all find something else to interest them in besides how I looked or what I would or would not eat.

"Well, I best be gettin' the rooms tidied," said Annie. "And then I'll take the tray back to the kitchen. Cook might need me, seein' that there's company." She left the room, sniffling.

I wondered what I should do when the children finished their hot cereal. Should I try to get them started on something? I couldn't remember what it was we were studying yesterday. What had I planned to do today? I hadn't the faintest idea. I picked up my cup and walked over to the window which overlooked the town and the harbor.

My throat felt dry; I gulped some tea. What would happen today? Would Captain Sears drum up some reason to send me packing? Would Mrs. Sears, having got wind of the escapades in the night, send for me and throw me out of the house? Could she have been awakened last night? Or by some strange unspoken conspiracy, would we all go on as if last night had never occurred?

I pictured us sitting in the drawing room on autumn evenings, me in my chair in the corner, Mrs. Sears dressed elaborately, Captain Sears drinking whiskey, chatting to her about the outfitting of his new ship, about what parties they would attend that week, about the sights he'd seen in his voyages when they'd stopped at tropical islands for supplies. And she, smiling, making the correct responses, the children interrupting, making demands. And all the while I would sit there in the background, thankful that they ignored me, that I was like a stick of furniture. Could it be that way? Did I want it to be that way? Did I want to remain here even though I had nowhere else to go?

I thought desperately that I must decide on some course of action, but for the life of me I did not know what to do.

I cursed myself for being such a weakling, a timid, dull girl who hadn't the presence of mind to help herself.

I thought of Miss Upton. But she could not help me. I had recently received a letter from her posted from Madeira. She was now fulfilling her dream of a voyage to Australia, and Madeira had been a port of call. She was far away; I would never see her again.

There was Miss Spooner. But no, I shuddered involuntarily, I could never go to her and confide the reason for wanting to leave Mrs. Sears's employ. She had assisted me once, very much against her will, and would not do so again, I was certain. Somehow also I felt she would blame me for Captain Sears's lecherous behavior. She would not regard me as an innocent party no matter how much I protested. I could not go to her.

There was no one. After my parents had died, I had no family. I was feeling very sorry for myself, wondering why I had ever been born.

What was the matter with me? My parents had stressed that it was something in me that would not be content, that it was a serious flaw in my character that I could never seem to find my place, that I could not seem to make friends or feel satisfied with the life that had been ordained for me. Yet I could not believe that it was ordained for me to be seduced by Captain Sears!

In India I had wandered through my childhood, never really feeling a part of anything, shying from what I saw around me. In New Bedford I had passed two more years of feeling little, doing little, just going from day to day placidly like a windup doll, looking after the children but having little desire in whether they learned what I was teaching or not, not really caring about anyone or anything, just doing what was expected of me with little emotion or determination. I had always done what was expected of me with a dull resignation that had characterized most of my life. I had actually done something by leaving India but then even that impetus had petered out and I was left grasping the one post which had been found for me. I had not even the gumption to look for another without references, not even now, because soon my money would run out and then where would I be? How would I live? I pictured myself going from door to door, farmhouse to farmhouse, begging for bread, water, a dirty bedraggled figure. Yet was that not better than staying in this house another day? That could yet happen even if I did not leave of my own accord. If I were tossed out bag-and-baggage, then that very well could be what would happen to me anyway. So should I embrace that future by my own choice or wait for it to be thrust upon me?

"Miss Cooke! Charles got porridge in my eye!"

I scarcely heard them. It was all so trivial. Who cared whether Charles had flicked a bit of his cereal onto Abigail's face? She would wipe it off and they would go on until next time one did the other a nuisance. I wished I could wipe off the memory of last night and go on as usual, too. But did I truly want to continue as usual? Hadn't I just been thinking how worthless and dull it all was, how I was little more than half a person with little feeling and contentment? But even that half-life was preferable to the nightmare I was now living. No matter what, I could not go on as though last night had never happened. I could not wipe it away as Abigail could wipe away the clump of oatmeal. I could not pretend it hadn't happened and continue my days ad nauseum, ad infinitum.

There were footsteps coming up the stairs. My heart began to race; I dropped the cup and saucer and stupidly, woodenly, stood there watching while they broke into pieces and the tea spilled, some of it seeping into the floorboards, the rest collecting in a dark puddle. I continued to stare at the mess, hearing the children clatter up to see who was coming. Then the footsteps halted outside the door and the children were silent.

Here it was. My orders to leave. I turned around almost in relief; for wasn't this finally a real action, a course I would have to take?

And I gave a slight gasp to see Captain Blaize standing there, tall and broad-shouldered, in the doorway, ignoring the children, his gray eyes looking across the room into my own, holding them, claiming them.

"Miss Cooke spilled her tea and broke her cup," announced Abigail, satisfied, to no one in particular. "And Charles tossed a spoonful of porridge in my eye."

His black brows were drawn together and his face was set in uncompromising lines. "Miss Cooke, I must speak with you. I assumed you and the children would be awake by now."

"Mama and Papa always sleep late but we don't do we, Abigail?" said Charles. "Abigail had to wake up Miss Cooke this morning. She'd locked her door."

Still I said nothing. Yes, we're awake. Yes, we've had breakfast. We should have begun our lessons now only I can't think of a blessed thing to do.

"Come out into the corridor. The children can be by themselves for a few minutes."

"Why should she? Why do you want to speak with her?" demanded Charles.

"Be quiet, Charles," I said, and in spite of myself, was drawn across the room as though I were walking through water, wondering what on earth this enigmatic, brooding man wanted with me. He motioned that we go out in the corridor and then followed behind me.

"What is it, Captain Blaize?" I asked abruptly. "I thought you would be leaving the house today."

"I am leaving," he said, "and that is why I've come to see you."

"There was no need for you to say good-bye. And if you've come to give me another opportunity to thank you for last night, I do thank you with all my heart. But it may be that you have only prolonged the inevitable," I said desperately, clasping my hands together, "either that or I must leave today with no references."

"Would that be so terrible?"

"Leaving with no references? I assure you it would. I must earn my own living, Captain Blaize, and without a recommendation from a previous employer the situation is near to hopeless. And I can't presume that Mrs. Sears will

85

write me an adequate reference if I leave so abruptly, whether she is aware of the cause or not."

"I have a solution that I believe to be the ideal one."

"A solution? For me?" I regarded him warily. "Do you know of a household which requires the services of a governess?"

"Oh, what I have in mind is a much better solution than that." There was a glint of amusement in his eyes. "And a far simpler one. It's this: I want you to marry me, Miss Cooke."

"Marry . . . you!" I whispered, my hands clutching into tight balls. "Is that what you said?"

"That's what I said. Your position in this house has become intolerable. I can assure you that as my wife your life would be far more agreeable."

"Captain Blaize, I can't but think you are trifling with me. And I don't find the situation amusing in the slightest."

"I assure you, Miss Cooke, that I am perfectly serious."

"But . . . we don't know each other. We know nothing of each other! How can you even consider that we be married?"

"You need a way out of this house, a secure future."

"Yes, but marriage—to a perfect stranger?" I colored, remembering that in a certain way he knew me better than anyone. "Besides," I went on hurriedly, "I'm not the sort of girl a man would want to marry."

He smiled. "And what kind of a girl is that, do you think? I believe you're exactly the sort of girl or lady, I should say."

My head was spinning. I couldn't think clearly or logically; he was robbing me of all rational thought.

"Come, Miss Cooke, I have no wish to further distress you, but the time has come for some plain speaking. Do you know how close you came to being raped last night?"

I closed my eyes in an agony of embarrassment, my face flaming, but the unrelenting voice went on.

"You cannot remain in this house another day—or another night. I cannot stay here indefinitely to thwart

Captain Sears's intentions, you know. And if you left, as you say, without a reference, where would you go?"

"I don't know. I can't . . . I can't think."

"Mrs. Sears told me last night at dinner that you are an orphan and have no real home, that you came from India two years ago and entered her employ. If you had had anywhere else to go, you would not have stayed in this position as long as you have. I am offering you a fine house, a life of leisure."

"I don't doubt that, Captain Blaize. It's not your possessions I am interested in. It's . . . ." *I don't know you,* my mind shrieked. How could I be your *wife?*

His brows knit. "Can you honestly say that you would prefer to stay here to perhaps be sacked and blamed for something you did nothing to encourage?"

"Of course not!"

"Or to leave today with nowhere to go, to be dragged down to God-knows-what fate?"

"I don't know what sort of fate I'll have if I go with you!" I cried, my eyes refusing to meet his.

There was a slight pause. "I will take care of you, Miranda. I'm not an ogre, you know, or a bluebeard."

I have only your word for that, I thought sullenly.

"There really is no alternative for you, my girl. Don't you see that?" He was becoming impatient.

"How can I answer you? I can't think . . ." Marry this tall dark stranger, this black-browed, scarred man I knew nothing about except that he was a whaler who had come to New Bedford to sell his ship. Except that he had taken me in his arms and kissed me passionately, hungrily, like Captain Sears had. No, not like Captain Sears. Never like Captain Sears. Whatever he was, he was not that sort of man at all. And I believed that he sincerely wished to help me, that I could trust him as I had never trusted Captain Sears. But there was something about him which made me uncomfortable, a smoldering intensity which he kept tightly reined. Unlike Captain Sears, very little of the real man, I felt, was on the surface. Only glimpses here and there . . .

87

"I knew that I must leave today, but I never thought . . . I've been so frightened," I said, more to myself than to him.

His face softened a trifle. He reached down to touch my hair for an instant. "My dear, you would do me much honor, you know."

"Couldn't I just . . . I don't know . . . don't you know anyone I could work for?"

"I hardly think any respectable matrons would take a recommendation from me, Miranda, even if I numbered many among my acquaintance, which I do not. I live on an island with my mother and her companion, and there is a small village of lobstermen, fishermen, and shipbuilders. I haven't any sort of employment to offer you. So, you see, I'm afraid it has to be marriage." His voice was apologetic though with that same underlying amusement.

"I'm sorry if I seem ungrateful, sir. I realize you are doing me a great honor by asking me to become your wife. It's just so unbelievable . . . that a person like you would wish to marry someone like me."

"You find that so difficult to believe?" A smile played around the corners of his mouth.

"I do indeed. And we are not acquainted with one another at all. You have no idea of what I am like, of what kind of wife I would be. And I have no idea of the type of husband you would be."

"We are acquainted in one way, are we not?" he asked softly. I could not mistake his meaning and flushed again.

"I . . . first tell me something about yourself . . . about your home."

"What do you wish to know?" His voice had altered slightly, hardened.

"You have decided not to be a whaler any longer?"

"I have," he answered curtly. "That life is over for me. I have both a shipbuilding business and a lumber mill which demand my attention. My father is dead and there is no one else to take them in hand. For a time I found whaling more exciting but, like the prodigal son, I returned to the island some months ago for good. In Thunder House

88

there is my mother and her companion. My mother does not enjoy good health and so it is likely we will see little of them. Well, Miranda, there it is. I do not think that the rugged landscape and relative isolation of life on a solitary island will daunt a girl who has endured a life in India such as I can imagine a missionary's life to be, not to mention the years spent in this house with those two children. So, what is your answer?"

"I . . ." I pressed a hand to my hot cheek. "It's just that I never imagined this is the way things would turn out."

"Things seldom happen the way you imagine them," he said coolly. "If anyone had predicted more than a year ago that I would return to Thunder Island to stay, I'd have scorned him for a fool."

Thunder Island. The name now had an ominous, menacing sound. And the bitter droop to his mouth did not reassure me. He had not wanted to return, I realized. And I recalled the way he had looked in the Bethel, almost blighted.

"You truly wish to marry me and take me back to your home?" I still could not believe it.

"I do. I can see strength and character in your lovely face and it reassures me."

"Oh no, I don't see how you could possibly see those things. I haven't much of either, I assure you," I said earnestly.

His face lightened then. "I don't believe you know yourself at all, do you? Will you marry me, Miranda? I won't ask you again."

I took a deep breath. "Are you always this impulsive, Captain Blaize?"

"I follow my instincts, if that's what you mean. And I'm rarely mistaken. At least—" He paused, his eyes narrowing.

"Very well, Captain Blaize. I will marry you," I said.

He did not show relief or joy at my acquiescence. He merely replied, "You have made a wise decision. I trust you will not regret it."

I hoped not indeed. What an odd thing to say, I

thought, after his careful persuasions. I felt rather light-headed and wondered at the way he had broken down all my doubts and defenses, sweeping aside my protests. But it did seem a miraculous solution to an otherwise dismal if not disastrous future. I fervently hoped that the same sort of future was not the one I would share with Captain Blaize.

"My Christian name is Nicholas," he went on. "I will now go and apprise your employer of our intentions. I wish to quit this house without further delay. Go and pack whatever you wish but you need bring nothing with you. Today we will order a complete trousseau for you and it will be shipped to Thunder Island on completion. We will depart for there tonight."

"Tonight!" I repeated dazedly. "But Captain — Nicholas, surely a minister can't be expected to marry us at a moment's notice?"

"We will be married on board ship after we embark. I will make the necessary arrangements with the captain."

"What are you doing out here, Miss Cooke? Don't you know you should be in here looking after us?" Charles was standing in the schoolroom doorway.

"I've just been asking Miss Cooke to marry me, Master Charles," said Nicholas.

"Asking Miss Cooke to marry you? Ha! That's a good one! Did you hear that, Abigail?"

"Did I hear what? Charles has drawn a picture of you, Miss Cooke, and put a huge wart on the end of your nose!" said Abigail, coming out into the corridor.

"Shut up, Abigail, you silly girl!" said her brother.

"I'll leave you to say your good-byes to the children while I seek out Sears."

"Yes, all right." I bit my lip.

"Don't look so downcast, my dear. Matters could be a good deal worse, you know." He went down the stairs and I followed the children back into the schoolroom.

"What did he mean, say your good-byes, what did he mean?"

"Well, Charles, Captain Blaize has just asked me to be

his wife. And I've agreed," I said wonderingly.

"You mean you are really going to marry him? How can you teach us if you do that? I don't believe it. Why would he wish to marry you—a sea captain like him? You're our governess. Governesses don't marry sea captains."

"Thank you, Charles, for graciously pointing that out. It is astonishing, isn't it? But it's true. I'm leaving with him in a little while."

"But you can't leave!" wailed Abigail. "You're ours— you belong to us! Who will look after us?"

"I know it seems very odd and sudden—it does to me, too. But I'm afraid I am leaving. I must. You'll soon have a new governess, probably a much better one."

It wasn't as if they were fond of me, I reminded myself. It was only that they were used to me and my abrupt departure was an upset in their routine. Still, I felt terribly guilty in leaving them this way and for several minutes tried to reassure them that they would have someone very soon to take my place.

"I hate Captain Blaize!" cried Abigail. "Papa's going to be very angry with you, Miss Cooke."

"I'm certain you're right," I said nervously. I dreaded the thought of facing him again.

After a while I went to my room and packed my gowns in a box with a few other things. I put on my cloak and bonnet. Then I went back to the schoolroom and told the children good-bye, standing in the doorway. Neither looked up from what they were doing; neither answered me. I might not have been there at all.

Clutching my box I descended the stairs to the first floor. I halted in the front hall, not knowing what to do or where to go, feeling like a fool. Where was Captain Blaize—Nicholas? It was difficult to think of him as Nicholas. It was near to impossible to think of him as my husband. Where was Captain Sears? I quaked at the thought of seeing him. And Mrs. Sears—but she probably was still sleeping. Should I go outside and stand on the porch? Should I wait here?

One of the maids came out of the drawing room and

gaped at me. "Goin' someplace, miss?" she asked, her startled gaze taking in my luggage beside me.

"Uh . . . yes . . . that is, yes, I'm leaving, Jane." I went red from the look on her face, and then a door down the hall opened and Nicholas came out.

I went over to him, wanting him to shield me from it all, wanting him to take me away as quickly as possible. He smiled reassuringly at me though his eyes held a hard expression. He reached for my hand and then, to my horror and confusion, he pulled me into the room.

Captain Sears was standing before the fireplace, scowling fiercely. When he saw me, his eyes narrowed. I looked down at the floor, tracing the pattern of the carpet with my eyes, trying to imagine myself somewhere else.

Nicholas said amiably, "I've been telling your employer that last night I could scarcely keep my eyes off you, Miranda, and swept you off your feet with my sudden proposal this morning. And now that I've explained the facts to you, sir, we must be on our way as we've a great deal to do. Thank you again for your hospitality."

"Just a minute, Blaize," said Captain Sears sneeringly. "Are you telling me you really want to wed this wench? You yourself implied last night she was not very appetizing. A dull poor girl of no consequence — and you, proud as Lucifer! What the hell went on last night between the two of you? And you had the gall to stop me from doing what you obviously were eager to do yourself! I contend that you want her for your own pleasure, not as a wife but a doxy, and she is stupid enough to believe you mean marriage!"

Nicholas dropped my arm and stepped forward. A muscle worked in his clenched jaw. When he spoke, his voice was like steel. "One more word from you, Sears, and I'll forget I was a guest in your home. I'll do what I should have done last night, teach you a much-needed lesson. And I wonder what Mrs. Sears would think if she were to learn you tried to rape your children's governess."

Captain Sears glared belligerently at Nicholas. "Get out of here, both of you!"

92

"With pleasure, sir. Come, Miranda," Nicholas said coldly and, taking my arm again, propelled me from the room out into the hall, where Jane still stood, dustpan in hand, staring at us.

"Is that yours?" he asked, gesturing to the box.

"Yes."

He picked it up along with his own bag. Just as we reached the door, we heard Captain Sears shout, "You're a pair of fools! Don't come back in a week or a month, demanding your precious job back or your ship, for that matter!"

"No chance of that," said Nicholas laughing, his anger suddenly gone.

The door was slammed behind us. "We're both well rid of that place, so cast away any final doubts you may have."

"I've never been so glad to leave a place in my life," I said breathlessly.

"Even to go off with me?" His mouth quirked. "Bless you for that. But first things first. I haven't had breakfast. I'm famished. How about you?"

"I am feeling rather weak," I admitted. "I didn't eat breakfast either."

"Let's find an inn and have some food, then. Do you mind a short walk?"

"Not at all. I like walking. I like being out of doors."

"Good. You'll have all the opportunities you want for that when we get to Thunder Island. There are no carriage paths, just riding and walking trails."

"Tell me about Thunder Island."

"Well, it's about five miles long and three miles across. I own most of it except for the village on the northern side, Nansett, which has the only harbor. The people there fish, and farm, and many of the men also work at my shipyard and lumber mill. It's quite beautiful in an untamed, remote sort of way. I hope you'll come to love it as I do. Unfortunately my mother has never grown accustomed to life there in thirty years. And since father's and sister's deaths her health has severely declined."

"What is the nature of her illness?"

He frowned. "I would say she has always suffered from discontent. She was the spoiled daughter of a wealthy Bostonian family—my father met her there on one of his trips. She was very beautiful and they were immediately drawn to one another. Her father approved his suit and so they were married after a short acquaintance. Soon after their marriage he brought her to Thunder Island. There's nothing to say but that she hated it from the very beginning."

"Why?"

He shrugged. "She missed the social life of Boston, the excitement of living in a big city. She's always been prone to bouts of depression which have made her truly ill. Years ago Father hired a companion for her, Sarah Thatcher, who is still with her today. They appear to be devoted to one another, but sometimes I question whether either of them do the other any good. At any rate, raising a family occupied her. She had three children; myself, then my sister, Julia, and then Emily. Emily is married and lives in Nansett. At Thunder House it's just my mother, Lavinia, Sarah, and soon, the two of us."

"Did . . . did something happen to Julia? You said . . . that one of your sisters died?"

"Julia was presumed drowned two years ago. She was my mother's favorite. My mother was never well, as I've said, and Julia's disappearance proved her undoing. Some days she doesn't seem to realize that Julia is gone, and then other days she's normal enough. We never know what to expect." He spoke aloofly, as if he had no real attachment to the events and people he described, as if he were relating a story. But I sensed a quiet despair behind the words, the same despair I had first sensed in him in the Seamen's Bethel.

"How dreadful for her. She must be so happy you have returned home to stay."

He turned his head to regard me, one eyebrow raised mockingly. "Nothing of the sort. Why should she?"

"But . . . her only son . . ."

94

"She's never been fond of me and has made no secret of that. She'll be terribly shocked by our marriage, of course." It was evident he took a grim pleasure in that.

"I hope she . . . that is . . . I want her to like me, to approve of our marrying."

His brows drew together. "Don't worry about her, Miranda. She and Sarah live lives of their own. They scarcely care what I do."

This did not sound promising but I hadn't the courage to ask any more. We had reached the inn and were shown into a private parlor. I waited until we were alone and then said haltingly, "I do want to thank you, Nicholas, for your proposal. You were right. I couldn't have remained in Captain Sears' employ after . . . last night."

"You need someone to look after you, my dear. I doubt if I'm truly the proper person but that's neither here nor there, is it? At least married to me you'll be safe from stupid fools like Sears. How old are you?"

"Twenty."

He shook his head. "You look even younger than that. Tell me something about yourself. You must have had a very interesting life so far."

"Oh no, I don't know how you could possibly think that."

"Let me be the judge of that. Tell me about your childhood in India, and why you decided to come to New Bedford."

And so encouraged by his present genial mood and interest, I talked about my past while we ate. He seemed to listen intently as though the things I said actually mattered to him and I slowly relaxed. I was feeling more at ease with him although to regard him as a man who soon would be my husband I could not without serious qualms.

He was a complex man. He had shown me several sides of his character: an impulsive, passionate side in the Bethel, though before that he seemed troubled, depressed. Then his sardonic anger at Captain Sears, his gentle but authoritative kindness with me that morning. He was used to getting his own way, I thought, used to taking what he

95

wanted from life with both hands. He had different moods and they might be hard to interpret, to deal with. He was easily amused, easily angered, but there was a brooding, hidden side of him, too, which vaguely disturbed me.

And tonight this man would become my husband and we would live together for better or for worse. The day had the dazed eerie quality of a nightmare, moving so swiftly and incredibly from one event to the next. It was difficult to believe that so much had happened that I had no alternative but to leave the Sears home with a man I scarcely knew. Oh, I had no doubt he would keep his word and marry me—I sensed he was not a man to go back on his word—but further than that I had no idea. I didn't know what sort of husband he would be or what would be required of me in my role as his wife. Was I expected to become the lady of the house, a fine hostess? If so, I would be a dismal failure. But that was what was required of wives of wealthy gentlemen, was it not?

I decided to make a clean breast of it. "Nicholas, I hope you realize that I'm not at all used to the sort of life you lead, or I imagine you must lead. I haven't a single accomplishment. And I'm not good at meeting people, or at conversation. I hope you won't be too disappointed. I just thought I ought to warn you." I spoke the words in a rush.

"Have no qualms about that, Miranda. We are a very quiet household. We do no real entertaining. As I've explained, my mother is little better than an invalid. And she dislikes the local people—she would scarcely invite any of them to dine. You will have nothing to do but be yourself, get used to Thunder Island—and to me."

Though his first words were reassuring, the last three he spoke dismayed me. Get used to him. Would that be possible, used to shared intimacies with this sardonic black-browed stranger? Sometimes his gray eyes softened, warmed when they rested on me, but more often I had noticed a hardness in them, a bitterness which I could not fathom. What sort of person was he really? Could we possibly be happy together? Would I ever become comfortable in his presence? Would I ever become used to him, as he had phrased it?

When he had drunk his second mug of coffee, Nicholas said, "I have some business matters to attend to this morning. Can you occupy yourself until one o'clock when we'll meet here for lunch?" He did not wait for an answer but went on, "After that I'll take you to the dressmaker's to order your trousseas. Miss Proctor's establishment comes highly recommended."

I had heard of Miss Proctor; she sewed gowns for all the ladies of New Bedford. Some said she was better than any seamstress in Boston. I had never dreamed she would be fashioning gowns for me. "All right, Nicholas."

He stood up, tossing some coins on the table. "Until one, then. Steer clear of the rougher streets of this town; I don't wish to come looking for you."

As though I were a child, I thought indignantly. That was apparently how he regarded me. Then he saw my annoyance and his lips twitched. "After all, you never know what may happen — even in so innocent a place as the Seamen's Bethel," he said. My face flamed but he was already striding away.

After buttoning my cloak and tying the strings of my bonnet, I went outside. It was a beautiful day, the air clear and sharp as crystal, the sky blue as the Wedgewood china Amelia Sears kept in her corner cupboard. In spite of myself I wondered what was going forward at the Sears house just now. I wondered if Captain and Mrs. Sears were discussing me, what they were saying about me. Even though I had been the one wronged and my leaving was no more than they deserved, I still could not help feeling that I had done something careless, furtive by leaving. That was the way Amelia Sears would regard it whether she was aware of my true motivation or not. And in running headlong from the Sears household to Captain Blaize, I wondered nervously if I might have exchanged the deep blue sea for the devil.

Nicholas had given me some money to purchase any items I might need and I had more than two hours of total freedom, both of which made a very unusual circumstance. I wandered about the sloping harbor area, poking in quaint shops which sold scrimshaw jewelry and nautical items. As I glimpsed the masts of ships anchored close by, I was reminded of Nicholas's decision to sell his bark and give up the life of a whaler. Was he regretting it? Would he come to regret it? Having known the excitement, the danger of Arctic whaling, would he be content to remain on land building ships—ships that others would command? Did part of him dread living at Thunder House with his unhappy mother? And what about Julia, the sister who had disappeared without a trace, who was "presumed drowned"? How odd. What did that mean? What could have happened to her?

There was a shop I had always wanted to look in, but it wasn't the kind which would have interested children and I had never had the nerve to browse inside when there was no way I could have afforded any of its luxuries. It sold soaps, perfumes, lace items, and other sorts of dainty, frivolous things to tempt the female citizens of New Bedford. With Nicholas's money in my reticule I felt almost like any of the other New Bedford ladies and I was determined to look about, even buy. With a new feeling of delight and near-abandon, for me, I selected several scented soaps, gardenia, rose, and lily of the valley. I picked up a crystal bottle of perfume from France and sniffed at its delectable scent. Then I fingered longingly a lovely lace shawl. Dare I buy it? Was I the sort who could wear it or would I look foolish in it? I had never possessed anything so pretty or frivolous in my life, except perhaps the glass colored bangles I used to collect in Bombay. But I was now the fiancée of a wealthy man, incredibly enough.

"May I help you, miss?" said the shop's proprietor, a tall gaunt woman with a pince-nez. She spoke politely but her gaze was doubtful as she surveyed me. I did not look as though I could make any noticeable purchases.

"Yes, I'd like to buy this shawl," I said in a rush before I could change my mind. "And this perfume."

Her manner altered slightly. "Of course, miss. And the

soaps?"

"Yes, and a bottle of hair rinse. Lavender-scented."

"Very good, miss. I'll wrap up these things for you."

The sum I paid her seemed enormous but there was still a good bit of money left over. I decided to buy an ivory brush and comb and mirror set, too. That really is enough now, Miranda, I thought rather hysterically. It was a strange feeling, seeing something in a shop and wanting it and being able to buy it. A heady feeling.

I was coming out of the shop, one arm clutching my purchases, when I saw her. Amelia Sears was driving down the street in her open carriage. She was coming toward me. She had not seen me yet but in a moment or so she would look this way. I mustn't let her see me, I thought wildly. I could not rid myself of the feeling that in some way I had done wrong; I had shirked me responsibilities, my obligations. She must not see me. Quickly I ducked into the next shop, moving back into the darkness of it, away from the naked sunlight of the street.

"Hello, miss. Ain't got the children today?" said a voice.

I turned, startled, my face growing even warmer, to see Mr. Carr, the ship carver who fashioned the nameboards and figureheads for ships. I had not even realized it was his shop I had blundered into.

"No . . . no, I haven't . . . no, they're not with me today," I babbled, feeling a fool, feeling that I *should* have them with me.

"The boy likes my shop," the man went on. "Tell him I'm working on another Indian now. He always likes my Indians. Tell him to come in. Bring him."

"Oh, I will," I said, smiling, nodding. "I'll bring him soon. He'll like it, I'm sure." What was I saying?

"Well, good day then," he said, picking up a small paintbrush.

"Good day." I went back into the sunlight. There was no sign of Amelia Sears or her carriage. I began to walk rapidly in the direction of the inn. Back there in our private parlor I would be anonymous.

Nicholas joined me less than an hour later. I had not

missed him; I had found it peaceful, soothing, to sit in a chair in front of the fire. I had so far forgot myself to even order a small glass of sherry.

When he returned, his mood had altered from his earlier affability. He was withdrawn and taciturn, and I felt my tranquility evaporating. He seemed absorbed in grim thoughts.

"Did the business matters you spoke of—did they not go well?" I asked diffidently.

"Hmmmm? Oh, Captain Sears' bank gave me a pretty price for the *Eagle,* so they went well, if that's what you mean. I wondered in fact whether he would renege on our agreement. But he knows a fine bark when he sees one."

"The *Eagle?*"

"My whaling ship. I named it for the bald eagles you will see on Thunder Island. They come to the coves at low tide to fish."

Our food was brought then but he did not eat much. He called for another tankard of ale and I searched my mind for some topic of conversation.

"I'm looking forward to seeing Thunder Island." That was not precisely true, but I was anxious to seem cheerful in the hopes that he might regain his good humor. "Tell me more about it, will you?"

He said heavily, "What do you wish to know?"

"Well, I'm curious about the people there. Tell me more about your younger sister, Emily."

"She's about your age. She married a lobsterman, Ben Somes. Now he's my foreman at the shipyard, not because he married my sister but because he's the best man for the job. My mother was not pleased at the match, to put it lightly. She had hoped for a great deal more, I suppose, for her only remaining daughter, a Boston season perhaps."

"Did Emily want that?"

"Absolutely not. She loves Thunder Island and she's been wild about Ben since they were children. I gave my permission for their marriage last spring because I was convinced she knew her own mind. Ben's the best sort, honest and solid as the earth, and a hard worker. I believe they are very happy. Emily is to have a child five months from now."

"I hope we can be friends. I mean, I hope she likes me. She'll think it very strange that we met one day and married the next, seeing that she's known her husband all her life."

"Don't fret about that. She's been urging me to get married, to find someone, as she says, the way she's found Ben. She'll be delighted with you and with me for bringing you to Thunder House." I got the distinct impression that he was talking in order to convince himself, as though he was the one who should be delighted and wasn't.

My heart sank. Was he having second thoughts? Was he wishing he hadn't been so rash as to ask me to marry him?

"Well," he said, "it's nearly time we were at the dress-maker's. I visited her shop this morning to examine her work, and I think you'll find it more than satisfactory. I explained to her that now you'll require warm clothing, the warmest fabrics. In the spring we can commission her to make cooler gowns for you. I hope cold weather does not daunt you."

"No, not at all. I like it—the heat was always so oppressive in India, so draining. Moreover one can always add more clothing to get warm, but what can one do in the heat?"

Chuckling, he said, "Pursuing that train of thought, I could think of something if you weren't such a little innocent." His gaze was warm on my face.

I blushed hotly. "I did not mean . . . I was merely trying to assure you . . ." Oh, dear, what a fool I was. I had sounded as silly and flirtatious as Amelia Sears without knowing it.

He sobered at my flustered embarrassment but still with a devilish gleam in his eye, he said, "Never mind, Miranda. I can assure you that it will never get so hot in Maine to warrant such extreme measures. If you've finished your lunch, we should be getting to the dressmaker's."

We walked to her shop in a rather constrained silence

101

and I again was thinking wildly, Is this real? What am I doing with this man? We passed a millinery where a silk blue bonnet trimmed with feathers was displayed in the window. "Oh, how lovely," I said without thinking.

"You must have that," said Nicholas. "It matches the blue of your eyes—a lapis lazuli blue. We'll go in there after your gowns have been ordered. I'll just tell the woman not to sell it to anyone else while we're at Miss Proctor's."

"Oh no, Nicholas, you don't have to. I didn't mean . . . I wasn't asking you to buy it for me, I really wasn't."

"Why on earth not? Why shouldn't you have a pretty bonnet? You're an odd girl—don't you know it's a husband's place, duty, even, to buy nice things for his wife? I told you, I'm buying a complete trousseau for you. You'll have an array of new bonnets and everything else you need."

Feeling slightly dazed I went with him into Miss Proctor's shop. She was a tiny birdlike woman of indeterminate age who flitted about, turning me in one direction and then the other.

"Take off your bonnet, miss. And I'll take your cloak, too. Oh, this will be a pleasure, sir. Your fiancée is quite, quite lovely. So few of my customers are actually worthy of my needle. Pour yourself a glass of port, Captain Blaize. I always keep it for my gentleman guests, you know. And we, my dear, will get to work."

Nicholas sat down on the armchair, wholly at ease, and helped himself to the decanter on the small table.

"We must take your measurements, my dear. Step this way, if you please." I followed her to the back of the shop, where we went behind a large chintz-covered screen. I noted the way her brows knit at the plainness of my gown and undergarments; it was obvious she was curious about the wealthy sea captain and the impoverished girl who stood before her.

"You'll require pretty camisoles, petticoats, and corsets. White, I think, with your coloring, rather than ecru. You've a slim figure, though nicely rounded in the right

102

places." She went on talking as she measured me, oblivious to my consternation. I prayed that Nicholas could not hear her comments.

"Let's begin choosing fabrics, shall we? You'll need the warmest softest woolens for the winters in Maine and I have the perfect cashmeres. Also velvets, satins and such for evening wear, and cotton for day dresses. I'll have you outfitted splendidly, my dear. Trust me. Your handsome fiancé wants the best for you."

Fluttering back and forth, she selected lengths of various materials and held them against my throat. "No, that won't do" or "ah, quite" were her exclamations. The colors which seemed to please her were delicate lavenders and mauves, rich roses and plums, sapphire and peacock blues, cherry red, wine reds—and all in such exquisite fabrics unlike anything I had ever possessed. I stood there, quite overwhelmed, feeling like Cinderella with her fairy godmother, marveling at the size and quality of the wardrobe which would be mine in a matter of weeks.

"I have two gowns partially made that I can have ready for you in several hours," Miss Proctor said, glancing with ill-concealed disfavor at my drab gown.

"Captain Blaize has booked passage for us on a vessel which leaves at half past seven."

"Then stop here on your way to the harbor and they will be ready. I only hope that two will suffice."

"Oh, I'm certain they will be quite ample, quite enough," I assured her, thinking that I had never had more than three gowns at a time in my life. But, of course, I couldn't tell her that. Not that she hadn't guessed it already; her sharp eyes missed little.

She helped me into my gray gown then assisted in pinning up my hair, which had become disarrayed. "Such beautiful hair," she said, "black with that sheen of blue. You really should not pin it up so severely, if you'll excuse my saying so, miss. It should be allowed to fall in curls over your shoulders. If you like, when I send your new clothes, I can include some pictures and instructions on hairstyles for you and your maid."

"My maid? Oh . . . thank you, Miss Proctor. That's very good of you."

"You musn't hide your looks, my dear. Captain Blaize is a fortunate man and I imagine there are many young ladies who would give a great deal to be in your shoes."

I did not know how to answer her. But in her occupation she doubtless automatically flattered her customers; I should not put a lot of stock in what she said.

I followed her to the front of the store, where she informed Nicholas that she would have a package for me ready at seven o'clock. He nodded and then coolly handed her a sum of money, which she accepted in the same cool manner.

"If these garments are satisfactory, we will require another set of gowns made for the warmer months," he told her.

"Yes, indeed, sir. I have the lady's measurements so you have only to order."

Next door at the millinery Nicholas purchased five bonnets for me: the blue one in the window and one of a lighter blue, a black satin, a red one with bunches of imitation cherries, and one of plum-colored taffeta. When I tried on each in turn, I did not recognize myself; I gazed at my reflection with much more interest than my parents would have thought seemly. But my eyes and skin looked different; I could not help feeling startled and pleased by the way I looked. The milliner announced they were exact copies of French bonnets.

Later that day we ordered several pairs of walking shoes, kid leather slippers in different colors, and gloves and muffs to match the new pelisses and cloaks Miss Proctor would sew for me. Finally, I said, "Nicholas, I'm terribly tired. Don't you think I have enough clothes now?"

He chuckled, flicking my cheek with one finger. "You're certainly an uncommon girl to say so, Miranda. But then you're not accustomed to frivolities." He took up the bandboxes, and the parcels wrapped in brown paper and tied with string, and we left the shop.

Uneasily I wondered if he had purchased clothes for

other women. He had certainly known what he was about, lounging in a dressmaker's shop as though it were a commonplace occurrence, and then unerringly selecting the rest of the things to round out my new wardrobe. With his dark good looks and wealth and arrogance he would not have lived the life of a monk. Or a missionary, I thought with a nervous giggle. His mind wasn't on those higher planes. Not a man who followed his instincts, who had chosen the most hazardous form of whaling as his career, who had pulled a strange girl into his arms and fiercely kissed her.

In a few hours we would be alone together as man and wife. Still, I need not fear him, I assured myself. He was a gentleman or he wouldn't have spared me the abhorrent attentions of Captain Sears. Surely he would not have rescued me from those only to inflict his own on me. But we would be married, and could do as he liked.

"Shall we go back to the inn for a glass of sherry and an early supper?" he asked.

The notion of food I found totally unappealing. "If you like," I said, trying to sound as casual as possible. It was probably as plain as day how nervous I was about the hours ahead.

"I've spoken with the captain of the ship, an old acquaintance of mine," Nicholas went on. "He knows of our plans and has agreed to marry us as soon as we are at sea."

I shivered slightly; the approaching dusk carried with it a chill. When we reached the inn, I sat down on the high-backed settle before the fire, slipping off my new bonnet and smoothing my hair. The landlord brought a very dusty bottle of sherry and two glasses. Nicholas half filled my glass before pouring a large one for himself.

Then he raised his glass, smiling crookedly, and said, "To our future, Miranda. And may heaven help our intentions."

Chapter Five

Two hours later I was in our cabin, the cabin Nicholas would share with me when we were married, aboard the ship which was conveying us to Thunder Island. The room was very luxurious, paneled in burled wood; there was a maroon velvet sofa against one wall, the other wall displaying a marble top bar with cupboard beneath. A tall mirror of Honduras mahogany with ivory inset stood in the corner and there was a large bed, which rocked with the movement of the ship. Blinds covered the porthole and in another corner there was a large copper bathtub.

Unfortunately I could derive little pleasure or consolation from my surroundings, as grand as they were. The contemplation of the hours ahead caused me the gravest anxiety. Soon after we had boarded, Nicholas had gone to the captain's quarters to get ready for the ceremony, leaving the privacy of the cabin to me. Now I was waiting for the summons which would result in my marriage to Captain Nicholas Blaize.

I had been childishly delighted with the contents of Miss Proctor's package. Enclosed were two gowns, one a periwinkle blue satin with full puffed sleeves to the elbow and a low heart-shaped bodice. The other was a ruby red walking dress of soft wool. Underneath the two carefully folded gowns was a white lawn nightgown lavishly trimmed with ribbons and lace. There were also a lace-edged camisole and several starched, flounced petticoats. Enchanted, I held the gowns before me and fingered the lovely delicate undergarments. Then I was panic-stricken at the realization that Nicholas would shortly be seeing me in these intimate garments, that they had been included for his pleasure as well as mine.

The cabin boy, Will, brought buckets of hot water and I washed with the rose-scented soap in the copper tub. I had unpinned my hair and the rising steam caused it to curl tightly as it streamed over my shoulders. I put on the camisole and the petticoats, laced the strings of my stays, and then slipped the blue satin gown over my head. It was a perfect fit. It took me a while to fasten the buttons in the back. Two I simply could not manage; I decided to draw the new lace shawl about my shoulders to conceal the area, should it gape. I twisted most of my hair into a knot and left a few ringlets spilling over my shoulders.

A new peculiar sense of triumph came over me as I gazed at my reflection in the mirror. I drew on crocheted lace gloves and sat down to wait, a victim to bewildering, paradoxical sentiments. In the meantime the gentle swaying of the waves had increased to a rolling gait and my stomach had begun to respond. Though whether it was due to the sea or the apprehension inside me, I could not be certain.

Will knocked at the door just then and he smiled shyly. He and I made an unsteady progress to the captain's quarters. It was rather an untidy room, crowded with furniture, books, maps, and instruments. Captain Miles himself was an elderly stocky man with a grizzled beard. The cabin boy and another sailor were there also, as witnesses. Again I was filled with the sensation that this was a dream, that none of it was actually happening to me.

Captain Miles grinned at me. "Well, well, quite a beauty, eh, Nicholas? Trust you, you young devil. If I'd found somethin' that pleasin', perhaps I'd have given up the sea, too." He chuckled.

"Let's not waste time, Miles," Nicholas cut in. "Doubtless Miss Cooke is tired after so long a day." His voice was cool, his face expressionless. He wore an evening suit of dark blue, the starched folds of his neckcloth standing out against his dark skin. I was struck anew by how handsome he was—and how formidable.

"In a hurry, are you?" said Captain Miles, and he grinned again. "Well, we may as well proceed." He picked up a small black book from his desk and came to stand before us.

Just that moment the ship gave a sudden lurch and I was thrown against Nicholas, who caught me to his broad chest. For an instant he held me to him, his eyes meeting my own. With faint wonder I felt him begin to tremble. Or was it only the swirling of the waves? Then he released me and I looked down at my clasped hands.

While Captain Miles read out the lines which bound me to Nicholas, I felt nothing but an odd numbness, a disbelief that any of this was real. Even when Nicholas took my left hand, slipped off the glove, and put a ring on my finger, it did not seem real. I stared at it, at the diamonds framing the large winking sapphire. It could not be mine; I could not be truly married.

But I was. Captain Miles closed the book with a snap and then handed me a pen, with which I was to sign the marriage certificate on his desk. The uneven motion of the ship made it difficult to write; my hand shook and a blot of ink marred the parchment. Then Nicholas took the pen from me and was signing his own name in bold lettering.

"Well, congratulations are in order, eh? I've some French brandy here. What do you say to a toast? Must have a ceremonial toast, y'know. You two lads can go now." Captain Miles set out three glasses and a bottle. Will and the other sailor bowed and left us.

Captain Miles handed me a drink. "To the both of you, eh?" he said as he gave a glass to Nicholas and then downed his own in one gulp. Nicholas drank, too, but I shook my head, finding the smell of it distasteful. I set my glass down on the desk.

The captain wiped his mouth, saying, "I've a ship to look to, and you don't need me for chaperone any longer. I hope the weather holds, ma'am, and you enjoy the journey

108

to Maine. Good night." He left the cabin while I had a wild impulse to call him back, to ask him all sorts of involved questions about navigation, about his travels, anything to keep him talking to us so that I would not have to go back to our stateroom with my new husband. But he was gone and we were alone.

"Shall we go, Miranda?" asked Nicholas, and I nodded dumbly. He took my arm and held it tightly as he guided me down the passageway. When we were inside our cabin, I moved abruptly away from him. The ship gave another toss and I stumbled against the bed, my lace shawl falling to the floor.

"I see you need a maid, my love," said my husband in amused tones: "I will have to suffice for the trip."

I had forgotten the undone buttons. I whirled around, flushing. "What do you mean?"

He said, "There's no need to look so alarmed, Miranda. I only meant that if you need me to fasten a few buttons, as you obviously do, I will oblige. I meant no more than that."

"Thank you," I said stiffly. "But I can manage just now." Still I stood there. What were we supposed to do now? Talk, play backgammon? I had noticed a game on the table.

Nicholas was watching me, a crease in his brow. Then he turned aside and sat down, pulling off one black boot. "Why don't you get some rest, Miranda? It's been a strange day for you, I realize."

"You mean — go to bed?" I asked rather wildly, and then felt the hot color flood my face.

His lips twisted. "Yes, go to bed."

"On that bed?" I asked foolishly.

"Where else?" His brows were raised, and though his face was still, I had the impression he was laughing at me.

"Uh . . . with you?" I said faintly, biting my lip as I stared at the floor.

"Well, married people commonly sleep together, you know, and there is only one bed."

I said nothing, fighting an urge to run from the room,

climb the narrow stairs and rush up on deck.

Then he seemed to relent. "Don't look like that, Miranda. I was only teasing you. I'm sleeping on the sofa tonight. I'm well aware of your feelings. I know you're not accustomed to me, to any of this. I have no intention of making any demands on you. You can sleep in blissful solitude," he said mockingly.

I closed my eyes, feeling weak with the sharp sudden thrust of relief. But I still had to remove my gown and put on my night attire. I still had to unpin my hair and take off some of my undergarments before climbing into bed, before shielding myself under the protective layer of bedclothes.

"Nicholas?"

"Yes, my dear?" He had shrugged off his coat and was untying his neckcloth.

"Could you . . . that is, I wondered . . . if you would put out the lights?"

"Put out the lights?"

"Yes, could you? I mean . . . you don't care to read or anything, do you?"

"Read?" Why was he repeating everything I said? "No, I don't care to read." Was there a slight emphasis on that last word or was it only my fevered imagination? "By all means, I'll put out the lamps."

I waited until he had done so and then said, "Thank you." As quickly as I could I unfastened my gown and tossed it over my head. I untied my stays and pulled off my petticoats. Then I reached for the nightgown I had laid across the bed and drew it over me, tying the satin ribbons to my neck.

"Everything all right, Miranda?" came Nicholas's voice in the dark, a hint of laughter in it.

"Yes, of course. Good night, Nicholas."

"Good night, my bride," he said ironically, and I heard his weight settle on the sofa.

Closing my eyes, I tried to still the rapid beating of my heart. We were married. I was Mrs. Nicholas Blaize. And nothing untoward had occurred. My husband had not

110

taken advantage of me, if a man could take advantage of his wife. Perhaps he was as relieved as I that we were sleeping in separate beds. Perhaps he had no desire to enforce his marital rights.

Marital rights. What hideous words. And yet I was married to a stranger who might do as he liked with me.

But at least not tonight. Perhaps he had no urge to touch me at all; perhaps ours would be a purely platonic relationship. He had made a gallant gesture by rescuing me from Captain Sears and a life of drudgery; perhaps that was as far as it would go.

I pictured us living in his house, talking contentedly, eating together, sitting by the fire, more like brother and sister than husband and wife. But even as I imagined it, I knew it was only a foolish dream. Even I in my innocence was aware of the unmistakable virility of the man I had married. No man who had kissed a girl the way he had kissed me would be content with that sort of existence.

The sound of a low rumbling snoring began from across the room and I giggled. How strange to hear a man snoring in my room. But now I had no doubts as to whether he was asleep. I could now succumb to the seeping drowsiness myself.

When I awoke the next morning, I found I was alone. I guessed Nicholas was up on deck, and I was grateful for his tact. Then I realized he would have seen me lying here sleeping, and I wondered if he had watched me with that intent scrutiny that characterized him. With heightened color I rose and washed my face and teeth in the basin. I then dressed hurriedly in my new red gown, afraid that at any moment the door might open and he would be there while I fumbled with my stays, while I pulled my white stockings over my legs. When I was ready, I looked at my reflection in the tall mirror, noticing how the ruby color made my skin seem rosier, how the soft folds of the fabric set off my figure as they clung the way no gown ever had before.

A knock came at the door. "Come in," I said faintly. It was Nicholas and he was carrying a tray with our

111

breakfast on it. "I just got this from the cabin boy. Everything's hot."

He set the tray down and turned to me. "Well, you look very pretty this morning. How did you sleep?"

"Oh . . . quite, quite . . . fine," I stammered, nodding like an idiot. "Um . . . and you?"

His mouth quirked. "I? Oh, well enough, Miranda. Not as comfortably as you on the bed, but well enough."

I took the cup of coffee he handed me, avoiding the dancing light in his eyes. "What is the day like?"

"Fair, though the captain thinks it might turn worse tonight and I'm inclined to agree with him. You won't be afraid if we run into a storm, will you? This is a sturdy ship, I assure you. You can go up on deck later if you wish. We're sailing around the tip of Cape Cod now and then we'll head further out to sea as we travel north."

He chatted amiably on a number of trivial subjects while we ate. I was hungry and enjoyed the grilled fish, scrambled eggs, and biscuits which had been prepared for us. After we had finished, he went up on deck with me and found a chair for me to sit on. He stayed with me awhile and then excused himself, saying he had promised a game of chess to Captain Miles.

To my surprise I was a little disappointed that he had gone, but I liked sitting in the warm sun feeling the salt-laced wind on my face, in my hair, breathing deeply the fresh air, listening to the raucous cries of a few gulls who ventured this far out over the ocean. All these things contributed to a sense of well-being greater than any I had known in a long while. I remained on deck until the late afternoon when the air turned brittle and cold and my cloak was not thick enough to ward off the penetrating gusts of wind. The water had become increasingly rough and there was a heavy blanket of gray coming from the south. It looked as though Captain Miles was right; we were in for a storm. I hoped not; I dreaded becoming seasick the way I had on my journey from Bombay. And I dreaded Nicholas seeing me that way.

Retiring to our cabin, I found him there. "I was just

coming to look for you," he said. "We're to dine with Captain Miles tonight. I hope that is agreeable to you."

"Yes, of course."

"I'll leave you to dress now." He was already dressed in black and did not seem quite as forbidding this evening.

"All right."

"I'll return in a short while to escort you then," and he was gone on the words.

Unbuttoning my red gown (I had left undone two buttons, wearing my black shawl across the back), I pulled it over my shoulders and folded it neatly in the trunk. Then I took out the blue satin, shook out its shimmering folds, and put it on. Again I realized with dismay that there were the same two buttons I could not fasten. Well, I could not keep on wearing the thing with two buttons undone. I would simply have to ask Nicholas to do them up for me. It was a very little thing, after all. I was not making any sort of overture. I had pinned up my hair and had just dabbed on some perfume when he returned.

"Ready, Miranda?" he asked, smiling. "That gown suits you, you know. You look delectable."

I flushed. "Um, Nicholas, I wonder if you'd help me to fasten my gown," I said in a rush.

"Certainly, my dear." He came over to me and I turned around, giving a slight start when I felt his fingers on my bare skin. "You smell delicious."

Was I supposed to thank him for saying that? I did not know how to take such compliments. Just then the ship plunged into a low hollow of waves and I stumbled forward. I would have fallen had he not caught me round the waist and held me against him.

And again I was conscious of a faint trembling of his body and I felt an answering trembling beginning inside me. He turned me around, his hands moving to my shoulders, until I faced him. He gazed down into my eyes and I could not look away, I could not pull away. His gaze dropped from my eyes to my mouth and then he was bending toward me. I closed my eyes before his lips touched mine. They were tentative at first, gentle, and I

113

moved my own under his in the same experimental way. He began to kiss me with increasing fervor, the way he had done in the chapel, and this time I did not struggle. He explored my mouth with his tongue while his arms crushed me to him possessively. My head was tilted back in the crook of his shoulder; I believe I would have swayed dizzily had he not held me the way he did. His lips traveled up the curve of my cheek to my temple, my eyelid, and then his face was buried in my neck. I shivered suddenly, and pushed him away. Immediately he relaxed his grip, one hand ruffling his hair.

"It's a pity," he said, his breathing ragged, "that we have to dine with the captain."

Confusedly I touched my hot cheeks as he released me. It was a blessing we were to dine with the captain, I thought. I had not been ready for this amorous side of Nicholas. And I was amazed at my response, at the fierce clamor of my senses as he plundered my mouth.

He moved across to the porthole and I adjusted a few pins which had come loose in my hair. My face looked flushed and dazed in the mirror, my lips red, my eyes dark.

"Well, as we must go . . . " he began, and I nodded, allowing him to lead me from the stateroom.

That evening passed in a fog. I ate automatically what was on my plate but said little and paid even less attention to the talk of the two men. I avoided Nicholas's eyes whenever possible. I was shocked and unnerved by the passion I had aroused in him; I could not stop replaying his kisses in my mind.

This was a development I had not expected, not yet, and I was at a loss to know what to do. I realized that it now seemed to Nicholas that I was ready for him to become my husband in the full sense of the word. If we had not had this engagement to dine with Captain Miles, then such an event might have occurred then and there.

I gulped my wine and asked for another glass, drinking that one quickly also. The trepidation I had felt yesterday seemed aimless, trivial to the tumult inside me now. For now I knew that Nicholas would not sleep patiently on the sofa another night biding his time, that after what had just taken place between us, he would not hesitate to take full possession of me. I thought hysterically of my hopes that we would live together as brother and sister—nothing could have been more absurd.

And my own treacherous senses had responded in a way that he could not mistake. I could not trust myself, and that realization frightened me even more than had his masterful embrace.

After dinner Will brought a bottle of brandy and this time I drank what I was poured. The liquid scorched my throat, making me grimace and cough indelicately. But then I had another sip, and another, and the heat coursed through me until I began to feel deliciously light and carefree. After the second glass I was able to look across the table at my husband and smile quite easily, even affectionately.

Very soon Nicholas was thanking Captain Miles for the dinner and saying it was time we retired. "I think Miranda has had a little too much brandy."

I heard all this in a pleasant fog. My mind was fuzzy but I was filled with a drowsy, heady contentment. I allowed him to help me up from the table, which to my surprise seemed to tilt before it righted itself.

"Is it the storm already?" I asked in a high, unnatural voice.

Nicholas looked at me concernedly, his hand taking my elbow. "Thank you, Captain Miles," I said as we turned to go. "Good night."

"Are you feeling all right, Miranda?" asked Nicholas when we were out in the corridor.

"Oh yes," I assured him, and then the wall seemed to lunge at me and I fell against it.

"I'm afraid you're tipsy, my love," he said, chuckling. To my surprise he swung me into his arms and carried me down the hall.

"I certainly am not. I've never been tipsy in my life!" I said in outraged tones.

"And I'll warrant you never drank as much in your life

115

as you did tonight."

We reached our stateroom and Nicholas carried me inside. I expected him to set me down but he went over to the bed. He sat down, still holding me. "I'm afraid you're going to feel poorly in the morning. I should have paid more attention to what you were drinking."

"I feel quite well now," I said with dignity.

"Can you get out of your gown by yourself, or shall I help you?" There was a tinge of color in his cheeks and I could feel the way his heart was thudding in his chest. I reached back, unfastening a few of the buttons, and then he turned me around and undid the rest. I began to giggle because the touch of his fingers tickled me.

"Silly child," he murmured, and his voice sounded strange. And when he turned me to him, again there was a fire at the back of his eyes which fascinated me.

He slid the gown off my shoulders and I watched it spill in a shimmering heap on the floor. He was pulling the pins from my hair. And then his hands were entangled in it, his fingers moving against my scalp and through my curls.

Of its own accord my hand reached up to stroke his cheek. "You will take care of me, won't you, Nicholas?" I asked softly.

With a quick indrawn breath he drew me to him, his face in my hair. Then his breath was hot on my skin and his mouth was moving from my earlobe along the curve of my cheek until his lips met mine with such unbridled force that my senses were instantly consumed with the feel and scent and taste of him. His mouth ravaged mine, which readily opened beneath his, and I began to kiss him as deeply as he was kissing me. His breathing was rapid and shallow when he held me away from him and I had the odd fancy I was drowning in his gray eyes. He began to untie the ribbons of my camisole, the touch of his hard fingers stirring me until I was shuddering with an unimagined delight. His kisses seared my soft flesh, his lips moving to my bare breasts. I touched his thick black locks while he nuzzled the hollow between. With one hand he was reaching up to take off my stockings, smoothing them

116

down my legs while I sighed in his ear. He pulled down each layer of petticoat with a growing urgency and then he was crushing me to him in a kind of frenzy.

"You're so beautiful, Miranda, so exquisite," he said thickly, pushing me back against the pillows. He let me go and began to remove his own clothing. I saw his massive shoulders and chest with its patch of black hairs before the candle was snuffed out and we were enveloped in the velvety darkness.

"Miranda," he said again with soft roughness and took me in his arms, his hard body bearing down on mine, his lips demanding my response. I put my arms around his neck and kissed him, reveling in the sensations rushing through me. With a sort of detached wonder I remembered I had feared this intimacy with him.

His body was moving over mine, his knee prodding my legs apart. I felt the steeliness of him straining into me and I submitted easily until there was a sudden vicious pain. Giving a small cry I tried to push him away, my hands on his chest, but I could not move, I could not break free of his powerful embrace. His mouth muffled the moans I was making as he kissed me, as he hurt me. Then his mouth was off mine and my chin was scratched by the hairs on his chest. He gave a deep groan, shuddering against me. I turned my cheek into the pillow.

Some moments later his voice came, huskily, "Miranda?" And his fingers were entwined in my hair and his cheek was pressed to my own.

I could not answer. There was a ringing in my ears and my head swam. The blackness in the room came into my head, and I slept.

Before I awakened fully, I was conscious of a pounding in my head aggravated by a sickening rollicking motion. The bed was swaying with the movement of the ship but that was not to blame for the spinning in my head. With these discomforts acknowledged and impossible to ignore, the last vestiges of sleep departed. I opened my eyes and looked miserably at the pitching cabin. I remembered the dinner with Captain Miles and the way I had drunk glass

117

after glass of wine. I had never drunk strong spirits in my life; the amount I had consumed last night was doubtless to blame for the churning in my stomach and the throbbing in my head.

With a shock I realized I was naked. For a few moments I was incredulous for I had never once slept that way. Then the later events of the night flashed into memory and I pulled the bedclothes over my head, overcome with shame and disbelief. Had I really allowed Nicholas to undress me, tolerated, no, welcomed, his mouth and hands on my bare flesh, his intimate caresses, his aggressive possession of me?

Humiliated, I let my mind dwell on what had occurred between us some hours ago. The brandy had so gone to my head that all decorum, all modesty had been swept aside. I had acted as eager as he, as though I had had experience in such matters! How could I face him today, remembering what he had done in the darkness? Thank heaven he was not now in the cabin.

But he is my husband, another part of me argued feebly. Yes, but still a veritable stranger to you. It's not as though you are in love with him or he with you. He said nothing about love, about caring for you. How could he? He doesn't know you any more than you know him. And you know very well you are no desirable ravishing creature. He is a man and you are a woman — the only available one at present, the most available one for him. He bought you, in a way.

In the midst of these battling sentiments I became aware of another feeling, increasingly urgent and no less painful. Oh no, I thought, not that! But it would not be denied. With difficulty I got out of the bed, reached for the chamberpot and was vilely unwell. Coughing and wiping my streaming eyes I climbed back into bed. I closed my eyes, waiting miserably for the spinning in my head to subside.

The second time I opened my eyes that morning it was hours later and I was no longer alone. Nicholas sat in the chair, fully dressed, watching me. When I looked at him,

118

he smiled. I thought he looked smug, stimulated, and I hastily averted my eyes.

I sat up, clutching the covers about me, noticing with vague relief that the throbbing in my head had disappeared and I no longer felt sick. But I was weak and there was a terrible taste in my mouth. And a terrible memory in my head.

My face burning, I said, "How long have you been there?"

Pushing his hands in his pockets, he replied, "A while. I came down once we were out of the storm."

"You were on deck in the middle of the storm?"

He nodded. I realized the raging elements had doubtless exhilarated him and that was the reason he looked the way he did. It could not be that he was relishing the events of last night.

"We hit a rather bad storm early this morning," he went on. "You slept through most of it, thanks to the brandy."

Thanks to the brandy! "Never mention that word to me again! I hate the stuff!" I cried, tears springing to my eyes.

"I'm sorry you were sick, my dear. As I said, I shouldn't have allowed you to drink so much."

"You doubtless planned it that way!" I said, knowing that wasn't true.

There was a pause. "I assure you, Miranda, that nothing was further from my intentions." He stood up and began to walk toward me.

"Don't come near me. Don't you touch me, Nicholas."

His black brows drew together. "What is it, my love? Are you still feeling unwell? It's nothing to be ashamed of; I've been seasick myself."

Mortified by his casual mention of my wretched illness, I bit my lip. "You wanted me to drink the brandy, didn't you? You wanted me to be drunk so you could . . . so we could . . ." I buried my face in my hands.

His voice was gentle. "I've said nothing was further from my mind. I know that things progressed more rapidly than you might have wished or anticipated but don't let that distress you. You are very charming, you know,

119

Miranda. I don't want you to feel any embarrassment or regret about last night. The brandy even helped, I think. It was perfectly natural, I assure you. You are my wife and I am your husband. And I—"

Looking up, I did not let him finish. "No, you're not truly my husband! You can't be—I can't believe it. It's a dream. It's all just a dream! I don't you know. I can't believe I married a man I didn't know and then let him . . . let you . . . I won't be your wife, your possession. Please . . . please just leave me alone."

He froze in his tracks at my words. His face whitened, tensed, until the scar in his cheek was scarcely noticeable. He stared at me for a long moment and then without a word he turned and left the cabin. The door shut with a bang and I fell back on the bed, wildly weeping.

I did not leave the stateroom all day. I still felt poorly and was unable to eat the food Will brought me. Nicholas did not come and I was miserable. I wondered how I could have spoken to him the way I had. I had sounded hysterical, ridiculous. I wondered what he would have said if I had let him speak and not sent him from the cabin.

Eventually that night I slept, though my sleep was disturbed by alarming, confusing dreams. Once I thought a cool hand touched my brow and a deep familiar voice said, "It's all right, Miranda. You're just dreaming." But even that may have only been part of a dream.

The next morning the sun was shining; I sat up to look through the porthole and saw the swelling, deep blue waves. I felt stronger and quite hungry though quite forlorn. I wondered where Nicholas was. Glancing about the room, I noticed with disgust that it was in chaos. My clothes were strewn here and there; the trunk gaped open; bandboxes and parcels that had been arranged against the wall the first night had slid about during the storm. After splashing some cold water on my face and cleaning my teeth, I began to straighten the cabin and was nearly finished when there was a knock at the door.

"Who is it?" I called, my heart beating quicker.

"Will, ma'am. I brung your hot water."

"Oh, thank you, Will. Set it outside the door, please."

When he had gone, I opened the door and carried the two buckets of steaming water inside the berth. With a little difficulty I poured each into the tub and then added some cold water from the basin.

I climbed into the tub and sank down in the soothing water, closing my eyes. I had washed my hair and was rinsing it with the lavender water when abruptly the door opened. I sat up with a jerk, sloshing water about, and tried to shield myself with my arms.

Nicholas eyed me sardonically as he shut the door. "Never fear, I haven't come to sully your precious virtue." He sluiced his face and neck with water from the basin. I noticed there were lines about his mouth and shadows under his eyes. My face scarlet, I bit my lip at the biting scorn in his voice.

"If you'd be so kind as to leave the cabin when you've finished, I can then bathe and dress. That way I shan't contaminate you with the repellent sight of my unclad state." Deliberately he pulled a chair near to the porthole and sat down with his back to me.

Suddenly the bathwater was cold. I reached for a towel and awkwardly climbed out of the tub, drying myself off. I donned my undergarments as quickly as possible and then put on the red cashmere gown. But again I could not reach two of the buttons.

Staring at the back of my husband's head as he sat reading, I stood there for a few moments dreading to break the frigid silence between us and ask his assistance. Why on earth did Miss Proctor sew so many buttons on her gowns, I thought irritably. My other gowns had always been easily fastened in the back. But Miss Proctor's gowns were impossible for their wearers to do up; all her customers had maids to assist them.

"Nicholas, would you help me, please? I . . . I don't seem to be able to do these buttons." I fervently hoped he would not think my request some ploy to win his attention.

He looked around, his lip curling, and said, "Why

certainly, my love. But you must come over here. I can't very well reach them across the room."

Walking over to him, I turned around nervously. Lifting up the heavy wet strands of my hair, I steeled myself to feel his fingers brush my skin. He swiftly did as I asked and I let my hair down. I felt I should say something, try to make amends in some small way. I hated this derisive side of him. And I had realized that I owed him a great deal, more than I could repay.

He had given me his name; he was giving me a new home, a new life. And I had been — I was — as much a stranger to him as he was to me. Did I not owe him as much as I could give, even myself?

"Uh, about yesterday morning," I began, still with my back to him, "I said some foolish things . . . it was partly that I was feeling so unwell, you see, and I . . . well, I wasn't used to . . ."

"You spoke your true feelings, those no longer obscured and distorted by the brandy," was his gruff response. "And I'm not a man to force my attentions on any woman, even the one to whom I have every right. I'll leave that to stupid lechers like Horace Sears. So don't worry. I'll not disturb you again." His voice had become harsh, uncompromising. "Just remember, my dear girl, that you welcomed my kisses before you ever touched the brandy, or have you conveniently forgotten that?"

My face flamed at his blunt rebuke. He was perfectly right. And I knew that brandy or no brandy I would doubtless have surrendered willingly to his heated embrace. Why had I blurted out those idiotic vindictive words, that I wouldn't be his wife, that he could not be my husband?

Tentatively I placed my hand on his arm. "Nicholas—"

"If you've finished you can get out," he said roughly, shaking off my hand. "I find I need some privacy, too."

I bit my lip, stepping back. Tears pricked my eyes but I refused to let him see them. Gathering my cloak in my arms, I left the cabin.

The fresh tangy air struck me as I ventured on deck. The

sun was very bright; I wished I had brought a bonnet, but nothing would have induced me to return to the cabin. I had not even combed my hair; it blew wildly in the wind like a gypsy's.

A few sailors were gawking at me though none said a word, doubtless for fear of Nicholas. I had noticed the respect they showed him. Standing by the railing, I watched the white-tipped waves.

I'm in a fix now, I thought dejectedly. A fine beginning to my married life. I was on my way to my new home with a surly embittered man, a man whose passionate embrace now seemed like a hazy dream. He was now a hostile stranger and for that I had only myself to blame. I had only myself to blame that it was our very intimacy which had caused this chilling estrangement between us.

And this was the way I was to be thrust into my new family—without even the support or encouragement of my husband to guide me. I had spurned the affection of my one friend in the world and this knowledge filled me with despair. I had only myself to blame for my bleak uncertain future.

Chapter Six

That day and the next I remained on deck, shunning the confinement of the cabin where in such a short time so many conflicting emotions had been felt. Will brought me a chair and I sat huddled in my cloak gazing at the vibrantly blue water. I was very forlorn; Nicholas avoided me and I him; it was a poor excuse for a honeymoon.

We again were sailing within sight of land but kept at a safe distance from the hazardous, jagged Maine coastline. The evening before, Nicholas had taken supper with me in the cabin, but he did not speak except to utter the merest trivialities. I ate from nervousness more than hunger, and the two of us pretended to be absorbed in our food. Nicholas sent Will for more wine and drank glass after glass which seemed to make him even more morose.

He quit the berth without a word after we had eaten and I wondered whether I had seen the last of him for that night. But after I had undressed, put on the lawn cotton nightgown, and was in bed, he returned.

"If you've no objection, or even if you have, I'll sleep in the bed tonight and not in that damned sofa where I passed a most uncomfortable night," he said coldly.

My face must have reflected the sudden alarm I felt because he added savagely, "Oh, for God's sake, girl, don't look like that! I'm not going to touch you!" He loosened his neckcloth and then bent to pull off his boots.

Wincing at his tone, I nevertheless stole a look at his chest and shoulders, tanned and muscular, before I turned

124

to the wall. I remembered the last time I had seen him like that before he had put out the lamp and taken me in his arms. But it did no good to dwell on that.

Moving over to the far side of the bed and facing the wall, I lay tensely waiting. The light was extinguished and Nicholas lay down beside me, pointedly leaving as large a space as possible between us. Just recently this man had been my ally, my protector, then my provider and lover, and now he was acting as though we were enemies.

Not that I sought his embrace, I hastily assured myself. I still cringed with embarrassment when I recalled our lovemaking. Yet Nicholas was the only person in my life now and I missed what warmth and friendliness had been between us.

The next morning I was awake before he. Crawling gingerly out of the bed so as not to disturb him, I washed my face and combed my hair and dressed again in the red cashmere gown. I wanted to look my best when we reached Thunder Island later that day.

Will came to the door with our breakfast. Bidding me good day, he set the tray down on the table. Before he turned to leave, he cast a quick glance at Nicholas asleep in the bed.

At the closing of the door, Nicholas stirred and sat up. He looked very large in the bed, his hair tousled. He wore no nightshirt.

"Good morning," I said brightly, looking away from him. "Our breakfast is here—I'll pour you a cup of coffee."

"First be so good as to hand me my trousers and I'll join you presently."

I did as he asked and then busied myself with arranging the dishes and food on the table. I heard Nicholas washing and moving around before he sat down across from me to pull on his boots.

"What time do you suppose we'll get to Thunder Island today?" I asked, handing him a cup of black coffee.

"Not as early as I'd hoped, it seems. But hopefully you'll have a glimpse of the island and house before sunset."

"Oh. I had hoped to arrive sooner than that—this afternoon, perhaps."

"The storm off the Cape blew us slightly off course," he said shortly.

It was another fair day, and after breakfast, I escaped to my favorite spot on deck. A few of the sailors spoke to me or nodded. If they considered it odd that the newlywed couple were apart the duration of the day, it was not apparent in their manner toward me.

Later Captain Miles came over. "We've a fine day to sail into Thunder Cove," he said jauntily.

"My husband told me it might be dark before we arrived. I was hoping to be able to see something of my new home."

"It's a sight, I'll grant you that. A grand mansion built from the local pink granite, looking like it sprang from the top of the cliff."

"Oh—I had no idea it was quite like that," I began, then flushed. "I mean, it sounds even more impressive that I was led to expect."

"Aye, I'm thinkin' you'll be glad to see the last of this steamer and go to a proper house."

I nodded. "Not that this isn't a perfectly beautiful ship, Captain Miles."

He grinned. "This is its first occasion to be used by honeymooners," he said.

"Oh," I said, giving a feeble smile. We were hardly that.

At noon I returned to the cabin only to find that Nicholas was not there. He was playing chess with Captain Miles, Will told me. Unaccountably annoyed, I ate my solitary lunch.

I took a book from the trunk after I had finished eating and sat down to read. But a drowsiness stole over me. The night before I had not slept until very late, conscious of that powerful body next to mine. I lay down on the bed and was soon lulled to sleep by the motion of the ship.

When I awoke, it was to hear the harsh cries of gulls flying near the ship. I looked out the porthole and realized it must be late afternoon. After arranging my hair and smoothing my gown, I climbed the stairs to the deck. We were passing small, spruce-covered islands, the distant ones rising from the water like tufts of moss. We had to be nearing Thunder Island.

I went below again and packed my belongings. I noticed then that Nicholas's things were already packed; he must have come in while I slept, I thought, disconcerted. Looking about the cabin, I was struck by how cosy and comforting it was. I had no desire, I realized, to leave it for the unknown place we were approaching. At that point depression hit me like a blow and I could not stop the tears from falling on my cheeks.

The door opened and Nicholas entered. Hastily I turned away, not wanting to give him further cause to despise me.

"We will be arriving at Thunder Island in less than an hour, Miranda," he said coolly. "It looks as though you'll be able to see the island at sunset."

I murmured something and then could not prevent a sniff from escaping. He came up behind me, took my shoulders, and turned me to face him. "You've been crying," he said in a gentler tone.

I shook my head, trying to smile and look cheerful. I must have failed dismally because he frowned and continued, "Surely the prospect of leaving this ship does not make you unhappy."

I sniffed. "You wouldn't understand, Nicholas." He was always at ease, always sure of himself in any company or situation. How could he possibly understand what I was feeling now? How could he comprehend my diffidence in meeting new people, the shyness which plagued me, he who had doubtless never been afraid of anything in his life?

"I should think you'd be overjoyed to know we no longer have to share a room. At Thunder House we'll each have our own bedroom which should cause you no end of gratification," he said sardonically.

I opened my mouth to protest but was at a loss for words. What was the point anyway? He was determined to dislike me. He turned away with a stifled exclamation and began to collect the baggage. "I'd advise you to come up soon if you care to see your new home," he said curtly as he left the stateroom.

His invitation was scarcely encouraging, but it was silly to remain down here when we were sailing closer and closer to the place which would be my home for the rest of my life. It gave me a jolt to think that way, and soon after, I went up on deck. I saw a great bulk of land in the distance.

Nicholas was standing against the rail, his legs apart, his hands folded behind his back. The wind ruffled his dark hair and his eyes were narrowed as though in speculation.

I approached him, the reluctance I felt overcome by curiosity. "Is that Thunder Island?" I asked, raising my voice against the wind.

"Yes, that's it." He turned to look at me and his gray eyes gleamed like pewter. Whatever else he was feeling it was apparent he loved his island.

We stood side by side, not speaking, as the sun sank below the mountain which was black against the tawny sky. Spruce and fir trees grew down to the water, even clinging to the rose-colored rocks which jutted out to sea. The forest looked dark and primeval and we saw no people.

We rounded one side of the island, sailing into a large cove. It was then that I saw Thunder House. It stood on the summit of the cliff above the cove. I was astonished by the size of it — it was far larger than any house in New Bedford. It was built in the Georgian style but had none of the grace which usually characterized such architecture. It was massive and imposing with long, opaque windows symmetrically placed. As Captain Miles had told me, it was constructed of the same reddish stone as the cliff. From this distance it was difficult to tell where the cliff stopped and the house began. The forest grew closely on both sides of the house, scarcely heeding its interruption.

The ship sailed as far into the cove as was safe, dropping anchor. A small boat was lowered so that Nicholas and I could go ashore. We said farewell to Captain Miles and I waved to Will. Nicholas followed a sailor down a rope ladder to the boat and waited for me to follow. I stood clutching the railing.

"Come on, Miranda, I won't let you fall," Nicholas called up from the bottom of the ladder.

I bit my lip, wishing we could properly dock. I had never descended a rope ladder; I hated the way it moved about, knocking against the side of the ship. How on earth could I manage it? All the eyes of the crew were on me; I felt like a fool; everyone was waiting for me to disembark. I took a deep breath and turned around, searching for the first rope rung with my foot. Two sailors had taken each arm until I could grasp the sides of the ladder; I did so and began the long unsteady descent. I could not look down; I kept my eyes fastened on the rungs before me. Nicholas was urging me on but I barely heard him. After what seemed like an eternity Nicholas caught me round the waist and helped me sit down in the boat. The sailor began to row us farther into Thunder Cove. I looked back at the ship and saw Will waving to me as he stood against the gunwale.

"How do we get up to the house?" I asked. It was now very high above us on top of the steep granite cliff. "Not another ladder!"

Nicholas smiled. "There are stone steps in the woods to the right of the house."

The chilled air smelled fragrantly of pine and fir trees. Nicholas assisted me out of the boat and over the boulders which littered the water's edge. The sailor followed with our baggage.

Twice I stumbled but Nicholas had a tight grip on me, saying after the second time, "You'll need to wear sturdy shoes when you go walking."

We went to the side of the cove and entered the woods, which at dusk looked gloomy and forbidding. What if we had arrived later than this, I thought, how could we have seen to make our way?

"What do you do in the dark, Nicholas?"

"Carry torches. But I do not advise you to walk about at

night."

The floor of the forest was carpeted by springy turf and scattered with pine needles. Following a path to a row of stone steps, we climbed while the balsam-scented air blew fresh and cold about us.

And then we were out of the woods and on a stone walkway which led to a door on the side of the house. Nicholas paid the sailor, who set down the bags, tipped his hat, and reentered the woods. Nicholas rapped the brass knocker on the door and we waited.

A few moments passed before the door was opened by an older man with a long, rather melancholy face, which nonetheless lit up when he saw us.

"Why, it's the captain! Welcome home, sir. We didn't think to see you back so soon."

"Hello, Amos. Miranda, this is Amos Trundy. He and his wife Martha have worked for us ever since I can remember."

"Ayeh, and a right wild one you were, too," said Amos, grinning, as he shook Nicholas's hand.

"Amos, this is my wife."

I caught a glimmer of surprise on his face before he said, "Welcome to Thunder House, ma'am."

"Thank you, Amos," I said, wondering whether I was also supposed to shake hands with him. I put out my own, smiling broadly, but he was stepping aside to get our baggage and so I pretended to brush back a stray curl with the same hand. In doing so I dropped one of the gloves I had removed and had to bend down to pick it up.

We were in a long corridor paneled in dark wood which reminded me of the inside of a ship. There was a large blue and white Chinese bowl, which looked very old, on a gleaming table flanked by two Chippendale chairs with claw-and-ball feet.

A door opened farther down the hallway and a woman came out. She was dressed in black and her hair was drawn back uncompromisingly from her face. She came toward us, registering neither surprise nor delight at our arrival.

"This is Sarah Thatcher, Miranda. Sarah, my wife."

Nicholas's voice was cool.

This then was his mother's companion. She extended her hand to me but there was no warmth, no welcome in the gesture. "How do you do? This is quite a surprise, Nicholas." And her eyes conveyed the implication that the surprise was not a pleasant one. Or was I too sensitive, too overwrought?

"How . . . how do you do, Sa—er, Miss Thatcher?" I said, stumbling over the words. Her gaze was speculating on my face and I flushed.

"How is Lavinia?" Nicholas asked curtly.

"Fairly well, at the moment. She is in the drawing room, if you care to go in."

I thought this was a strange way to talk to Nicholas, but he merely nodded and took my elbow. We followed her into a spacious, beautifully appointed room.

The walls were papered in an elaborate print of exotic birds in blues and greens. There was a handsomely carved mantel, which was painted blue as was the crown molding around the ceiling and the woodwork framing the door and windows. The room was furnished with mahogany pieces in the opulent style of a century ago. There was a secretaire against one wall and a carved tall-case clock against another. From the ceiling were suspended two crystal chandeliers.

A woman was seated on the sofa, her white hair coiled high on her head. It was obvious that she had once been beautiful, but now she was faded and frail-looking with violet shadows beneath her eyes.

"Why, Nicholas! Are you back so soon? I thought I heard voices. And who, may I ask, is this young woman?"

"Hello, Lavinia. This is your new daughter-in-law, Miranda. My wife."

A look of amazement came over her face and I felt the hot color seeping into my own. I made a rather feeble attempt at a smile, twisting my gloves in my hands.

"Your wife! Well! This is indeed a surprise. How very like you, Nicholas. Come and sit beside me, my child, and tell me how you captured my arrogant son."

I gaped at her, not knowing what on earth to say. Nicholas had stiffened at her words. "We are very tired from the journey, Lavinia, and would like to go to our rooms before dinner," he said.

"Of course, Nicholas. We'll meet again soon, Miranda. We have plenty of time to get to know one another—there is ample time for everything on Thunder Island, as you'll learn."

"Send Morwenna up, please. She is to be Miranda's personal maid, if you've no objection."

"No, why should I have? I warn you, though, Miranda, she's rather inexperienced. You will have to train her since you've brought no maid of your own, I take it, and she is hardly accustomed to looking after a lady. Is that all your baggage?"

"Yes, that's all," I answered faintly, overcome at the thought of having to train a maid.

"Well, it seems my son must have been in a great hurry if you hadn't time to bring with you more things than that!" Her glance invited me to share her amusement.

"The rest of her things are being shipped here," said Nicholas smoothly. "I was in a hurry to return, as you guessed, Lavinia. Come, Miranda. Dinner will be served in one hour."

With no further talk he led me out of the drawing room and across the hall to the staircase. I was confused and troubled by the undercurrents I had noticed in that room. Neither of the two women had acted affectionately toward my husband, nor had he acted that way to them. And their manner toward me was scarcely welcoming. I had been assuring myself that my nervousness would vanish as soon as I met them but instead it was intensifying. Lavinia's gaze had been sharp as it passed over my worn plain cloak, in contrast to my elegant bonnet, and I could tell she was wondering where on earth Nicholas had found me. I also was aware that she had guessed I had never had any more baggage than that which Amos had carried in, and her asking about it had been merely to belabor the point.

It was odd that Nicholas used his mother's given name when he spoke to her. That only seemed to set them apart further from each other. And Sarah Thatcher had been even less friendly than Lavinia. What sort of a household was this? I wondered unhappily.

On the second-story landing I paused to study a large mural. It was a tropical scene of a bay and a sandy beach with mountains in the distance wreathed in clouds. Underneath a group of palm trees stood some brown-skinned people who were waving at a ship as it sailed into the bay. The women wore garlands of flowers and colorful skirts.

"That was my great-grandfather's ship you see there," explained Nicholas. "It was painted by a traveling artist from Boston at the latter part of last century. He wanted a reminder of the islands he had visited in the South Seas — and of the women, I daresay. He was a trader in the Orient, and so was his father before him. It was my grandfather who began the shipbuilding business. He had no love for the sea, felt no lure, and neither had my father. They were fortunate."

I looked up at him, puzzled by his words, but I wasn't bold enough to ask what he meant.

"Lavinia and Sarah live on this floor, down that corridor in the south wing. Our rooms, yours and mine, are on the floor above at the northern end. The corresponding ones on this floor are no longer in use."

Glancing across to the other side of the landing, I noticed two doors which presumably led to the unused wing. They were shut.

I followed him up the second stairway, which was carpeted in blue as was the hallway which led to our rooms. It seemed the Blaize family liked to surround itself with the colors of the sea, whether or not they felt its lure. Silver sconces lit the hall, which was also paneled in dark wood, giving the impression of a ship's cabin.

Nicholas stopped and opened a door close to the end of the long hallway. "This will be your room. The rooms on this floor were meant to be guest rooms, but since returning from my last voyage, I've moved up here. My room is

133

next to yours. If you don't like the furnishings in here, you can order new materials and things."

Catching my breath in delight, I clasped my hands together. "Oh, but I do like it, Nicholas! I . . . I can't believe it's mine." It was a very feminine room done in shades of apricot and white. Brocade curtains were drawn back from the four-poster bed and swags of the same fabric adorned the tall windows, which faced the sea. I could hear the waves crashing on the rocks in Thunder Cove. Delft tiles framed the fireplace and on the mantel were two blue and white Chinese vases. There was a highboy with shell motif and two wing chairs drawn up to the fireplace. On opposite walls were two doors; one, I guessed, led to a powder room and the other connected Nicholas's room with mine.

"Thank you, Nicholas," I said fervently. "It's more than I ever dreamed of."

His face softened a little. "I'm gratified it meets with your approval. Your trunk should have been brought up by now. Morwenna will bring you hot water. Ask her for anything you require. And now, if you'll excuse me, I shall also bathe and dress for dinner."

I sat down in front of the fire which burned cheerfully in the hearth. Already I felt better in this lovely room; I was only sorry I could not have dinner in here tonight instead of having to return downstairs. A knock came at the door. "Come in," I said.

The door was opened by an auburn-haired girl with soft brown eyes and a warm complexion. She smiled shyly and curtsyed. "Good eve to 'ee, ma'am."

"Good evening. Are you Morwenna?"

"Aye, Mrs. Blaize."

"I don't think I've ever heard that name before."

" 'Tis a Cornish name, ma'am. I come from Cornwall, in England."

"England! How did you get to Thunder Island?"

"The master hired me in Boston to help out Jenny and Mary. But now I'm to be a lady's maid. I'm sorry to tell 'ee, ma'am, that I've no experience."

134

"Oh, I've no experience either . . . in having a maid, I mean. We should suit one another very well. But tell me, why did you leave your home in Cornwall?"

"Oh, ma'am, there be rare poverty there. And when my father was drowned while fishin' there weren't no reason to stay."

"You had no other family?"

She shook her head. "My three brothers all died in a mining accident four years ago. The shaft flooded. I worked in a tavern in Truro until I'd enough money to sail to America."

"I'm sorry, I mean about your family. I'm an orphan myself. All this" — I gestured to the room — "all this is very new to me. What do you think of Thunder Island?"

"Oh, 'tis pretty, I reckon, but wild, and the woods so thick and dark. In Cornwall the cliffs over the sea be grass-covered but here the woods creep right down to the shore. Not that this b'ain't a fine house," she added hastily.

"Yes, it is. It will take some getting used to; I've never lived in a house so large. I imagine I'll have a hard time learning my way about at first. I worked in a fine house but not one like this."

"You worked, ma'am?" she asked, opening her eyes wide.

"Yes," I said ruefully. "I was a governess. Not a very good one, I'm afraid." She was looking more and more surprised and I thought, oh dear, perhaps that's not the way I should be speaking to my maid, admitting my incompetence and unease. I had so much to learn about being a rich gentleman's wife.

But now she was regarding me with awe. "And now 'ee be the mistress of Thunder House. 'Tis like a fairy story, ma'am."

I smiled but my heart felt heavy. "I daresay it seems so. Now I had better have my bath or I'll be late for dinner on my first night here."

I bathed in the powder room while Morwenna unpacked my boxes. She laid out the blue satin gown for me to wear.

135

I looked at it, reminded of the second time I had worn it. Nicholas had slipped it off my shoulders, his kisses burning my flesh. Putting a hand to my flushed cheek, I started to tell Morwenna that I wouldn't wear it. But that was a foolish reaction. It was becoming, and besides, I had nothing else suitable for dinner at Thunder House.

Morwenna helped me into it, exclaiming with delight. I was infected by her high spirits and the two of us giggled while she tried to arrange my hair. Her face was a cheerful one, her manner warm and enthusiastic; such could not be said of the two women I had met earlier. I was grateful to Nicholas for hiring her.

Nicholas strode through the doorway dressed in a dark suit, which fit his broad shoulders and narrow waist exactly. "Are you ready, Miranda?"

"Yes." I wondered what he would say if I asked to dine alone in my room rather than eat in state downstairs with the others. He did not refer to my appearance; after one glance he did not look at me again. He seemed miles away and there was a rather grim look to his face.

We entered the dining room, Lavinia and Sarah just behind us. Nicholas nodded to me to sit at the end of the long table and I moved to do so only to be stopped by Lavinia saying deliberately, "Why don't you sit on Nicholas's right, my dear? It will facilitate conversation between you."

I blushed and stammered an apology, thinking that we had not sat down and already I had committed a social gaffe. Naturally it was her place to sit at the end of the table; this was her house.

Nicholas looked across at her, frowning, before he pulled out the chair across from Sarah for me to sit down. He took his place at the head of the table while Lavinia sat at the other end. Two girls wearing kerchiefs to hold back their hair served us, one pouring wine and the other ladling soup into bowls.

"Miranda, how pretty you look! Such a beautiful gown," cooed Lavinia. "You'll have to be tolerant of us in our old things."

"No false modesty, Lavinia," said Nicholas curtly.

She did look regal in a black taffeta gown, which set off her fine-boned features and white hair. Sarah wore a gown similar to the one she had worn earlier. She did not speak to us, her face as tight as wax, her manner as unyielding.

"Now, Miranda, we are eager to learn how you and my son met," said Lavinia. "Don't disappoint us."

I threw Nicholas a rather dismayed glance. What could I say? I had no idea where to begin relating the strange events of the past week.

He looked across at his mother, his lips quirked. "You'll be happy to know that I rescued her from a life of drudgery. She's far too pretty for that sort of life, don't you agree, Lavinia?"

"Oh, indeed. Just what sort of drudgery were you involved in, Miranda?"

"I . . . I was a governess."

Her eyebrows rose. "How very curious. I don't believe we've ever had a governess in the family. And my impulsive son seized you from that life? How touching. You must have made quite an impression on him, Miranda."

I colored, not knowing how to respond to her mocking tone of voice. She made me feel gauche and foolish. I took a sip of the lobster bisque, which was laced with sherry.

"Oh, she did, Lavinia. I knew when I saw her that I had to have her," Nicholas answered in the same bantering tone.

"And did she also have a similar reaction?"

This time I could not mistake her meaning. She was intimating that I had married Nicholas for his money. I wished I could come up with some clever retort but instead I just sat staring into my soup as though I expected something to emerge from it.

"You mistake the matter," countered Nicholas silkily. "It took all my powers of persuasion to convince Miranda to become my wife."

"Indeed. That must have been a novel experience for you, Nicholas. Who were your parents, my dear?"

Did she want to know their names? "They were mission-

137

aries in India, Mrs. Blaize. In the Bombay Presidency. They were teachers. And so was I."

If I had said they were gypsies, she couldn't have looked more astounded. "Missionaries, did you say? Now I know with certainty that never have we had a missionary in the family. How very peculiar. Nicholas, you surprise me more and more." She continued to regard me as though I were some sort of new species which fascinated and repelled her.

"Miranda's parents died in a cholera epidemic over two years ago and she left there for New Bedford, where she worked as a governess," said Nicholas. "I met her in her employer's home."

"Well, that is very interesting," she said faintly. "And my son wisked you off to Thunder Island? I wonder how you will like it."

"I'm certain I'll find it most enjoyable," I said. But that sounded ridiculous, as though it were a book to read. I tried again. "It's very beautiful, isn't it?"

But she went on as though I had not spoken. "You see, Miranda, I, too, came here as a new bride. Mine was a very different way of life, let me tell you, than the one I came to at Thunder Island. We were rather frivolous and I missed those parties, the gay social rounds. Not that that should trouble you with your background. But later I had my family to keep me busy. Nicholas was a very active, demanding baby, not at all like the one that followed. And there was this house. It was magnificent, even by Boston standards. My husband's family always liked to live on a grand scale, although no one ever comes to visit! It's far too remote for that.

"I think the Blaize men regard themselves as despots of a tiny kingdom untouched by the outside world. Here they've been lords of the land, and some of them lords of the sea. Or they have tried to be. Nicholas has that in his blood, you know. I find it very difficult to accept that you are content to remain on land, Nicholas, when a few short years ago you could hardly bear to be home between voyages."

138

Nicholas's mouth had tightened at her words, but when he spoke, his voice was cool. "You have only to look at Miranda, Lavinia, for your answer to that. My wife and my shipyard will keep me content."

My soup spoon, ill placed in the bowl, clattered onto the china plate beneath it. And then as if that were not bad enough, it tipped off the plate and landed with a thud onto the floor. I reached down to retrieve it but one of the maids was already setting another at my place. I realize I should have left it on the carpet to be picked up when the room was straightened. But it was too late now; I was holding it in my hand. With a feeble smile I handed it to the girl. Imagining what Lavinia's expression was as she watched these proceedings, I wished I could just sink under the table and be done with it.

"You actually sold the *Eagle?*" Lavinia was asking after what seemed like a very long pause in the conversation.

"I did."

"I didn't believe you would be able to part with it. Wonders never cease," she said lightly. "Sell your ship, bring home a wife. What will you be at next, I wonder?"

Warily I looked up to see Nicholas scowling across the table at his mother. But she was chuckling as though she found him delightfully amusing.

The dinner we were eating had been very well prepared, but eaten in this uneasy atmosphere, the meal was impossible to enjoy. Every bite I put in my mouth I feared would become lodged in my throat. Would every meal, every occasion, spent in the company of Lavinia and Sarah be this uncomfortable, this unnatural? If so, I wondered how I could endure it. Honey-coated barbs flew back between mother and son while Sarah sat silent and dour — was this what Thunder House was really like? And I was revealing to them how foreign my life had been to the one they led; I was conscious I was making a poor impression.

And Nicholas. How could a man like him, so self-assured, so determined, live in this atmosphere? Perhaps it had made him what he was. I wondered sincerely why he wished to remain on Thunder Island. I saw now how foolish had been my words to him about his mother appreciating his decision to settle here for good. It was obvious they had little fondness for one another; I could not help but question what it had been like for him to grow up in such a house, his mother openly preferring her second child, Julia.

"I'm looking forward to meeting Julia," I said in an attempt to break the awkward silence that had arisen.

There was a sudden breathless stillness in the room which was palpable. Gasping, Sarah looked across at Lavinia, who had turned sickly pale, the shadows under her eyes a deep purple.

What on earth had I said? Oh God, I realized with a stab of horrified self-loathing. You said *Julia*, and she's the one who . . .

"Miranda means Emily, Lavinia. She is still confused by all the new faces and names," said Nicholas calmly.

Lavinia turned to him, rather dazed. "Of course, Nicholas. It was just so . . . unexpected, hearing her name like that."

Emily, Emily, went my agonized mind. How could you have made such an error? "I'm terribly sorry, Mrs. Blaize. I can't think how I could have said . . ."

"It's all right, Miranda," said Nicholas. "Such mistakes are easily made." His eyes were compelling me to say no more, to stop my flustered apologies. I put a hand to my burning face.

"Emily, yes," went on Lavinia. "Yes, you would not credit it, Miranda. She lives like a pioneer woman; she even makes soaps and butter and lard. With her upbringing! But it was the life she chose and Nicholas did not discourage her." She looked pointedly at her son, who was pouring himself another glass of wine.

"Nicholas tells me she is to have a child," I said.

"Do have some of this blueberry pie, Miranda. It's a specialty of Martha's."

"Thank you," I murmured, disconcerted by the way she ignored my mention of Emily's condition.

Glancing at Sarah across from me I saw she was smirking at my chance words, at my discomfiture. It appeared that Emily's pregnancy was something Lavinia tried to ignore — or worse, had I committed another faux pas? Perhaps Lavinia was one of those women who did not like to comment on such things. Or perhaps she merely didn't want it commented on by me.

Finally the meal came to an end. Sarah rose, stating flatly, "Your mother is tired, Nicholas. I'm sure you can see that. If you'll excuse us, we will retire now."

"Yes, I am a little weary. Dear Sarah, so devoted, so protective. She has been a great comfort to me all these years, Miranda."

"Good night, Lavinia, Sarah," said Nicholas, rising. They left the room and Nicholas sat down again, pouring himself a glass of port. "Perhaps you'd care to retire now," he said, frowning. "Can you find your way back to your room?"

I realized this was a dismissal. "I think so." I stood up, wanting to say something, anything, which might help dispell the atmosphere created at dinner. I wanted to tell him how sorry I was for my thoughtless words, for my gaucheness, how sorry I was that I had given him cause to be ashamed of me.

"Nicholas, I . . ."

"Well, what is it?" he snapped. "Are you going to thank me for bringing you to this house of warmth and family feeling? Well, no words are necessary. But this is my house and no matter what the circumstances, I'm not going back to sea. Although they'd certainly be gratified if I did."

"But why, Nicholas? Is it me? Is Lavinia angry with you for bringing me here? I know I wasn't exactly a success tonight," I said, inviting him to smile at the gracelessness I had displayed. But he did not. I bit my lip.

"That's the least of it, if your presence even comes into it. No, Miranda, I'm afraid her feelings are a great deal more complicated than that." His face had darkened, the small scar above his jaw paling in contrast.

"How did you get that scar?" I asked, momentarily diverted.

A smile I did not like curved his lips. "It was a souvenir of my last voyage, just so I'll never forget it," he said with bitter humor. "Now go to bed."

I had no choice but to obey him. Who was I to try and reach him, to ask him to confide in me, to offer comfort or understanding to a man like him? But he had deflected his mother's attempts to slight me and for that I was grateful.

I went up to my room and rang for Morwenna to help me out of my gown. She got out the nightgown and asked me, "Do 'ee want tea or coffee in the morning, ma'am?"

"Tea will be fine. But isn't breakfast served downstairs?"

"No, ma'am. Trays be brought to the rooms here."

Breakfast in bed! "Oh. Well, good night, Morwenna, and thank you."

When I was in bed and had blown out the candle, I listened to the water hissing in the cove below. The house was silent. I felt very alone. The splendid luxury of Thunder House could not cloak the turmoil which seethed within its walls. Until late I strained my ears for sounds on the other side of the connecting door, but I heard nothing except the mournful, relentless sea until finally I fell asleep.

Chapter Seven

I was awakened the next morning by muffled voices coming from Nicholas's room. I gathered he was talking to one of the servants.

Rising, I went to the window. A scene of breathtaking beauty was displayed before me. Far below in the cove the murmuring waves foamed over the pink granite rocks in spumes of silvery green. Tall spruce trees lined the sides of the cliff like sentinels, some perched valiantly on over-hanging boulders. Captain Miles's ship was nowhere in sight; I presumed it had sailed away soon after we embarked. A bald eagle, its tail and head tipped with white, drifted gracefully over the calm water in search of food. It was low tide.

There was a slight expanse of lawn which halted abruptly at the edge of the cliff; there was no fence to protect the unwary from the sheer drop to Thunder Cove below. I would not care to walk that lawn at night.

With a little difficulty I managed to raise the window. As I did so, a sharp blast of chilled air rushed in, carrying with it the tang of sea air and the scent of fir trees. Collecting my shawl, which was draped over a chair, I drew it about my shoulders and leaned slightly out of the window. In the distance on one side rose Bald Mountain, its rounded crest smoothly granite, its slopes thick with evergreens.

A knock came at the door. I did not turn around but merely said, "Come in," expecting to see Morwenna with my breakfast.

"So what do you think of your new home by daylight? Does this view meet with your approval?"

Whirling around, I said, "Oh, Nicholas, it's you! I mean yes, yes, it's beautiful." Every nerve was alive in my body at the sight of him; I shivered slightly in the cold wind.

He moved to shut the window while I sat down, hugging my shawl about me.

"I did not hear you come in last night, Nicholas."

He leaned back against the closed window, his hands in his pockets. He was already dressed in a hunting-green riding coat belted at the waist, brown leather breeches, and black boots. A scarf was carelessly knotted around his neck. He looked very much at one with the wilderness outside.

"No, you wouldn't have. I was out walking until dawn."

"Walking—all night?"

He grinned, his even teeth white in his dark face, his eyes gleaming like pewter as they looked into mine.

"Yes, I know every inch of the island—and I carried a torch."

The nocturnal excursion seemed to have agreed with him; the grim tension was gone from his face; he looked stimulated. "I wondered whether you'd care to see some of the island after you've had your breakfast," he said.

"Why, yes, Nicholas, I'd like that."

"Very well, then, I'll return for you in an hour."

After he had gone, I pulled the bellrope for Morwenna and she came shortly with my breakfast tray. "My husband is going to take me round the island. You can get out the black merino gown and my black cloak and my black poke bonnet."

She did as I instructed but there was a puzzled, almost dismayed expression on her face. "Forgive me, ma'am," she said, "but be these all your clothes? With you the new mistress and all I was wondrin' . . ."

Even my maid was disappointed in me. "Those are all the things I have for the time being," I said apologetically. "The red cashmere walking dress and the blue satin are

144

new; the other things were mine when I worked. But my husband has ordered a complete trousseau for me and when that comes you'll have more to look after."

"I hope I haven't made 'ee angry, ma'am."

"Of course, not Morwenna. I know I'm not at all what people would expect."

I was surprised to hear her say, "It be a real pleasure for me to serve 'ee, Mrs. Blaize."

Embarrassed, I said, "Thank you. That means a great deal to me. Now I had better get ready. My husband, I'm certain, likes punctuality. That is, he would wish me to be ready when he asks." And so I was when Nicholas strode into my room, which seemed all the more feminine by contrast.

"I thought we'd go over to Nansett. It's under two miles, and the path is easy to follow once you've learned the way."

We went downstairs and out a door at the back of the house. Here was a large lawn landscaped by hedges and edged by groves of slim white birches. Amos stood holding the reins of a horse and nodded to me.

"Oh Nicholas, perhaps I should have said . . . I don't ride," I said, biting my lip.

"I didn't suppose you did, Miranda," he said. "That's why Amos has just brought out one horse. You can ride behind me. Come, I'll help you mount." He lifted me onto the horse and then climbed astride in front of me. He nudged the animal forward and I nearly slipped off the saddle, gasping as I did so.

"You'll have to hold on to me. Surely you'd rather put your arms about my waist than risk a fall." He sounded amused.

With heightened color I hesitatingly clasped my arms around his waist and held on as we rode away from the house and entered the woods. That path was rather uneven with stones and tree roots poking up. There were birch trees as far as the eye could see with patches of wispy tall grass growing between them. The forest was dappled with sunlight and the air had grown warmer, protected from the

145

sea breezes. There were faint splashes of autumn color heralding the glories to come; some of the birch leaves were tipped bright yellow.

As we drew farther into the forest, it became shadier. Lush ferns carpeted the floor and in places vivid green moss cushioned the horse's hooves. The birches gave way to sugar maples, which promised a riotous blaze of color in the coming weeks. Balsam firs, perfuming the air with their spicy fragrance, mingled with the oaks, aspens, and dogwoods. A few trees grew on their sides, their trunks weirdly contorted and spotted with lichen.

The path came out onto a swamp, whose still surface was coated with pale green growth. Dead trees clustered at one end of the glade like thin gray wraiths. Wispy tamaracks grew around the sides of the bog. Winterberry shrubs glowed red, startlingly beautiful against the blue-gray water. A mountain rose before us on the opposite side.

We skirted the swamp, which Nicholas call Blackett's Glade. "In midsummer the pink swamp roses bloom here in thickets — that's a pretty sight. Just remember to be careful if you go near the water. These swamps can be treacherous. And we're still too far from the village for anyone to hear you if you called for help."

The path took us into the forest again and soon we had begun to climb. The trees grew densely here, the sky mere slits of blue.

"We're following a lower slope of Bald Mountain now," Nicholas told me. "In a short while we'll come to an open place where you'll have a view both of the top of the mountain and of the countryside below."

"How much of this is your land, Nicholas?"

"All that we've covered and a good deal more. I own all of Thunder Island except for Nansett and a few fields at the back of it where the people farm."

The forest was thinning and soon we were free of it. To the side rose the rocky summit of Bald Mountain.

"Do you see the way the mountain is rounded smooth at the top and its face chiseled with giant steps? Years ago a

146

Swiss professor, a scientist, at Harvard theorized that a major part of the earth was once covered by ice. Ice that was several thousands of feet thick."

I shuddered. "I can't imagine it."

"It seems probable that Thunder Island was covered and sheared by those glaciers. There are a number of inland lakes and ponds which have no inlet to the sea, nor are they fed by mountain streams. It is likely that ice, moving very slowly, gouged out valleys and then, when it eventually melted, the water basins remained. The theory describes how fractured boulders were plucked from cliffsides and deposited at the shoreline, thus forming our rocky, jagged coast. This process took place over thousands of years; man has only inhabited Thunder Island for several hundred. Makes one feel rather insignificant, doesn't it?"

"If anything could make *you* feel insignificant, Nicholas, I daresay that could," I said shyly, and he laughed.

We rode on along the stony path of the mountain. The wind was sharper up here, but invigorating. Nicholas pointed out the northern bayberry bushes with their green-gray berries, from which the villagers made soap and candles. Mountain cranberry crept over the exposed ridges, its leaves small and glossy. The height of the granite mountain rose steeply to our left; to our right the tree tops made a prickly blanket which stretched far across to the sapphire ocean. Blackett's Glade could be glimpsed below, and in the far distance behind us was a lake enclosed by black-green spruces.

When I turned forward in the saddle, we were descending into the woods and all was once again hushed and shadowed. We rode until we came to a low stone wall at the edge of the forest matted with moss and leaves.

"This marks the end of my land," said Nicholas. "The next field belongs to a few of the villagers, who use part of it to grow corn, as you can see. We'll have to dismount here."

He got off the horse and then lifted me to the ground, his hands firm around my waist. When he set me down, he did not loosen his hold. I looked up into his face and found myself unable to look away from his warm gaze. His eyes lowered to my mouth and he bent forward while my heartbeat quickened.

Just then a voice called, "Mawnin', Nicholas!"

Nicholas jerked his head up, releasing me. A man was coming toward us. He was tall and leanly built with a handsome, square-jawed face and fair hair.

"Good day to you, Ben," said Nicholas, his arm outstretched.

The two men clasped hands warmly. "Miranda, this is Ben Somes, my brother-in-law. Ben, I'd like you to meet my wife."

"Hello, Ben."

He shook my hand, giving me a slow, wide smile, which I thought very attractive. "We heard you'd come, Mrs. Blaize. From Minnie Slocum, who got it from one of the sailors. Tell it to that bahskit and it's all over town! You both come to the house for a mug-up. Emily'd never forgive me if she knew I'd seen you and not brought you back. Happy as a clam, she is, with the news."

We stepped over the stone wall, walking across the field. Nicholas led the horse while Ben and I walked side by side. We passed a stone grist mill, its trim and its wheel painted red.

"Did the men get the timber and cordwood loaded onto Captain Miles' ship?"

"Ayeh. First thing this mawnin.' Did he give you a fair price for it?"

"Not without some wrangling, as usual. But I held out. How's Emily?"

"Well, and she'll be all the better for seein' you and Miranda here."

"Nicholas, did you say that Captain Miles bought lumber and took it back?"

"Yes, bound for Boston. Thunder Island is plentiful in white pine, oak, and ash trees, which are used for building or for making furniture. Ships like Captain Miles' stop here frequently to load the logs and transport them to

148

ports."

We made our way through a copse of trees, which separated the field from the outskirts of the village. The buildings were scattered on streets which wound their way down to the small harbor. The simple clapboard cottages were painted white and trimmed with black or dark green shutters. Windowboxes with cheerful flowers or trailing ivy adorned many of them. The smell of the sea was strong as we walked down a central street and one could hear the raucous cries of gulls. Below, small crafts were moored near the dock. Nanset was a quaint, picturesque village.

"Where is everyone?" I asked.

"The men are either at the lumber mill or shipyard, or out checking their lobster traps. The men have many occupations here—that of fisherman, sailor, farmer, lumber man, shipwright, and carpenter. The women, I imagine," Nicholas added with a smile, "are stealing glimpses of you from behind their curtains."

We had reached a pretty cottage surrounded by a white picket fence. Yellow and orange chrysanthemums bloomed in the doorway and there was a vegetable garden to the side of the house.

Ben opened the door, calling, "Emily! Look who I met at the stone wall!"

Nicholas and I followed him inside. It was cozy and charming with country furniture and lace curtains at the windows. A large decoy of a Canadian goose stood on the rustic mantel; two chairs upholstered in red were drawn up to the fireplace.

Into the room came a young woman with dark hair and fine-boned features which reminded me of Lavinia.

"Nicholas!" she cried happily, throwing her arms around her brother. I was surprised to see him pat her slightly rounded stomach after he had kissed her on the cheek.

"You look bonny, as usual," he said. "How's this one doing?"

"Oh, we're both fine. But introduce me to your lovely bride!"

149

"Miranda, this is my sister, Emily."

She kissed me affectionately, drawing her arm through mine. "I'm so glad you've come, Miranda. I do hope you'll like Thunder Island. It must seem quite a different country from New Bedford but I hope you'll grow used to it soon, used to all of us. Nicholas, it's so good to have you back. Come and have some chowder with us, both of you."

In the kitchen a trestle table was set for lunch. Bunches of dried herbs hung from the exposed beams in the ceiling and a large cast iron pot simmered over the fire.

"It smells delicious," I said. "Can I help you?" The shyness which normally overcame me when making new acquaintances was rapidly evaporating.

"You can set two more places with those bowls and plates from the hutch. I'll get the utensils."

We sat round the table while Emily ladled the redolent fish chowder into four bowls. She passed round a plate of rolls accompanied by raspberry preserves and butter. There was also a sharp yellow cheese she confessed to have made herself. I thought her remarkable. And here in her comfortable kitchen I had no qualms that I would spill my soup or do something equally clumsy.

Naturally she was curious about how Nicholas and I had met and decided to marry. When Nicholas explained briefly, omitting the part that Captain Sears had played, she exclaimed, "I don't wonder at it at all. Nicholas always knows his own mind; it must have been love at first sight!"

I flushed, her words putting me quite out of countenance, but Nicholas said, his lips quirked, "You should know, Emily. Even as a child you chased Ben shamelessly."

"Ayeh, she did," said her husband, a smile glinting in his eyes. "I finally had no choice but to marry her."

She laughed, not in the least offended. "I had no choice. Ben was always too bashful."

That could never be said of Nicholas, I thought.

It was a pleasant hour we spent with the two of them. The devotion they felt for each other was readily apparent, and if it made me a little wistful, I did not mind. The atmosphere in this charming cosy cottage was far removed

150

from the atmosphere at Thunder House; it was no wonder that Emily had longed to escape to a new life with Ben.

After lunch the men retired to the parlor and I helped Emily clear the table and clean the dishes. She talked with enthusiasm of the child she was carrying and I was touched by her eager anticipation. Many women in her place did not refer to their condition and the rest of us were supposed to act as though we did not notice the altered shape of her body and the reason for it. When the baby did come, it was viewed as a pleasant surprise. But Emily was proud of her condition.

"Perhaps you'll be expecting a child soon, too, Miranda," she said.

"Oh, I don't think that's very likely," I blurted out, and then my face grew hot when I realized what I had implied.

She took my hands in hers. "Miranda, it's all right. Remember, you and Nicholas scarcely know one another. These matters take time. But things will improve between you—you must first grow accustomed to one another. I can see how proud Nicholas is of you."

"Proud—of me? Oh, no, I'm sure you're mistaken."

"That I'm not, I assure you. You're beautiful and very sweet. You've a kind heart, I can tell. And Nicholas needs someone like you. He's had a hard time of it this last year . . . not that he shows it much. But things will be much better now that you are here, I'm confident of that. This is the best thing which could have happened."

I had not the heart to disillusion her. She wanted to believe that Nicholas and I would fall in love and that I would be able to ease his black moods. If she only knew the sort of beginning our married life had had! But it was better she didn't know. And I hadn't the courage to ask her what lay at the back of the hard time he had had.

Nicholas came in the kitchen then and asked if I were ready to leave. "We don't want to tire you out, Em."

"Don't be silly! It's been wonderful to have you both here. You must come back very soon, Miranda; don't wait for Nicholas to bring you."

"I won't. Thank you, Emily, for making me feel so

151

welcome. I've enjoyed being here very much."

We said good-bye to Ben, and Nicholas untied the horse. Then we began to retrace our steps up the winding narrow street.

"Did you really enjoy yourself there?" Nicholas asked me.

"Yes, Nicholas, I liked both of them very much. I'm . . . I'm glad you have a sister like Emily."

"Ben makes her a fine husband. And she's much happier keeping busy than Lavinia is sitting idly."

A woman with flyaway gray hair came out of her cottage as we passed and made a pretense of sweeping her porch. But her eyes were on me.

"There's Minnie Slocum," said Nicholas between irritation and amusement. "She wants to see you, naturally. Hello, Minnie," he called.

"Good day, Captain Nicholas," said the woman, who had dropped her broom and was hurrying across her lawn to meet us. "And this is the new Mrs. Blaize. I'm right glad to meet you, ma'am."

"How do you do, Mrs. Slocum?" I asked, extending my hand.

"Been at Mrs. Somes', have you? I saw the horse outside."

"I'm sure you did," said Nicholas.

"Well, I like to keep my eyes and ears open, Captain. One of the men from the ship told me you'd brung a bride to the house. He said some of the sailors couldn't stop watching her!"

I quite was taken aback but Nicholas said dryly, "I'm delighted to learn she met with the approval of the crew. And now if you'll excuse us, Minnie . . ."

"Happiness and health to you both," she said. I thanked her while Nicholas nodded.

We continued up the hill past a small white church with a pointed spire. Bunches of Indian corn hung on its two front doors. "How charming," I said.

"I daresay you'd like to attend services once in a while," he said.

"Yes, I would. Could we?"

"If it would please you, then of course. After all, we first met in a chapel, did we not?"

His good humor encouraged me to ask diffidently, "Why were you there, Nicholas? You've never said. And you looked so . . ." Reluctant to pursue my questioning, I looked up at him to gauge his reaction.

But he did not appear to be listening. His gaze was fixed on something on the side street of the church. It was a young woman. Not something, but someone. A most definite someone. Mesmerized, I stared at her as we drew closer.

She was beautiful. Corn-colored hair rippled over her shoulders. She moved toward us in graceful sensual glides. Her eyes were violet-blue and slightly tilted, her red lips full and provocative over a clefted chin. She wore a simple dark blue gown which did nothing to diminish her ripe lush beauty.

Biting my lip, I glanced at Nicholas. If her effect on me was to make me feel awkward, plain, and self-conscious, then what effect did she have on him? His face told me nothing. Yet the warm contented feeling which had filled me since being in Emily's cottage was draining out of me like water through a sieve.

"Hello, Nicholas," she said. "We heard you had returned." Even her voice was distinctive, smooth and rich as honey.

"How are you, Heather?" he asked, smiling. But was there a trace of something in his voice, a shade of unease? Or was I merely imagining it?

She smiled slowly. "Oh, I'm as you see." Her eyes traveled to me.

"Miranda, this is Heather MacLeod. Her father used to be pastor of the church here. Heather, this is my wife."

"I'm pleased to meet you, Miranda," she said, holding out her hand.

"How . . . how do you do, Heather?"

"Would you care to come inside the manse? I know Mother would love to meet you. She was most interested

153

when we heard the news this morning."

Glancing at Nicholas, I hoped he would decline. But he nodded and said easily, "All right. After all, I'm introducing Miranda to the island. And she's already met Minnie Slocum."

Heather laughed. "That woman! I'm certain she wouldn't let you leave Nansett without making Miranda's acquaintance; she was doubtless watching for you all morning. Do you remember that time, Nicholas, when she rushed to tell you she'd seen Emily kissing Ben? Or when she had to be the one to wait at the dock and tell Joe Everett his wife had had a son when he'd been out trapping all day?"

They laughed together with the ease of old friends and I smiled, wanting to be a part of them, but I didn't know Joe Everett or his wife. We followed Heather to the other side of the church, where there was a large frame house painted white with black shutters and trim. A porch encircled the front; we walked up the steps and across to the front door. I was very reluctant to enter this young woman's house as though by entering I would cross some invisible boundary, move into an intimacy with her that I would regret. And there would be no going back once it was done, no restoring of that protective barrier.

"Miranda looks chilled; let's get out of this wind," Heather said, opening the door. And then we were inside.

A maid took my cloak and bonnet while Heather told her to bring a pot of tea. My heart sank. It seemed we would be staying for a while. We went into the parlor, which was furnished rather shabbily; the upholstery was gold velvet with that shiny look which comes from a lot of wear. I felt better as I looked around; it was a rather endearing sort of room; there was nothing to intimidate me here. And Heather was also a minister's daughter — it was foolish of me to be ill at ease with her.

"Well, how nice this is!" said a soft voice. A woman was coming down the hall staircase, her face alight with pleasure as she looked at the three of us seated in the parlor. "Nicholas, how good to see you!"

He rose and took her hand and she held her cheek for him to kiss. "Hello, Katherine. You're looking well."

She was a very handsome woman, tall and buxom. In her youth she must have been just as beautiful as Heather with the same tilted violet blue eyes, the same dimpled chin. She wore a mauve gown, simple like Heather's but elegantly cut.

"And this must be the lovely bride we've heard about— news travels fast on Thunder Island, my dear! How good of you, Nicholas, to bring her by. I wondered when we would get to meet her. I'm Katherine MacLeod." She took my hand in both of hers and gave it a little squeeze, her eyes smiling into mine.

"How do you do, Mrs. MacLeod?"

"Oh, call me Katherine, my dear."

"I'm Miranda."

"Such a pretty name. Shakespeare, isn't it? Are your parents fond of Shakespeare?"

"My father was. Once he tried to direct his Indian pupils in a performance of *Macbeth*. It wasn't too successful, I'm afraid."

She laughed. "That must have been something to see. Indian pupils, you said. Do you mean the Indians we have or the ones from India?"

"From India. I was born and raised there, in Bombay. My parents were missionaries."

"How fascinating! You don't say! What a remarkable girl you must be!"

"Oh no, although they were . . . remarkable people."

"My husband was a minister also. When he was young he had aspirations to be a missionary, but working on an island off the coast of Maine was as far as he got! Poor Bruce, he wasn't exactly the adventuresome sort. But a wonderful man all the same. We miss him, don't we, Heather?"

Heather nodded. She was pouring the tea.

"He's been gone three years, you see, Miranda," said Katherine. "But it's odd, sometimes I still think I hear his steps on the stairs."

155

"I lost my parents," I said. "They died of cholera."

"And then you came to America?" she asked solemnly.

"Yes, they were originally from New England and so I booked passage on a ship to New Bedford, wanting to get away."

"Nicholas met you in New Bedford? We knew he'd gone there to sell the *Eagle*."

"We met at the home of my employer. I was a governess."

Nicholas and Heather were speaking in low voices. I wished I could hear their conversation but Katherine was asking, "And he proposed to you? What a lovely romantic story. Heather, did you hear that?"

Heather was laughing at something Nicholas had said. She looked toward us. "What was that, Mother?"

I blushed, wishing Katherine wouldn't say anything further, but she went on, "Miranda was a governess at the house in New Bedford where Nicholas was a guest. He must have swept her off her feet. You both have just restored my faith in romance."

I did not look at Nicholas to see what effect her words had on him; I took a sip of tea. But it was very hot and scalded my tongue, making me cough.

"I'm sorry, Miranda. I should have warned you it was still quite hot," said Katherine, chagrined. "Are you all right?"

"Yes, of course," I said, smiling idiotically. I took another sip, my face red. If only people would stop exclaiming how romantic it all was, our meeting and marrying the way we did. It was nothing like that, I thought forlornly. It was furtive—almost sordid. At least Captain Sears's part in it was. And I had wondered ever since if Nicholas was regretting his impulsiveness.

Katherine MacLeod seemed to guess some of my feelings, for she reached out a hand and touched my arm. "Don't mind me, my dear. I'm just an old busybody like Minnie Slocum. But I had a happy marriage and I like to observe them in others."

I nodded, smiling, to show her that I was not offended.

How could I be when she was so warm and friendly, so interested in me? I was too sensitive. Why was I so tense, so prone to self-consciousness? I had not been that way at Emily's earlier, and Katherine was not one to make me feel that way either.

It was Heather, I thought heavily. It was she who reminded me of who and what I was — not the cherished wife of a handsome wealthy man but the obscure insecure girl I was. Not that the aspirations of her birth were any higher than my own. But her grace and polish and the air of allure she had, which was as natural to her as breathing, all combined to make me feel woefully inadequate, dull in comparison. And she did all this unintentionally, to give her her due. I could not fault her for that.

At last Nicholas was setting down his tea cup and rising, saying that we had to be on our way. "I must go over to the shipyard this afternoon and see how things have progressed. Ben had some things he wanted to discuss with me."

"Thank you for the tea," I said.

"Do come and see us again soon," said Katherine. And Heather smiled, her violet eyes like pools at dusk.

We rode back to Thunder House, speaking little. I wondered what Nicholas was thinking about but naturally I did not ask him. He and Heather were old friends; he was obviously a welcome, frequent visitor in their home. She had been serene, poised, totally at ease with him. Was it possible he could have known her all these years and not fallen in love with her?

When we reached the house, he lifted me down from the horse, saying, "I'll see you later this evening, Miranda."

"All right, Nicholas. Thank you for taking me to Nansett."

He nodded absently and rode away. I had no desire to return to my room. Crossing the side lawn, I went into the woods and descended the stone steps which led to Thunder Cove.

The tide was moving in, lashing at the impassive rocks with great splashes and booms. The walls of the cliff echoed the crashing of the waves as I picked my way carefully across the cove. Tiny dog whelks clung to the moist rocks, and golden clumps of seaweed crackled and swayed in the rising water. Under the cliff, yellow wild roses grew defiantly between the stark gray boulders.

As I rounded the cove, guided by the line of spruce trees which perched above me, I paused and glanced back at Thunder House. The slight lawn was not visible from this angle and the house rose majestically from the salmon-hued granite which formed its foundation. It looked even larger from here than it had from the ship, a lofty massive defense against the primeval forces of the elements below. The long opaque windows did not relieve its somber formidable look. It was not a house which welcomed and beckoned. I fancied it looked down at me on the shore, contemptuous and aloof. You are not worthy of me, it seemed to say. Who are you to aspire to be my mistress? But I don't aspire to that, I was tempted to say. I know I'm not right for such a place, for such a man.

Turning away, I stepped and hopped over the rocks, stumbling here and there but determined to go on. I wanted to see what lay beyond Thunder Cove. The sound of the sea was deafening.

After I had reached the edge of the cove, the going was not as rugged. Narrow flat boulders of white-striped gray made easy walkways. The sun was warm on my face, the breeze fairly mild. Gulls swooped over the water in graceful turns; some huddled on rocks. The sea trickled into the cracks between the stones where tiny spiders scurried. Pieces of driftwood were scattered about, bleached and smooth.

Ahead of me a huge monolith rose dramatically from the water's edge, its surface creased and scarred. Doubtless Nicholas would call it a legacy from the glaciers. It certainly looked singular as it loomed above the shoreline When I had reached it, I touched its cold hard face.

"Like the Selkie's Throne, do you?"

An old man was coming toward me from the opposite side of the monolith, a pipe in his hand and a red bandanna tied around his neck.

"What did you call it?"

"It's the Selkie's Throne. The Great Selkie is said to hold court here."

"Who is the Great Selkie?"

The man took a puff on his pipe, studying me. "Ye cud be the captain's wife."

"Yes, I am. And you are . . . ?"

"Noah Todd, the lighthouse keeper."

"There's a lighthouse on Thunder Island?"

"Ayeh." He jerked his thumb behind him. "Down around there a ways. A place like this got to have a lighthouse, specially when the fog's so thick ye cud stick a knife through it."

"You were telling me about the Selkie."

" 'Tis an old Scots legend. It's said he—or they—comes ashore in misty murky weather when the sea is as calm as a lake. He grows legs when on land and his fins disappear."

"Are you saying he's a fish who sits on a throne?" I asked, smiling at the image.

Noah regarded me gravely. "He's dahk and sleek as a seal, but he's paht man, too. He's half-seal, half-human. But he's got no soul like a human bein' has. He cud steal ye away if he'd a mind to. They say he comes ashore and calls to the mortal bride he desires. She can't resist him. Then they both go down to the fah dahk dephs of the sea. It's said he's handsome though with odd slanted eyes and hair black and close as fur, streaked with silver. He steals a mortal bride and she becomes a soulless creature like he is."

"That . . . that's ridiculous. Surely no one around here believes that?" I asked uneasily.

He shrugged his shoulders, puffing on his pipe. "A tale, I said. Who can tell?"

"Oh. I see. Well, thank you for telling it to me. I should be getting back now."

"Ye cud come to the lighthouse one day if ye've a mind to."

"Perhaps I will. Good-bye, Noah."

159

"Good-bye, Mrs. Nicholas."

I turned around, heading back in the direction of Thunder House. Even in the bright sunlight when the sky was a rich blue his words had unnerved me. The image he had described was as eerie as it was compelling. I had no trouble conjuring up that dark sleek creature, resembling a man in form, sitting atop the monolith while the mist muffled the sound of the waves and shrouded the shore. Thunder Island would be a different place in those conditions, an alien place where we were at the mercy of the elements and those who inhabited the kingdom of the sea.

Why, I was sounding like the old man, I thought with a shaky inward laugh. It was contagious. A Scots legend, he had said. A Celtic legend that doubtless went back to the pre-Roman days of ancient Britain. He was an eccentric, of course, living alone at the lighthouse, constantly surveying the changing moods of the sea. That was likely to make anyone suggestible, though I found it difficult to believe that others in Nansett gave credence to the existence of such creatures as selkies. Still, the very earnestness with which he had described the legend had disturbed me. I was glad of the golden brightness of the day and the sharp clarity of the air.

I made my way back along the shore to the house and this time I did not pause to scrutinize it. I looked forward to returning to my lovely room and being alone. Perhaps I could ask Morwenna for some tea. I would enjoy sitting in one of the apricot wing chairs without having to worry that I would do or say something foolish or regrettable. What time would Nicholas return, I wondered.

When I was ascending the stairway to the third floor, my name was called and I looked around in dismay.

"Miranda? I've been looking for you. Amos said Nicholas brought you back nearly two hours ago," said Sarah, an accusing tone in her voice.

"Oh yes, he did, but I've been walking along the shore. I'm sorry I wasn't here—was it anything important?"

"Well, I hardly know what you would consider important, Miranda. But the mistress would like you to join her

160

in a quarter of an hour for tea."

My heart sank. "Very well, Sarah. I'll just change my gown," I said, conscious that my hair was tumbling out of my bonnet and the hem of my gown was wet and muddy. "Where shall I . . ."

"Down that hall, the third door on your right."

"Thank you, Sarah. I'll be along shortly."

She nodded coolly and I turned and continued up the stairs. When I rounded the bend in the stairs, I saw she had not moved; she was still regarding me, her face expressionless, her hands folded across her waist.

There went my hope of having the rest of the afternoon to myself. Resignedly I opened the armoire and took out the red cashmere gown. Undressing, I slipped it over my head and then rang for Morwenna to help me fasten the buttons. I could not get used to the idea of having a maid even though Miss Proctor's gowns seemed to require the assistance of one.

The sea breeze had blown my hair wild and woolly; Morwenna smoothed it and pinned it up as best she could. I was dreading this enforced visit with Lavinia and Sarah no matter in what guise it had been offered.

I went downstairs to the second floor and knocked at the door Sarah had instructed. She opened it and I walked into a beautiful sitting room. It was done in yellow and white with gold-painted furniture in the French style. There was an ormolu clock on the mantel, and pretty china boxes of various sizes and shapes were set on fragile little tables about the room. The windows did not face the sea; instead the wide lawn and distant birches created a tranquil idyllic backdrop for the room.

"Ah, Miranda," said Lavinia, who sat on a settee with a tea table before her, "how nice of you to join us. I hear you have been gone the entire day." She said it as though she could not imagine what I had been doing to occupy myself. "Sit down and tell me how you take your tea." She poured me a cup from the silver teapot and handed it to me. "Tell me what you've been doing with yourself. What did you find to interest you on Thunder Island?"

"Nicholas took me on a ride. We passed a swamp—"

"Oh, that would be Blackett's Glade. A man named Blackett was drowned there in the last century. Dreadful, gloomy place. I've always detested it."

"Yes, well . . . Nicholas said in the summer when the swamp roses bloom around it, it's lovely."

She gave a deprecating half-smile. "Nicholas is a Blaize, my dear. He considers every part of Thunder Island worth admiration."

"Uh, we rode to Nansett and had luncheon with Emily and Ben."

"Oh? I wondered if you had met her today. Her husband is a man of few words, isn't he?"

I smiled. "I'm becoming used to that. So is Nicholas a man of few words."

Her lids dropped. She handed me a plate of cinnamon cookies. "And I daresay you ate in her cosy kitchen. Nicholas has offered her money to enlarge the cottage but so far she's refused it—quite foolishly, I might add."

"It was a pleasant, warm room."

"I daresay it *was* warm with that cooking stove right next to one! I declare I would feel quite suffocated."

"She's a very good cook," I pointed out, feeling more and more uncomfortable. It was in very poor taste for her to criticize her daughter's lifestyle to me.

"Martha gave Emily some lessons when we knew she was determined to be married and Nicholas had given his permission. I hope she isn't regretting her impulsiveness. Both my son and my daughter—so impulsive, so head-strong, rushing into things without thinking."

I bit my lip. "As Nicholas did in his marriage to me," I said quietly.

Lavinia gave a light brittle laugh. "As you say, Miranda. You will forgive me for saying that I was never more shocked in my life than I was last night when he brought you in and introduced you as his wife, was I, Sarah? But then Nicholas has never been in the least predictable. He's a difficult man to live with, not like his father Roger was. I don't envy you at all. You haven't much experience with men, have you?"

"N—none, not really."

"I thought not. I wonder how you'll deal with Nicholas. I can't quite reconcile the two of you together in my mind. Did he truly see you one day and propose to you the next? Do tell us the details; Sarah and I have so little to divert us here."

"There's not all that much to tell, Mrs. Blaize," I said uneasily, twisting my wedding ring around my finger.

"Nonsense. A whirlwind courtship like that and not much to tell?"

"Well, it was all very sudden as you've imagined. I had been requested to bring the children to the drawing room one evening because a visitor was there. It was Nicholas." Glancing from Lavinia's amused curious countenance to Sarah's stolid one I wondered what to say next.

"Did you speak to him in the drawing room?"

I shook my head, feeling my face growing hot. "It was later that—we spoke."

"Later? Do you mean that night? How did that happen? Were you asked to dine with the family?"

"Oh no, nothing like that. I was never asked to . . . that is—" Lavinia had exchanged glances with Sarah.

I didn't know how to go on. It was obvious to both women that I had no wish to continue, but I hadn't the courage to tell them that it was none of their business. There was a lump in my throat. I swallowed some tea hoping that it would dissolve, but it didn't.

"So when did you and Nicholas actually first speak to one another?"

My hands were in my lap, clenching and unclenching themselves in tight clammy fists. My nails were digging into my palms. Why was she pressing me? Why did she have to go on and on? Did she have to make me more miserable than I was already?

"Well, Miranda, the way you're refusing to tell us makes me think you've done something very naughty," she said archly, wagging a finger at me.

This goaded me as it was meant to. "It wasn't I, it was

163

my employer, Captain Sears." And then I knew I shouldn't have said anything further because now she would not let up.

"Your employer? And what did he do? What has he got to do with Nicholas?"

Bending my head, I stared at my sapphire and diamond wedding ring. "He . . . he came into my room. Nicholas heard us and he—he stopped him." Are you satisfied now, I wanted to ask, is that diverting enough for you?

"Heavens! I hardly expected anything quite so . . . so melodramatic. What a sordid little story, to be sure. I had no idea . . . You've certainly shown my son to me in a new light. A gallant knight in armor, no less."

"He was gallant, yes," I answered, biting my lip.

"But then he carried it rather far, didn't he?"

"What do you mean?" I asked, although I knew.

"Well, after all, Miranda, he didn't have to *marry* you, did he? Or is there something else you're not telling me?"

"No! That is all. He asked me to marry him the next day."

"And naturally you accepted. What a fortunate girl you are, Miranda! To be so adept at taking a dreadful turn of events and turning it into such a promising one. You must be very clever."

"I don't understand what you mean, Mrs. Blaize. It just . . . happened. Everything happened so quickly. One minute I was in total despair and the next Nicholas was taking me away from the Sears house. Nicholas was . . . very kind. I was—I am—grateful to him."

"I'm quite certain you are," Lavinia said, her eyebrows raised. "Although surely you are not giving yourself enough credit? An impoverished girl suddenly married to a most eligible man! That took some doing, certainly."

I gazed at her in dismay, unable to think of anything to say in my own defense. She made it sound as if Nicholas had picked me up out of the gutter, as if I had manipulated Captain Sears's behavior and that of Nicholas for my own ends, to win myself a rich husband.

"Nicholas felt sorry for you, didn't he? Even I can see

you have something in your face which would appeal to some men—a helplessness, an innocence. Though I can imagine that it will prove very hard to hold that interest. I hope you have not cooked your own goose, my child. Marrying Nicholas might not turn out to be the panacea to your problems after all. It may seem like a happy resolution now, but—you don't know Nicholas at all well, do you?"

I was at a loss to understand her except to realize that she did not approve of Nicholas's marriage to me and she did not care how often she made me aware of that. The only consolation I had was in knowing that she had no affection for her son and his happiness was scarcely a concern of hers. She was critical of Emily's marriage to Ben Somes and now Nicholas had scandalized her by bringing me home. As far as she was concerned, both her children had foolishly married beneath them and she had little faith in the success of either alliance.

But she seemed to feel she had said enough for one afternoon. She had left me in no doubt as to her true feelings and now she was content to change the subject. "So what else did you do today?"

Why did I answer her? Why didn't I just get up and leave the room? But of course I didn't do that. "I met the old lighthouse keeper this afternoon."

She rolled her eyes. "Noah Todd, that dotty old fool. Roger's father made him lighthouse keeper more than fifty years ago. I don't think he's ever going to have the courtesy to die and give the position to someone younger, more important. Nicholas won't hear of dismissing him. Just like Nicholas to be contrary like that. I believe he does it just for spite."

"I don't believe Nicholas would risk people's lives out of spite."

"Oh you don't? Did you hear that, Sarah?" They both smirked.

I flushed. "Noah was rather strange. He told me of an odd legendary creature—the Great Selkie. He seemed to believe that it comes ashore with sinister purposes. Even

165

ashore to Thunder Island, where it steals mortal brides and takes them back to the sea with it."

Lavinia's cup and saucer crashed to the floor, the liquid staining the carpet. Her face was white, her lips bloodless. Suddenly she looked old, feeble. The change was so startling that I was alarmed. One moment her manner had been mocking and patronizing; now she was reduced to a quaking terror-stricken woman.

"What is it?" I asked in a panic. "What have I said?"

Sarah was at her side, putting an arm across her frail shoulders. "Now, now, dearest, it's only a foolish legend."

Both women had momentarily forgotten my presence. Lavinia's eyes stared wildly into Sarah's. "Why must they start that again? I can't bear it—I just can't bear it, not again!"

"There, there, Lavinia. Noah's just an old fool and so will I tell him when next I see him. No one believes that tale, no one at all. Now sit back and relax and I'll pour you another cup of tea."

"No, no! I couldn't swallow it. In heaven's name, why must they keep on about that dreadful creature? It's unhuman, it's wicked!"

I was stricken with remorse at the reaction my idle words had caused. "I'm sorry, Lavinia. I didn't know what I was saying. I didn't mean to . . ."

Sarah looked across at me then and froze my apology. I recoiled from the baleful accusing expression on her face. "You knew exactly what you were doing, Miranda! It made you uncomfortable to hear the truth spoken about you and so you chose that way to pay Lavinia back. How revoltingly petty, how cruel to strike out that way at a sick woman! I hope Nicholas finds out soon what sort of a girl he's married. He'll be repenting at leisure, that's for certain. But he'll have only himself to blame. And he's used to that! You deserve one another."

I did not stay to hear any more. I hurried out, stumbling into a table on my way, tears stinging my eyes and obscuring my vision, and fled to my room.

Chapter Eight

By that evening I was very sore from the morning's riding excursion; I was not used to sitting aside a horse. But I paid little attention to the physical discomfort. My mind kept playing over and over Sarah's malignant expression, her accusations that I had deliberately brought on Lavinia's bewildering transformation. Had I made her truly ill, I wondered wretchedly. How long would it take for her to recover?

I had thoroughly alienated my mother-in-law and her companion in less than twenty-four hours. Good work, I thought. Would Nicholas be angry with me? But surely he would realize that I had not intended to hurt Lavinia. How could I when I had no idea of the way she would react to the mention of the selkie creature? What possible significance did she attach to it? She could not be genuinely afraid that such beings existed and sought to harm her.

Curling up on my bed, I turned my face to the wall. One thing was certain: I could not face any of them this evening. I could not go down to supper and sit with Lavinia and Sarah with the memory of this afternoon so sharp and painful. And Nicholas would notice something; he might even press the point when we were all in attendance. I could not sit there while Sarah told Nicholas how I had upset his mother so gravely. Or even if she said nothing, her eyes would follow me, hate-filled, accusatory. I could not face her, especially.

When Morwenna came to help me dress for dinner, I

told her I was not feeling well and would not go downstairs. I didn't want anything to eat, I assured her. I stayed in bed, thinking of excuses to continue to remain in my room tomorrow and not have to see any of them even then. At least Nicholas spent his days at the shipyard. And Sarah and Lavinia would likely wish to avoid me even as I wished to avoid them. Days might pass before we were forced to meet again, I thought, feeling relieved. Thunder House was so large I could evade them for the present.

Movements in the room next to mine alerted me to Nicholas's presence. Oh no, I thought, dismayed, he must have returned from the shipyard. Unless it was one of the servants, laying the fire or something like that. I hoped it was. I fervently hoped that Nicholas would not come in and speak to me. Perhaps I could pretend to be asleep. . . .

There was a knock on my door. I held my breath, praying he would go away if I did not answer.

"Miranda, are you in there? I want to talk to you."

"Come in," I mumbled.

Nicholas opened the door and walked into the room, dressed in evening clothes. He looked very tall and forbidding from where I lay in bed. Hastily I sat up, not wanting to be in such a position. He might be reminded of another occasion on board ship when we had lain together. . . .

"Morwenna says you are unwell, that you aren't coming downstairs for dinner," he said, a pucker in his brow.

I said nothing, fingering the delicate lace border of the bedsheet.

"What is wrong? I see you are already dressed for bed." He sat down beside me. "Are you really ill?"

"Ummm. N—not exactly."

His eyes narrowed. "Oh, I think I . . . it's something you don't wish to talk about, is that it? A temporary discomfort? My dear child, there's no need to look like that. I am your husband, after all."

My face flamed. "It's nothing like that . . . like what you are thinking. It's merely that I am sore from riding and I . . . I have a headache."

168

"Is that all?"

"Can't that be enough?"

"I merely wondered whether something had upset you. Whether you were trying to avoid me," he said, his mouth quirking.

"Why should you think that?" I asked in a muffled voice.

"Well, Sarah and Lavinia have withdrawn for the night, taking dinner in their rooms. And when Morwenna told me you were doing the same, I got the impression everyone was avoiding me."

"I'm confident no one wished to do that, Nicholas," I said in spite of myself.

"Not even you?" The teasing glint in his eyes flustered me.

"It wasn't exactly you I wished to avoid, you see," I said slowly.

"Who, then?" He seemed to relax a little, leaning closer to me.

"Well, you see . . . this afternoon I took tea with your mother and Sarah and . . ." I began, smoothing the bumpy lace pattern of the sheet over and over.

"And?" he prompted, his tone suddenly grim.

"It was something I said—not meaning to, of course—that frightened Lavinia, agitated her. I'm sorry, Nicholas. I'm afraid, you see, that I'm to blame for her remaining in her room tonight. But I didn't mean anything by it. I didn't hurt her intentionally, I promise you."

He took my hands in his. "Of course you didn't, Miranda. I know you well enough to know there's not a malicious bone in your body."

"Sarah said . . . she thought I meant to hurt Lavinia by what I said. That I had spoken deliberately to make her ill. She was so angry with me."

"What did you say? Come, you can tell me. I won't be angry with you."

Still I hesitated, pushing back my hair.

"You're not afraid of me, are you, Miranda?" he asked swiftly, his brow knit.

I bit my lip. "After you left me at the house I went for a walk along the shore. I came upon Noah Todd, the old lighthouse keeper. He pointed out what he called the Selkie's Throne to me, and he described such a creature coming ashore in the mist in search of . . . of a bride. I thought it was a very peculiar story and so I mentioned it to Lavinia and Sarah when we were having tea. Lavinia had been asking me about myself, about you and me, making it seem as though I had . . . almost tricked you into marrying me or something equally awful. I was anxious to talk about something else and so I mentioned Noah and his obsession. But I never dreamed it would have the effect on Lavinia that it did! I never meant to make her ill."

He shook his head. "You're not to blame, Miranda. You couldn't have known what significance it has for her."

"She doesn't really believe in its existence, does she?"

"I don't know. But you see, when my sister Julia disappeared evidently some people . . . some very foolish people . . . began to suggest —"

"Nicholas! You surely don't mean — she doesn't believe one of these seal creatures actually came ashore and took Julia!"

He shrugged. "A demon lover, they spoke of. Oh yes, there were those, I learned later from Amos, who stated quite calmly that Julia must have been taken by a selkie. The Scots brought that hideous legend to Thunder Island a hundred years ago. It only enhanced their story that late in the day that Julia disappeared it had become foggy and the sea calm — supposedly ripe conditions for such a thing. Did Noah mention Julia in particular to you?"

"No, Nicholas. He just sort of . . . warned me, as though I might be a likely candidate, I suppose. But does your mother truly think that's what happened to Julia?"

He sighed heavily. "Apparently the idea became fixed in her mind in the weeks following Julia's disappearance. I was at sea as I've told you so I can only relate what I've heard. I did not come home until weeks afterward. Because Julia's body was never found, the idea that she had been . . . stolen away by supernatural means began to prey on Lavinia's mind. Somehow the thought that my sister was doomed to an undying life with a soulless creature — foolish as it sounds — seemed more horrifying to her than if she had merely drowned. Martha told me that one night Lavinia got out of bed, made her way downstairs in the dark and out the front door unbeknownst to anyone. It was only when she began to scream, 'Why did you take her? Bring her back!' while standing on the cliff above the cove that the household was aroused and she was restrained."

I could only stare at him in horror.

"Pretty tale, isn't it? Even now when these bad spells come on her, Sarah has to give her laudanum drops."

"Oh, if only I had not said anything," I cried, stricken.

"How could you know, Miranda? My mother lost my father several years ago. She collapsed totally then and had a very gradual recovery. She was — very angry with me for leaving Thunder Island and the shipyard. Then when Julia was gone . . . well, it's been too much for her. Her mind, her spirit has never recovered from the shock."

"I can tell she's very unhappy, Nicholas," I said sadly. "If she weren't, she wouldn't try so hard to — but that's neither here nor there. I'm sorry for her."

"We must make our own happiness, Miranda. My mother has never learned that. Even when my father was alive she was subject to episodes of deep melancholy. She's always been moody and discontended. She's never accepted life as it is on Thunder Island and tried to make the best of it. With Julia gone she has little to interest her."

"But there's Emily and the baby — her own grandchild to look forward to."

"I'm afraid she has little interest in either. She has lost a husband and a child with much suffering and cares little about what or who remains." He shrugged.

"What was Julia like?"

"She was like my mother, I suppose. She had been molded carefully into being like her. They were always together, that is, when Sarah was not giving us lessons the way she did when we were children. But Julia spent the rest of her time at Lavinia's side, sewing, playing with her dolls, talking of whatever interested them. When she grew older, she was a fine lady like my mother; they both considered themselves too good for Thunder Island. Even as a child Julia rarely spent time with other children in Nansett the way I and later Emily did. She stayed close to Lavinia's side, which, naturally, my mother encouraged. Lavinia doted on Julia; she was very proud of her. Poor Emily was always being compared to her, and not favorably, reminded that she hadn't her grace, her bearing. Emily was a tomboy, preferring to climb trees and hunt for gulls' eggs rather than practicing her curtsies and the proper way to pour tea. Julia was to have a fine Boston season, for which Lavinia and she were preparing when she was lost."

"And you say no trace of her was ever found?"

"No. They searched, of course, but found nothing. And for Emily things only got worse after that. Sometimes Lavinia couldn't bear the sight of her. No wonder on my return last winter she begged to marry Ben. They had been planning to wait another year but she couldn't endure living in Thunder House any longer."

"What do you believe actually happened to Julia?"

"There are several versions of what might have happened. The most likely is that she was caught on Seal Island at high tide and attempted to wade or swim back. The current would have carried her out to sea."

"Where is Seal Island?"

"On the opposite side of the island from here. It's a tiny island, uninhabited, which is linked to Thunder Island by a causeway. At low tide the causeway is wide and one can easily walk across it, but within a very short time after the tide has turned, it is covered with water up to ten feet deep. She may have thought she could make it back, having no wish to remain on the island until the tide swung again another six or seven hours later. For an islander living all her life here, Julia was remarkably ignorant of the workings of the sea, of nature. She rarely

172

left Thunder House."

"Except for that day."

He nodded. "Except for that day. I did wonder at the time. She was not fond of roaming about on her own. But that particular day she must have. At any rate she may have lost her footing in the fog and fallen from a cliff, her body washing out to sea."

"Was it very foggy?"

"So I've been told. Not earlier in the day, but by late afternoon it was. No one knows precisely what time she disappeared. If she was drowned off Seal Island, it had to have been close to high tide, which on that day was at midafternoon. Before dusk the fog rolled in from the sea. Lavinia and Emily had taken luncheon with her but never saw her again after that. It was not until they all gathered for dinner that she was missed and by then the house, the entire island was enshrouded in fog.

"Lavinia became quite agitated and ordered that the house and grounds be searched. But because of the weather a thorough search out of doors was impossible. The men's torches did not cut through the mist and their voices did not carry. No one could have heard her if she had called for help."

I shuddered. "How horrible."

"The next day the fog cleared off by late morning, and though Amos and Seth searched carefully, assisted by the men in Nansett, her body was never recovered, never washed ashore."

"There's no chance that she might have left the island of her own accord?"

His black brows drew together. "Run away, you mean? No. No ships were sighted that day. And what would her motivation have been? She was very excited about Lavinia's plans to take her to Boston for the season. They were convinced she would make a brilliant marriage there; they thought of little else. She would not have left Thunder Island before they were due to travel to Boston."

"I suppose not. And no one saw her that afternoon, anywhere?"

He shook his head. "I'm afraid it's a mystery which will never be satisfactorily solved. And it's a lesson to you, Miranda, to take care when you go out walking. And now I have an idea." He smiled slightly. "Why don't I ask Jenny or Mary to bring us a supper tray up here?"

"You mean, here . . . in my room?"

"That's what I said."

"But I'm not hungry," I said in sudden panic.

"So? I'm not going to force you to eat. You don't have to eat anything if you don't wish to," he said gently, amused.

"If—if you like," I said reluctantly.

He stiffened. "If I like! What about you, Miranda? I certainly don't wish to force my unwelcome presence on you!"

I didn't want him sitting in here with me, sharing a comfortable meal, acting as though we were like any other married couple. There were other things married people did together . . . and I was already dressed for bed, as he had remarked.

"Well, then, since you put it that way, Nicholas, I don't think so. I'm sorry but I'm very tired. It's been a very long day . . . so many things to get used to. And I'd like to take a hot bath; it might help relieve my sore muscles. I—I'd rather be alone if you don't mind."

"Whether I mind or not has little to do with it," he said, standing up, his eyes like gray granite, his mouth hard. "Good night, Miranda. I hope you sleep well." And he stalked out while I gazed contritely after him. But I had not wanted him to remain in my room indefinitely, to sit with me in cosy intimacy over a meal. Husband or not, I still felt very ill at ease in his presence, especially when we were alone. After the day I had had, I simply could not endure more time with him, wondering desperately if he would try to touch me, to kiss me—or worse.

Morwenna brought me hot water and I soaked in the tub, relieved to be able to relax freely and alone. "Have you ever heard of a creature called a selkie?" I asked her.

"Course I have, ma'am. We Cornish folk do know of

such things," she answered matter-of-factly.

"What do you know of it, then?"

"Well, they be terrible handsome and dark, with hair that grows close to the head like the skin of a seal. They live forever down in the sea in a crystal palace with floors of coral. But it be lonely down there and so from time to time they come ashore, shed their seal skins, and search for mortal brides. 'Tis said they call and a maiden that hears can't resist. They can't speak like we do but they make an odd sort of singing sound. They take their brides down to the bottom of the sea to their palace where the roof be made of waving golden and brown seaweed. But it be truly the hair of the drowned brides, for when they try to escape the selkies they always drown. As long as a girl bides with a selkie she can breathe under the water, but if she leaves, the water will choke her and drown her. When my mother was a girl she knew a girl that were took."

"But surely you don't believe that, Morwenna. She can't have been!"

" 'Tis true right enough, ma'am, I do tell 'ee. She went down to the beach one night and all they found o' her the next morning were the red ribbon she wore in her hair."

"But she may have drowned, or sailed away in a boat. A dozen things could have happened rather than that she was . . . spirited away by the song of a seal to his crystal and coral palace. After all, no one's ever seen a selkie. Have they?" I asked in spite of myself.

"Oh aye, ma'am. Plenty o' folks 've seen 'em afore," she insisted. "Else we wouldn't know what they be like."

"But there are always people who claim to see all sorts of things, Morwenna. It doesn't mean they actually exist."

She pursed her lips. " 'Ee's been down to the Selkie's Throne, haven't 'ee?"

"Yes," I admitted reluctantly, "though I thought it just a tall stone, which it is."

" 'Tis one thing to some and another to others, ma'am. 'Ee's not used to livin' by the sea like I be. Else 'ee'd know that there be such creatures, though they do rarely come ashore. And when I see a seal I always say a prayer and

175

hold up my hand, which 'ee ought to do, Mrs. Blaize."

Two days later I was still stiff and so I was not disappointed when I awoke and saw that it was raining. Wisps of mist floated eerily past my windows. The treetops were concealed in the dense whiteness and the sound of the waves in the cove was barely audible.

As I stared outside I was reminded of the legend of the Great Selkie, shuddering when I thought of walking outside in that clammy ominous stillness to be approached by who knew what. Was that what Julia had done? Had she been overtaken by the rising fog, lost her footing and fallen, her broken body then washing out to sea? Had she attempted to wade across that covered causeway, confident she could make it to Thunder Island before the water got too deep? If the fog had been drifting in the way it was now, she would have been even more anxious to reach the warmth and safety of Thunder House rather than face spending the night in that chilling, blinding moisture. But it was odd that no one had seen her, that no trace of her had been found. A wealthy beautiful girl—I was certain she had been beautiful—with everything to live for, with the prospect of a season in Boston society before her, an untimely end—it made such a compelling story. It was no wonder that some of the local people wanted to attach bizarre, supernatural connotations to her disappearance. It was human nature. Even I was fascinated and longed to know what had actually happened. And I hadn't even known her. No wonder that those who had had indulged in rampant speculations. It was just unfortunate that their idle talk had come to Lavinia's ears and so disturbed her. She had had enough heartache to bear without imagining her beloved daughter dragged to the depths of the sea to a palace canopied with the long waving hair of other drowned brides who had sought to escape the slippery embrace of their demon lovers, the evil mermen, the selkies.

After I was dressed and had eaten my breakfast, I

decided to look around some of the house. I would avoid
the corridor where Lavinia and Sarah had their rooms, but
there were many more rooms to peer into. I might even get
lost; I found something pleasant in that thought. It might
be diverting to get lost in a house this size. After all no one
could say I was trespassing, not in a mansion which
belonged to my husband. And there would be no one to
pry, to criticize, to intimidate me.

I would begin with the rooms off this hallway. There
were several bedrooms but I soon discovered they did not
yield much of interest. The furniture was swathed in
sheets; they were obviously guest rooms which were never
or seldom used.

I could imagine people arriving by ship for house
parties, these rooms light and cheerful — and occupied.
But the dust on the mantels was thick; the hearth had no
held a fire's blaze in a long time; the windows were rather
dingy; cobwebs shrouded the corners of the walls. All the
rooms of this floor had been guest rooms, Nicholas had
said. I guessed mine was the only room which had been
kept in readiness for a female guest.

And then there was Nicholas's room. I wondered if I
had the nerve to peek inside, and decided I did. Why not?
It was perfectly safe — he had left for the shipyard hours
ago and would not return until the evening. Why shouldn't
I look into his room? If a servant chanced to come in, I
could say I was looking for something he had told me was
there. But no one would come in. Morwenna had straightened his room while I ate breakfast and then she had
turned mine out before going downstairs to help the other
women. I was alone on this floor. And I had a mounting
curiosity to see the inside of my husband's bedroom.
Glancing up and down the corridor, I knocked softly at his
door. There was no answer, as I had expected, and so I
twisted the doorknob and pushed open the door.

It was a large chamber but appeared rather smaller
because it was cluttered with so many things. There was
the usual furniture — horsehair sofa, massive four-poster
bed with wine-red hangings tied back with gold tassels like

the curtains at the windows, large arm chairs, tables. But these things were quickly registered and then were forgotten.

It was the other items in the room which caught and claimed my attention. All sorts of instruments hung on the walls — and from my two years in New Bedford I could easily identify them as whaling instruments. There were spades, knives, tackle, a needle of giant proportions, hooks, harpoons — all these were suspended on the walls, displayed in an almost venerated way. And then on the tables were various nautical items such as a chronometer, a brass telescope with woven case and lanyard, a sextant, a brass speaking trumpet, a telltale compass. All these were set down as though they were to be used at any time, as though this room were the captain's aboard ship. I could almost feel the waves rolling under my feet; I could almost smell the sea.

Nicholas must have taken all these things from his ship and set them up here. There was a name board against one wall with goldleafed letters, *The Eagle*. And it was the most poignant sight of all.

I realized I had given little thought to my husband since marrying him. I had been so caught up with my own insecurities and worries that I had not been concerned with him. This room brought that home to me with a jolt. Nicholas had created a ship's stateroom within the walls of Thunder House, a room which was meant to remind him of his days at sea. After giving up the sea he had returned to Thunder House, taken a room in this wing on this floor, and filled it with memories. He must miss his old life terribly, I thought. Perhaps that was why he had visited the Seamen's Bethel, to be reminded again that he was at heart a seafarer.

"What the hell are you doing in here?"

Whirling around, I saw with horror that Nicholas was standing in the doorway. He strode in and grasped my arm, his eyes burning furiously into mine. "What are you doing in my room?"

"I — I —" I stammered idiotically. What could I say? I

was prying and there was no denying it. "I thought you were at the shipyard," I said lamely, as though that were justification enough.

"Obviously. Nothing else could have induced you to step one foot inside this room," he said sardonically.

"Nicholas, please, you're hurting me."

He released my arm and I rubbed where he had gripped it so tightly.

"Well, now that you're here perhaps you'd like a tour. You see before you many useless relics of an anything-but-novel past." His voice was casual but his eyes were cold.

"Were they from your whaling ship?"

"Clever girl. They were. I thought I'd bring them up here to keep me company, to remind me of the glorious past." Once again his tones were bitingly scornful.

"I didn't realize you missed it so. Whaling, I mean," I said quietly.

An ugly smile twisted his lips. "What would you like to see first? Would you like me to explain to you how a chronometer works, or how to use a sextant? Would you like to look through that telescope? Better yet, infinitely better, would you like to hear some of my experiences?"

Dismayed, I stared at him not knowing what to say. Then I remembered what had provoked my curiosity before. "What is that large thing that looks like a needle?"

"That, my dearest wife, is a head needle. It's used only in Arctic whaling. It's inserted through the blubber in a whale's head and then connected to a chain strap. The needle and chain are then drawn through the blubber and the chain ends linked together to form the lifting strap. The head is then lifted on board so that precious commodity, the baleen, can be removed from the whale's mouth." He related all this quite caustically and then added, "Would you care to see a piece of scrimshaw made from baleen?"

I nodded, biting my lip. He went to one of the tables and picked up a long object. It had been decorated with a scene but it was not an example of the delicate ivory scrimshaw I was used to seeing; it was dark brown with a

179

dull finish.

"Not very pretty, is it?" he asked ironically, reading my thoughts. "But it's now the most valuable product of the whaling industry, did you know that? For umbrellas and ladies' corsets. You're not distressed by my vulgarly mentioning such garments, are you, Miranda? We can't have you distressed, can we? But the truth is I sailed to the frozen Arctic with thirty men for ladies' corsets. Amusing, isn't it? Bloody amusing." He set his jaw; his scar was pale in his dark skin.

I was at a loss to understand him. Then he growled, "Well, you've satisfied your curiosity. The tour is over. Now get out."

I did not need a second order from him; I turned and left the room, eager to be away from him. But I could not go to my room—it was too close to his. Instead of going back there, I hurried down the hallway and the staircase to the second floor. Anxious to get out of sight in case I should hear his footsteps on the stairs, I opened the doors leading to another passageway.

It was very quiet with the kind of hush that seems melancholy. I opened a door to a room on my right. I was in a magnificent bedroom, larger than my own, which also faced the sea. The casement windows were diamond-paned, framed by elegant rose damask curtains which swept the floor like the gown of a beautiful woman. I walked in, my kid shoes slipping into the plush carpet, noticing the Italian marble fireplace, the shell-pink moiré covering the walls, the two cherry corner cupboards with glass fronts, the bed with its lace canopy and silk-and-lace pillows. I picked up one or two of the pillows and set them down again. Who did the room belong to, I wondered. Who came in to burrow down in all this soft luxury?

And then I saw the portrait. When I saw it, I wondered why I had not noticed it first off. It was large with an ornate gold frame. A girl sat serenely in a white gown tied with a pink sash, her bonnet trimmed with pink ribbons. Her eyes were a gray-blue, her rose mouth formed a slight smile, her cheeks were delicately flushed.

"Julia," I breathed, knowing it was she, that she was the owner of this splendid room, the occupant who would never return, who would never toss aside the silk pillows and recline in that bed. But the room did not know it. It had an expectant air, as though she could come in at any minute and untie the strings of her straw bonnet, set it on a chair, and pull the bellrope for tea before going over to sit on the rose brocade loveseat by the hearth. If I closed my eyes, I could imagine her sitting there, picking up the book of poetry on the small table and leafing through it to her favorite selection.

With great daring I went to the large wardrobe and pulled it open. It was filled with lovely gowns and there was a faint scent of lavender which wafted toward me. I drew aside each gown, admiring the exquisite fabrics and delicate or vibrant colors. These, too, gave the impression they were waiting to be worn, waiting for their owner to open the wardrobe and choose carefully what she would wear. On the left side of the wardrobe were several shelves on which were placed pairs of shoes for very small feet. So many gowns, so many pairs of shoes, for one young woman. Underneath the shelves were three drawers; I opened each to find special underclothes, petticoats, shawls, all the fripperies of a well-to-do-girl.

I shouldn't be here, I thought guiltily. I shouldn't be looking at her clothes, snooping about where I had no business. It was furtive, ugly. Why am I examining the belongings of a dead girl in a room that hasn't been used in two years?

But it didn't look as if it hadn't been used. It looked as if she had merely been gone for a short time, that she would return shortly to wear these gowns, button these shoes, tie these shawls, put on these bonnets. No attempt had been made to close off the room, to clear it of signs of its last occupant. One of the maids must have come in to clean it — unlike the rooms I had seen earlier.

I looked back at the portrait above the marble mantel. She was lovely, serene, self-assured, as though she had everything she wanted, as though life pleased her very well.

181

She could not know she was to die so young, that she would not return to gaze at her portrait.

I was still looking into her painted features, imagining them animated with life and youth, when I heard footsteps in the corridor.

Hurry! I thought. I must not be found here, of all places! It was bad enough in Nicholas's room but here it would be fatal. I glanced wildly about the room, looking for a place to hide.

The wardrobe. It was the only place. I stepped in, pushing the clothes to one side, and then stood at the back, drawing the gowns across to conceal me. But I had left the wardrobe door ajar. I could see a crack of light where the doors did not meet. It was too late to reach out and try to coax it shut. Someone had entered the room.

"Oh my dear, what a time you've been. We had no idea where you'd got to this afternoon. It was very naughty of you to go off without telling me. You know how I worry, what a silly state when I get into. Especially when it's foggy. Oh, this terrible place." It was Lavinia. Did she know I was here, was she talking to me?

No, I realized with a chill moving down my spine. It was not me she was sweetly scolding; it was not me she had been worried about. It was Julia. She was talking to Julia, who had been dead for two years. But who or what did she see in the room?

"Look, darling, the book of dress designs I wrote for came by ship today. We can go through it and decide which ones you'll like best for the Boston season, and then as soon as we get there we can go to the best dressmaker's shop and order them for you. I'm particularly fond of this one. I think it would so become you with your lovely long neck and this style would show it off to best advantage. What do you think, my dear?"

It was Lavinia's voice, no doubt about that, but a Lavinia I had never heard. She spoke in such lovingly happy tones, quite different from the ones I had heard her use previously.

"Yes, white silk would be admirable. And I do think a

182

pale blue—for your eyes. And, of course, your favorite shade of rose—in taffeta, I think. And here are several pages of the newest fashions in riding habits. You must have a few of those for early morning and late afternoon rides, and for house parties in the country."

It was pitiful the way she went on, making plans, discussing a new wardrobe for a girl who had never gone to Boston, who would never go to Boston. Who would never wear those habits, take those rides in the city or the country.

"I must say, Jenny did a poor job of turning this room today," the voice continued. "You know you always leave your poetry book just so, and your bed pillows look disarranged. She didn't even close your wardrobe properly."

Holding my breath in fright, I heard her coming over to where I was hiding. Please don't let her open the door, I begged, please don't let her find me here.

She didn't. She merely closed the door so it was very dark inside the wardrobe and the smell of lavender was strong. How long would she stay there, I thought. How long must I stand here?

She was going on in the same bright animated voice about what they would do in Boston, whom they might meet, what entertainments they would attend, what old friends she would be reunited with, while I stood in the wardrobe with that oppressive scent of lavender, listening to her conversing with her beloved daughter. Her mind was truly unhinged, I thought with alarm. She carried on this pathetic charade to keep her daughter alive here at Thunder House, rather than admit she had drowned and her body washed out to sea, where it had likely made food for the fish. I felt sick myself just thinking about it. Poor mad Lavinia. Suddenly I didn't hate her anymore. No matter what she believed of me, no matter what she said to me, I realized now that she was seriously ill. Her cruel mockery, her taunts and criticisms could only hurt me temporarily. I would try to remember this and the next time try not to take what she said about me to heart.

Just then I heard another voice and for one heartstopping frozen moment I thought — it's Julia! Her spirit is speaking to her grieving mother! But then I realized it was Sarah who had come in search of her mistress.

"Come, Lavinia, you shouldn't be in this part of the house. It's cold in here."

"Why don't they come and light a fire then? What's wrong with those stupid girls? Don't they know that my darling needs a fire? I shall have to speak to them quite severely."

"I'll give them your message, dear. But let's go back to your sitting room, shall we? There's a nice fire there and Martha has brought up our lunch. Some nice lobster salad, just the way you like it. And then you can have a nice rest . . ." her voice faded away. They had left the room.

Taking a deep breath, I moved the gowns aside and pushed open the wardrobe doors. Thank heaven neither of them had discovered me cowering in here. Would Lavinia have known me? I was vastly relieved that I had not found out what her reaction would have been. It was unnerving enough hearing her carry on that macabre one-sided conversation and straining in spite of myself for an answer.

As I went across the room to the door, I looked up at the portrait of Julia again. Was there a trace of sadness on that lovely face, a premonition of what was to come? No, I decided. She looked complacent, tranquil, confident. She could not have known the fate in store for her.

I went out of the room and gingerly opened the doors to reveal several more bedrooms. There was another large chamber, which I assumed had been Emily's room as it was also kept clean and ready for use. I gathered there were times she returned to Thunder House. If Julia's room was in this part of the house, doubtless Emily's was too.

At the far end of the corridor was a sitting room. The chairs and sofa were covered in a pretty chintz fabric of pink cabbage roses against a muted green background. There was a piano at one end of the room, and bookshelves were built into the walls on either side of the fireplace. The windows looked out over the lawn and the woods beyond. It was a restful comfortable room where one could be at peace, be restored. I wondered whether I might have the use of it. There was no sitting room on my corridor and this would be ideal. Already I loved the room, and I could not see myself sitting contentedly in the sea-colored drawing room downstairs. Should I ask Nicholas whether I could come here? No, I couldn't ask him anything after our awkward, puzzling confrontation this morning. I have never seen him in just such a mood. And he doubtless would have returned to the shipyard by now.

But it was cold in this room, cold and damp. No fires had been lit in this part of the house in the recent past, radiating their comforting glows about the rooms, flickering shadows on the walls. Some of the rooms were aired and dusted occasionally but not warmed.

Could I ring for a fire to be lit in here? No. I imagined the servants talking. "That new Mrs. Blaize wants a fire in Miss Julia's and Miss Emily's sitting room." "No! Don't she know that wing's closed off? The missus wouldn't like it if she knew someone was in there . . ." No, I couldn't ask them; I had better wait and ask Nicholas first.

But the sight of the piano had stirred in me the half-remembered enjoyment I used to derive from playing. I had not played since leaving India and had probably forgotten much of what I had learned, but I sat down on the tapestry-cushioned seat and hesitatingly began to pick out the pieces which were stored in my head. I played for a while, happily surprised that my fingers remembered more than I expected. I was terribly rusty, of course, not having played in nearly three years, but I could still enjoy myself. When I had played all I could recall, I lifted the piano bench to see if there were any books of music inside. I found Beethoven's "Für Elise" and "Moonlight Sonata" and played both haunting melodies, stumbling rather badly in places, to my vexation. I should begin practicing again, I thought. Could I come here and play every day?

My fingers were becoming stiff with the damp chill of

185

the room. I had stayed here long enough. Someone might wonder where I was, after all. Panic-stricken, I suddenly was reminded that it was well past noon. The servants had doubtless been waiting to serve my lunch and most inconveniently I had not appeared. I didn't even know where I was supposed to take my luncheon — in the splendor of the dining room, alone? I hoped not.

Before I left the sitting room, I quickly scanned the bookshelves for a book to read. There were a few novels by Jane Austen, several uplifting tracts of a moral and spiritual nature, a collection of Shakespearean plays, some stories by Washington Irving, some volumes of poetry, and then my eye was caught by a book entitled *Julia, or the Illuminated Baron,* by Sally Wood. This for some reason sounded enticing, perhaps because the heroine of the novel had the same name as the girl who had sat in this room and played that piano, and I took it down from the shelf. Then I stole back down the long passageway, through the doors to the landing and up to my room.

There I was relieved to find a covered tray, which upon inspection, yielded a plate of cold lobster salad and a roll. Morwenna or one of the others had doubtless left it for me; I wondered contritely if I had upset their routine by not appearing at lunchtime.

I ate my lunch and then while the rain fell outside I enjoyably devoured the gothic romance set in a dangerous chateau in eighteenth-century France. So far were the events in the book from my own dull experiences that I was thrilled by the adventures of the hero and heroine as they endured kidnappings, haunted tombs, and other such melodramatic happenings.

By late afternoon I was more than halfway through the book and the light was dying. I closed the book, laid it on the table, and got up to stretch my legs. Looking out the window, I was startled to see nothing but a thick whiteness. The clouds had descended, or the mist had risen, enveloping Thunder House in an impenetrable shroud.

Hours had passed since the fire in my room was lit, and the sight of the congealed vapor made me shiver. The fog must have settled over the entire island, cloaking us in a mysterious, isolated world.

I had an odd fancy that perhaps there was no other world, that it had all vanished in the mist, and we at Thunder House were the only people remaining, wrapped in smothering veils of cloud and sea. I was alone in the world with a sour-faced hostile woman, a mad heartbroken mother-in-law, and a bitter sardonic husband.

I turned from the window and pulled the bellrope for Morwenna. When she came, I asked her to bank up the fire.

"I left your luncheon for 'ee, ma'am, not knowin' where 'ee were." She regarded me doubtfully.

"Yes, thank you, Morwenna."

"The master said to tell 'ee he won't be home for dinner, ma'am, and I'm to ask when 'ee'd like your dinner served."

"Where is Nich—Captain Blaize?"

"He be gone to the shipyard. 'Tis likely he'll be gone all night, he said, because the mist was rising."

"How is Mrs. Blaize?"

"She's stayed the whole day in her room, I reckon. No one ain't been in to see her besides Miss Thatcher, and Martha to bring their meals."

It was not Thunder House which was cut off from the world, I realized; it was I. But after the way Nicholas had acted this morning when he discovered me in his room, I was relieved not to have to face him tonight. I wondered whether he was deliberately avoiding me. Nonetheless, I felt strangely alone and defenseless. Lavinia was ill in her room attended by no one but that silent stern Sarah and I was stairs and corridors away in my own little corner of the house. But at least I was not forced to dine with the two women with Nicholas gone.

"I'll take my dinner in half an hour, Morwenna, if that's convenient to Martha, of course. After that I'd like to bathe and retire early."

And so my evening was spent. After I had settled in for the night, I read by wavering candlelight until late. When I at last blew out the guttering candle and the fire was dying in the hearth, I heard with relief the sound of the hissing waves in the cove and knew that the mist must be lifting. By morning it would be gone and my foolish fancies with it.

The house was silent, but then up here it was not possible to hear people moving about on the floors below. I wished that Nicholas was sleeping in the next room. Just knowing he was there would help me to feel secure. Instead there was nothing but silence, blackness, and empty rooms. When at last I fell asleep, I began to dream.

I was walking along the shore listening to the cries of the gulls and the lapping of the waves against the rocks. It was a serenely beautiful day but I could not rid myself of an inexplicable feeling of dread. As I walked farther, I looked out to sea and noticed a mountainous cloud billowing across the horizon. While I watched, it began to roll in from the ocean, drawing closer and closer, devouring the sun and obscuring the blue sky, swallowing the swooping gulls and stilling the motion of the waves.

Frantically I began to run toward the forest but I stumbled over a boulder and then found myself unable to rise. My legs refused to support me. I looked back toward the water, crying out, but my voice was absorbed in the sulphurous mist as it engulfed me. Fighting desperately for breath, I clawed through the chilling sodden mass.

I heard a peculiar eerie melancholy sort of singing and then suddenly an arm reached about my neck and I was being slowly dragged over the rocks to the ocean. I struggled frantically but the powerful grip did not lessen. Cold clumps of seaweed slithered over my face; their rank odor filled my nostrils and open mouth.

Abruptly, then, as in dreams, the mist vanished, revealing a steel-colored sea and sky. And I was looking into the face of the Great Selkie, dark and evil, with slanted, lashless eyes, its seal skin partially concealing its manly nakedness. I screamed and screamed, desperately fighting its dank smothering embrace as I was drawn inevitably to the sea.

"Wake up, Miranda, wake up! It's only a dream. You've

just been dreaming. You're perfectly safe—nothing can hurt you. I'm here and you're safe in our house. Don't, Miranda, it's I, Nicholas. Come on, open your eyes."

A feeble light cast shadows over the room. Nicholas was beside me, his hand smoothing my fevered brow and hair. He had lit the candle on the night table and by its light I realized I was in my own room. The nightmare was over.

Trembling, I cried, "It was so horrible, Nicholas!"

"What frightened you so? What were you dreaming of?"

I shook my head, afraid to describe it for fear it would somehow be invoked.

"Tell me, Miranda," he ordered. "What was it? You were crying out for dear life."

I sat up slowly. "It was the . . . the selkie." I spoke the word with an effort. "It was taking me away . . . to the sea. I could smell it . . . and the water was so cold, and the mist . . . It was singing." I gave a shudder.

He put his arms around me and I rested my head on his broad bare chest, scarcely realizing that I did so. "You're safe now, my love. Nothing can take you from this house—or from me, not even the Great Selkie. You know that I'd never let anything hurt you, don't you?"

"Oh Nicholas!"

"Come now, it's all over. You're shivering. You had better get back under the blankets."

"Nicholas . . . please, please don't leave me!" I was still clinging to him.

He hesitated before putting an arm around me again. "I guess old Noah and his tales brought this on. What's this you've been reading?" He picked up the gothic tale beside my bed and shook his head. "No wonder. You are too susceptible, Miranda. But I'm here to look after you and you're perfectly safe. Didn't I promise to take care of you?"

"I'm sorry for disturbing you, Nicholas," I said ruefully. The chilling effect of the dream was receding and I was beginning to feel foolish as one does after describing a dream which was horrifying only before it was put into words.

"My dear girl, don't be ridiculous. I'm your husband, after all. Who else should calm you in the night?" Tenderly he stroked the line of my cheek and then abruptly took his hand away.

Yet we're not like any ordinary husband and wife, I thought. And this morning you spoke to me as though you hated me. "I thought you were staying away all night."

"I decided to come back to the house when the mist began to clear. The truth is I couldn't sleep over in Nansett knowing you slept here." His voice was light with its usual ironical tone. "Well, you need to get some sleep. If you need me for any reason, you have only to call. I can leave the connecting door open if you like."

My face was growing warm. "No, please don't, Nicholas."

He gave a stifled exclamation. "For God's sake, Miranda, I was only thinking of you. I had no nefarious intentions in mind. But I should have known better than to suggest that you wouldn't want a protective barrier between us. I'll bid you good night."

He was up and striding from the room when I said in a small voice, "No, that's not what I meant. I meant . . ." I bit my lip.

He stopped, tensing. There was a pause. "What did you mean, Miranda?" I could sense he was straining for my reply but I could not go on.

"Well, Miranda?"

"It was nothing, Nicholas. Just . . ." I shook my head. "I won't keep you from your bed any longer."

"What about your bed?"

"What . . . what do you mean?" I asked, my heart beating quicker.

"What about keeping me from your bed?" I could not read his expression in the dim light of the room.

"I . . . I'm sorry, Nicholas."

"Damn it, girl! I don't want you to be sorry! It's just that the sight of you . . . oh, go to bed, Miranda, and allow me to do the same!" With those words he had left my room and shut the door behind him.

Why didn't you stop him? Why didn't you call after him and tell him that you wanted him to stay? You fool! He was waiting for your invitation — he said he wasn't going to force himself on you. Well, he will just have to wait a while longer, I answered myself. I'm not ready to tell him I want him to make love to me; I'm just not ready yet. And how could I say such a thing, or convey such a desire? It's not as though we are in love with one another; it's not as though I mean anything to him. And I probably am not a very enticing specimen to him anyway, no matter what he had said about the sight of me. How could I be? I knew nothing about pleasing men. I buried my face in the pillow.

When I awoke, the room was filled with sunlight. Going to the window, I looked out with delight at the lapis water and salmon-colored rocks of Thunder Cove. The black-green spruces stood sturdily along the edge of the precipice and puffs of fleecy clouds scudded across the faded blue sky. I remembered the events of the night — my terrifying dream, the way I had clung to Nicholas, not wanting him to leave me, the way he had waited for me to ask him to stay.

When Morwenna came with my breakfast, I asked, "Has Captain Nicholas gone out?"

"Yes, Mrs. Blaize. He left for the shipyard soon after dawn, I heard Amos say."

I told Morwenna that I did not want any breakfast, that I would just drink tea. While she was taking the food back to the kitchen, I got dressed in one of my old gowns. The strained muscles no longer bothered me and I decided to go for a long walk, exploring more of the island.

Setting out across the wide lawn behind the house, I entered the birch woods. The floor of the forest was soggy from yesterday's rain; a damp earthy smell lingered in the sun-sparkled air.

When I came to Blackett's Glade, I did not take the path which skirted it but kept on straight ahead. I hoped this path would lead me to the opposite side of Thunder Island. I drew deeper into the woods and heard the

191

scufflings of animals, the whistles of birds.

After I had walked a long while, I saw through the trees a large glassy lake, doubtless the one I had spotted from the slope of Bald Mountain. When I reached its edge, I sat down on a tree which had uprooted and fallen on its side. There was not a ripple on the lake's surface, nothing but the reflection of the towering spruces to shadow its blue sheen.

I was wishing I had eaten my breakfast since it was by now about noon, but I had no desire to return to the confines of Thunder House. After a short rest I followed the path to the other side of the serene secretive lake and penetrated the deep woods beyond. They were dark and gloomy and I could not help looking over my shoulder from time to time, my ears listening instinctively for stealthy sounds.

Increasingly I wondered whether I should turn around and go back before I became truly lost, but I walked on a bit more until I began to hear a muffled roaring sound which grew as the trees thinned and the sunlight blazed ahead. And then I was out of the woods.

I stood high on a cliff above the sea. Under me the surf shot continually into the air with such incredible force that the ground and air shook with the booming vibration and I was flecked with spray. Countless years of tides and surf had carved a narrow chasm in a boulder, launching the surging waves fifty or more feet into the air. This spectacular display was all the more awe-inspiring after the sedate gloom of the woods.

Out in the ocean a man was lifting something out of the water, probably a lobster trap since many of the colorful buoys bobbed on the surface.

There was a miniature island which sat about one-half mile off the coast. That must be Seal Island, I thought, the one linked to Thunder Island at low tide by a causeway. Just now that causeway was barely visible, a gray trickle of pebbles and sand. Someday, when the tide was right, I would walk across it.

Feeling by now very hungry and rather tired, and conscious of the three miles or so to travel back to the house, I turned from the cliff and reentered the forest. After I had passed the lake, now darkened by the afternoon sun, and gone farther into the woods, I reached a pale green meadow strewn with Michaelmas daisies and Queen Anne's lace. Three deer were grazing at the far end and did not notice me.

I realized I must have taken the wrong path at the lake and so I retraced my steps. When I eventually found the uprooted tree on which I had rested, this showed me the right path and I continued the last mile or so of my trek without error. At last I saw Thunder House rising through the trees and I hurried inside and up to my room, where I rang for Morwenna.

When she came, I asked her timidly if I might have some tea and sandwiches. "I'm sorry I missed luncheon, tell Martha, but I've been out walking. I do hope it's no trouble."

"How could it be, ma'am? You be the master's wife, after all." She shook her head as though she found me perplexing.

After I had eaten and rested, Morwenna came back to fix my bath. When I was dressed again in the blue satin, I sat nervously waiting for Nicholas to come. I had heard him return from the shipyard and I assumed he was also changing for dinner. I wondered whether Lavinia and Sarah would be joining us in the dining room. Strangely restless, I got up and went down the hall to the Palladian window which stood over the stairway looking out over the back lawn. The sun was dropping behind the forest, its beams shooting streams of gold between the black trunks. I watched as the tawny sky paled and dulled in the blue-violet dusk.

"There you are, Miranda." Nicholas was coming toward me dressed in a black suit with a silver embroidered waistcoat. He was pulling at his stock as though it was too tight, a frown about his mouth. "I'm sorry to have kept you waiting but we're rather behind schedule at the shipyard." His voice was cool, his manner aloof. "But it's still a little early for dinner. Would you care to go down to the drawing room and have a glass of sherry?"

"Oh, if you like." Then I winced because I knew he didn't like me to sound so uncertain. "Yes, that would be agreeable." That sounded worse, too formal. "Will your mother and Sarah be there, do you think?" I couldn't help asking.

He cocked an eyebrow. "Perhaps. But that should have no bearing on what we do."

But it does, I thought. I don't want to see them. I don't even want to eat with them, much less pass the next half hour or so before dinner with them. But I went downstairs with him to the drawing room.

I was relieved to see it was empty. Nicholas poured two glasses of Madeira from the decanter and sat down across from me. I sipped my wine, my heart thumping uncomfortably.

"And what did you find to occupy you today?" he asked.

"I walked across the island to the place where the surf pounds up from the boulder, up to the cliff. It was so breathtaking, Nicholas, so . . . I don't know. I've never seen water shoot up that high in such powerful gushes. And I saw Seal Island across the causeway. Thunder Island is very beautiful, Nicholas, you were right."

"I'm glad it meets with your approval."

"Yes, it does. I mean, I like it here very much."

"Is that so? I'm gratified to hear it. I have had serious doubts about bringing you here at all."

I bit my lip, coloring. The curtness with which he responded to my attempts at making amends stung me. And he *had* been wishing we had never married, just as I feared. In a rush the words came out. "I'm sorry, Nicholas, for everything, for not being the right sort of wife, for not . . . I tried to warn you how it would be; I knew you would come to regret your proposal." I rose and set down my wineglass, clinging to the shreds of dignity I had left. "I don't believe I want any dinner after all. Please convey my excuses to your mother."

In a flurry of skirts I moved quickly to the door, hoping he had not noticed my eyes were filling with tears. But just as I was reaching for the doorknob, he caught my arm.

"When are you going to stop running away, or sending me away?" he asked angrily, and then he pulled me roughly into his arms and crushed my trembling lips beneath his. His mouth devoured mine searchingly, urgently, and I began to respond, pressing my body against his, my arms going around his neck. I felt his hand caressing my neck, moving down to where the bodice of my gown shielded my breasts. I gave a little moan, a sudden flood of weakness overtaking me.

And then he was lifting his mouth from mine and setting me gently aside. He tugged at his neckcloth, his breathing rapid, his face tinged with color. "You see, Miranda, how easily I can lose control with you?"

Flushing, I looked away. And then the door opened and one of the maids was announcing dinner. I smoothed my hair and adjusted my gown while Nicholas watched me, his gray eyes shining like pewter. Then he took my arm and we went to the dining room.

Chapter Nine

"Come in, darlings," cooed Lavinia as we entered the dining room. To see her sitting there at the end of the table perfectly composed, her lips curved in a faint smile, it was almost impossible to connect her with the pitiful woman she had been the day before. Nicholas pulled out a chair for me and then sat down himself.

"I understand you've been spending nearly all your time at the shipyard," Lavinia went on while our soup was being served. "I wonder that Miranda does not consider herself ill-used. But then your marriage is not exactly a . . . shall I say the usual sort, is it? And you are fond of traipsing about out-of-doors, are you not, child? You had better make the most of these days before the weather changes and you are housebound. Oh, the dreadful winters here, Miranda! One can scarcely venture outside!"

"Come, Lavinia," said Nicholas, piqued, "you know it is not as bad as all that! You needn't paint such a harsh picture for Miranda. If we were inland, the winters would be ten times worse — we'd be buried under feet of snow for months. But on Thunder Island the ocean acts as a buffer to ward off the severest weather conditions."

"So you claim, Nicholas, but never do I feel so isolated and trapped as when the winter comes."

"As Father used to suggest quite often, you can easily go to Boston and stay with friends or rent a house for the season if the prospect of another winter here is too daunting. I can book passage for you on a ship later this

196

month, if you wish."

Her eyes narrowed. "That would please you, wouldn't it? If Sarah and I left Thunder House to you and this girl. How cruel of you, Nicholas, to suggest turning me out! This is still my home too. Besides," she continued in lighter tones, "I have nothing in common with the people back there, leading the dull provincial life that I do here. What on earth would I talk to them about—the lobstering, or perhaps the lumber mill?" She laughed shrilly.

Nicholas's mouth tightened. I feared he was going to make some biting retort so I said hastily, "I saw a lobster-man checking his trap today. It looked like hard work."

"Lifting the trap from the water, do you mean?" said Lavinia. "I would scarcely call that hard work for a man."

"It is difficult and hazardous, Miranda, especially in the winter," said Nicholas, as though his mother had not spoken. "I've often in the past been out with Ben Somes in his boat."

"Finally, here is the capon!" announced Lavinia. "Sometimes I don't know what it is they are doing in the kitchen. I hope Martha made the port wine sauce. Ah, yes."

"Perhaps you have some recipes you'd like to give to Martha," Nicholas suggested to me.

I began to demur, flushing, but Lavinia cut in scornfully, "I have no doubt she is well versed in the making of curries! Really, Nicholas, you know I cannot abide any highly spiced foods."

I bit my lip. "As a matter of fact, I don't have any experience in cooking, Mrs. Blaize, curries or otherwise, I'm afraid."

She gave me her freezing superior smile. "Of course not, my child. I never expected it of you at all. Nicholas has no notion of these things. And just now you must become accustomed to Thunder House and the island."

"Accustomed to it as you did, Lavinia?" asked Nicholas bluntly. "And you did not even have the excuse of a mother-in-law who was determined to discourage and disparage you."

Her eyebrows rose; she looked limpidly at him. "Why,

Nicholas, how can you talk so? If I don't mince words when I talk with Miranda, it's only so that she knows what's in store for her, spending her life in this place."

"I like Thunder Island," I said, twisting my ring round and round. "I think it's the most beautiful place I have ever seen."

"I daresay it is, my child, considering what you have known. Anything, any place would be an improvement in your life. You've done very well for yourself."

I could not answer her, thoroughly cowed by the unveiled contempt in her voice.

"I congratulate you on your perception, Lavinia," came Nicholas's voice, as smooth as silk. "That's what I had in mind when I proposed to Miranda. I knew she possessed the strength of character to make the best of things. An all-too-rare quality, wouldn't you agree?"

"That's enough, Nicholas," said Sarah. "Have you forgotten all respect due to your mother that you address her in such a manner? But you've never had any feelings for anyone but yourself!"

"It's all right, Sarah, really it is," said Lavinia tolerantly. "If you or I carried what he does on his conscience, we should perhaps not be held accountable for the things we say."

Nicholas's face went dark until the scar was white in his cheek. Without a word he got up from the table, threw down his napkin, and strode from the room. I looked after him in dismay.

"Perhaps we can now finish our meal in peace for once," said Sarah coldly.

"Poor Nicholas, I shouldn't have said that, I suppose," said Lavinia with not a touch of remorse. "It wasn't very thoughtful of me. I don't like to remind him of the past, you know that, Sarah. I know it's over and done with—the terrible damage has already been done and he has to live with that. But he can be so cruel to me sometimes."

"He's a selfish brute," Sarah said between clenched teeth. "He always has been."

"Yes, I don't understand how I could have failed so

dismally with him. Even as a child he was impossible," said Lavinia, shaking her head. "The things he would do and say, the trouble he would get into. He is so different from his father. Roger had a very different temperament, didn't he, Sarah? So mild, so dependable, never doing foolish impulsive things. Always good-humored. Remember the way he used to try and cheer me up?"

"He didn't like to see you down in the dumps, that's certain," was Sarah's answer.

Lavinia sighed heavily. "I don't think I want any more dinner. Would you help me up to my room?"

"Of course, dearest."

"Forgive us for leaving you, Miranda. I believe I shouldn't have come down tonight. I tend to forget how Nicholas affects me. I should have listened to you, Sarah. You warned me I didn't quite have my strength back."

You were strong enough to cut Nicholas to the quick, I thought wretchedly. You were strong enough to belittle me.

I waited until I was certain they had had time to reach their rooms and then I hurried upstairs to look for Nicholas. But he was not in his room. Nor was he anywhere else on the third floor. Where could he have gone, I wondered anxiously. He might not even be in the house. With scarcely a thought I took my cloak from its peg in the armoire, rushing back downstairs and out the side door.

"Nicholas! Nicholas!" I called into the damp chilly air.

"You needn't shout. I'm right here," came his voice near me. He walked forward under the lamplight of the house.

"Oh Nicholas," I cried in relief. "I was so worried—I mean . . . I thought you'd gone out into the night," I finished lamely.

"And you were coming in search of me? Foolish child, haven't I told you it's dangerous for you to go out after dark? You might lose your footing if you ventured near the cliff, not to mention being lost in the forest."

"I know. But I was . . . I was concerned about you. After what happened at dinner tonight—"

"I don't want to hear another word on the subject!" he broke in savagely. "And if you had my memories you wouldn't either!"

I flinched. "I'm sorry, Nicholas. I didn't mean to . . . it's just that I don't understand."

"Be grateful for that. Be grateful you have nothing to berate yourself with. I'm sorry I lost my temper with Lavinia. Usually I don't allow her to provoke me—she's altogether too pitiable—but when she was deliberately cutting you down I couldn't help but respond in kind. Come, let's go inside the house. I could do with some brandy."

He took my arm and we went indoors. At the foot of the stairs he paused, saying, "You go on up to bed, Miranda."

"But Nicholas . . . I want to . . . that is, I'll sit with you if you like."

He shook his head, the lines around his mouth hard. "I'm afraid I'd be poor company tonight. Go on, go upstairs. I'm going to do some paperwork for the shipyard."

He treats me as a child, I thought unhappily. He doesn't want to share his troubles with me. I'm nothing to him in any way that matters. Slowly I went up to my room and got ready for bed.

I lay awake until late, but Nicholas did not come.

Some days later I walked to Nansett. It was a gray morning, the ashen rippled clouds hanging low in the sky. The woods seemed especially dark and cheerless. It was as though they possessed a melancholy secret which they guarded closely and resistively. Or perhaps all of this was only due to my mood.

Swirls of mist hid the top of Bald Mountain, but the path which traversed its side was clear. Before long I had reached the village and was on my way to Emily's cottage when a voice called out, "Good morning, Miranda."

Katherine MacLeod was crouched in her yard. She rose, smiling, and I saw she had been cutting chrysanthemums, purple and yellow. For an instant the sight of them reminded me of the flowers strewn on the temple floors in Bombay.

"Good morning, Mrs. MacLeod."

"Katherine."

"Very well, Katherine," I acknowledged, smiling.

"Would you care to come in for a cup of coffee? I have to put these in water."

"They're very pretty."

"Thank you. I always love the autumn, don't you? The mums blooming, the leaves turning, the pumpkins and gourds—symbols of the harvest and all that. There's such an expectant stimulating feeling about it, I always think."

"I think I know what you mean." I followed her inside and she asked me to take a seat in the parlor while she found a large vase for the flowers and ordered the coffee prepared.

Taking off my cloak and lapis bonnet, I sat down in one of the comfortable but worn chairs. The piano in the corner did not look worn, however. It was highly polished and well kept up. I wondered whether Heather played. She probably did—and beautifully. She wasn't in the room, perhaps not even in the house, and yet already I was conscious of feeling inferior. But I genuinely liked Katherine.

She returned soon carrying a vase full of the flowers, which she set on the piano. "There, that's nice."

"I was admiring your piano. It looks like a very fine one," I said.

She nodded, a little sadly, I thought. "It was a wedding gift from my dear husband. Far more than he could afford, but he knew I loved to play and took pride in me. You see, I grew up in Camden. My father was a minister also and we never could afford a piano, although I played and practiced very often on the one that belonged to our church."

"That's how it was with me, too," I said warmly. "I took piano lessons in Bombay but, of course, we didn't have our own instrument."

"Oh, do you play, too, Miranda? How delightful!

201

Heather has never taken to it, I'm sorry to say. Not that she hasn't other accomplishments, of course. She paints, you know—rather well, I believe." She smiled. "But I would say that, wouldn't I, being her mother?"

"I'm sure she's very talented," I said wistfully.

"Would you play for me, Miranda? I would enjoy it very much."

"Oh no, I couldn't. I was playing the other day and was sadly disappointed at how rusty I sounded. I haven't played in years, you see. But I would love to hear you play."

She rose and went to the piano, beginning to play with much expression and skill. The music washed over me in peaceful waves. She was very good, better than anyone I had ever heard.

The maid brought in a tray of coffee, sugar, and cream and a plate of cinnamon buns. "That was beautiful, Katherine. I can see why your husband was so proud of you."

While she had been playing, an idea had been forming in my mind. I bit my lip, wondering whether I should ask her as she held out the plate of cinnamon buns to me. I accepted my cup of coffee with a word of thanks and then began tentatively, "I've just had an idea, Katherine. I wondered whether . . . well, I wanted to ask you . . . would you be willing to give me piano lessons? I badly need them and I would enjoy studying with you. It would be nice if . . . if I improved enough to play for . . . for Nicholas sometime."

"Why, Miranda, what a charming idea!" she exclaimed, her face turning pink. "I would love to give you lessons. I've taught in the past but lately there hasn't been any demand for a piano instructress in Nansett! And it would give us a chance to get to know each other better. I still play for the church services here as I did when Bruce was the minister. Mr. Whitcomb, my husband's replacement, most kindly asked that I continue."

"I'm certain he considers himself fortunate to have you play the hymns and such. I would be very grateful to you,

202

Katherine, if you helped me improve my playing."

"Is there a piano at Thunder House you could use?"

"Well, there is one in the sitting room that must have belonged to Julia and Emily. I discovered it when I was exploring the house the other day. I can ask Nicholas if I may use it. No one is using it now, after all. It's a bit out of tune but considerably better than the one I used to play in Bombay!"

"Julia was very gifted," Katherine said, nodding. "She was one of my pupils, you know, my very best. I taught Emily also but not for long." She smiled. "I could never convince her to practice, and without practice even the gifted are lost. With practice even someone who is not especially talented can become skilled and derive enjoyment from playing, not to mention giving enjoyment to others. I'm certain Nicholas would love to have you play for him in the evenings. Why don't you play for me now and then I'll have an idea of what we should work to improve."

"All right," I said nervously, and went over to the piano. I played a short piece from memory, stumbling and apologizing, my face red, and then I sight-read a piece she selected.

"Yes, I think I can help you a great deal, Miranda. You have a nice touch and you give attention to dynamics as many do not. You lack confidence and so you make mistakes. And, of course, you haven't played in a long time. But I believe by studying with me, if you practice, you'll see a significant improvement in a few months' time."

I clasped my hands together. "Thank you, Katherine. When shall we begin?"

"Well, if you don't have anything to do now, we could have a short lesson. I have some music I can go over with you which you can take home to practice, and you need to work on scales to limber up your fingers and give more confidence and vigor to your playing."

"Ugh, I always hated scales," I said, adding hastily, "but I'm willing to practice them, of course." I had a great deal of time on my hands and this would give me something constructive to do. I also thought that the money she would earn from giving me lessons would be helpful. I was certain Nicholas would be generous in paying her.

I pictured myself sitting in Julia's sitting room wearing the blue satin gown, silver candelabra lit on the piano, playing for Nicholas, who sat listening to me admiringly, congratulating himself on having acquired a wife with such musical ability. Naturally in that pleasant dream my playing was vastly different from what it was in reality. But with Katherine's help it would improve.

So I stayed in the parlor and worked with her for the next hour. She was a good teacher and quickly put me at ease, encouraging me, correcting me, making me repeat stanzas until she was satisfied with my progress. I played rather badly at first but under her inspiring tutelage I was confident that I would be playing better soon.

When I was getting up to leave, tired but exhilarated, Heather came in. Today she wore a forest green gown in which she looked radiant, and she was carrying a large basket of vegetables under her arm. An extraordinary thought came to me that she resembled a pagan goddess of the harvest with a ripe luscious beauty. Immediately I felt too thin and pale and drab.

"Hello, Miranda," she said: "Oh, are you going? I'm sorry I missed your visit; I've been across at the Everetts. They sent you these, Mother."

"That was good of them," said Katherine. "What do you think, Heather? I'm going to be giving Miranda piano lessons. So you'll be seeing a good deal of her."

"Oh. Well, you'll enjoy that, Mother, having a pupil again. It's been a long while, hasn't it, since . . ."

"Since Julia." Katherine nodded. "Yes, I've missed teaching her."

"Oh, I'm not like Julia, I'm afraid," I said ruefully. "I don't possess her talent. But your mother has been kind enough to agree to teach me anyway."

"Then she can play for Nicholas, you see, Heather. A fine man like him ought to have an accomplished wife."

Suddenly the thought of my entertaining my husband seemed foolish, even presuming. I was eager to leave the manse. "Well, thank you, Katherine. I'll see you again soon. I'm going to stop over at Emily's now."

"Give her my love, won't you?" I nodded and I left their house, grateful that Heather hadn't been present to hear me play. Even though she did not play herself, nonetheless I was reluctant for her to listen to the mistakes I made. I wondered what sorts of pictures she painted, what sorts of subjects.

I went on down the winding street to Emily and Ben's cottage and knocked on the door. When Emily opened it, she was obviously pleased to see me. "You've caught me making bread. Come in and we'll have a talk while I work. I was hoping you would come by again soon."

We went into the kitchen and I sat down, watching her knead the dough. I wondered at the life she had chosen after being raised in such luxury. Yet this simple house radiated love and contentment whereas Thunder House, in all its splendor, teemed with baffling, complicated, even ugly, emotions.

"I've just come from Katherine MacLeod's. She sent you her love. I stayed there longer than I expected — she's agreed to give me piano lessons and I've just had my first one."

"Oh Miranda, I am glad. I didn't know you played. I was all thumbs when it came to the piano," she said smiling, scratching her cheek with a floury hand.

"I don't play at all well myself. But Katherine thinks she can help me. I used to enjoy playing when I was younger, in India. I'm going to ask Nicholas tonight if I can use your sister's piano. Do you think he will mind?"

"Why should he? No one else plays it and it's just sitting there collecting dust, I've no doubt."

"You don't think he'll mind my using her sitting room? I don't want to do anything to make him angry. I think it's a charming room. I know . . . I probably shouldn't have been in that part of the house but I was exploring one day and . . ."

"I'm certain he won't mind, Miranda. You have every right to take what rooms you'd like and use them. I know Nicholas would agree with me."

I was silent, thinking of how Lavinia had come into her daughter's bedroom while I had been shut in the armoire and had carried on a conversation as though Julia had actually been present. But I couldn't mention that to Emily. I didn't know her well enough to approach such a delicate subject nor did I wish to distress her. Most significantly, who was I to presume to discuss the poor woman with her only daughter? Emily had been very kind to me but she might be inclined to tell me it was none of my business. I had no desire to risk a snub from her. I was also tempted to ask her if she could shed some light on what had passed between Nicholas and Lavinia recently, but I couldn't bring myself to mention that either. She seemed to think that I knew all about Nicholas's past and I was embarrassed to admit I didn't, as though it were a failing on my part. Also I hesitated to discuss Nicholas with anyone, even his sister; it seemed somehow disloyal. Lastly I took a craven comfort in being in the dark; I wasn't certain that I truly wanted to know what lay at the root of his black moods, his biting sarcasm, his mother's heedless words.

I was afraid that Emily would say, "Nicholas misses the sea. He gave it up last year because he felt obligated to come back to the shipyard business, but he's never gotten over it and longs to return." I didn't want to hear those words spoken aloud; they would be so terribly certain, so final. And I would know then that there was nothing anyone could do to make a difference, to help fill the void in his life.

And there was something else, some sort of tragedy associated with his last voyage. . . .

So I spoke none of what was in my mind. We conversed on light matters while the dough rose and then I said I didn't want to tire her, that I should be getting back to Thunder House.

I made my way up the street and across the cornfield to

the stone wall. There were muddy patches in the hushed woods from the recent rains and a damp earthy smell penetrated the air. It was when I was following the path which crept alongside the lower slope of the mountain that it happened.

I was looking out over the island at the tops of the spruces which reached across to the white-crested gray waves when suddenly from my right side, from the higher slope of the mountain, came a rumbling crashing sound. Startled, I stopped in my tracks as an enormous boulder came toward me, rolling over and over, crushing bushes in its wake, chipping and smashing smaller rocks, which also began their abrupt descent. I stood transfixed, terrified, not knowing which way to move to get out of the boulder's path. It was charging at me; it would smash my body as easily as it would a bush; there was nothing I could do to prevent it. I could not even scream.

Then suddenly just as I was putting my arms in front of my face, it veered off sharply to the side and thundered on down the mountain just to the rear of where I stood. For a few frozen moments I watched its turbulent progress as it thudded over stones and slammed into evergreens, again veering off erratically until I heard it finally lodge somewhere below in the woods. The other stones it had ousted rolled nearby but did not touch me.

Shaking, I began to run along the path until the mountain was behind me and I was once again in the silent gloomy woods, a blessed silence, a blessed gloominess. And then I slowed my pace, catching my breath, the blood pounding in my ears like violent drumbeats. I had come very close to being killed and I had not been able to move to save myself. It was a miracle that the boulder had not struck me. The rain we had had must have loosened the rocks which clung to the higher slopes of the mountain until that huge one began its hazardous plummet.

I sat down on a tree stump and covered my face with my hands, taking deep sobbing breaths until some of my equinamity was restored. I had not been struck; I was perfectly well; in the future when I walked that path I would have to be prepared for a similar occurrence so that I could react. But surely such a thing would not happen again. It had been a freak accident; the odds were that I would never suffer such an experience again.

But what a close scrape it had been; I had come within inches of a horrible death. It gave the phrase "one fell blow" a hideous new meaning for me. I hurried through the woods until I came out at Blackett's Glade and then skirted the pond, which was eerily silver as it reflected the overcast sky.

On the other side of the glade I again entered the woods and rushed on, eager to reach Thunder House and my own room. Stiff sharp roots caught at my gown, loose stones in the path caused me to stumble, but I hurried on, scarcely heeding them, not caring that my clothes were dusty, muddy, and doubtless torn, that my hair was untidily tumbling down my back and over my shoulders, that my face was stung by gnats and scratched by overhanging branches I did not carefully avoid.

After I had continued for a while, the woods became denser, the way more and more difficult to follow. In my harried state I must have taken a wrong turn at Blackett's Glade. If I had taken the right path, I would have reached Thunder House by now. But I had been so agitated by my narrow brush with death that I had not paid attention to where I was going.

I turned around to try and retrace my steps but the path I had trudged on was not clear. I realized it had not been a real path at all but a trail which I had more or less forged myself. Traipsing over stones and green spongy moss and newly fallen leaves, I tried to figure out which way I had come. Was it by that fallen log over there; had I passed that small puddle half-covered with leaves?

Suddenly nothing looked familiar; I could not remember any particular landmark. I was lost. I felt like such a childish fool — I could not even take a walk without causing some calamity. I stood for a while gazing hopelessly in every direction, noticing with alarm how dark the woods were growing. It couldn't be more than midafternoon, I reckoned, but with the sky so gray it seemed later. And if I didn't find my way back soon, it *would* be much later—and darker.

Wait a minute, I thought briskly. There's no need to panic. That's one good thing about living on an island—you can only go so far and then you come to the shore. So even though I was lost now, if I kept walking I would eventually reach the water's edge and follow the shoreline until I came to the house even if it took hours. I tried not to think that it might be night before I reached the house, or that I might never come to the shore but just wander about the woods in circles. No, I would not think of those possibilities.

I was reminded of the story of Hansel and Gretel and how they had been lost in the forest after nightfall when the breadcrumbs they had dropped to blaze their trail had been eaten by birds. There had been nothing left to mark their trail. I wished I had somehow marked the way *I* had come.

But there was nothing to do except to plod on determinedly in one direction, hoping it would not be long before I came out by the water or spotted familiar surroundings which would lead me to Thunder House. I found myself looking over my shoulder, listening even, for what I did not know, and I tried to make less noise as I trampled through the underbrush. This was very difficult as I was hampered by my long skirts and the leaves which carpeted the floor of the forest were already brittle and dry.

Clenching my hands into fists, I continued walking, assuring myself that I was perfectly safe, that I couldn't be truly lost, that there was nothing to fear. But it was no use. The trees were closing in on me, the trunks closer together, blocking my path, obscuring the poor light. The panic I felt was rising no matter how hard I tried to suppress it. Soon it was given full rein and I began to run, not caring how many times I nearly fell, not caring how my gown and cloak tore, or how my leather shoes were scraped, not caring how the twigs stingingly brushed my cheeks, about

209

anything except I had to find my way out of this primeval menacing forest before I began to scream and scream like some wild demented creature.

Just then the woods suddenly halted and I broke free of them. I was in a clearing. I still had no notion where I was but at least I was out of the woods for a time. In the clearing stood a small cottage with a thatched roof. It was like something out of a fairy tale, and I was reminded again of Hansel and Gretel and how they had stumbled onto an enchanting gingerbread cottage. But in the cottage had lurked an evil witch. . . .

I wondered whom this cottage belonged to. I could stop and inquire the way back to Thunder House. Yet as I drew closer, I realized the house could not be inhabited. Even before I went up the flagged walkway and knocked on the little arched door, I was aware that it was not lived in. The grass and weeds in the clearing had grown tall and dense; the windows were streaked with grime; the chimney was cold and bare.

Still, I was curious about it. Even in its melancholy neglected state it was charming and I wondered who its last occupants had been. There was no sign of a garden of any sort so it must have been a very long time since people had lived there. I tried the doorknob and was surprised to find that it turned in my hand, opening the door.

Cautiously I peered inside, noticing at once a musty unpleasant odor. Suddenly a large dark thing came tearing at me and I screamed before I realized it was a bird which was hurtling toward the light of the open door. It flew past me, sweeping my face with its feathery wing. Shuddering I watched it fly out and then pulled the door shut behind me, hoping it was the only occupant of the cottage.

Slowly my eyes became adjusted to the gloom and I could make out pieces of furniture. I stood at the entrance to a sort of parlor which was the only room in the cottage. My nose wrinkled at the combined smells of dust, dampness, mice, and bird droppings. I saw that the upholstery was faded and torn and stained with moisture, and that the curtains at the windows had once been white but were now yellowed and limp. It was obvious that it had once been an attractive room, but years of neglect and treatment by various forest animals and birds had brought it to its sad moldering state. From the outside it hadn't looked as dreary and decaying, but inside, the illusion of an enchanted cottage was swiftly dispelled.

I wandered about the room in the half-light for a few moments before realizing with fresh consternation that I was wasting time, that I still had no idea where I was, that the afternoon was inexorably drawing into evening. For all I knew I could be even farther from Thunder House than I had been while tearing through the woods. Even though the cottage was dreary and forlorn, it was an improvement on the darkening closing woods.

But I had to continue on or else I might not find my way out of them before nightfall. Going outside, I shut the little wooden door with its quaint arched top and looked about, trying to decide which way to go. And then I noticed a path, overgrown and bristly but a path all the same which must lead somewhere in particular. At least I could attempt to follow it instead of straggling aimlessly through the thick forest.

Feeling heartened, I began to tramp down the path, trying to ignore the fact that the light was dimming, that it was already evening. I walked quickly, relieved that the path did not end abruptly but wound its way through the woods. Before too long I came upon a graveyard, the sight of which may have further dismayed me had I not spotted the name "Roger Blaize" engraved on a plaque on the mausoleum. If this was the Blaize family cemetery, then surely I must be nearing the house.

I hurried on and after a while saw the trees thin out and the pink granite structure loom in the distance. With a huge sigh of relief I slowed my hectic pace and trudged toward the house. I had come out of the woods on the south side of the house, a way I had not come before.

When I came around the back, I saw Amos walking a horse on the gravel driveway and he stopped to lift his cap and nod at me. He looked at me curiously and I realized again how disheveled and unkempt I must appear. I hoped I would see no one else before reaching my room.

But as luck would have it I met Sarah on the second-story landing and her eyes flickered over me, shocked, disgusted. I was certain that she would waste no time in telling Lavinia about the disgraceful state I had come home in. My face scarlet, I tried to nod coolly at her before going up the stairs to the third floor.

When I reached my room and glanced in the mirror, I could understand her scandalized expression. My face was scratched with red welts, my hair was sprinkled with bits of leaves and pine needles, my bonnet was covered with a thick layer of grime and stood awry on my head, my skirts were ripped and spattered with mud. I looked like a fright, I thought, and had a wild desire to laugh. But Morwenna might come in and hear me and then tell the other servants that the master's new wife stood before the mirror, laughing at her reflection.

"I thought I heard you come in, Miranda," said a voice behind me.

"Oh! Hello, Nicholas," I said weakly. He would come in just now.

"What on earth has happened to you? What have you been doing, climbing trees or something? Martha said you'd gone out this morning and not come back for lunch."

"Should I have?" I asked anxiously. "I'm sorry, Nicholas."

"For God's sake, Miranda, you don't have to apologize." His voice was irritable. "You're the mistress of the house; you can do anything you like! It's just that I didn't know where you'd got to and it's dusk outside. I was just going to get Amos and Seth and start looking for you."

"I'm sorry if I've inconvenienced or worried you. I went to Nansett earlier today and on my way back took the wrong path. I was wandering through the woods or I would have been home hours ago."

He sighed. "Well, at least you're home safe and sound. I'm going to summon Morwenna for some water. You

212

need those cuts washed. It looks as though you've been bitten by gnats, too. I'll fix you up and then you can have a bath before dinner." He shook his head; he seemed very annoyed with me. "You look like an untidy child."

"I'm certain that's what Sarah thought, too," I said woefully, biting my lip.

"Oh Miranda, who gives a damn what that woman thinks? It's just that I was afraid something had happened to you."

"You were? Well, as a matter of fact, something almost did."

His black brows drew together. "What are you talking about?"

"I was almost knocked down by a boulder as I was coming across Bald Mountain earlier this afternoon. And it upset me so much I took the wrong path by mistake."

"A boulder?" he repeated. "Good Lord! I wonder if I should let you out of my sight!" He shook his head.

I sat forlornly while he dabbed at my face with a wet cloth and then applied some ointment on the swollen insect bites. I felt like a child who had wandered off and caused trouble. I couldn't even be trusted to find my own way home before upsetting household routine.

"I came upon a little cottage in the woods," I said to change the subject. "It looked as though it was once a very charming place, but now's it going to ruin."

"You must mean the Folly," he said. "My father had it built many years ago for my mother, as a wedding present in fact. He thought it might amuse her, I suppose. But she never liked going there so he left it alone. We used to play there some as children but no one's been in the place for years, I suppose."

"That's a shame. I was thinking what a lovely charming home it would make someone if it were fixed up," I said wistfully.

He regarded me somberly. "Were you?" he paused, sighing. "It's difficult for you here at Thunder House, isn't it?"

"Difficult?" I didn't want to annoy him further. "Why

213

. . . why do you say that?"

"Well, you can't tell me it's been exactly easy for you so far. And you always seem so . . . oh, never mind. Let's drop it, shall we? You had better bathe and dress for dinner."

"Wait, Nicholas. There is something I want to ask you."

He seemed to tense slightly. "What is it?"

"There is a sitting room on the second floor which I believed belonged to your sisters."

"Well, what of it?" He had relaxed, his voice was less curt.

"I wondered . . . that is . . . I'd like to use it, if I may."

"Is that all? Naturally you may use it. Just tell one of the servants to sweep and dust it for you and to light a fire in there tomorrow. You're welcome to it."

"Oh thank you, Nicholas, thank you very much," I said, suddenly happy.

"What a strange girl you are. You act as if I've given you some sort of present. You're my wife, Miranda, you can use any room you'd like."

"I would like to go there and practice the piano every day. And there are some books to read and—"

"I didn't know you played the piano."

"Oh, not well, I'm afraid. But Katherine MacLeod is going to give me lessons so I will improve," I said shyly.

"Is she? When did all this come about? You have been a busy little bee."

"Just today. I saw her this morning and she gave me my first lesson. Is . . . is that all right, Nicholas?"

"Of course it's all right. Why shouldn't it be? I understand she's a gifted pianist. I know my father was fond of hearing her play in church, and he wanted Julia and Emily to take lessons with her. Here's Morwenna. I'll leave you so you can get ready."

The twilight was settling over Thunder Cove. The sun had managed to break through the clouds in its descent and in the distance the water was a shimmering green, the sky above a lavender haze crowned with opalescent clouds. Directly below, the waves beat against the rose-colored

214

rocks in the eternal struggle of sea against land.

I had a bath and then dressed in the blue satin gown, which that day Miranda had cleaned and pressed. When Nicholas returned, I was ready to go downstairs.

"I have something for you, Miranda." He drew a long velvet box from his breast pocket. "A real present this time."

"Oh Nicholas, I don't need any presents," I protested, embarrassed.

"Isn't it a husband's privilege to give presents to his wife? Come, open it."

Smiling shyly, I took the box from him and opened it. Inside was a necklace of sapphires and diamonds. "Oh Nicholas! How perfectly lovely—though I don't think I'm at all the sort of person who could wear it."

"It's yours now, Miranda; I hope you will wear it. After all, that was my intention—and it matches your wedding ring, and more importantly, your eyes. I should have given it to you before this. Now that you are married to me, naturally the family jewels belong to you. I'm sorry I've been remiss."

"Oh, that's all right, Nicholas. I'm not used to jewelry, and besides, I don't really feel married," I said brightly, trying to put him at ease, and then clapped a hand to my mouth when I realized what I had said.

"Don't you? No, I don't suppose you do at that. What a blow to my conceit. But you haven't let me be a proper husband to you, have you?" His voice was light but his face had hardened, his eyes were shuttered.

"I didn't mean precisely that, Nicholas . . ." Twisting my ring, I regarded him pleadingly. Oh, you fool, I thought, whatever made you say such a thing? "I was only trying to say—"

"It doesn't matter, Miranda! Hurry up and put on the damn thing so we can have dinner," he ordered.

Hastily I fastened it around my neck, shivering slightly at the feel of the cold stones against my throat. We went downstairs. I was desperately trying to think of something to say to break the stiff silence which had arisen between us but, of course, I could come up with nothing. It was an awkward dinner, which we ate alone as Lavinia and Sarah were dining upstairs. Nicholas sat grimly drinking his wine and I stared at my plate, thoroughly depressed.

Nicholas said finally, "You look exhausted, Miranda. And little wonder at the kind of day you've had. Go upstairs and get some rest." His mouth was tight; he did not look at me.

He's always telling me to go to bed, I thought, just like a child. Is that truly how he regards me? "Very well, Nicholas," I said, biting my lip. "Thank you very much for the necklace. It's really quite beautiful."

He nodded absently and I left the room. I did not want to go upstairs and sit alone; I was too wound up to do so. When I reached the second-story landing, I noticed the doors which closed off the corridor to Julia's room and I had an idea. I would go and practice the piano. Perhaps playing would soothe me.

Taking a candle from the several on the lowboy in the hall, I lit it and opened the corridor doors. It was dark and cold in that hall but this did not deter me. However, I left the doors open, reluctant to close myself off in the shadowy passageway.

On impulse I paused at Julia's door and went in her old room. Holding the candle high above my head I looked over the beautiful room, my eyes going inevitably to the portrait where she sat with the faint supercilious smile on her face so like Lavinia's. In the shadowy light her gown glowed a ghostly white and for a moment I thought it stirred. But it was only the wavering candlelight passing over it which created the illusion of movement. Even so I was relieved to shut the door and move on down the hall.

When I reached the sitting room, I went in and set the candle on the piano. Shivering in the chilly room, I considered summoning one of the servants to request that a fire be laid and lit. But no, I wanted to be alone in the room. This room comforted me even in its present state; perhaps a servant's entrance would destroy that effect.

Sitting down on the piano bench, I opened the piano

and began to play from memory. The light from the single candle was not bright enough for me to read music tonight. To warm up my stiff fingers I played a few scales, beginning *piano* and gradually working up to *fortissimo* as Katherine had instructed. Eventually my depression was buried as I became engrossed in the practicing. When my fingers were ready, I began to play "Moonlight Sonata," which I remembered from having played it so often in India. The melancholy gentle beauty of it filled the room and I realized I was playing it better than I ever had before. It was as though my fingers were possessed of a talent better than I had displayed until now. I played and played, feeling my eyes fill with tears, but I was not truly sad—it was just something in the music which evoked this response. I could feel the descriptions of moonlight in the piece.

So absorbed was I that at first I did not sense or hear the presence of anyone else in the room. I had left the door open intentionally because the moonlight was spilling down the passageway from the Palladian window at the end of the corridor. But as I was nearing the end of the piece, there was a quick indrawn gasp followed by a muffled thud behind me. I started and turned around.

Lavinia was staring at me like someone seeing a specter. She looked like a ghost herself in a white filmy dressing gown, her white hair falling over her shoulders, her face as white as her gown in the moonlight. She had dropped her candle, which had fallen unlit to the floor. I realized with a shock that she had heard my playing, that it had lured her here.

"Julia! Oh, my darling girl! Why did you stay away so long before coming back to me? I haven't heard you playing in so long—so long. But tonight I heard, as I've thought I have in the past, and here you are. I've missed you so terribly, Julia. I knew you'd come back. He brought you back, didn't he? He knew you couldn't dwell forever in his kingdom beneath the sea. He knew you had to return to the warm sunlight and soft breezes and clear air. He's brought you back and here you are and now

217

everything will be fine, my darling, everything will be just as it was before."

She spoke sweetly, plaintively, and I stared at her in horror as cold prickles ran down the back of my neck. There was a sick feeling in my stomach. For Lavinia was not speaking to me, Miranda, the daughter-in-law she despised; she was speaking to her lost well-loved daughter Julia, whom she believed had been stolen by the Great Selkie.

She was mad, I thought. I couldn't move. I was terrified that if I did, something would happen—she would touch me or collapse and I couldn't bear that. I licked my lips and tried to swallow. Should I speak to her? But what would I do if she realized that I was not Julia? Would the shock be too much for her?

"Please play some more for me, Julia. You know I always loved to hear you play. Begin again at the beginning and I can imagine the moonlight outside coming to life. I'll sit right here. It's cold in this room, isn't it? You should have called someone to light a fire."

Mesmerized, I could only gaze at her. Why did Sarah not come? Where on earth was she? What could I do? I turned back to the piano, my heart racing, a cold sweat over me, and began the piece again. But this time the magic was gone. I could not play it properly and stumbled over the notes, over the keys, my trembling fingers going of their own accord and not to my wish.

And then the spell was broken in more ways than one. Lavinia gave a great awful shriek and leapt up from the sofa. I stopped playing, more frightened than I had been up to now. She continued to shriek like some wounded animal in terrible pain and anguish while I stared at her, appalled, my hands pressed to my cheeks, aghast at what I had done. I had shown myself to be not Julia, but Miranda.

"You stupid stupid girl!" she cried wildly. "How dare you? How *dare* you come in here and play? And wearing her necklace! How could you do this to me? Oh, you're cruel and vicious! I hate you! I hate you!"

218

She was coming toward me; she was grasping me by the arms. I tried to shake her off, moaning, while she regarded me with utter loathing and despair. Tears came to my own eyes as her nails dug into my bare arms.

Suddenly Sarah was in the room prying Lavinia away from me, her features distorted with emotion—shock and concern for Lavinia, and hatred for me. Lavinia collapsed, sobbing, on Sarah's shoulder while the other woman folded her in her arms.

"Oh Sarah, I thought . . . I thought it was *Julia!* I thought my own dearest girl had come back to me. But it was only her!" She sobbed in the most heartbreaking manner.

"I'm sorry, Lavinia, I'm so sorry," I babbled over and over, also weeping, loathing myself for the unwitting deception I had played, for being only her son's wife instead of her beloved daughter returned from the grave.

"What in the name of God is going on here?" thundered a voice. Nicholas stood at the entrance to the room.

"It's all your wife's fault—ask her!" shouted Sarah. "There, there, my dear, it's all right, I'm here," she said to Lavinia, patting her shoulder.

"Oh Nicholas, I'm sorry. She heard me playing the piano and thought—she thought I was Julia. She asked me to keep playing and then it suddenly struck her that I was not Julia. I'd hoped . . . I didn't know what to do—"

"Of course it struck her, you little fool! How could you ever play as well as Julia?" cried Sarah viciously.

Nicholas turned to Sarah. "How could you have let her come down here?" he asked between clenched teeth.

"I thought she was settled in bed! I had left her and gone to my room for the night. I don't care what you say, Nicholas, I won't lock her in her room! She's still the mistress of this house! This girl here, this girl you've married, she knew what she was doing. She has been torturing Lavinia, trying to drive her out of her mind! All because Lavinia spotted her for the scheming adventuress she is! First she mentioned—oh, so casually—that dreadful creature, and now this, trying to play like she is Julia to further torment your poor mother! I won't have it, do you hear? I will not stand by and let her do this! I'll kill her first, Nicholas! I swear I will!"

"Get out of here, Sarah, and take her with you," ordered Nicholas harshly. "Do as I say, damn it!" The scar carved into his cheek stood out like the new moon on a dark night.

"I won't, not until I've spoken my mind. You've brought this little upstart into this house—your mother's house—and the two of you are trying to destroy her!"

"No, it wasn't like that at all—" I cut in, appalled. "I didn't want to hurt her, to remind her. I didn't think anyone could hear my playing; I didn't think anyone would know I was here. Then when Lavinia came in and began to talk to me, I couldn't tell her I wasn't Julia! I didn't know what would happen if I did that. I was only trying to help her. I didn't mean to make her worse. She began to scream . . . oh Nicholas, you must believe me! I wasn't trying to have anyone believe I was Julia! You must believe me, Nicholas!"

"You must believe me, Nicholas," mimicked Sarah shrilly. "You must believe me! Why in hell did you come in here in the first place? You have no right to be in here! Didn't you notice the doors closing off this passageway? You must have—you opened them! You're trying to drive Lavinia insane, to torment her until she can't take any more! This was Julia's room, her piano, and yet you came in and played until Lavinia heard you, until you lured her here! You wanted her to hear you or else why did you leave all the doors open? You wanted her to think it was Julia come back!"

"No! No!" I cried, shaking my head, wringing my hands.

"She's wearing her necklace," cried Lavinia, pointing at me. "She's wearing Julia's sapphires! Give them back to me!" And she flung herself out of Sarah's arms and at me, yanking hard at the necklace until the clasp broke across the back of my neck. I cried out in pain, rubbing where it had snapped.

Nicholas gripped her shoulders and pulled her away from me. But she turned on him, a raging virago, her eyes burning, her face paper-white. "Don't touch me, Nicholas Blaize! It's all your fault! You bringing this little nobody to my house to take my place, to wear Julia's jewels, to use her room, her piano! You gave her that necklace, didn't you? How dare you take Julia's jewels? And to let *her* wear them!"

"The jewels are mine now, Mother, and as Miranda is my wife, they belong to her," said Nicholas quietly, his voice like steel. "Julia is gone; she can't wear them anymore."

"Where is Julia? Where is my precious girl, can you tell me that? In the sea! Oh why did I ever come to this godforsaken place? I hate the sea—I can't bear it! Roger knew that and he always said I'd get used to it—used to that dreadful roaring sound in my ears day and night, night and day, never ceasing! Well, it took my Julia! My sweet girl, the only child I ever really wanted, not like you and Emily, who always did whatever you pleased and didn't care who was hurt because of it! Roger was barely cold in his grave and you took off whaling, shirking all your responsibilities. You had to be a whaler, didn't you, and look what came of that! You got what you deserved, abandoning your father's business, leaving us here, leaving Julia to be lost! I wish you had never come back! Why weren't you killed too? Your reckless foolhardiness murdered all those other men—why didn't you die too? You weren't doing us any good by being alive—you weren't here to save your sister! And then you come back when it's too late and think you can take up shipbuilding again. But you've got blood on your hands, Nicholas Blaize! And you damn everything you touch! Think of that every time you take your wife in your arms. Does she know you sent a score of men to their deaths? Does she know you for the man you really are? I wish you were both in hell!"

Then the alarming rigidity left her body and she crumpled on the floor, her face in her hands, rocking back and forth on her knees. Sarah bent down to her and helped her up. She led her unresisting from the room. We heard them go down the hall and soon they were out of earshot.

I was still riveted in place. I looked down at the sapphires spilling across the floor. They looked dark and evil in the gloom of the room. I could not believe what had taken place in here; I had the uncanny feeling that it had all been a horrible melodramatic play in which we all took parts, reciting lines which had been written down for us. It could not have been real—those things could not have been said in earnest. It had been a masque, a drama, a tragedy. But not real.

But Nicholas's face, gray and frozen, was real; my trembling was real; the horrid nausea I felt was real. Nicholas picked up the candlestick Lavinia had dropped and hurled it across the room into the hearth. Then he turned on his heel and left.

Chapter Ten

I do not remember leaving the sitting room and going up to the third floor to my own room. But there I was sitting by the dying fire recalling Nicholas's face, watching him hurl the candlestick, shuddering at the impact it made as it struck the flinty surface and rolled onto the carpet. And then I remembered the gasp I had made, the sudden turn back to him, only to watch as he stalked from the room without a word or a backward glance. And I kept hearing his mother crying, "You've got blood on your hands, Nicholas Blaize! You damn everything you touch!" And then I was crying again, painful wrenching sobs which wracked my body with blows until I eventually fell asleep from sheer exhaustion.

Sometime in the night I awoke, dreaming it all again, replaying the play, re-acting the act, dramatizing the drama in my head until I woke shivering, parched, drained. The fire was dead, the room lit silvery in the moonlight which streaked across the water and shot into the room. Shakily I got up from the chair and went across to Nicholas's door, opening it. His room was also invaded by the razor-sharp steely moonlight. But he was not there. The moonlight shone on the brass instruments, illuminating the gold letters of the name board which spelled *Eagle*.

"Would you like to hear some of my experiences?" he had asked. The bitterly sarcastic words seem to float on the air. The despair in this room was a live creature writhing to return to a time before tragedy, before desolate disappointment, before violence. It reeked of a deplored recklessness and a profound hopelessness, hopes that had been brutally wrecked in the savage sea.

And I saw a man, dark head bent, sitting in a chapel built for mariners, while on the walls were enscribed memorials to dead men, men lost in the vast primitive sea. I saw a hard narrow mouth, bleak wintry eyes that were haunted, shuttered, turned inward in self-blame and guilt. I saw a cheek with its telltale token impossible to remove, to overlook.

This room was choked with momentos of some tragedy I could not yet imagine, of an aching desire to set back the clock, to sail the seas in search of the great bowhead whales in victory. It was a desire now thwarted, a dream trampled in stark grinding defeat. I understood and I did not understand. I imagined and I could not imagine. I wondered; I could only wonder.

I next remember my room dim and shadowy in the light of emerging dawn and I was again sitting in the chair wearing my blue satin gown. And there were footsteps in the room next to mine. I flew across to the door and opened it.

Nicholas was sitting down pulling off his boots. I looked at them, fascinated by the way the clumps of mud stuck to the sides of the soles and heels, the brown paste sullying their shiny blackness. His hands were streaked with grime; no more did he wipe them.

"Where . . . where have you been, Nicholas? I waited up for you—you never came in."

"Did you?" he asked without looking at me.

"Yes, of course. I wanted . . . I wanted to be with you. You stormed out so abruptly last night—"

"I don't want to talk or listen or even think about what happened last night, do you hear?" His eyes blazed into mine, his face thunderous.

Flinching, I cursed myself for my tactlessness. "I was only going to tell you that I'm sorry my playing caused such a . . . turmoil and I won't use Julia's room anymore. I won't play the piano anymore."

"If it weren't the piano, it would have been something else, don't you see that? It will always be something else. I should never have married you, Miranda. I should never

224

have brought you here. I was a damned fool—there's blood on my hands just as she said. The blood of decent brave men, men I led astray." He gave a brief hard laugh. "Perhaps even what Captain Sears had in store for you would have been preferable to what I've brought you to—it certainly wouldn't have been any worse."

I started to protest but he cut me off again. "You should have married someone else—a boy with no past to burden him, to inflict on others. I should never have married. I had determined never to do so before—why didn't I hold on to that resolve? I actually thought I was helping you by proposing! What a cursed fool I am!"

I gazed at him in helpless desperation, wanting to say something to comfort him, to object to his harsh words, to assuage his hurt. But I just stood there in crippled silence until he said more calmly, "If you don't mind, Miranda, perhaps you'd leave me now. I have to bathe and dress before going to the shipyard and it's obvious you barely slept. Go back to bed."

Suddenly I found my tongue. "You *were* helping me then, Nicholas, you were! And I'm glad we're married, terribly glad! How can you say what . . . what Captain Sears had in store for me would have been better? How can you even *think* such a thing? You don't really mean it, do you, Nicholas?" And when he did not answer, I cried, "Please, Nicholas!"

His eyes were bleak. "What do you wish me to say, Miranda? That I did the right thing in marrying you, that we are very happy here at Thunder House, that our life together is a great success? Have you forgotten how you recoiled from me the morning after I made love to you? Lavinia's right—I soil everything I touch."

"But that was . . . that was just because I was so . . . I was unused to everything. It wasn't really because of you!"

His mouth twisted. "No? But you've made it very clear at other times how you feel about any intimacy with me. Well, I have only myself to blame. That's what I get for marrying a girl like you."

"What do you mean 'a girl like me'? I'm not a child,

Nicholas, you can talk to me. You can't listen to your mother's ravings and take them to heart. She'll say anything to hurt you, so will Sarah. You don't believe that I played the piano deliberately to remind her of Julia, do you? Just as I don't believe whatever happened on that Arctic voyage was your fault the way she said it was."

"You don't know what you're talking about, Miranda," he said. "You want me to talk, do you, you want to listen? Very well then, I sailed with thirty men to the Arctic, to that frozen wasteland at the top of the world where the icebergs are jagged razor-sharp pieces of hell which trap a ship, blocking its passage until there is nothing but that stark whiteness on all sides, mountains of it, lavender in the dusk, golden in the sunlight. And there is the sound of drifting ice boulders crunching into ice fields, the moans of men freezing with cold, men throwing themselves into the water, sliding off the ice with great terrible cries, men running across the ice fields as though they offered some hope of salvation while others wanted to ram the ship into the ice to only have it crack and splinter apart and sink, men fighting men they once liked and respected but now which the Arctic had transformed to savage beasts — is this what you wanted to hear, Miranda? Is this the truth you wanted to know about your husband? That I was so bloody determined to whale in the Arctic that I caused the deaths of nineteen men? That I couldn't stop after two successful expeditions but had to return to again pit my luck against that frozen hell up there? And then to have disaster strike. To live the rest of my life wanting only to set back the clock, to give those men back to their families? I had my reckless daring, my stupid pride crushed by an impregnable tower of ice. Is this what you wished to hear? That you married a man so arrogant he thought he couldn't be defeated? That he pushed on farther north even though there were signs of an early freeze, a freeze which would lock men into an evil savage zone for weeks before releasing the survivors as mere remnants of humanity? You see, I can't forget. I will never forget. I will not let myself forget. All these things remind

226

me, castigate me."

"Then get rid of them, Nicholas! Get rid of them! You're doing yourself terrible harm keeping them around you, surrounding yourself with unspeakable memories!" I spoke without thinking and scarcely recognized my own voice, my own words. "Get rid of them, I beg you!"

"I will never get rid of them," he ground out brutally, his face stormy. "Now get out, Miranda! I've told you what you wanted to know. We won't speak of this again."

I stepped back through the doorway to my room, and taking the knob in my stiff cold grasp, I pulled shut the door. Catching sight of my reflection in the tall mirror I felt an aversion add to my corroding dejection. There was something repellent about wearing evening finery when the dawn emerged. It was out of place, unsavory like an overripe piece of fruit turning brown in spots or a rose past its full bloom, drooping its head dispiritedly. My hair was frowzy, my gown was creased and bunched up, my face smudged with sleep and scraped with traces of the snagging branches into which I had blundered yesterday. I looked ridiculous; I felt worthless. And Nicholas wished he hadn't married me. He wanted to be alone with his memorials to a once glorious, then tragic past.

Pulling off my gown, I did not care when I heard it tear. It fell to my feet and I kicked it aside before climbing in bed and huddling under the bedclothes. For a while I tried to sleep, tried to escape at least for a short time, but I finally got out of bed. After splashing cold water on my face, I combed through my tangled curls and then dressed in one of my old gowns. I pulled the bellrope for Morwenna and when she came I asked her for a pot of coffee. Her expression was pitying; she would not meet my eyes. I imagined the servants were privy to the terrible scene last night and that they knew that Nicholas had stormed out afterward, not returning until dawn.

"I'm going out, Morwenna," I told her abruptly when she had brought the coffee. "I won't be back for luncheon."

"Martha fixed 'ee some blueberry hotcakes, ma'am.

Won't 'ee have a bite or two?"

I shook my head. "I couldn't eat a thing."

Outside the air was crisp, the vibrant blue sky scalloped with clouds. The woods were just beginning to glint with color. Though still mostly green, the maples whispered of forthcoming corals, reds, and golds. I walked to Nansett quickly with no more than a slight pause and a swift glance up the slope of Bald Mountain. The terror I had felt yesterday seemed almost trivial in the light of later events.

I hurried over the stone wall and past the grist mill until I reached the village. The cottages were brilliantly white in the sunlight as, one after another, they queued down to the deep blue water. I was glad my poke bonnet obscured part of my face; I nodded at the few people I passed, having no choice but to do so. I reached Emily's house with a certain relief and knocked at the door. Please let her be in, I prayed.

She was. She asked me inside, looking troubled when she saw my expression. "What is it, Miranda?"

I sat down. "It's Nicholas. And it's I, too. In fact the whole dreadful thing was my fault." I bit my lip, not knowing how to continue.

"Tell me what has happened," she said gently.

"Last night I was playing the piano—Julia's piano. You recall me telling you I was going to ask Nicholas if I might practice on it for my lessons with Katherine MacLeod?"

She nodded. "Yes, I was certain he would agree."

"Well, he did agree, and so last night I went in the sitting room and began to play. After I had been there awhile, your mother came in. Oh Emily, it was so awful—she thought I was Julia! She didn't know me, she was talking to me as though I were Julia come back from the dead!"

Emily's face had paled. "Go on," she said.

"She asked me to keep on playing for her, and she sat down on the sofa. I . . . I didn't know what to do. I was afraid not to do as she asked—I didn't know where Sarah was. I was afraid that if I refused or left the room, she might get worse.

"Well, she got worse—much worse. I began to play again and I was so agitated that I made lots of mistakes, could scarcely play the piece. She realized all of a sudden who I was and began shrieking hideously and then Sarah came and shouted at me and then Nicholas was there, too, and Mrs. Blaize was saying these horrible things to him and he just stood there like a statue until Sarah took your mother away. Then Nicholas left and was gone all night.

"This morning I went into his room—he had come back—and he talked about his last whaling expedition, but there is so much about it, about everything that I don't understand. Do you know his room is filled with things . . . things he used on his voyages . . . things that torture him? They are like sacred momentos, but to punish him, not to make him happy. Emily, I need to know about that last voyage, and I thought of coming to you."

She shook her head. "I assumed you knew, Miranda. I thought Nicholas would have told you and would have prepared you for our mother."

"He did mention that sometimes she was not herself, that there were times she didn't remember Julia was dead, but I had no idea . . . I couldn't imagine that she would say the sorts of things she did. This morning was the first time Nicholas spoke of his whaling experiences to me— and that was only after I had pressed him. I don't think I wanted to know before, I wanted to hide from whatever I sensed in him at times—the anger, the bitterness. He was right to think of me as a child. But I know I can't hide from any of it any longer. And so I would appreciate it if you would tell me everything you know."

"Well, I only know what Nicholas told Ben and what Ben heard from some of the other men who returned with Nicholas. Most of the crew were not local men but the survivors came here first before sailing home. But I daresay I should begin by telling you that Nicholas was always fascinated with whaling and longed to make his mark in the trade. Many of the ships built in my father's shipyard were whaling barks so Nicholas knew all about

229

it — it wasn't just an outlandish whim. As a boy he'd sit in Jock's tavern and listen for hours to the stories whalers would tell while they were on shore between voyages. Our mother disapproved of his interest, of his rubbing elbows with those types, as she called them, but her attitude, her scoldings and punishments did not deter him or quell his longing to experience that sort of life firsthand.

"When he was older, nearly a young man, he came to work in the shipyard with Father. He learned all aspects of the business but he was restless — he still wanted to try his hand at whaling. It frustrated him very much that he was building vessels he couldn't travel on himself. At one point he was determined to go, but Father had a heart attack and so Nicholas stayed on to take over much of the responsibility for the mill and yard. Mother kept reminding him that Father's health wasn't good and that his place was here. Then several years later Father had another attack, this time a fatal one, and soon after, Nicholas announced that he had signed himself on as a hand on a whaling ship out of Nantucket. Mother was in a rage over what she called his selfishness, his rashness, that Father wasn't cold in his grave before Nicholas had to rush off like a fool. He was always strong-willed, unpredictable, impulsive, and she hated those qualities in him. At any rate, Nicholas was gone for nearly three years. After he had acquired the expertise needed, he purchased the *Eagle*. And began commandeering his own expeditions.

"He decided to sail to the Arctic to hunt the bowhead whales for the hundreds of pounds of baleen they would yield. It's the most hazardous form of whaling — and for something so mundane as women's corsets! His first voyage was successful and very profitable. So was his second. Nicholas was always daring and shrewd. But the last one was a catastrophe."

"And that's the reason he stopped whaling and decided to sell the *Eagle*?"

Emily nodded, her eyes somber. "They had already caught several bowhead. It was September — a year ago, as a matter of fact — and apparently there had been signs of an early freeze but Nicholas thought . . . well, he presumed they would sail from the region without any trouble. He had had two successful runs up there before and he was resolved to get the maximum amount of baleen the ship would hold."

"But something happened so that they couldn't leave."

"The *Eagle* became lodged in ice one night. There was nothing they could do but wait for the ice fields to drift away again and free them. But it was weeks before that happened, and in the meantime some of the crew began to go mad from the waiting and the cold. Also there was the white glare of the sun on the ice—do you know that can drive one crazy?"

"Nicholas ordered there was to be no liquor consumption but somehow some of the men became inflamed with alcohol and ran out across the ice, never to be seen again. Others jumped into the icy waters. There were arguments, even an attempted mutiny." She paused. "It was a horrible nightmare, worse than you or I can ever imagine. A few of the men froze to death. The scar on Nicholas's face—one of the men tried to stab him with a kitchen knife during the mutiny attempt."

I could not say anything; I could only stare at her in horror.

"Of course he did all he could to keep the crew steady those weeks but in those conditions . . . he was one of the fortunate few who survived. Eleven out of the original thirty. Nicholas swore he'd never subject men to those dangers again. For a time after he had returned, he would do nothing but sit in his room surrounded by those tools and things, staring out to sea. He'd lugged them up to Thunder House from the battered ship. He moved into the wing where you now have your room.

"I wasn't married then—I was still living at home—but nothing I did or said was of any use. He avoided all of us, taking his meals alone, walking for hours at night, rarely speaking. Julia had been lost while he was away on his second voyage so Mother, when she saw him, blamed him for her disappearance. She told him to leave Thunder

House and he did, spending the winter in Nova Scotia. Later she said his neglect had caused Julia's death, and the Arctic disaster that followed was his retribution. Eventually he began working again at the shipyard and began to show a renewed interest in it, throwing himself into work there to build it back to the flourishing business it had once been. He repaired the *Eagle* and then, as you know, sailed her to New Bedford in search of a buyer.

"Ben told me that the money he made from the sale is all being sent to the families of the men who died in the Arctic. I believe he visited a number of them when he was in New Bedford since some of the men came from there, before he sold the ship to your former employer."

An image of him sitting in the Bethel came to me, his face shielded by one hand, his shoulders slumped forward before he lifted his bleak face to mine. "Whales are not the only victims," I had murmured — and he had heard me. He had doubtless been visiting the grieving families that day, or was preparing to do so. And he must have reached out to me for some sort of comfort — an angel, he had called me — when he was in dire need. But it was a comfort I had not been able to give then, a pain I had not been able to fathom. His manner had alarmed me. But now I sensed that in that desperate ardent embrace he had gripped and held on to me for dear life, as a drowning man would reach for and cling to a life preserver in the midst of the choking tossing sea.

I had not understood then and I had fled from him, shocked and frightened. Then Providence had again thrown us together in Captain Sears's house. But it had been a different Nicholas then. An arrogant man with iron control as he lounged at ease in the drawing room. Then later had come the flash of blazing anger at Captain Sears, which was swiftly suppressed when he turned to me with kindness, gentleness.

And the following day my abject misery and his startling proposal of marriage, which seemed to be made almost in spite of himself, out of pity for me, I had thought.

232

All these things I saw more clearly now and my mind moved ahead in sequence to our wedding voyage, his passionate possession of me as though he were seeking something in me to bring him peace, to soothe the anguished raging in his blood, in his heart, in his head where the memories were still alive, fresh, and intolerable. And I had rejected him, thrown back his pain in his face in my own petty self-conscious reaction to an act which was vitally human, undeniably fundamental.

After that he had turned icily hostile and it was little wonder. And he had spurned my company, retreating into his former black thoughts, seizing them as he had earlier seized me. He had continued to hold on to them because, as I knew, even in misery there could be a certain security, a reason to do nothing because all things were proved futile.

I saw all this; I knew it all to be so. And I knew something else with fully as much assurance. I loved Nicholas, loved him with a potent desperation, a towering urgency that had been bottled inside me until now when it surged forth in triumph. This was what I wanted, this was what my life had been missing—a place of wild natural beauty and a man to love to the exclusion of all else. I had found both of these things on Thunder Island. But even as the flame soared from my insignificant soul, I knew that my love was as hopeless and terrible as Nicholas's memories, that he could not return my love. He was an embittered shell of a man who was flinging me from him even as he gathered, welcomed those memories to himself. He lived haunted, and he lived alone. There was no place for me. Whatever I might have done before, whatever I could have offered him, was impossible now; he did not want it; he had ceased to seek it. There was nothing I could do.

Looking over at Emily, I said weakly, "Thank you for telling me all this Emily. I'll go now—I know you have things to do."

"No, Miranda, sit still. We'll have some tea."

I shook my head firmly. "No, I really don't want anything. I think I'll go for a long walk. First I have to tell

233

Katherine I won't be going through with my plan to take piano lessons. It's not worth it now. And then I'm going to go for a walk."

She regarded me helplessly. "Very well, Miranda. I know I've given you a great deal to take in. But I don't think you should give up your music lessons."

"I'm not going to play Julia's piano again, Emily. It's hers even though she's gone and I never should have intruded," I said stiffly.

"I can understand how you feel, I really can. After all, I escaped from that house when I married Ben. I was very much in love with him but I was also eager to leave Thunder House. But you . . ." Her voice trailed off and she looked away, shrugging. I knew what she had neglected to say—I couldn't leave. There was nowhere I could go.

"Good-bye," I said. "And I am glad you told me all you did. It was time I knew."

When I had left her, I trudged up the street to what had been the manse when Katherine MacLeod's husband was the local pastor. The sight of the pristine white house with its black shutters was comforting, steadying. I went up on the porch where pots of mums had been arranged cosily. The maid showed me into the parlor and Katherine soon joined me, looking strikingly handsome in a periwinkle blue gown which matched her violet-blue eyes.

"I'm sorry to bother you, Katherine, when I took up so much of your time yesterday . . ."

She waved away my apologies. "You're always welcome here, my dear. I'm very fond of your husband, and Emily, too, of course, so I want us to be good friends."

"Well, I've come by to tell you that I won't be able to take lessons as we've planned."

"Oh? I'm very disappointed to hear that."

"You see, the piano I'd hoped to use—Julia's—well, Mrs. Blaize was very upset when she overheard me playing it. So I think it would be better for all concerned if I don't again."

"Hmmmm. I see what you mean. But is that the reason? Because you don't want to distress Lavinia Blaize? There must be another piano for you to use."

"I believe that is the only one in Thunder House."

"Oh, not at the house. I was thinking of one here in Nansett. I don't want you to give up your lessons before we've scarcely begun, Miranda. I think you have a talent worth developing."

"Thank you, Katherine, but—"

"I know!" she exclaimed, her face brightening. "You can use the piano at the church—next door! The building is deserted most of the day except when the women are preparing it for a service and so you would have plenty of privacy. And it might be a pleasant place for you to sit and practice. Why, it's the ideal solution!"

"Do you really think so? That it would be all right? I would like to continue our lessons, it's just I didn't want to—"

"You didn't want to upset Lavinia again, I understand perfectly. And your sentiments do you credit. But I believe that if one has a talent, even a small one, it's one's duty to cultivate it. I encourage Heather in her painting and I want to encourage you in your music. And I know the Reverend Whitcomb won't mind. After all, no one uses the church piano besides myself. You must go there and practice."

"When do you think would be a good time?"

"Oh, the afternoons would probably be best because the building is swept and dusted some mornings a week. Yes, I think the afternoons would be ideal. Is that agreeable to you?"

I smiled. "Yes, Katherine. Thank you very much." I felt a little break in my depression.

"I'm glad you came to me with your problem."

"So am I. I feel better already."

"Good. Perhaps you'd join me for a cup of tea."

"Oh, I don't wish to trouble you. I'm going for a long walk, perhaps over to Seal Island if I can get across."

"Then you'll need a cup of tea and some of my blue-berry muffins to strengthen you if you mean to walk all the way there. No, don't argue. I was indulging in a bit of

235

loneliness, missing my husband, and I'm delighted you've taken me out of it. I'll just tell Janet to fix us a tray and be right back."

I was studying the collection of porcelain figurines in the curio cabinet when she returned. "These are lovely," I said.

"My husband gave each one to me at different times over the years. Sometimes at Christmas, sometimes at a birthday or to mark our wedding anniversary. He knew how fond I was of pretty things and he often felt badly that he wasn't able to give me more in the way of material possessions. I used to say, "But Bruce, I have you and Heather—what more could I wish for?" And it wasn't as though I were used to luxuries. But still it bothered him— he wanted more for Heather and me even though we were content and had always been. What is it?"

"Oh, I'm sorry . . . I was thinking about Mrs. Blaize. I understand she has never been content on Thunder Island, and her husband was able to give her everything in the way of material possessions. There's such a contrast between you, although I shouldn't really say that."

She shook her head. "Poor Lavinia. We could have been friends. I came to Thunder Island as a new bride shortly after she did, but she made it clear she wanted to have as little to do as possible with any of us at Nansett."

"That's a shame. A friendship with you might have helped her."

"She and Roger did give several dinner parties back in those early years. But it was evident she had no intention of deepening our acquaintance. She entertained us because it was the proper thing to do, to invite the minister and his wife to dinner. And there were no others in Nansett she considered welcoming to her house. Still, I enjoyed those occasions at Thunder House—it's such a beautiful place. All those lovely rooms filled with such treasures. Oh well, I wasn't quite of her background though naturally I was educated, brought up properly as a minister's daughter. But we had little money, you see. It was difficult for my mother, on an equal position socially with the wealthy

236

citizens of Camden but a far cry from them financially. Still, that's what being in a minister's family is all about — as you must know very well yourself, Miranda."

"Well, it was different for me. All the missionaries were poor and we rarely came into contact with the other white people who lived in Bombay. But I can understand how it must have been. And it was Lavinia's loss, not to have you as a friend."

She smiled and clasped my hand. "You're very dear, do you know that? Nicholas is very fortunate to have you. Oh, he's no fool, that's certain. He must have seen instantly what you were like. He needs someone like you."

"Oh, I don't know . . ." I said, reddening. "I think things are worse for him since I came." I stopped, wondering how I could have revealed so much. But she was such an easy person to talk to — it was the effect she had on me. She radiated warmth; she had nurturing qualities which made you wish to confide in her. She must have been a great help to her husband.

"I'm sure you are wrong, Miranda. But there is always a period of adjustment after two people are married. And you knew one another for such a brief period of time before. It's only natural that things should seem bewildering, even difficult, at first. Nicholas has been . . . preoccupied for a long time. I assume you know about what happened to his ship and his crew?"

"Yes, some things he told me and then Emily explained rather more."

"Well, it's good you know. You can help him achieve a measure of acceptance, of peace with the past, and you can help him look ahead. A child would be a very good thing, I think, for both of you."

I flushed again and she went on hastily, "I'm sorry, Miranda. That was very presumptuous of me, I'm afraid. But I'm already so fond of you and I do know something of your situation. I've known Nicholas all his life, remember. So please do not be offended by my plain speaking."

I squeezed her hand. "I'm not at all offended, Katherine. I'm grateful for your interest. Perhaps you are

237

right. But—that's for the future, isn't it? And now I've taken up enough of your time. I better leave now if I'm going to walk across to Seal Island today."

"That's a walk I enjoy myself," she said. "You know, I assume, about the causeway and how it's flooded at high tide?"

"Yes, Nicholas told me. He warned me to be careful."

"I was nearly stranded there once myself. But I was able to wade across without much difficulty. There's a point before which you can do so safely but then after the water is a certain depth it becomes dangerous. Bruce was concerned when I told him I had waded across, but he admired me, too. I was always more adventuresome than he. We were perfect foils for one another."

She ushered me out and we said good-bye on the porch. "Thank you for solving my dilemma—about the piano playing, I mean."

"I'm so glad I could. And it's a fairly good instrument—one of the men here tunes it from time to time."

Waving at her, I went up the street and turned away from the village. Once in the woods I paid careful attention to the way I was going and tried to push the frightful discoveries I had made today to the back of my mind. I would give myself up to the beauty of the afternoon. Judging from the sun's angle it was about noon.

I passed Blackett's Glade, following the path through the forest to the lake, which glittered like a thousand tiny stars in the sunlight. I continued until I had reached the spot where the woods halted at the cliff's edge, where the mighty spruces' branches were stunted by the ocean wind. As I walked along the cliff, I noticed blueberry bushes growing in profusion. Eventually the high cliff descended steeply and jaggedly to a mass of boulders. On higher ground spidery grass grew in patches among the rose-colored rocks; closer to the shoreline the pools of water trapped between the rocks were the color of strong tea. Silvery-green barnacles crusted the stones.

The causeway which led to Seal Island was littered with shells and clumps of brown, glossy seaweed. The breeze was tangy and mild. I untied the strings of my bonnet and took it off, shaking my hair loose.

When I reached the island, I walked along the shore, lifting my skirts as I stepped across the gray slabs of rock. The tiny balls of bladder wrack popped as I stepped on them; their shapes reminded me of amber-colored strawberries.

Here the ocean did not crash and boom; it lapped the shore placatingly. Looking back across to Thunder Island, I could see the rounded crest of Bald Mountain as it rose above the black-green forests. Ahead of me three white seagulls stood motionless on a boulder which jutted out over the water.

After a while the rocks stopped and I came to a small beach of caramel-colored sand. I discovered that it was not sand at all but a generous spilling of crushed shells. I sat down to rest, judging that I was about halfway round the island. From here it was not possible to see Thunder Island; I might have been the only person in the world as I sat there on that deserted beach on that uninhabited island. One lone seal, its dark fur streaked with white, lounged on a broad flat rock in the sun. I remembered what Morwenna had said about holding up one's hand and saying a prayer at the sight of a seal in case it was not only a seal but a selkie.

There was no noise. The bluish-green waves were placid. Even the gulls were silent. It was almost eerie, that stillness. I decided to explore the interior of the island before going back to the causeway. Climbing over some steplike boulders on the far side of the beach, I entered the woods along a soft, mossy path. It smelled damp, fresh, and earthy in there where the sun could not easily penetrate.

A sudden harsh sound startled me then, coming so quickly after my quiet, lonely vigil by the water. But it was only a blue jay, soon joined by others, pursuing an owl from tree to tree. I pitied the owl, caught by daylight, venturing into a place and time it did not belong.

The trees opened up to a field of golden gorse, Queen

239

Anne's lace and yellow daisies. The sun was warm; flies buzzed past me, crickets chirped in the tall grass. A few apple trees cropped up here and there like hands, twisted and knobby.

If I walked across the field and through the opposite stretch of woods, I should reach the shore which faced Thunder Island that much quicker. I was mindful of what Nicholas had said about the onset of high tide, and even though I believed I had plenty of time to cross the causeway, there was no reason to delay and risk being stranded. The very thought made me hurry across the field to the woods.

I walked along a path I assumed would lead me to the rocky shore but after I had gone a long while, the path twisting and turning before me, I began to worry that I was lost. But that notion was a foolish one because Seal Island was a small place — it couldn't be more than a half-mile across. The sun was now high overhead and I wondered uneasily how long it would be before the causeway was impassable.

When at length I did emerge from the woods onto the shore I saw with dismay that the huge bulk of Thunder Island was still nowhere in sight. The path must merely have rambled haphazardly over the island instead of cutting directly across it. But I had no intention of reentering those woods and trying to find a shortcut to the causeway. I would just have to walk along the shore until I reached it.

The sky was hazy now, I noted, but the implications of that did not occur to me, so intent was I in climbing over the rocks. I was impatient for a glimpse of Thunder Island around the next bend. My haste made me careless and in my eagerness to jump from one boulder to another, I missed my footing. My ankle turned under me and become lodged in a crevice. The initial pain was sharp and intense. Moaning, I sat down heavily and lifted my foot from out between the rocks. My boot was badly scraped but that hardly mattered now. But I did not see how I was to continue clambering along the shore, much less to traverse the three miles or more back across Thunder

Island to the house.

After a while the vicious pain subsided, but each step I took was uncomfortable, making my progress slow indeed. I went along, putting most of my weight on the other foot until finally the island rounded off again and I could see the trees of Thunder Island. A blanket of low smoky clouds covered the top of Bald Mountain and cast a milky film over the blue sky. It looked as though the clouds were moving this way. Perched on a huge boulder, I searched for the welcome sight of the causeway.

But it was not there. Nothing but greenish-gray water, sullen and dismal. Ahead I saw the huge limb, smooth and pale as marble, which marked where the causeway should be but there was no avenue of gray pebbles leading to Thunder Island. It had disappeared; it was hidden somewhere under the bayberry ocean.

Panicking, I started to run over the remaining rocks, ignoring the shooting pain in my ankle, until I reached the tree limb which by now was partly submerged in the water. I stared out at the waves which lapped so gently, so deceitfully, over the edge of the causeway. I looked as though I expected the causeway to suddenly emerge, comfortingly dry and wide enough for me to cross. But it did not. It was not there.

Perhaps it was not yet so deep; perhaps I could wade across safely as Katherine had been able to do. Her husband had admired her for having had the courage to do such a thing. I walked into the icy water with no thought as to my clothes and went forward a few steps. To my horror the water quickly reached my waist; I had no way of knowing how much deeper it would get over the half-mile distance. And the tide was moving it rapidly. Swimming the length was out of the question.

In despair I turned and waded back to dry land, shivering as the breeze—when had it turned so cool?—pierced my heavily sodden clothes. The gray clouds now covered the sky above Thunder Island; the day which had begun warm and bright now held the damp chill of promised rain. I stood there, wondering what on earth I was going to do.

The causeway would not be passable for another six or seven hours yet and by then it would be past twilight, and cold. How stupid I had been not to tell Morwenna where I was going—but I had only decided later. Katherine knew but if no one asked her, then what good did her knowing do me?

I put on my bonnet but took off my wet cloak, wringing the water from its folds. Sitting on a large flat rock I pulled up my wet skirts and took off my shoes and stockings. The bracing icy water had numbed my throbbing ankle but now it was beginning to pain me again.

Fighting back tears, I tried to stay calm by assuring myself that I was, after all, in no danger, I had only to wait until the causeway was open again. I tried not to dwell on the fact that it would be dark when I would have to walk the width of Thunder Island before reaching the house.

What an idiot I was—Nicholas had been right in his chiding estimation of me yesterday, that I was little better than a child who could not be let out of his sight. From one day to the next I could not help doing foolish things.

The thought flickered into my head that this was like the day Julia had disappeared. She had gone out walking and no one had ever seen her again. And she had never returned. But I would not think of that. Oh, don't let me think of that!

There was nothing to do but sit and wait. I was in no danger, I reminded myself. I just had to stay calm. Looking out over the water, I glimpsed some colorful shapes bobbing on the surface. The lobster traps! Perhaps someone would come to check them as I had seen the man doing the other day. I hoped above hope that they hadn't already been checked while I was exploring Seal Island. I strained my eyes for the sight of a boat or a person walking along the opposite shore but there was nothing.

I would not give up hope. There were many people living on Thunder Island—why shouldn't at least one of them come near here so that I could signal for help? It was more than a possibility. I had only to wait.

It was later when the breeze had grown stronger and the sky stormy that I began to be truly frightened. It was not a witless mounting panic which I might control with an effort, but a cold insidious dread which crept into my mind little by little and would not be allayed. The tide was covering all but the top twigs of the huge limb, and I watched it desperately for a sign that the water had begun to recede. Gray spiders scurried nearby, seeking shelter under the rocks, and behind me the dark spruces huddled against the encroaching elements.

I wondered whether I should go inside the island to the field. It would doubtless be warmer there away from the wind. But then I wouldn't know if anyone came within sight of the island. And I had to know. Recklessly, beyond thought or caring, I began to shout for help. It did not matter that there was no one to hear me. I shouted until my throat ached.

The iron gray sky was reflected in the choppy water. Even the slightly turning leaves had lost their vibrancy. The island seemed an alien place and I could not help glancing over my shoulder from time to time.

Nicholas had suggested that Julia may have lost her life by attempting to swim from Seal Island to Thunder Island. The tide change was up to ten or more feet, he had said, and the current strong. Had she sat here as I was and become so desperate and frightened that she could not wait for low tide but had tried instead to wade or swim across? If such had indeed been the case, what had made her attempt such a reckless thing?

Could someone or some thing—have so terrified her that she had braved the cold waves in order to escape?

Stop it, I commanded. You will not do this to yourself. You are the only inhabitant on this island except for a few small birds and animals. And one seal with black slanted eyes, doubtless very strong and smelling of brine. . . .

Quickly I began to imagine what everyone at home was doing. Morwenna—had she begun to wonder at my prolonged absence? Nicholas—had he returned from the shipyard yet? What were Sarah and Lavinia doing now — not that they would be in any way concerned for me. Was it possible that Emily might have paid her mother a visit this afternoon and remarked that I surely should have come back by now? I imagined them sitting in Lavinia's sitting room, drinking tea, eating molasses cookies. And Emily saying, "I wonder why Miranda hasn't come home yet. Surely she should have returned from her walk already." And Lavinia coolly answering, "Oh, she often roams outdoors all day. The servants complain she is never here to eat her lunch and they find it quite trying anticipating her needs and movements. I can't think what she finds so enthralling about Thunder Island." And they would talk of something else, convinced that I was content wandering the woods or shore. But, of course, nothing like that had occurred. Lavinia was doubtless prostrate in her room and Emily would not wish to see her mother so soon after hearing about last night's scene.

Indeed, why should anyone worry that something untoward had happened to me? Why should it occur to anyone that I might be hurt or in trouble? It might occur to Nicholas, of course, seeing that I had begun to make a habit of things like this. But he was likely too preoccupied with his work and his dark emotions to give me a thought. Perhaps he wouldn't even return to the house tonight. It wasn't as though he wanted to be with me, I thought miserably, when he had been wishing that he had never married me.

No one was worried about me, I knew with a leaden certainty. I had been warned several times about the causeway and the tide, and it was assumed that I would take heed of those warnings.

My ankle was throbbing badly. There was no way I would be able to cross three miles of rugged terrain even if I managed to cross the causeway. There was nothing I could do. I did not even have the means to build a fire to alert someone to my presence here.

A thick gray wall now hovered over Thunder Island and was approaching the shore where I sat. I reached for my damp cloak and covered myself with it. Before long, wisps of mist began to float about me, rising from the ground like specters from the grave. I was the alien on this land of fog and rock and spruce; I was the one who did not belong. Like the owl which had ventured out in daylight and was then pursued relentlessly by the outraged birds of the day. Would something come soon to pursue me, outraged at my trespass?

The opposite landscape was misty and distant, a vague image, not sea, not land. The shapes and colors of the forest were blurred and muted by the fog bank. There still were no sounds except for the soft washing of the waves over the stones. Even the seagulls had disappeared, as if Seal Island in its present state were no longer their domain.

Don't let the mist rise, I pleaded. Don't let me be blinded in it! That I could not bear. Rain, yes, darkness, perhaps; but not that dreadful cloying wetness. It's unnatural somehow, evil.

And no one would be able to hear me scream. . . .

Suddenly I noticed that the water seemed slightly lower on the tree limb—or was it merely my hopeful imagination? No, it was a bit lower. So the tide had turned. Yet I still had several hours to wait before the causeway would be crossable and by then it would be dark. I imagined myself stumbling in the dark, veering to one side of the causeway and then the other, not being able to follow its course, splashing into the water, which seemed to be on all sides.

In the meantime the mist was rising, drawing its impenetrable veil over the defenseless land. And as it rose, it brought with it creatures who were not human, who came up from the dark deep caverns of the sea to cloak themselves in the shielding fog. Creatures who sang eerie tuneless songs, creatures with black slanted eyes and dark dripping hair like glossy seaweed, creatures who shed their seal skins and took the form of men. Selkies who possessed no souls, living forever in their kingdoms beneath the sea, stealing earthly brides for company. Brides who

245

would drown if they fought the slithery embrace of their demon lovers, their long waving hair forming the roof of the crystal-and-coral palace far below the tumultuous waves. How many of them were down there in those icy bottomless depths, how many unsuspecting maidens had been dragged below the surface to fulfill the loathsome needs of the Great Selkie himself?

"Shut up, you fool!" I shouted aloud. "That's quite enough of that!" But my voice sounded lost and mournful instead of briskly reassuring. My last vestige of control broke and then I was screaming as loud as I could, sharp piercing screams which rose again and again from my throat but which did not seem to come from me.

For in that eerie dim world I could believe that such creatures existed, that they emerged from the water and captured their prey. And only hours earlier I had come upon a seal and it had gazed at me from out of its black eyes. Morwenna had said selkies were irresistible, that they were like dark handsome men. Once one gazed at you, you were its prisoner forever.

A sound came to my ears then, a soft splashing sound. It's nothing, my mind cried, nothing but the lapping of the water over the rocks. But no, it was louder than that and it was coming closer.

It was coming from the sea. Like some creature swimming toward the shore, sliding through the waves, gliding through the mist until its fins became legs. Legs which carried it up on the pebbled shore where it would gather me close to its dank chest so like a seal's pelt.

A dark shape was looming up from the sea; I could barely make it out in the fog. My throat was choking with a horror unimaginable but I could not move, I could not run.

And I knew I would not be able to flee its drenched powerful hold as it bore me back with it to the ocean fathoms, my long hair waving like dark glossy seaweed.

Chapter Eleven

I heard my demon lover calling to me in the mist. I did not answer; I could not answer. The vague shape was nearing the shore; I watched, fascinated, beyond reason, beyond fear.

"Is someone there? Can you hear me?"

It was a voice and the voice was human. And suddenly I realized that the looming shape was a man standing in a small boat.

"Yes, Yes!" I shouted. "Help!"

"Don't be afraid, I'm coming."

"I've hurt my ankle. I can't walk."

"I'll come get you." He jumped from the boat, wading the few feet to the shore. His voice I had never heard before; he was a man I did not recognize. But he was undoubtedly a man and no dark sleek creature, soaking and smelling of brine.

"I'm so glad you've come. I thought . . . well, I can't tell you what I thought." My relief was so intense I felt giddy, light-headed.

He was tall and lean with fair hair, which waved over his forehead under a blue knit cap. He bent down beside me. "Put your arms about my neck."

I did as he asked and he lifted me in his arms, carrying me to the boat where he gently set me down. Then he climbed in and sat on the plank opposite me.

"Thank you, sir. I thought I'd never get off that dreadful place," I said, my teeth chattering.

"Don't imagine it's a pleasant place in the fog, with night comin' on. Sorry I've nothing to put round you. Not that it'd be dry now anyways. But I'll have you home as quick as I can."

"I'm Mrs. Blaize. Mrs. Nicholas Blaize."

"Ayeh, I thought so. Didn't he wahrn you 'bout the tides? And 'bout how fast the weather can change? Nicholas ought to take better care of you," he said crisply.

"He did warn me, but I twisted my ankle and could not hurry back to the causeway before it flooded."

"Happens to others round here. It's an easy thing to happen. It's a good thing I came by to check my traps." He nodded toward several huge buckets, in which swam several gray lobsters.

"Yes, I'm so glad, so grateful to you. No one else came by all afternoon."

"I'm Zeke Somes."

"Ben's brother? Oh! My name is Miranda."

"Pretty name. Suits you. We can get back to Nansett in maybe an hour, maybe more. Then we'll get a horse and I'll ride you back to the house. But it's a ways round the island and I know you're cold. You better have some of this."

He reached inside his double-breasted navy coat and pulled out a flask. "Drink this. It's whiskey—good for cold and shock."

"Thank you." I drank deeply, gratefully, the strong drink burning its way down my chilled body. I handed it back to him and he took a swig.

The fog had not grown any thicker, I noticed with relief. Zeke was rowing close to land but not too close, avoiding the jagged peaks of rock which thrust up near the shore.

Soon exhaustion hit me like a wave. The whiskey had helped to numb the pain in my ankle. It was also beginning to give the illusion of warmth and comfort. I was safe now, and before long would be home in my warm bed with a fire blazing and crackling in the hearth. My teeth had stopped chattering and I no longer felt miserable.

"Tell me about trapping lobsters," I said drowsily. "How do you do it?"

"Well, we use traps made of oak slats and filled with nettin'. The trap's divided into two pahrts—a "kitchen" and a "pahrlor." Lobsters are scavengers—they eat dead fish. So you slip a dead fish into the kitchen as bait. A lobster swims through the eye, which is shaped like a funnel, and it can't get back out. It can only go forward to try to escape and there it is, stuck in the pahrlor—or I hope it is when I come to check."

"What do your buoys look like?"

"They're red with blue stripes runnin' across. Everyone's are different, I guess you know, so we can tell 'em apahrt. Ben's are red with yellow stripes, not that he does much lobsterin' anymore."

"Do you also work at the lumber mill or shipyard?"

"Nope. I like bein' my own man," he said, his voice strangely rough, "not workin' for others. Ben and I are different that way. He works for Nicholas and likes it. And he's married to Emily."

"Are you married?"

He shook his head. We glided over the water as darkness fell. And finally came the wavering lights from the cottages of Nansett. Zeke rowed to the pebbly shore and then got out and pulled the boat onto land. Then he lifted me in his strong sinewy arms and carried me from the shore to the street.

No one was about as it was the supper hour. I was rather relieved that we did not meet anyone because now that I was safe and secure, I was conscious of being held by a man I scarcely knew, I, a married woman.

"Where are you taking me?" I asked, a trifle uncomfortably.

"To my house. Must get somethin' hot in you and those clothes dry before we ride to Thunder House."

I did not want to offend him and so I did not object. Also it had begun to rain in earnest and I was relieved when we reached a small cottage not far from the harbor. Zeke opened the door and carried me inside, depositing me gingerly on a chair before the fireplace.

"I'll build up this fire and find you somethin' to wear. Then we'll have some food."

I was too tired to answer. The euphoric feeling of the

whiskey was gone and I was cold again. There was a throbbing in both my head and my ankle. I couldn't see much of the interior of the cottage, but at least it was dry and smelled pleasantly of woodsmoke.

When he had banked up the fire into a roaring blaze, he stood up, saying, "You can undress in the bedroom, Miranda. And I'll go over to Ben's and get somethin' of Emily's for you to weahr. Ben can ride to the house and let them know you're all right."

"Thank you, Zeke. That's thoughtful of you." I followed him into the bedroom. He lit a candle and I saw that the narrow rope bed was rumpled and untidy, and there was a film of dust on the bare wooden floor. It was a sparse room, leaving no clues as to the personality of its owner.

I felt slightly uncomfortable at being in a man's room, even though it could be said that we were bound by family ties. But I had to get off the heavy damp gown and layers of petticoats. After I had done so, I took a blanket from Zeke's bed and wrapped it around me. The harsh wool pricked my skin but at least I was warm.

After a short time had passed, I heard Zeke return and moved to the bedroom door. "I brought you a gown of Emily's and a shawl. I'll hand them to you if you open the door."

I opened the door a little and slipped a bare arm through to take the bundle he held out. "Thank you, Zeke."

I closed the door and quickly put on the gown. Emily had also included a pair of stockings; I pulled them on and buttoned one of my boots, leaving the other one loose about my sore foot. My hair was in a wild disordered state but I had no comb to untangle the curls which spilled in riotous abandon over my shoulders.

Zeke stood beside a tavern table in the keeping room. He had filled two mugs with fresh coffee and set out two pewter plates with slices of bread and cheese.

"Mmmmm. That looks wonderful and the coffee smells delicious."

He looked down, his voice gruff. "I know it's not what you're used to, livin' up at the house."

"Nothing could look better to me just now," I told him earnestly. "Let's eat, shall we?"

Slowly his face creased into a smile. "So eat."

The coffee was strong and good and there was cream with it. It revived me completely as did the bread and cheese. I ate heartily. Zeke did not eat much but sat there watching me and drinking his mug of coffee he had laced with whiskey from the flask.

"You wahrm enough?" he asked once.

"Oh, yes. I'm feeling much much better. I'll never be able to thank you enough for coming along and rescuing me. I'm afraid to think what might have happened to me if you'd not come along."

He frowned into his mug. "Your husband should take better care of you, like I said."

"It was my own fault. He did tell me about the causeway flooding so quickly but I didn't really believe it could happen as quickly as it did. When I walked over to Seal Island, I thought I had plenty of time. I didn't imagine that in an hour or so it would be covered—and already so deep."

"It's tricky, that's a fact," he said grudgingly. He seemed to want to blame Nicholas for my carelessness, which puzzled me.

"Do you know Nicholas well?" I asked timidly.

He gave the slightest snort. "I guess you could say I do. I know him better than most folks round here."

"Oh, how silly of me. Of course you must have been friends all your lives like he and Ben have been."

His pale blue eyes penetrated mine. There was something in his expression, in his face I did not understand. "Nicholas and me 've never been friends."

"Oh," I said, flushing. "Well, I understood from Emily that Ben and he . . . and I just assumed . . ." I was making matters worse as usual.

"Ben and me are different in a lot of ways, like I said. One of the ways is how we feel about *Captain* Nicholas.

251

But Ben wasn't with us in the Arctic, Ben didn't see how bloody boneheaded Nicholas was."

"You were on the *Eagle* with Nicholas—when the ship was trapped in the ice?"

He set down his mug sharply, a muscle working in his jaw. "I was."

"But then you know how hard Nicholas tried to keep the crew steady. You know what a terrible time it was—and how Nicholas still feels he's to blame."

"It's damn right he should blame himself. It was no thanks to him we didn't all die or go mad up there like the others did. If he hadn't been so lily-livered some of the others might've been saved too."

I stared at him in consternation. "What do you mean, Zeke?"

His voice was low but every word was flinty. "That bastard wouldn't give the ohrder to let the ship break up the ice herself. It's been done before, I told him. Men were freezin' to death, crazy with pain and fear. And the way the sun glared on the ice. But he wouldn't give the ohrder, the filthy cowahrd. No matter what a few of us said. He wouldn't drive the ship into the ice. It was his fault those men died; we'd all 've died if the ice didn't shift and cut us adrift the way it finally did. If it hadn't we'd all be dead and Nicholas'd be in hell for murder."

"But I thought . . . that ramming the ice like that would have broken up the ship."

"That's what he said, that's what he told *you*. But some of us know different. And we tried to take matters into our own hands."

His words triggered a recent memory. "Emily told me that there was an attempted mutiny," I said slowly. "Were you involved in that, Zeke, a criminal offense to wrest command from a ship's captain?"

"When the captain's a lazy stupid bounder risking the lives of thirty men, they've got the right to try and save themselves! But some of the poor devils defended him, challenged us. They couldn't see him for what he was, the bloody fools."

"Surely he's paid for his part in that disaster, Zeke. He's suffered agonizingly. He still is."

"And he ought to keep doin' that 'til his dyin' day, Miranda."

"You shouldn't talk that way to me, Zeke. He is my husband," I said coldly.

He waved my words away impatiently. "Oh, I've heard about the two of you, about how you wed when you hardly knew each other. Everybody knows that. How could you know what sohrt he is, the sohrt too soft to give an ohrder to save men's lives?"

"Nicholas might be many things, Zeke, but there's one thing I'm positive about. He is no coward." My voice was firm.

He started to make a sharp retort but instead he stopped, his face softening as he looked at mine. "Well, youh're loyal. Nicholas has the devil's own luck, I'll say that for him. And now I've offended you and you'll likely never speak to me again."

I shook my head. "How could I? You took me off Seal Island and brought me here to get warm and dry. And gave me supper. I'll never disregard you."

"Nicholas won't like it," he said bluntly.

"I'm sorry that there is such bad feeling between you but you have been very kind to me."

"I guess weh're related in a way."

"Well . . ." I did not think that anyone could claim that because his brother had married my husband's sister we were in any way kin to one another. But I did not say so. I just smiled.

"Perhaps you should take me to Thunder House now," I said diffidently. "They will surely all be wondering—"

But I did not finish what I had begun to say. A loud persistent pounding at the door interrupted me. Zeke rose, his jaw clenched, to answer it. I suppose we both knew instantly who it was. I had a sudden sick feeling at the pit of my stomach.

But before Zeke had crossed the room, the door was flung open and Nicholas came in. His hair was flattened to his head in shiny locks, his black cloak was dripping wet. His fierce gaze took in everything: Zeke's hard defiant expression, my face, flushed and startled, the remains of food on the table, my clothes drying on the floor by the fire.

"Well, what a cozy little domestic scene this is," he said silkily. "Perhaps I shouldn't be interrupting."

"Zeke was just going to take me home, Nicholas," I said nervously, rising from the table and gripping its edge. I actually felt guilty even though I knew there was no reason.

"After first plying you with whiskey and taking off your clothes, I suppose? Or do I have that order wrong?"

I went scarlet with humiliation. From a distance I heard Zeke's voice.

"She was cold and wet, you damn fool. Likely she'll be sick from this day." Zeke's frame, tall as Nicholas's but not as broad, was stiff with contempt.

Ignoring Zeke, Nicholas strode over to me, saying furiously, "What the hell are you doing here, Miranda? Why did you come here instead of going directly back to Thunder House?"

I just stared at him, speechless, wincing at his expression and harsh manner.

"Didn't Ben tell you, Nicholas?" asked Zeke insolently. "I found her stranded on Seal Island. She was there for hours. You should take better care of your wife."

"I don't need you to tell me my duty, damn you!"

"Is that a fact? I was thinkin' you needed someone to. Because it looks like you take no more care of your wife here than you did of your ship—"

He got no further. Nicholas had lunged across and struck him on the jaw with a smashing blow. "No, Nicholas!" I cried too late. Zeke fell back over a chair onto the floor. Then he slowly sat up, his face twisted with loathing. His lip had been cut; I saw the blood trickle down his chin before he wiped it away. "I should 've killed you then," he said.

"Nicholas, no more!" I shouted, hurrying over to him

254

and clutching his arm. "That's enough. Zeke was being kind to me. He may even have saved my life; he was checking his traps and heard me screaming. If he hadn't I—"

Nicholas turned his black-browed scowling gaze on me. "Didn't I warn you about Seal Island, you foolish girl? Didn't I tell you about that bloody causeway and how quickly it floods?"

Flinching, I let go of his arm and stepped back a pace. Zeke got to his feet, rubbing his already darkening jaw. "She'd hurt her ankle. She couldn't make it back, don't you understand? And I figured she needed a change of clothes and somethin' to eat quick."

"And you supplied the change of clothing?" asked my husband sarcastically.

"Emily did, Nicholas," I said. "You have no cause to reproach Zeke for his behavior toward me. No cause and no right to reproach either of us."

"If you knew anything at all about this man, Miranda, you'd agree I have plenty of cause."

"Face it, Nicholas, she could have died out there and you none the wiser," said Zeke, sneering. "So it seems you owe me a little gratitude for returning Miranda to you. That sticks in your craw, doesn't it?"

"She's Mrs. Blaize to you!" Nicholas snapped viciously, the scar white in his cheek. "Don't you dare call her anything else!" And to me he flung, "Get your clothes, Miranda. We're getting out of here."

"Thank you, Zeke," I said brokenly. He gave a short nod, his eyes averted, his fists clenched.

Retrieving my damp things, I bundled them into my cloak. Nicholas took the bundle from my trembling grasp and impatiently swung me off my feet, carrying me through the open door of the cottage. Tossing me on the horse, he climbed up behind me and then slapped the animal on its flank. We set off galloping into the dark rainy night. Nicholas's arm was like a pincer around my waist; he gripped me to him cruelly so that my breathing was short and my heart thudded unnaturally.

When we neared the stone wall which marked the beginning of his estate, he pulled the horse roughly to a stop. "I want it understood you are to have nothing to do with Zeke Somes, Miranda. Is that clear?" His voice was stony.

Suddenly it was my turn to be angry and I was shocked at the words which tumbled from my mouth. "How could you, Nicholas? How could you treat him like that after he rescued me, after he rowed me all the way back to Nansett! He took care of me—"

"Damn his hide for that!" he cut in brutally.

"I suppose you would rather he had left me there to—that he had not come along at all. That would have been preferable to you than having to be grateful to Zeke. You probably wish I was still on that island!" My voice rose shrilly.

"Don't be a little fool! Of course I'm relieved you're safe! If you only knew—but it would have to be that blackguard!"

"You didn't come looking for me. Thank heaven someone did."

At that he flung himself off the horse and pulled me roughly down, his hands gripping my shoulders in a painful steely hold. "Where the hell do you think I've been? I've been searching for you for hours, my girl! But I never dreamed you'd be so foolish as to cross over to Seal Island after I'd warned you particularly against it!"

"You should know by now I do all sorts of foolish things, Nicholas! And I suppose it's my fault I turned my ankle, too."

"You should have taken better care. Yesterday you were lost in the woods—today you were stranded on the island in the mist—what new horrors will you think up for tomorrow?"

"I'm sure something will occur to me," I said spitefully.

"And you'll meet your death likely as not!"

"Not this time, thanks to Zeke."

"Shut up!" he said savagely. "I don't want to hear his name again! He's a sullen moody bastard who never

256

learned to take orders and he nearly cost the loss of even more lives on the *Eagle*. It was your Zeke who led the attempted mutiny, Miranda, it was your Zeke who tried to force me to drive the ship into the ice! He was as mad as some of the others — only a madman would insist on doing such a crazy thing — it was sheer suicide! He tried to kill me that day in the stateroom but he only succeeded in cutting my face. I'd been warned, you see, and so I was prepared for him. He'd talked his nonsense to some of the others until they believed him, the poor desperate fools. There was a bloody brawl and he was nearly stabbed himself. I managed to stop those that would have killed him. He hates me even more because he knows he owes his life to me. So now you owe yours to him — I owe him for saving you! God, how damned ironic! But no matter how he treated you today, you are to have nothing further to do with him. He's not to be trusted. That was obvious from the pleasant domestic scene I interrupted."

"What do you mean? He merely prepared some food and coffee. Anyone would have done the same in the circumstances."

Nicholas took my chin in his hand. "Do you want to know why he's not to be trusted, Miranda? Do I have to spell it out for you? Your usually touching naiveté is wearing rather thin just now. What do you think Captain Sears wanted from you? When I think of you there in Zeke Somes's cottage, I could — ! But you're my wife, my girl! And as my wife, I'm ordering you to steer clear of him!"

My defiance now thoroughly quelled, I did not protest again. Nor did I struggle when his mouth came down hard and insistent on mine and his hand cupped my breast painfully. He kissed me as though he hated me, which he most likely did, and I was numb, immobile in his grasp.

"Never forget for a moment that you belong to me, Miranda," he said harshly. "Perhaps I was a fool to marry you, to bring you here, but it's done. And there's no undoing it, no matter what you or I may wish. 'Til death do us part,' just remember that."

We rode home in silence. I was too exhausted, too

shaken to do more than lean back against Nicholas, hardly caring if I swayed in the saddle and fell off the horse. My ankle hurt a great deal and I longed for my soft bed. When we reached the house, Nicholas lifted me off the horse and carried me inside.

Lavinia and Sarah met us at the foot of the stairs. "So there you are, Miranda," said Lavinia severely. "Much ado about nothing, as I told you, Nicholas. When Ben rode over to tell us you were at his brother's cottage, Nicholas had just come in from combing the shoreline to the lighthouse, and Amos and Seth had been scouring the woods with torches. Though they could see but little in this weather. Now you see what can happen when you wander off the way you've been doing."

"I'm sorry to have caused so much trouble," I said weakly.

"Sarah, send Morwenna up with some bandages," said Nicholas over his shoulder as we went up the stairs. In my room he set me down on the bed. I was shivering and reached out to the fire as if I could never be warm enough.

After shrugging off his wet cloak, he went over to the armoire and rummaged through some drawers until he had found a shawl, which he draped over my shoulders. Clutching it around me, I gave a start when he took hold of my foot.

"I need to get your stocking off, Miranda, to look at your ankle," he said.

I let him lift up my gown and unroll my stocking. Holding my swollen ankle, he examined it while sitting beside me on the bed. "Where is that girl?" he asked irritably. "This should have been wrapped up hours ago, but Somes can thank his lucky stars that he didn't extend his — kindness — to pulling up your skirts!"

"Nicholas, you're hurting me," I protested, wincing, trying to pull my foot away.

He released me. "I was just assuring myself that no bones were broken. But I think you'll be fine in a few days. For the present you must remain in the house and use your ankle as little as possible."

I would miss my next piano lesson, I thought glumly. "Could someone take a message to Katherine MacLeod to tell her I won't be there in the morning? She was to give me a piano lesson."

"Certainly, though it's likely by tomorrow she will have heard all about it and will draw her own conclusions. In Nansett news travels quickly."

Morwenna came in at that moment crying, "Thank the Lord you be safely back, ma'am. I be worried to death that you'd not return!"

Nicholas's brows drew together. "That she'd not return? What foolishness is that? Give me those things and then leave us." I gave her a feeble smile and she bobbed a curtsy before quitting the room.

He bound my foot deftly with a long bandage and secured it. "There. How does that feel?"

"Better," I admitted. "It doesn't throb nearly as much. Thank you."

He continued to hold my bare leg in his hands. I tried to move it out of his lap but he would not free it. I yawned suggestfully, my hand over my mouth, hoping he would take the hint and leave me to go to bed. But he did not.

"You led me quite a chase this evening, my girl," he said.

"I'm not a child, Nicholas. I don't like it when you talk to me as one and treat me like one. The way you call me 'my girl' as though I were still in my teens."

His lips quirked. "And in reality you are much older, of course. Twenty, I think you said?"

I frowned. "You know what I mean. The way you treat me — the way you spoke to me in front of Zeke. It was . . . humiliating."

His eyebrows rose. "Well, this is a new development. Pray continue."

"Don't make fun of me, Nicholas. I'm only trying to say . . . that is, I don't appreciate you scolding me, bullying me whether in front of people or when we are alone. I daresay I do seem to you to be little more than a child but I assure you —"

259

"On the contrary, I don't think of you as a child at all. It would be a great deal easier if I did." There was a warm caressing note to his voice which instantly set my heart fluttering. I looked away from him, nervously pushing my tangled curls behind my ears. He went on, "In fact, I thought it was you who have been trying to hide behind your innocence, your inexperience."

"I don't know what you're talking about," I said in muffled tones, the color rising in my face. "And now, if you'd please excuse me, I'm tired. I'd like to go to bed."

"How refreshing to hear you say that. I'd very much like to go to bed, too. But in order to do that, you'll have to take off Emily's gown, won't you?" His gaze flickered over me and dropped to my bare leg. Again I tried to inch away but he began to slide his hands over my skin, up my leg.

"Don't, Nicholas," I said, conscious that my heart was racing inside my breast and my skin tingled from his touch.

"And why not?" he asked, still with the smile playing about the corners of his mouth. But there was a look in his eyes now that I could not mistake—an intensity, a smoldering.

Leaning toward me he slowly drew me to him. I shut my eyes and felt him kiss me lightly, his tongue a soft wet caress, his lips moving tenderly, excitingly over mine until I was shivering. His mouth continued its tantalizing onslaught on mine and I was conscious of a trembling fire brewing inside me, a honeyed intoxication seeping through my body.

I turned my head, wanting to feel his tongue on my neck and earlobe, shuddering when it tickled my skin. Gathering my hair in his hands, he pulled my mouth to his again. I began a tentative exploration of his mouth and he bruised my lips with the unbridled force of his kisses.

Oh, Nicholas, I love you, I thought but did not say it aloud. He began to undo the buttons at the back of my gown. Slowly he drew the sleeves down my arms. When the gown hung about my waist, his feverish gaze moved over my bare shoulders to where my breasts rose from

260

under the lacy trim of my camisole. He reached out a finger and traced a line from the pulse beating at my throat down to the crevice between my breasts. I could feel my face warm with color and yet I did not want him to stop.

Lifting me slightly, he urged the gown over my thighs until I was free of it and it lay discarded on the floor. "Why, Miranda, where are your petticoats?" he asked, his words slurred but his voice still with its mocking note. He had shrugged aside his shirt and was taking off his trousers.

"Uh . . . well, they were soaked so I . . . I took them off before . . ." I held my breath, afraid he would become angry again.

"Well, that makes things a little easier, doesn't it? Not as many layers." He began to unlace the satin ribbon of my camisole until it gaped open. I turned my flushed countenance away from the longing reflected in his eyes.

"Are you afraid of me, Miranda?" he asked softly, his fingers tweaking one long curl.

"N—no . . . I don't know," I said haltingly. "I don't understand you."

"Don't try to understand, just give yourself to me," he said hoarsely in my ear, his breathing quick and ragged. And then he took my yielding body in his arms and bent down to kiss my breasts, his tongue paving a throbbing trail from one peak to the other. The feel of his warm mouth inflamed me and I grasped him round the neck, my fingers in his thick dark hair. And then he was pushing me back against the pillow and lowering his hard body on top of my pliant one which nonetheless was crying out with an unfamiliar bold urgency, demanding to be placated, its burning to be quenched.

"You're so beautiful, Miranda," he murmured, his voice scarcely recognizable, "I don't want to hurt you again."

"You won't, Nicholas," I whispered but I could not help giving a slight gasp when he entered me, though not from pain.

Immediately he paused, his face buried in my hair where

261

it spilled across the pillow, but I pressed my fingers into his shoulderblades. "Don't stop now," I breathed, not caring what I said, my desire as avidly potent as his.

He moved inside me, gently at first, but when I lifted my hips to his, he began to drive into me with an increasing force he could restrain no longer. His breath was hot on my cheek and I felt the thunder in his heart as he took fierce possession of me. And soon he was groaning again and again and I was gasping and we were clutching one another in a desperate gratification so intense, so consuming that it was as though our souls melded and became one. I knew a total ecstasy, a triumphant joy unlike any I had ever experienced. And then he kissed my warm cheeks, my eyelids, my sighing mouth, his heartbeat slackening to a placid thudding, his powerful body tamed, subdued in my arms.

When I awoke the next morning, the sun was streaming in and I was disappointed to see that I was alone in the bed. Why had Nicholas not woken me when he had risen? Last night's memories were fresh in my mind and I longed to be cradled in his reassuring hold. But he was not in my room nor in his. I wished wholeheartedly that he had not left me to wake and breakfast alone. It made me wonder if perhaps I had misinterpreted the amorous passion he had displayed.

At the window I watched the sun glittering on the blue water in a silver sheen. The ocean was as still as a mountain lake and no lingering traces of fog remained to film the air. My ankle was a bit painful when I put my weight on it but not nearly as sore as I had expected. The bandaging Nicholas had done last night had relieved it a good deal.

Morwenna came in carrying a breakfast tray. "Mmmm, that looks wonderful," I said. "I could eat a horse this morning, but toast, eggs, and grilled fish will do me fine. Martha is really an excellent cook. I've been very amiss not to go to the kitchen and meet her. She probably thinks I'm very rude and I don't blame her. I don't know why the notion never occurred to me before now. Tell her, please,

Morwenna, that I'll be along later after I've dressed."

"Captain Nicholas said you're not to leave this floor, Mrs. Blaize."

"Oh, that's ridiculous. I'm not an invalid. I can walk some, see? I'll have my breakfast and then you can bring hot water for my bath, if you would. Then I'll dress and go speak to Martha and the others. It's time I properly introduced myself to them all."

She nodded and I sat down on the chair before the table where she had laid my breakfast tray. And I thought as I ate that food had never tasted so good. Then I sank into a scented softened tub of steaming water and washed my hair.

After I had dressed and combed my hair, leaving it down over my shoulders to dry, I slowly made my way down the hall. It was a bit tricky limping down the two flights of stairs but I managed to do so without too much difficulty, gripping the bannister for support. I was slightly embarrassed that I had never gone to the kitchen before. In the past two weeks of living in Thunder House I had not considered trespassing on the servants' domain, confident they would regard my presence an unwelcome intrusion. But now I did not see it that way at all. And I had also been too shy to speak to the servants in my husband's house. But now I realized that it was only proper that I establish some contact between us. I knew that the names of the maids were Jenny and Mary but I hadn't even learned which was which. I had been too self-conscious, too absorbed in myself and my own anxieites to show them any courtesy. And that was lamentable.

The two girls were there with Morwenna and there was a large older woman who wore a starched white cap on her head. "Good morning," I said. "I know you are all busy but I just wanted to come in and meet each of you personally — except for Morwenna, of course. What a wonderful room this is."

The floor was flagged stone; from the great ceiling beams hung dried herbs and flowers and bunches of garlic cloves. Copper pots of all sizes gleamed from hooks on the walls and beams; there were two brick ovens to the sides of the huge hearth, and a great pine table stood in the center of the room.

"I'm right glad you've come, Mrs. Blaize. I'm Martha Trundy," said the older woman. She held out her hand and I took it, smiling.

"Hello, Martha. I've been enjoying your cooking so that I feel as though I know you already."

She beamed. "Bless your heart, ma'am. I'm glad you like our down-east cookin'. It's poached salmon tonight, just caught by Seth, with a cream-and-dill sauce. One of the captain's favorites."

"It sounds delicious."

"This is Jenny," she told me, nodding at one of the girls. "And that's Mary. You know my husband, Amos, who tends to the horses and grounds. And there's also Seth who does the heavy work indoors and some huntin' and fishin' too. And Morwenna here. That's all of us."

"Mrs. Blaize doesn't have her own maid?"

"No, the girls here clean her rooms as they do the others in the house. Miss Thatcher's always looked after Mrs. Blaize."

"How long have you and Amos been at Thunder House, Martha?"

"We came years ago—before the girls were bohrn. We lived in Nansett and had only been married a shohrt time when Mr. Roger asked us to come and see to the house and the missus. She was a new bride then, just come from Boston, and the old cook had died."

"And when did Sarah—Miss Thatcher—come?"

"Oh, 'bout a year or so later when the missus was expectin' Nicholas. Mr. Roger thought she ought to have another woman with her here at the house."

A woman not from Nansett, I supposed. I wondered whether it had been about that time that she had rebuffed Katherine MacLeod's overtures of friendship. What a shame, I thought. Two refined cultured women living on the same small island yet never meeting as friends do. It was apparent that Katherine could never have had much in common with the other women of Nansett yet Lavinia had looked down her nose at her also, lumping all the local women together as unfit to socialize with.

Just then Sarah appeared in the doorway, her face stiff and disapproving. "Where's Mrs. Blaize's luncheon tray, Martha? You're late with it again. It is precisely three minutes past twelve."

"I'm afraid it's my fault, Sarah. I've been visiting with Martha," I said.

"As you say, Miranda."

"One of the girls'll bring it right up, Miss Thatcher," said Martha, and I was surprised to see that she was not ruffled by Sarah's brusqueness.

"Well, I know you're busy at this time of day, Martha, so I won't disturb you any longer," I told her.

"I'm right pleased you came by, ma'am, and I hope you'll come again soon."

Going up to my room, I put my foot up while I sat on one of the wing chairs. I was rather bored and wondered what I should do to pass the time. I had never done embroidery or needlework the way other ladies in my position did. I was certain that Julia had embroidered exquisitely — she had been so accomplished in all feminine pursuits.

I pictured her sitting on the rose-and-green chintz-covered sofa in her sitting room, the afternoon sun shining through the tall windows and kindling the birch leaves at the edge of the forest. She would have sat serenely at her stitchery, confident in her beauty, in her worth, looking forward to the day when she would make her debut in Boston society.

And yet that day had never come, despite her beauty, despite her worth, despite her accomplishments. Instead she had been lost. What a swift abrupt end to such a promising life, I thought. If indeed she had drowned the way everyone assumed. There was something ominous in the fact that her body had never been recovered, had never washed ashore. In spite of oneself it made one wonder about what had actually happened on the day of her disappearance.

Thinking of the sitting room had given me an idea. I could go down there and take one of the books from the shelves to read. I would not stay in the room but there could be no harm in my borrowing a book. By now Lavinia had doubtless finished her lunch and would be resting. Perhaps she was already asleep. No one would be the wiser if I stole down that closed corridor and made my way to the sitting room at the end of the hall.

I limped downstairs, pausing on the second-story landing next to the mural depicting the South Sea Island. There were no sounds, not even the low murmur of voices coming from Sarah's and Lavinia's rooms.

I was passing the door to Julia's bedroom when I had the impulse to open it, to look inside just briefly. Glancing down the corridor, I was reassured that the doors were still closed the way I had left them. It would not do to have left them open, announcing my presence in this hushed, almost-sacred domain.

Julia's room was exactly as I had seen it before. It was obvious the maids had been in there to clean this morning because the casement windows had been opened slightly to let in the fresh air. The sheer curtains under the damask ones blew gently in the breeze, lifting and billowing toward me like ghostly arms. I went over to the bed, looking down at the silk and lace pillows, at the lace-and-linen coverlet, at the airy bed curtains tied back with pink ribbons. How ethereal the whole effect was, as though Julia hadn't been a flesh-and blood girl at all but some fragile fairylike creature deigning to reside in Thunder House.

Her portrait drew me and I gazed upon her delicate features, the winsome smile about her mouth, the flush of roses in her cheeks, the soft lights in her light brown hair. But surely hair of that color deserved to be called deep golden and not light brown at all.

On the mantel were two Sevres candlesticks glazed in bright hues and a Dresden shepherdess with white complexion, rosebud mouth, and blond ringlets peeping out coyly from under her bonnet. What a pretty thing, I thought, enchanted. Of course Julia would have had such a charming piece of porcelain to enhance her room. And I took it down from the mantle to closer examine it.

But it slipped from my fingers and crashed to the floor by the hearth where there was no carpet to protect it or muffle its fall. The smashing tinkling sound seemed to go on forever and I stared hopelessly down at the broken remains of the little shepherdess, dread and dismay seeping through me like some poison liquid I had swallowed.

I had not closed the door of the room and now I wondered if anyone could have heard the crash. But surely not. The doors were closed to the landing. Swiftly I bent down and began to pick up the small pieces. One was a section of her lovely little face—her rosebud mouth—and I looked at it with shame. I could not glance up at the portrait lest I discern some sign of reproach on Julia's painted features. Instead I gathered up the pieces and stood up, wondering what to do with them.

Why had I come in here? I had no right to disturb the sanctity of this room, the memorial to a graceful accomplished girl so unlike myself. I had proven that by carelessly dropping the Dresden shepherdess. I shouldn't be in here handling these lovely things, gawking at Julia's belongings like some wistful impressionable child. I had to leave immediately.

But to my horror I heard the unmistakable sound of the doors opening in the corridor; I heard footsteps treading softly down the hall. Quickly I put my hands behind me, still clutching the jagged shards of porcelain. The footsteps neared the room where I stood and I watched, breathless, stricken, as Sarah came into view.

"So it's you," she said coldly. "I thought it might be. What was that noise I heard?"

"N—noise? I . . . I don't know . . . what you mean," I stammered, reddening.

"Yes, Miranda. I was walking through the landing when I distinctly heard a crash of some sort, even though the doors were closed. This room isn't that far down the hall, you know. What did you do? What did you break?"

"I . . . I . . ."

"What are you hiding behind your back?" She strode over to me and I stepped back, squeezing the broken pieces as though to shield them from her sight.

She smiled slightly, her eyes bearing into mine, and then reached around me, seizing one of my wrists.

"You've cut your hand, Miranda," she said.

I looked down, startled and dismayed to see blood dripping from my palm. There was a long gash in the ball of my hand; I had not felt the sharp edge of the china pierce my skin. "It's nothing," I said faintly, and pressed at it with my other wrist.

Carefully she took the pieces of the shepherdess from my numb grasp and set them down on the mantel. "You know you have no right to be here. What were you doing? What made you come in?"

"I . . . I heard a noise—I thought one of the servants—"

"You heard nothing. If you had heard someone on this corridor, you wouldn't have come. It was curiosity which brought you here, wasn't it? Or the desire to imagine yourself to be someone you can never be, in a room that is so beautiful you can scarcely take it in. Or perhaps you were planning a new torment for Lavinia."

"No, Sarah . . ."

"That was one of her favorite things, that shepherdess. She had had it since she was five years old. Even as a child she knew to be careful with things, to take care of them. She wasn't the sort of child who picked up things with a vulgar curiosity and then ruined them. And you've broken it with one careless sweep of your hand, haven't you? You who have never had lovely things, who have no idea how to look after them, to cherish them. Instead you come in here and you begin to destroy."

"No . . . I didn't mean to . . . I'm sorry . . . I know I shouldn't have touched it."

Her lip curled ever so slightly. "Nicholas should never have married you; he should never have brought you here. Did you have any idea of what it would be like coming to this house and being married to a man like Nicholas,

268

brought up in the finest surroundings with the best of everything?"

"It—all of this—it hasn't made him happy. It hasn't kept him from suffering—it isn't as though he's been loved . . ."

"What do you know of happiness? What do you know of love? You married Nicholas to escape whatever wretched life you had—God knows why a man as proud as he would marry someone like you. And you're wrong when you say he hasn't had love. His father spoiled him, ruining him by not curbing his son's temper and rashness. His sister Emily has always worshipped the ground he's walked on. And he could have had Heather MacLeod for the asking—we all knew that. At least she's got poise, some breeding."

I felt the color drain from my face. Her smile was sardonic.

"Oh, didn't you know about Heather MacLeod? Didn't you know Nicholas was once in love with her and she with him? Didn't he tell you everyone assumed they would get married after he returned from the Arctic?"

My lips were cracked, my mouth parched. "No . . . he didn't tell me."

"That's why we were so shocked when he brought you here. We at least had been prepared for him to marry Heather. She used to come to dinner here, did you know that? Even though Lavinia had never associated with her mother, even Lavinia admitted the girl had dignity, bearing, grace."

"What happened between them?" I asked, and my voice sounded shrill, unnatural.

Sarah shrugged. "Oh, Nicholas came back from his last Arctic expedition and wouldn't have anything to do with anyone. At first he shut himself up in his room and refused to see any of us, even Heather. We didn't expect that to last forever, though, and it didn't. It was just a matter of time before he began supervising work at the shipyard and mill and repairing the *Eagle*. Emily married Ben and we assumed Nicholas would eventually regain his

269

peace of mind and go back to Heather. But instead he went to New Bedford and returned with you. Heather we could have understood. They had known each other all their lives and seemed so suited. How could a man like Nicholas not be drawn to Heather MacLeod? None of the men in Nansett have ever been able to keep their eyes off her for years now. But she never encouraged any of them. It was Nicholas. Everyone assumed they would marry someday when Nicholas stopped his gallivanting and was ready to settle down. She must resent you terribly, Miranda. I wonder if now Nicholas is not already regretting that he so impulsively chose you instead of her. We've watched you try to be the lady Laviana is, the lady Julia was, and yes, even the lady that Heather is despite her being penniless. They belong in a house such as this and you never will."

"Emily chose to leave this house," I said, biting my lip.

"Yes, and threw herself away on a poor lobsterman! Oh, I don't care what exalted title or position Nicholas has given him! He's still nothing but a simple fisherman, which is all he'll ever be. He's as out of place in this house as you are!"

"I . . . I'm not going to listen to any more, Sarah." I stumbled across the room but her voice followed me.

"Just remember this, Miranda. Nicholas became a changed man after his Arctic disaster. But he's beginning to come out of that, out of the self-pity and guilt which he's wallowed in for the past year. And one day he is going to turn to you and wonder whatever possessed him to take you for his wife. And then your troubles will have just begun. You will never be mistress of Thunder House, not in any sense of the word."

Chapter Twelve

I left Sarah as quickly as I was able, limping away to put as much distance from her gloating contemptuous face as I could. I was haunted by the memory of the first time I had laid eyes on Heather MacLeod and thought her so voluptuous, so alluring. And there had been something I had vaguely sensed in Nicholas's manner toward her. I now knew the reason for the slight restraint he had shown and thought he had hid his feelings rather well. For him to come face to face with his former love, a love he had spurned for whatever reason, while he was with his new bride must have been disconcerting in the extreme.

She had not displayed any unease; there had not been the least amount of reproach in the way she had regarded him. I wondered now why that was. Something, though, made hideous sense to me. When Nicholas had returned from his last Arctic voyage a year ago, he had rejected consolation from everyone—Heather included. He had not been able to face work at the shipyard; he had not felt like resuming his romance with Heather. He must have cut off their relationship because in that state he had not been able to look to the future, to plan ahead. He could do nothing but dwell on the Arctic disaster, for which he held himself accountable.

I wondered what Heather's reaction had been to his rebuff. Had she thought to leave him alone for a time, hoping he would return to her after he had come to grips with the past? Had she been patiently biding her time, assured that his feelings for her would rekindle once the shock of the tragedy had worn off?

But this had not been the case. After he began to emerge from his depression and remorse, he had sailed to New Bedford to sell the *Eagle*. And he had met and married me instead. What on earth could have motivated such an extreme action on his part when Heather had been waiting in the wings?

I knew he had taken pity on me. He had been carried away by a protective instinct on the night Captain Sears had come to my bedroom. For months he had been consumed by guilt for those lives lost in the Arctic. He had doubtless been punishing himself when he had pushed Heather away, when he had shirked any happiness which might have been his. He had suffered along with all those others who had suffered. He had not allowed himself to forget the disaster, to put it behind him. But though the suffering of those crewmen had been of short duration, his was prolonged and had endured for months. It was still going on.

He had filled his room with morbid reminders of a terrible occurrence. He had been vulnerable, a prey to his emotions. And for a man like Nicholas that must have been a new experience. When I had seen him in the Bethel, he had been so weighed down with self-blame that he had scarcely known what he was doing. He had reached out to me for comfort and then he had prevented Captain Sears from ravishing me. Had he done that because he had seen a right he might do by me when there had been little he could do for his wretched crew? Had some part of him urged him to spare me Captain Sears's advances because that at least was something he might do, exercise a control over? Had he rescued me as he had been unable to rescue the nineteen men who had sailed with him and died? Had my fear and helplessness sparked a memory in his mind, struck a chord which then resulted in his saving me from Captain Sears? I thought I could see that; I thought that was what must have happened.

And then the next day, still spurred on by his anger and

his shame, had he proposed marriage perhaps hoping that in marrying and protecting me he might find some sort of peace, that he might be vindicated because he had come to the aid of a poor defenseless young woman? I could see it all so clearly now. He would help me as he had not been able to help those poor men whose sanity and reason had frozen bit by bit in the Arctic, pieces of their minds dropping off like icicles. He would perform a good deed by giving me his name and possessions; he would be purged, reprieved. He had been desperate to atone for his arrogance, his belief that nothing could blemish his luck and shrewdness, and in my forlorn situation he had seen a way to do this.

But this had not happened. He had not found peace. He was still tormented by dark thoughts; he still prowled Thunder Island at night, a prey to guilt and blame. Did he, had be begun to regret his hasty decision of marrying me?

Even in his lovemaking of last night, which I had interpreted as quite another thing in my naiveté—even in that he had just been seeking some sort of temporary comfort, his anguish burning itself out briefly. But he did not love me; he had never professed to love me. Last night he had made love to me, his kisses and the feel of him stirring feelings in me which could not be denied as I had stirred feelings in him. Yet it was because he was a man and I was a woman. It was not as though I were in any way special to him. I was his wife and it was my duty to submit to his needs. Love had no place in our uneasy union. What I had seen as genuine caring was no more than his being a victim of his own lust and the availability of a woman. Nicholas had gazed at me, desired me, and then taken me, but his heart had not been involved. And I wondered whether his lovemaking had had its roots in Zeke Somes's rescuing me from Seal Island. He had bitterly resented Zeke's part in that. Perhaps by possessing me last night he had been merely displaying his claim over me, asserting that only he had rights to me after what he had deemed Zeke's insolent interference. I belonged to him and no one else, and I was not to forget that.

Yet how could I forget it? I could not forget it even if I wanted to. For I loved my husband, loved him with an aching heart which longed to have my deepest yearnings reciprocated, with a heart which longed to take over his hurt and pain to myself. But this I could not do. I was as helpless to help him as he had been to sail out of the ice fields with his ship and crew intact, unscathed. He did not want my help; he turned to me only for brief respites when the needs of his body made themselves undeniable. But he was no closer to loving me than he had been when we had first set eyes on each other in the chapel for mariners. Something in me had appealed to him, had aroused his protective instincts but that was all. And I knew that I had not proven to be the redeeming angel he had hoped for. How could I release him from the black world he inhabited, enclosed on all sides by walls of brick — the bricks molded from shame and sealed with penitence? How could I strive to tear down those bricks? I might strike at them, shaving off films of red dust, but I would never be able to make any real dent or impression in that wall. Never would I be able to sever those bricks.

So where did that leave us? Heather continued to be there waiting in the wings. Did she still hope or even assume that Nicholas would return to her? Had his love for her frozen in the Arctic tragedy, was there a chance of it surging forth again? Would they resume their former relationship? Would he fall in love with her again and deplore his marriage to me?

I could only sit and wait for the future to happen, to learn whether or not I would lose my new husband. But if one had never gained, could one actually lose? Nicholas had never been mine. Out of pity he had married a helpless pitiful creature — a creature I now despised though from whom I could not separate.

When Nicholas returned from the shipyard that evening, he looked into my room as I supposed he would. I was esconsed before the fire, my foot raised on a stool, attired already in my dressing gown. Before he could say any-

274

thing, I told him my foot was paining me rather badly and I would not go down to dinner.

"I'm sorry to hear that, Miranda," he said. "I'll stay and keep you company."

"No, Nicholas. I'd rather you didn't. I mean, it's not necessary. Morwenna is perfectly capable of looking after me." On top of all the things which had been made clear to me today I also could not forget that he had seen fit to leave my bed without waking me this morning. That in itself seemed a sign that what had occurred between us was meant for the night, for dreams, and would not carry over to the light of day, to reality.

I was not watching him; I was staring at one of the Delft tiles on the hearth as though there was some secretive significance to be found in it.

"As you wish," came his voice after a very long pause, and I heard the door close behind him.

The next day my ankle was back to normal and so I decided to walk to Nansett to practice on the church piano. My hand where I had cut it yesterday was healing already; it would not hamper my playing. I had missed a lesson already and had not practiced since that horrible night when Lavinia had come upon me in Julia's sitting room. But Katherine's encouragement had bolstered my resolution to become a better player and it was time I began practicing again. I had not made a success of governessing, nor of being the proper wife for Nicholas. I was determined to succeed at something if only to be an adequate musician, deriving a certain security in the discipline required and a certain solace in the beauty of music.

Outside, the forest blazed with glorious colors. The maples glowed from burgundy to scarlet, coral edged with gold; the oaks burnished mahogany; the birches fraily yellow. The trees were a magnificent sight clad in their autumn leaves; the air was fresh and brisk but not cold. It was October.

It was in the stretch of woods on the other side of Blackett's Glade before the path began to incline steeply up the slope of Bald Mountain that I spied them. The man

275

was tall and broad with black hair; the woman's corn-silk hair fell over her shoulders like a cloak of gold. She was nearly as tall as he. I halted in my tracks peering through the trees at them, identifying them instantly as Nicholas and Heather. They were not touching but I thought there was a familiar intimacy in the way they stood together. Her head was bent as if she was deeply troubled by something. I was not close enough to hear what they were saying and I had no wish to go closer. It would be terrible if they heard a sudden movement and turned to see me there. They must not see me; I could think of nothing but that I should avoid their gazes at all costs.

Leaning back a little behind a tree trunk, I watched them. I wondered what they were talking about, if they were talking about me. I thought I could imagine Nicholas saying, "I don't know why on earth I married her, Heather. It was a momentary madness, I swear to you. Don't let her come between us." And Heather, looking into his eyes with her fascinating violet-blue ones, saying, "We won't allow her to come between us. She is nothing to us. Our love is stronger than any man-made alliance."

I held my breath, my fingers clutching the hard rough surface of the tree, waiting for him to bend a little to kiss her, but he did not. Instead he went off in one direction, leaving her to follow the path up the mountain.

My heart hammering, I did not move for quite a while. I wanted both of them to have enough time to get where they were going, to be as far away as possible before I continued on my way. I was tempted to slink back to Thunder House, to nurse my wounds in the sheltered privacy of my room, but I did not give in to the temptation.

Finally I let go the tree trunk which I had been gripping all the while and continued the trek to Nansett. In a haze I made my way to the church and pulled open the heavy wooden door by its iron ring and went inside. I stood in the vestibule, trying to adjust to the gloom. The doors to the sanctuary were closed but I opened them, relieved to see that it was much lighter in there, the light pouring in

276

the arched pointed windows.

The piano was in the front to the left of the pulpit. I walked down the aisle. It was very quiet and cool in the church but I thought I could hear my heart pounding and feel drops of sweat on my brow. Sitting down on the piano stool, I opened the instrument and set the music I had brought in front of me. I began to play and the notes sounded harsh in my ears. Today my playing was brisk, aggressive. My eyes rarely left the music and I played for a long while. When I finally got up to leave, I scarcely remembered what I had played. I had no idea if I had played well or with many mistakes. It did not matter. I had played because the piano was there, because my fingers were trained to find the notes my eyes read.

When I left the church, it was late in the afternoon and all feeling, all energy had been drained from me. I went slowly through the woods, not caring this time if I should come upon Nicholas and Heather and they see me.

Heavily I went up the two flights of stairs to my room. When I opened the door, I was startled to see many boxes piled on the floor and on the bed. Morwenna was opening one of them with a pair of scissors.

"What's all this?" I asked.

She jumped up. "Oh, ma'am! They're all yourn! Your new clothes. They've come on the ship today—such lovely, lovely things!"

Together we went through the boxes. There were numerous gowns of gorgeous fabrics and hues with many pairs of slippers of soft kid leather to match. There were sweet nightgowns and dressing gowns with ruffles or with Juliet sleeves; camisoles and petticoats and pantalettes frothy with lace; warm woolen pelisses in plum, lapis blue, and cherry red, each trimmed with fur or velvet; cashmere shawls, paisley shawls, and organdy fichus. Morwenna insisted I begin trying on the different gowns and I was swept along by her enthusiasm.

"Now you be dressed proper," declared my maid with satisfaction. "The captain—he'll be ever so proud of you."

"Do you think so?" I asked wistfully, looking doubtfully

at my reflection in the mirror.

Just then the door opened to Nicholas's room and he stood there. "So your trousseau arrived on the ship. Good." He still wore his work clothes and his hair was ruffled, untidy. I thought he looked terribly handsome. "I have a surprise for you," he said.

"A surprise?" I repeated.

"Yes, we've had a dinner invitation for tonight. I thought you might enjoy eating some place other than here."

"Emily's?" I inquired eagerly. "How nice of her."

He shook his head. "No, not Emily. Katherine MacLeod has asked us to dine with her and Heather tonight."

I could not keep the dismay from my expression or my voice. "Oh. Surely it's rather short notice?"

His eyebrows rose. "I hardly thought that you would be one to cavil at that. I thought you liked Katherine. And on Thunder Island we don't hold so tightly to etiquette."

"Of course not, Nicholas. And I do like Katherine very much. It's just . . . well, it took me by surprise, that's all. I had not thought to go out again tonight."

"Oh, were you out today?" Was there a shade of unease in his voice; did the pucker in his brows become more pronounced?

"Yes, I went to the church in Nansett to practice this afternoon," I said breathlessly.

"To the church? You walked to Nansett?"

"Yes, Katherine suggested that I practice there."

He *was* frowning. "Are you telling me that your ankle was well enough to take you over a mile of rough terrain and back again, when last night it pained you so that you had to be alone?"

I opened my mouth, could think of nothing to say, and gave a poor uncomfortable attempt at a smile.

"Well, get ready. We have to ride to Nansett within the hour." His voice was hard.

"Very well, Nicholas."

I chose to wear a plum taffeta gown with full dropped sleeves that buttoned tightly at the wrists. I would wear the

278

pelisse with the fur collar and the plum satin bonnet Nicholas had bought for me in New Bedford. If nothing else, I would try and look as presentable as possible; I hoped desperately that I would not betray my chagrin at coming face to face with Heather after I had seen her in the woods with my husband.

Morwenna helped me dress and, following an illustration and instructions Miss Proctor had enclosed, arranged my hair in thick curls which hung glossy and black over my shoulders. I put on my pelisse, tied the ribbons of my bonnet, pulled on my gloves, and was ready when Nicholas came.

"You look very pretty, Miranda," he said gruffly. He hesitated and then came over to me and bent his head. And I stepped back, flushing, looking everywhere but at his face.

"Shouldn't we go?" I asked, fidgeting with the ribbons under my chin. "We mustn't be late, after all."

There was a pause before he answered coolly, "Yes, let's go."

We went downstairs and he lifted me on the horse Amos had brought round for us. Then we were off and I was reminded with a sharp pang of the dark ride we had taken in the rain when he had kissed me fiercely. But tonight it was not dark; it was twilight and the woods were filled with a smoky lavender light. And Nicholas did not attempt to kiss me.

It was dark by the time we reached Nansett and there were lighted candles in the parlor windows of the old manse. The maid showed us into the parlor, where Heather and Katherine were already seated.

"Ah, here you both are," said Katherine, rising and coming across to greet us.

I smiled faintly at Heather, who was looking ravishing in a russet velvet gown. It accentuated her peaches-and-cream complexion and the light of the candles burnished her hair to gold.

Katherine sat down beside me on the sofa while Nicholas took the chair next to Heather. "How beautiful you look tonight," said Katherine to me, and I was grateful, thinking her kind to say so whether I actually did or not.

"I understand tomorrow is the launching day for the new ship, Nicholas," said Heather.

"Yes, the deck planking was finished today."

"Launching day—does that mean the ship is ready to be sailed?" I asked, diverted from my own thoughts for the moment.

"Not yet," said Nicholas. "It means the ship is ready to be put in the water. You see, a launching cradle, resting on greased ways, is first built under the ship. The support structures—the ramps and staging—that were built up around the ship are cleared away. Then the ship is wedged up off the keel blocks and onto the launching cradle. The cradle is then cut loose and the ship slides stern first into the water. But it's not yet ready to be sailed; more work has to be done—carpentry work, joiner work. And then the rigging of the masts is done last. A whaling ship has three masts. The topgallant, royal, and skysail yards must be rigged. The running rigging is done and the sails bent on. Only then is the job complete and the ship ready to be sailed. But the launching day is a very important one, an occasion for celebration." I was surprised to hear him talking easily with no trace of feelings associated with his last whaling endeavor. In fact, he sounded enthusiastic about the work at the shipyard and full of energy. His smile at Heather had been no more than casual and friendly, but I could not rid my mind of the still picture of them together in the woods.

"You shouldn't miss the launching day, Miranda," said Heather.

Katherine stood up saying it was time to go in to dinner and I set down the glass of sherry I had scarcely touched. Katherine took my arm affectionately, which left Nicholas and Heather to follow behind us. I wanted to look over my shoulder to try and interpret any glances between them but I was afraid of what I might see.

Katherine sat at the head of the table with Heather opposite her and Nicholas and I across from one another. I had not been in the dining room before and it had the same past-its-prime, shabbily genteel look of the parlor—the velvet curtains fraying a little, the sheers behind them yellowing. But the table looked most attractive with a large arrangement of mums in the center of the Quaker lace tablecloth and I thought a cosy, comfortable house it was.

"Your mother tells me you are an artist, Heather," I said. "What sort of pictures do you paint?"

She smiled at me. "Portraits. I find painting faces fascinating—trying to detect that particular something which defines one's personality and then attempting to depict it on canvas. I'm not very good though. I'd like to be much better."

"Don't let her fool you, Miranda," said Nicholas, flashing what I thought was an especially warm smile at Heather. "She's really very good. You've been to Julia's room and seen the portrait, haven't you? Heather painted it."

"Oh, that was several years ago," said Heather with a wave of her hand. "I hope I've improved since then."

"I think it's a marvelous painting, Heather," I admitted. "Did she sit for it?"

"Yes, I came to Thunder House every day for a while, didn't I, Nicholas? And then later, of course, I was able to finish it without her there. But she was a good subject and a good model. She could sit serenely like that for hours and not get restless."

I said nothing, imagining if it were I who were being painted. I would have doubtless sat fidgety and self-conscious, like a gauche adolescent. Julia, of course, had never been like that. I was certain Heather had not either.

As if echoing my thoughts Katherine said, "Such a lovely girl, Julia," and she shook her head.

"Perhaps you'd permit me to paint you sometime, Miranda," said Heather.

"Oh, what a good idea," exclaimed Katherine. "It would make such a wonderful present for Nicholas."

Nicholas's eyes were on my face as though considering,

but he did not say anything and I reddened. It was obvious he was not interested in commissioning a portrait of me.

We had lamb roast with herbs and new potatoes. It was very good but I hadn't much of an appetite.

"I used the piano in the church this afternoon," I said to Katherine when Nicholas and Heather were occupied in a conversation about some of the workers at the shipyard.

"I'm so pleased, Miranda. I'm glad you changed your mind about stopping the lessons."

"I'm sorry about missing the second one this week. You see, I got stranded on Seal Island and—"

"Yes, we heard all about that. How dreadful for you! And we had just been talking of the very thing that morning."

"It was foolish of me. And when the weather began to change, I was afraid that when the causeway did clear I would not be able to see my way across it, and across Thunder Island to the house."

"It was certainly fortunate for you that Zeke Somes was out checking his traps."

I nodded, stealing a glance at Nicholas, worried that the mention of Zeke's name might bother him. But I need not have worried. He and Heather were still deep in conversation. I heard the name "Noah" and realized they must be talking about the old man at the lighthouse.

"Nicholas and Heather were once stranded on Seal Island, weren't you, Heather?" asked Katherine. They looked over at her.

"Together?" I asked stupidly, and then bit my lip. Of course they had been together—what else could she have meant?

"I was still in my teens," said Heather. "It was years ago." She looked annoyed at Katherine for mentioning it.

"It was the day of your sixteenth birthday—I well remember," said Katherine. "You and Nicholas were supposed to be helping me decorate the house since your father had hurt his back and couldn't reach to hang any garlands or lanterns. Roger said I could borrow Nicholas from the shipyard to help me. The two of you went in

282

search of bittersweet branches, do you remember?"

"Nicholas said the best bittersweet grew on Seal Island," said Heather, smiling in remembrance.

"It did. And I had no idea you'd take so long cutting it that we'd be caught by the tide," said Nicholas, his lips quirked.

Why were they talking about this? As Heather had said, it had been years ago. She was somewhere in her middle twenties now and Nicholas was thirty or a little more. Why were they dredging it up? And I had not noticed any bittersweet growing on Seal Island.

"Did you make it back for the party?" I heard myself asking.

"They were two hours late," said Katherine. "I was furious. We couldn't imagine where they were. It was still light when the causeway cleared so they managed to see their way back."

I took a meager comfort in this; surely being stranded on a deserted island during the day was less shocking than if they had passed the night there.

"Had you begun the party?" I asked.

"Oh yes, what else could we do? Everyone had arrived and of course they were hungry. Bruce said he was certain that they would return at any time and so we were to start the festivities and dancing."

"What a stir you must have created when you did appear," I said, and was astonished at the spite in my voice.

Nicholas frowned at me. "It was all long ago," he said. "And it wasn't as though we were the first that that had happened to."

"Well, the way you scolded me, Nicholas, I never would have thought that such a thing had happened to you," I said lightly.

"Yes, Miranda, it's happened to many people in Nansett. So you're in good company," said Katherine.

I found little consolation in the knowledge that the good company included my husband, who had been alone for six or seven hours on an uninhabited island with this tall goddess, who even at sixteen must have been very striking.

After dinner we moved back into the parlor for coffee and cake. Nicholas seemed to grow restless and I was ill at ease despite my affection for Katherine. So when he rose to go, I was relieved. We said good-bye, thanking them for the dinner, and Katherine said, "Next week we can have another lesson. Meanwhile, keep up your practicing. Now I wonder what Janet did with your things. They're not on the umbrella stand. Heather, go ask her."

When Heather had gone, Katherine said, "Oh, she may have put them in Heather's studio. I'll go see." Curious to see the studio, I followed her across the hall and into a room.

"Yes, here they are. Your pelisse and bonnet, Miranda. Such a charming one. And here is Nicholas's cloak. I'll take it to him."

She went past me and out of the room while I stood stockstill, my eyes riveted on a large portrait hanging on the wall. A portrait of Nicholas.

He stood on the deck of a ship, the water swirling in the background. He looked handsome, and arrogant, and there was an expression on his face of anticipated excitement, of an upcoming event he eagerly awaited. It must have been painted when he had first become a whaling captain. I wondered if he had modeled for it, but I cast that notion aside. No, that wasn't something Nicholas would do. Heather must have painted it with his face in her mind. She doubtless knew every inch of it . . . and she kept his image in her studio. . . .

Slowly I turned and walked from the room, mechanically putting on my bonnet and tying it. Katherine took my hand, kissing my cheek. "You feel so cold, Miranda. Button up your pelisse—it's a chilly night. October is here now."

"Thank you, Katherine," I said dully, and went out with Nicholas.

"Are you cold?" he asked as we rode out of Nansett.

"No," I murmured.

"Did you enjoy yourself tonight?"

"Yes."

"Heather tells me her mother is very fond of you, that she finds you very charming."

"Oh." Rather like a child, I thought, or worse yet, a doll.

"I wondered whether you'd care to come to the shipyard tomorrow for the launching. All of the village will be there and it's an exciting event to watch." There was a note in his voice of barely suppressed eagerness. Vaguely I wondered why he was so anxious to have me there.

"All right, Nicholas. After all, I haven't yet seen a ship you have built."

"That's just what I was thinking, my love. Come to the shipyard before noon. We launch at noon. Do you know the way?"

He proceeded to tell me how to get there and soon we had reached Thunder House. "You go on inside, Miranda. I'll stable the horse and be up shortly." He lifted me down from the saddle but his arms did not release me. They enfolded my waist and drew me against him. But I began to struggle and push him away. Scenes, both real and imagined, flitted through my mind — Nicholas and Heather in the woods, Nicholas and Heather alone in Seal Island, Heather dining at Thunder House with Nicholas while Lavinia looked on in benign approval.

These images flooded my mind and I could not bear their stinging intrusions. I cried, "Don't Nicholas! Leave me alone!" And then I was fleeing inside the house and up the stairs. When later I heard him go into the room next door, I held my breath but I needn't have worried — he did not disturb me. And my relief became a desolation.

In the morning Morwenna was agog with excitement over the launching day. It seemed the entire household was going — the only exceptions being, predictably, Lavinia and Sarah.

"Have you ever seen a launching?" I asked Morwenna.

"No, but I be told 'tis a grand sight. Be you going, ma'am?"

"I suppose so," I said listlessly. "My husband asked me

to."

" 'Twill be wonderful, I hear. Jenny and Mary have seen many of them and they do say 'ee never gets tired of seeing it."

I dressed in a wine-red cashmere gown and then put on my blue pelisse with the velvet collar and cuffs and the blue silk bonnet with died feathers swept across the brim. I picked up the white fur muff and was ready. I could tell Morwenna was anxious to hurry along to the shipyard so I had dismissed her, saying I could finish my toilette myself. The other servants had also gone ahead.

I went down the paneled hall and descended the stairs to the second floor. A voice, raised and excited, came to my ears and I recognized it as Lavinia's. She sounded happy, carefree. It brought to mind the last time I had heard her speaking that way—in the sitting room in the moonlight and the time before when I had stood behind the closed doors of the wardrobe in Julia's room, muffled in clothes and oppressed with the scent of lavender.

Hardly knowing why I did so, I moved down the corridor, my slippers making no sound on the carpeted floor. As I approached Lavinia's room, the voice became more audible and I noticed that her door was ajar.

"Oh, Julia, darling, I can scarcely wait for our trip to Boston! You'll adore it there, I promise. So many fine mansions, townhouses, the elegant entertainments we shall attend—balls, soirées . . . the excitement, the frivolous excitement like nothing you've known on Thunder Island."

There was a brief pause and then she hurried on, "Now, Julia, no indulging in a fit of nerves. It's not like you. Why else am I taking you if not to find a grand husband? I want to show you that there is more to life than Thunder Island with its dark forests, gloomy swamps, and fishermen's cottages. That there are wide cobblestoned streets with fashionable shops and lofty buildings and beautifully cultivated parks, not at all like the riotous expression of nature on this wild island. That there are people who are not concerned with sea voyages and farming and sawmills and lobster traps. With your looks you'll have your pick of the most eligible bachelors, and the dowry Roger left you is a generous one. One thing about your father, he was always generous with those he loved."

Even though I had twice before heard her talking to her dead daughter, I could not help turning cold, my mouth becoming dry. Was Sarah in there with her? Did she sit silently while her mistress indulged in these pathetic fantasies?

Her voice had begun again and this time my heartbeat quickened and I began to tremble. For somehow her muddled mind had jumped to the present and yet she was still talking to Julia, talking about *me*.

"You would not credit it, Julia! It's more than I can bear. Your brother has brought that dull girl of no account to live in Thunder House. Yes, he's actually married her— I can still scarcely believe it! I know you did not consider Heather MacLeod a good enough wife for Nicholas but believe me, she would have been a great improvement on this girl. Heather I could have understood and Roger was always fond of her. But this girl—who in the world is she? She's a dreadful nobody! And Nicholas has actually said that she can use your room and wear your jewelry! It's abominable. And I have to sit by and watch her. I never wanted her here. Nicholas has abandoned all filial feeling and is allowing her to take your place and mine. I won't have it! I won't have it, I tell you!"

There was a soothing voice which I recognized as belonging to Sarah but I did not stay to hear any more. I should never have ventured down this hall in the first place.

I now believed that Lavinia was mad in a threatening, sinister way and I was afraid of her. I had not truly feared her up until now but her last words had been so filled with venom that I believed she would have gladly done me grievous harm if she had known I stood outside her door.

I went down the stairs and outside. The wind gusted strongly, swirling the colorful leaves from the trees to the needle-covered forest floor. The late morning sun glinted on the maples, some brilliantly crimson, some the vibrant shade of ripe pumpkins on the vine. The dark soothing balsams and spruces mingled with the blazing leaves, and the woods were filled with their fragrance. Blackett's Glade wore a lonely forlorn air even on this bright day, the slender gray wraiths of dead trees adding to the swamp's dreary forsaken look. Even the water was a dull gray-blue and the reflected bulk of Bald Mountain nothing but a massive murky shade.

With Nicholas's directions to the shipyard in mind, I walked through a section of woods I had never traveled before, but I now knew instinctively that I was headed toward the shore so it must be the right way. A mountain stream, brisk and teeming, spilled over the glossy black stepping-stones in its path. Under a pearly blue haze Bald Mountain's smooth granite ridges were dotted with wine-red bushes. A sparrow called out its song, "Old Sam Peabody, Peabody, Peabody," and soon another echoed it.

I heard the activity of the shipyard long before I reached it. There was the sound of a crowd of people, of hammering, and then a dreadful piercing ringing noise that I could not identify. As I drew closer, it became louder and I put my hands over my ears. But then it stopped and did not come again. Through the trees ahead I glimpsed the blue of the sea and knew I was nearly there. And it was an impressive sight which met my eyes when I cleared the forest and looked across a wide stretch of grass and sand to the shipyard.

There was a long open-loft building near the shore and inside it was the bark. There were no sides on the building but the bark was partially concealed by the mass of support structures which had been constructed around it. All around the ship and near to me were crowds of people—men, women, and children. The men were working for the most part except for the older ones, who were standing and watching, pipes in their mouths, hands in their pockets. The children were running around excitedly but their mothers were careful to see that they kept a safe distance from the staging that was slowly being taken down from about the ship.

I saw Martha and Amos and a little ways off the three maids, nudging each other and giggling as they watched the young men working. I envied them their carefree joy, unhampered by worries or doubts. I felt years older and quite sedate, a bit numb even. The excitement, the thrills passing through the crowds, could not touch me.

"Miranda, I'm glad you've come!" It was Emily and she was hurrying up to me, a little breathless.

"Hello, Emily, I'm glad you're here also. I was feeling a little lost."

"I asked Nicholas if you were coming and he said he didn't know. I assured him you would not miss so important an event as a launching."

"When will they do it?"

"First they take down all the staging and the ship is wedged onto the cradle. The cradle is heavily greased so the ship can slide from it into the water. It won't be too long now."

"Have you seen Ben?"

She shook her head. "Come with me. We can look for both Nicholas and Ben. Nicholas told me to be sure and tell him when you got here. I've been keeping an eye out for you." We went through the throngs of people toward the huge open-loft structure. We passed Katherine standing with a group of women; she waved at me. I did not see Heather.

There were men climbing on the support structures, tearing beams and posts apart, ousting nails from wood. "What was that awful ringing noise I heard before?" I asked Emily.

"Oh, a few of the caulkers were working on the other ship in the second building. They were driving oakum, or tarred hemp, into the seams between the planks. It helps to keep the ship tight. The beetles, or mallets, they use make that terrible sound. Often it makes the caulkers go deaf if they do it long enough."

Suddenly I noticed Nicholas standing on the deck of the ship talking to Ben. "They're they are," cried Emily, and she called up to them, waving.

Nicholas looked down. Was that relief I saw in his face when he spotted me? Could it be that he was happy to see me, even after last night when I had spurned his embrace? I felt shy, out of place in this hectic scene.

He was coming down, climbing down the support ramps, Ben behind him. I smiled and said hello to Ben, who, like Nicholas, had rolled up his shirt sleeves and discarded his jacket. Their shirts were open at the throat.

"So you came after all," said Nicholas quietly to me while Ben put his arm around Emily's shoulders and pointed something out to her on deck. "I didn't think you would."

I flushed. "Morwenna told me I couldn't think of missing a launching day."

"I can only be happy that you took your maid's advice since my own invitation did not move you," he said coolly, his mouth tightening.

I bit my lip. "The ship looks fine, Nicholas, beautiful, really."

He gave me a swift keen look. "Do you really think so? I admit to being rather proud of it myself," he said, and there was a tinge of color in his cheeks.

"Well, I know I mustn't keep you; you must be very busy just now," I said.

"I am, at that. Well, I better get back on deck." He moved away but then looked back. "Thank you for coming, Miranda. I'll talk to you later."

I nodded and he went off with Ben.

"Miranda, there's someone I must speak to," said Emily. "Why don't you go close where you can better watch the action and I'll come find you in a little while?"

"All right." I felt rather in the way already but as she suggested I went closer to the ship and drew underneath a portion of the support structures which had not yet begun to be disassembled. All around me were shouts, laughing, the noise of hammers and of wood breaking, but the sounds were dim in my ears. On deck behind and above me were men and women eagerly awaiting the moment the ship would slide into the sea.

"Hello, Miranda."

It was Zeke. He wore the same navy blue coat with brass buttons, and his pale hair glinted in the sun. An ugly bruise married his jaw.

"Oh, hello, Zeke. I'm surprised to see you here. I mean—" Why didn't I ever think before the words tumbled from my mouth?

"Didn't think I'd be at Nicholas's launching? No, I didn't plan on it—but then I thought you might be here."

I looked up at him uncertainly. "I didn't know whether I'd come either but I had heard it's something not to be missed. And everyone around here, it's apparent, feels the same way."

"Ayeh. Everyone's proud and rightly so, I expect. They've worked hard for this day. And Nicholas is a sight better shipbuilder than he is a whaler."

"Zeke, you really shouldn't talk that way about my husband to me," I said.

"So he's poisoned you against me, has he?"

"Of course not. It's just that the . . . the hatred . . . between you makes me uncomfortable. And it's really none of my business."

"I doubt Nicholas'd agree with you there," said Zeke, but his quick anger had subsided.

I looked up toward the ship and saw with a slight shock that Nicholas was staring down at us. He did not look pleased. Clenching my hands inside my fur muff, I bit my lip.

Zeke saw him, too. "Well, I won't keep you talkin' any longer, Miranda. No need to rile Nicholas." He seemed amused. He nodded at me and moved off in the crowd. I looked back up at Nicholas but he had disappeared from view. I wished that he hadn't seen me talking to Zeke but it couldn't be helped. And where was Emily?

I suddenly wished I had not come. Perhaps I could go back to Thunder House now. Nicholas was preoccupied— he would doubtless not notice if I left. I was in no mood to join in the festive spirit of the day; all around me were people enjoying a holiday but I felt strangely removed

291

from all of them.

Just as I turned to go, there was a rending crashing noise above me and I glanced up, my heart in my mouth, to see a large portion of scaffolding falling. Just as on the slope of Bald Mountain when that boulder had hurtled toward me, I could not move.

Like the boulder, shrieked my terrified mind. Just as the large wooden mass was almost on me, I jumped back and to the side, stumbling and falling on the grass. The scaffolding hit the ground next to me with a tremendous impact and I felt the ground vibrate with its force. Staring mesmerized at the thick sturdy beams nailed together, I realized I would now be dead if they had struck me the way they had the ground.

There were screams from all directions, shouts, and running. "Are you all right, Mrs. Blaize?" "Dear God, did you see that?" "Ayeh, she could've been killed all right." "Where's the captain? Get him, you fool!" Then "Get back, get back, give her air!"

Shaking violently, I felt very chilled with a cold that burned like ice. I could not take my eyes from the portion of support structure which had collapsed within inches of where I was sprawled on the grass. How had it come to fall just as I stood under it?

Then Nicholas was beside me, his face white, his eyes darkly gray as smoke, unfathomable. My bonnet was off; I was cradled in his arms, my head pressed to his chest; he was saying my name over and over.

"Oh Miranda, are you all right? What a horrible thing to have happen!" cried Emily. "Look at her, Nicholas, she's shaking all over."

"Tell Ben to get some brandy from one of the men. They always bring full flasks on launching day." His voice was grim.

She was gone and then Katherine was beside me. "My poor child, I just heard what happened. Is there anything I can do for her, Nicholas? She's as white as a sheet."

"Emily's gone for some brandy. That was the last portion of the supports, I take it?"

"Yes, the ship seems to be clear of them. But what a dangerous thing — I've never witnessed such an accident on any launching day I've ever attended! Poor Miranda!"

"Here's some brandy, Nicholas," said Ben. "Is she all right?"

"She will be when she's had a swig or two of this. It'll stop the shuddering." He lifted the pewter flask to my lips and tilted it. "Drink some of this, sweet."

I swallowed, then choked and sputtered. "That's all right, have a bit more," ordered Nicholas.

"Her color's coming back a little," said a voice I recognized as Heather's.

I closed my eyes, not wanting to see or hear any of them. But the violent trembling had stopped.

"She better go back to the house, Nicholas," said Sarah. "I'll take her."

Sarah! What was Sarah doing here? "No, I'm not going with her," I said, my voice returning.

"It's all right, Miranda," said Katherine soothingly. "You're perfectly safe now. It's all over and you have nothing to fear any longer. It's all over."

"I just don't know how it happened," Ben was saying. "Unless the ramp somehow got loose after the other parts were taken down. But how in the world . . . it's never happened before."

"God only knows. I was on the starboard side then," said Nicholas. "No one seems to have seen it actually begin to fall. We hadn't begun on that section yet — the men were working on the other parts."

"Nicholas, you must get back. I'll sit with her," said Katherine.

"I will, too," said Emily. "You and Ben need to go on with the launching. Since Miranda doesn't want to go back to Thunder House, she can sit here on the grass and we'll take care of her. Then later you can take her back."

Nicholas seemed to hesitate, not releasing his hold on me.

"Nicholas, you must proceed with the launching. Afterward you can take her back, like I said. Come, Miranda, sit here by me and have another sip of brandy," urged Emily.

"No, thank you," I said about the brandy but began to struggle to my feet with Nicholas's help.

"Are you certain you are all right, Miranda?" he asked, his black brows drawn together.

I nodded and Emily motioned him and Ben away. "Sometimes I think men make even more of matters than do women," she said to Katherine. "Nicholas's face was as pale as Miranda's. But she'll be just fine in a little while, won't you, darling? We can sit and watch all the excitement from here."

The crowd was losing interest in us and moving away, spreading out to find places from which to watch the ship enter the ocean for the first time. Katherine sat on one side of me and Emily on the other. Heather had left us, probably moving closer to the ship when she saw her mother had the situation well in hand. Sarah had also disappeared.

I sat on the grassy incline, the gale off the water blowing my hair, the salty tang of it on my lips, in my nostrils. "Look, there it goes!" cried Emily, and I turned to look at the sleek ship as it moved gracefully, sliding off the greased ways and nosing into the sea amid tumultuous cheers, whistles, shouts and applause. The ship was launched.

Chapter Thirteen

"What a splendid sight!" Katherine said. "I never get tired of seeing it. Bruce and I used to love to watch all of Roger's ships when they were launched."

"I'm so pleased that Nicholas has taken a renewed interest in the business," said Emily. "I think he's finally starting to put the past behind him. That's likely due to you, Miranda."

I stared at her, giving a rather hysterical laugh. She and Katherine exchanged glances. But they couldn't know what incredible notion had struck me when I had looked up at the wrenching, splitting sound of wood, when my mind had played back the sight of the boulder hurtling toward me from down the mountain. In the heart-stopping moment when time had stood still I had had a wild impression that those support structures had been deliberately shoved from their height to bear down on me like a wall of mighty ladders. Fantastic as it seemed—and the rational part of my mind was trying to convince the impressionable part how fantastic such a notion really was—I could not shake it off. Could someone have actually meant to harm me? Could someone actually have meant to kill me? But surely that was absurd. It had been a freak accident, nothing more. Yet following so quickly after the other freak accident on the slope of Bald Mountain . . . Nonsense, they had both been coincidences. Everyone in his life has close calls with death—but do they usually follow one after the other?

Who in the world would want to kill *you?* I asked myself in self-disgust. What significance can your life or death be to anyone? How can you threaten anyone enough that he or she would wish to kill you? Your frightening experience has temporarily unhinged your mind and you are imagining all sorts of crazy things.

All right, said the other side of my mind. I admit it sounds ridiculous but just for a few moments let's examine all the possibilities—all the possible suspects. Crowds of people had stood on the deck just as the structure had fallen—any one of them could have cut the ropes and sent the structure toppling over. With all the confusion going on up there and on all sides of the open loft, it would not have been too difficult for someone to do exactly that without attracting attention. But who?

Nicholas, I thought with a dull thrust of pain. It could have been he. He had admitted it had been a mistake for us to marry. If he had already resumed his former relationship with Heather, he would be ruing his impulsive marriage to me. He would be wishing he could be rid of me. Together they might be plotting my demise so that they would be able to marry in the future. Was that what they had been discussing in the woods yesterday? Naturally my death would have to look like an accident. And what better opportunity than an occasion such as a launching day celebration when throngs of people would be milling about, all busy with work and socializing. In all the commotion there would likely be no witnesses. The structure would have suddenly given way, collapsed on me and—what a terrible tragedy, everyone would have said. How horrible for Nicholas—and on his day of triumph, too. I recalled the eagerness Nicholas had displayed when he suggested that I come today. Heather had also made a point of telling me I shouldn't miss such an important

296

event.

The image of Sarah came into my mind. What on earth had she been doing here, miles from Thunder House? Had she left Lavinia alone? I had heard them talking before I had left the house. Could Sarah have followed me to the shipyard? Surely Lavinia herself could not have walked all the way here. No, no matter how much she disliked me, I couldn't imagine her trudging across the island and then somehow having the strength and agility to climb on deck and send the structure crashing down. But Sarah could have. Sarah was a strong formidable woman and she was devoted to Lavinia to an almost obsessive degree. She might have thought that by killing me she could bring Lavinia some sort of peace. Lavinia bitterly resented me — that was obvious to everyone, even the servants. She despised me for having the presumption to marry into her family and she hated me for the position I held in the household as the only young woman. She saw that as a usurption of Julia's place. I had played Julia's piano, my fingers pressing the keys as hers had done, my eyes following the printed notes of music as hers had. And Nicholas had given me her necklace to wear — a family necklace, but one to which Lavinia protested I had no right. Also, both the women hated Nicholas. Lavinia blamed him for Julia's death because he had not been on Thunder Island to look after his family and so Julia had disappeared. Not only was this cruel and unjust, it was illogical. But Lavinia's mind did not work logically; it acted solely on her emotions. By ridding Nicholas of me she might feel the slate was clean. Julia gone, Miranda gone. Sarah could have come as her envoy, with or without her approval, with or without her entreaty.

And then I realized that if someone had actually tried to harm me, it very well could have been Heather acting alone, not as Nicholas's partner in crime. She was a tall strong young woman; she had lived in Nansett all her life; she had doubtless attended many launchings; she knew about the structures built up around the ship during construction and how they were then removed, broken

297

down. She had always struck me as very capable and confident. Could she also be calculating and ruthless?

She kept a portrait of Nicholas in her studio. At one time she had been special in his life. They had been childhood friends who had grown up together, although Nicholas was a few years older, and as they reached adulthood they had drawn even closer. True, Sarah had told me that when he had returned from his last Arctic voyage, his feelings for her had changed, but he had turned from everyone then and shut himself in a hard cold shell.

After marrying me and bringing me to Thunder House out of a misplaced sense of guilt and pity, he might now be realizing that he had been a fool. Heather could have been his for the asking—a far superior wife in every way to him than I. He must be realizing that more and more each day. If he was truly coming to terms with his past and putting it behind him, it was not unlikely that he had begun to wish he had married Heather before sailing to New Bedford and finding an insipid gauche girl like me. Now could he be trying to rid himself of the undesirable wife he had married in a fit of madness? Were his episodes of love-making only to keep me from suspecting his true sinister intentions?

Unless it were Heather acting alone. If she had never stopped loving him, then she might be hoping that if I were out of the way, he would return to her. Perhaps he had told her in the woods yesterday that he regretted marrying me and wished the act could be undone. And so she was taking matters into her own hands. . . .

And since I was allowing my mind free rein in considering all these dreadful possibilities, I also wondered whether the boulder had been a first attempt to murder me. Some strong person could have lain in wait for me, prodded the boulder until it rolled down the mountain and gained in momentum to crush all in its path. But no, said the other side of my mind, that *is* ludicrous. You're really stretching things a bit far—with all of this! It's just that you've had two severe shocks and those added to all the strain and stress of the past few weeks—well, all that is enough to addle anyone's wits. Calm down and be sensible.

The cheers and laughter from the crowd went on about me. Everywhere people were shouting, chattering, eating, dancing to the sea shanties being sung and played but none of it touched me. Someone was robustly singing "What Shall We Do with the Drunken Sailor?" with a fiddle accompaniment. I recognized Noah Todd, the lighthouse keeper, as the fiddler. The music went on; the new ship rocked in the choppy water; the wind blew from the sea; the people talked and made merry. But there was an illusory quality about the whole lively scene as though it took place on a stage. And I, as the sole viewer, was also the sole inhabitant of the real world.

"Hooray and up she rises, hooray and up she rises, hooray and up she rises, early in the morning!" went on the voices, and I had the uncanny feeling that they would vanish behind the curtain when the song was over. It seemed too perfect a set—the sleek new ship on the blue water, the grassy incline descending to the sandy shore, the celebrating villagers reveling in the day's events.

The music stopped and Noah put down his violin. He wore a red shirt tucked into his trousers and a blue bandanna knotted around his neck. He looked toward where I was sitting with Emily and Katherine and walked over to us.

"Ye haven't come to see my lighthouse yet, Mrs. Blaize," he said, wagging a finger at me. "It's down the beach from the Selkie's Throne."

"No, I'm sorry, Noah. I'll come soon, though."

Nodding, he shambled off.

"It's a wonder Nicholas still keeps Noah on as keeper," Katherine said, shaking her head. "I can't imagine he would be much good if there were an actual shipwreck. He's so old now that his mind wanders; one never knows what he's going to say or do."

I was trying to dispel the detached feeling I had had so I said, "I see what you mean. He told me to beware of

299

selkies the first time I met him." I smiled faintly.

"That's precisely what I was talking about. He's quite senile, I'm afraid. But I know Nicholas feels a loyalty to him."

"Oh, I don't think Noah's quite that far gone," said Emily, quick to defend her brother. "He's not the only one in Nansett who tells those old legends. And he does have Tom Cameron to help him, after all. Nicholas knows it would destroy him to be dismissed. That lighthouse is his whole life—and Tom is very often there to help him. The lighthouse is a very pretty sight, Miranda. You should go and see it. Noah adores to have visitors."

"I will."

Nicholas and Ben were making their way up the grassy dune in our direction. When they reached us Ben said, "Well, she's done. There won't be any more work done today."

"What happens now?" I asked.

"Oh, the festivities will continue for a while longer, until nightfall undoubtedly," said Nicholas. "But you still look a trifle pale, Miranda. I'll take you home."

"Yes, I'm feeling a little weary myself," admitted Emily. "I think I should go home, too, Ben."

"And I suppose I'll find Heather and tell her I'm returning to Nansett also," said Katherine. "Wait for me and I'll walk with the two of you."

"All right, Katherine," said Emily. "Congratulations, Nicholas. It's a beautiful ship, just as good as any Father built. I'm very proud of you and Ben."

Nicholas bent to kiss her cheek and then we said good-bye. He put his arm around my shoulders and we walked to the place where he had tied his horse. "Are you certain you are all right, Miranda? That was a nasty shock for you."

"Yes, I'm fine, Nicholas. For a time I felt—but as you said, it was a nasty shock. I suppose such scares can start one considering all sorts of frightful things. But I'm all right now."

He looked puzzled and that part of my mind which had

leaped wildly to the conclusion that it might have been no accident, that part, sinking but game, gave its last warning that I not be fooled by his tender solicitious manner. But I pushed that last thought ruthlessly aside — I loved this man and I would not believe that he had tried to kill me. He might wish he had not married me, but I could not believe now that he was plotting my murder. Oh, Nicholas, I thought, you wouldn't, would you. . . .

When we reached the house, he went upstairs with me. I was conscious that we were alone in the house except for the two women on the floor below. The servants were still at the shipyard.

I said, "Nicholas, I'm sorry to have taken you away from the festivities. After all your work you deserve to celebrate also."

"My dear girl — oh, I forgot, you don't like me to refer to you that way. Miranda, my dearest, don't be foolish. I had no desire to stay there without you."

"I wonder what Sarah was doing there. I mean, shouldn't she have been here with your mother?"

"I asked her the same thing. Evidently Lavinia had had another bad spell this morning and became very agitated. Sarah had to sedate her with laudanum. When Lavinia was resting peacefully, she decided to walk over to the shipyard." He shrugged. "Even Sarah needs time away from Lavinia, after all. She knew she would be asleep for hours."

"I suppose so." I had overheard Lavinia in the throes of her "bad spell," possibly just before Sarah had administered the laudanum drops.

"Miranda —" Nicholas ruffled his dark locks with his fingers.

"Yes?" I asked tensely.

"Last night . . . when we got back from Katherine's — and even before that — I haven't understood — I don't understand — why you've seemed so distant. I had thought we were finally . . . I know you were angry with me about Zeke, but after that — the way you gave yourself to me, well, I automatically assumed that you were finally . . .

becoming used to me, that you no longer minded being alone with me. At least I very much hoped so. But then everything was changed — again. Tell me, Miranda, what is wrong between us?"

With heightened color I remembered Sarah's words about Heather and the way they had stood close together in the woods. But I couldn't tell him any of that — I couldn't let him see how hurt I was because then he would realize I was in love with him. . . .

"Last night I wasn't in the mood to go to Katherine's, Nicholas, as much as I like her, and I'm feeling rather tired just now. I don't feel up to . . . to being questioned by you," I said irritably.

"I know you've suffered a shock today, my dear. It meant a great deal to me to see you at the shipyard. Last night when you ran from me, I didn't know what to think. I was at my wits' end. And then — when that structure fell and nearly crushed you, I could only think that it was my fault; I was to blame. You might have been killed and all because I had entreated you to come to the launching."

He put out a hand and touched my cheek. "What is it, Miranda? Something's troubling you. You've . . . hardened toward me."

"It's nothing, Nicholas," I said dully. "Nothing and everything."

His black brows drew together and his hand dropped to his side. "What do you mean?"

I sighed. "Well, you're the one who has said that we shouldn't have married, that I shouldn't have come here. How do you expect me to take that?"

"I may have said that but I've also said and done a great many foolish things! And you have seemed so . . . lost, so unhappy much of the time. I have wondered whether I did a very selfish thing in marrying you."

"No more selfish than I did in accepting your proposal," I said tightly. I must not be drawn in by the tender caressing note in his voice, by the warm glint in his gray eyes. The shadow of Heather MacLeod was between us and to me it was as solid as the walls of Thunder House.

"Now, please, Nicholas. I would like to be alone."

He stiffened, his eyes narrowing swiftly. "Forgive me. I only wanted to — but it doesn't matter. It's plain to me how you feel. You cannot bear to be in the same room with me. I was obviously only fooling myself when I thought anything had changed."

When he was gone, I lay down on my bed, my head aching viciously. I felt so confused by all the thoughts whirling in my head; by Nicholas's manner, which had just now seemed affectionate; by my own response to him, which I had had to suppress; by Heather's place in all this . . . I did not know what to think. I could not trust my own feelings, my own instincts. I no longer felt that every gesture, every word, was suspect by any and all the way I had at the shipyard, but even now I was reluctant to trust Nicholas, not with that tall beautiful goddess living in Nansett. It was inconceivable to me that he might be falling in love with me, that he might have actually chosen me *over* Heather.

The following day I went down to the first floor with the intention of exploring more of the house. The servants' quarters were at the back, near to the kitchen. But it was not those rooms which interested me but the rooms in the front of the house, the rooms which faced the sea.

Walking down the long hallway which linked the front and rear entrances of Thunder House, I paused outside two immense paneled doors with polished brass knobs. Turning both knobs, I pulled open the doors. In the gray light the room was shadowy, cavernous.

It was a ballroom. There was no mistake about that. Rows of chairs and tables were draped with sheets against each wall. There was a dais at the far end of the room where the musicians would sit. The curtainless windows loomed from floor to ceiling; the floor was parquet. The chandeliers when lit would radiate with a festive sparkling brilliance.

A damp musty smell clung to the room; it had apparently not been used in years. Indeed, I wondered whether

303

it had ever been used. It seemed almost an aberration for Thunder House to have a room such as this, meant for huge lavish entertainments. It was likely that Nicholas's great-grandfather had designed his house in the way that all great houses were designed—with a ballroom. Whether it were used or not was perhaps unimportant.

I closed the doors and turned to investigate the room opposite. It was a library. There was a circular leather-top desk in one corner with two mahogany-and-cane chairs drawn up to it. On the table, or desk, were what looked like plans of various ships. On three of the walls were bookshelves, on the other was a group of nautical prints and framed maps. It was a masculine room; I had no doubt that it was used by my husband when he was working on shipyard business. Unlike his bedroom, though, with its harsh reminders of the past, this room had no such pretentions. There was a pleasant smell of old bound books; it was a comfortable, useful room.

I went down to the kitchen. Martha was there alone; I assumed the girls were tidying up the house. "Good morning."

"Good mawnin', Mrs. Blaize. And how are you feelin'? That was a nasty close call yesterday, wasn't it?"

I nodded. She went on, "Captain Nicholas says no one saw it stahrt to fall. Never had such a thing happen on launchin' day before. I expect the captain had words for the men—and questions. He was real upset last night—wouldn't touch his dinner, just like you."

I was eager to change the subject; I had not come down here to talk about yesterday. "Martha, I have just been in the ballroom. When was the last time that a ball was given here?"

"I don't know. Not since Amos and I came here. Seems a shame, don't it? This house looks like it was built for lots of folks and parties and such. But there's never been much of that." She shrugged.

"This house badly needs gaiety, doesn't it?" I said slowly, an idea dawning in my head. Why shouldn't Nicholas and I give a ball, a party for all the people who lived on Thunder Island?

I went back up to my room in growing excitement. It was a wonderful idea. I was certain Martha would do everything she could to help me, to carry out my wishes. It was something I would enjoy planning and executing, with her help, of course.

I imagined the room decorated in an autumn theme with the chandeliers lit and echoing with the sounds of fiddles and dancing feet. I hoped that Nicholas would be in favor of the idea; I would ask him tonight at dinner. Suddenly I had the desire to be with him again, to hear his voice, to watch the expressions move across his features, to see that certain look in his eyes when sometimes they looked into mine. I couldn't spend the rest of my life here feeling sorry for myself—that was the worst kind of self-indulgence, I could almost hear my mother saying. I smiled; I felt almost happy.

That evening I dressed in a dark blue velvet gown with a square neckline and leg-of-mutton sleeves. When I was ready, I knocked on Nicholas's door but got no answer in reply so I went on down to the first floor.

He was in the drawing room. He wore his customary black evening clothes with a waistcoat of gray satin and a black silk neckcloth. My heart gave a flutter.

"Good evening, Nicholas," I said shyly. "Where are Lavinia and Sarah?"

His lip curled. "If it is the two of them you wish to dine with, you will have to go to Lavinia's sitting room. They're not coming down tonight. So I'm very much afraid you are forced to be alone with me. Of course, Martha hasn't served yet—if you think quickly, you can invent some excuse to leave."

Dismayed at the sardonic note in his voice, I said lightly, "The ability to think quickly has never been one of my attributes."

Swallowing his wine, he set down his glass with a snap and said curtly, "It comes too damnably easy to me."

Jenny announced then that dinner was ready. "Too late," he said with a slight sneer, "you are doomed to spend the

305

next hour in my company."

Biting my lip, I went with him into the dining room and sat down at the table. I was wondering whether I had the nerve to bring up the subject I had been thinking about all afternoon.

While Jenny served our soup and poured the wine, I cast glances at him, phrasing my request in my head. Finally she left the room and I said, "Nicholas, I've been thinking. We should give a ball."

He looked up, distracted. "A ball, did you say? What nonsense is this, Miranda?"

"It's not nonsense at all. There's that enormous ballroom — why not use it?"

He shook his head. "You never cease to surprise me."

I did not know how to respond to this so I went on, "I want us — you and I — to give a party for the people of Thunder Island. Not a formal glittering ball — they wouldn't enjoy that and I doubt if I would. But a sort of fete with music and country dancing and food and drink. You know the sort of thing I mean. Don't you think everyone would enjoy that?"

"By everyone do you mean Lavinia and Sarah?" he asked, but the sting was gone from his voice.

"Oh, I daresay they won't much like the idea when I present it to them. I know that. But that shouldn't stop us, should it? Why don't we make it a celebration before the long winter?"

"What do we have to celebrate?" he asked rather bitterly.

"Well . . . the success of the shipyard, the harvest time, anything."

"Do you know your eyes are sparkling and there are roses in your cheeks?" he said musingly. "You look — radiant. Poor Miranda. You don't have much fun, do you?"

"I don't know," I said, disconcerted. "But I think this could be a special night everyone would enjoy. Well, what do you say? May I start planning it?"

His lips quirked. "Why not? When do you mean to have this splendid event?"

"Oh, at the end of this month or the first week in November."

"Very well, my love. You have my full approval."

I smiled broadly. "Thank you, Nicholas. You won't regret it. I promise you won't. Perhaps even Lavinia and Sarah will have a pleasant time." I paused before adding wryly, "Still, I may not tell them for a day or two yet. I'll wait until I've discussed things with Martha."

"Well, I don't envy you broaching the subject with them, but we'll pay no mind to what they say. You can have your ball or celebration or fete or whatever you wish to call it. And I'm certain that there won't be one person in Nansett who won't be delighted to come."

"Thank you, Nicholas." I smiled happily across the table at him and this time his pensive scrutiny of me did not make me uncomfortable. My mind was too full of plans and flickering images of the upcoming event. I gave scant attention to the realization that a few short weeks ago I could never have considered hostessing any sort of party, much less a huge lavish affair such as this. It was just another of the strange inexplicable turn of events which had occurred in my life since coming across Nicholas Blaize in the Seamen's Bethel. Absorbed in this event, I would have plenty to occupy my time and my mind so that the doubts and questions would be pushed aside.

When we had finished the blackberry cobbler Martha had baked for our dessert, some of my uncertainty returned. What were Nicholas's plans for the evening? Would he make any attempt to prolong our evening together?

He did not. He got up and poured himself a large brandy from the decanter on the sideboard, saying, "If you'll excuse me, I have some work to do on the new plans for a ship." He spoke coolly, distantly.

And I said airily, "Yes, I, too, have work to do before Martha and I begin discussing the preparations. I'd like to have things worked out in my head before I speak to her. Good night, Nicholas."

"Good night," he said with what I considered unnecessary curtness.

The next morning I had a piano lesson. I took the path which led to Nansett and paused on the slope of the mountain to look down over the radiant intricate cover of trees which was Thunder Island. Fir trees bristled amid the wispy ethereal golden birches and abundant flame-bright sugar maples. The sky was a robin's egg blue, a rich contrast to the harvest leaves.

Glancing up to the summit, I deliberately stood there a few moments longer. No large stones made their rapid helter-skelter progress toward me. My spirits had improved considerably in the past couple of days; I was resolved to try and make the best of things. I had something now to look forward to—the approaching ball. And I had the wild beauty of Thunder Island to surround me. And I had friends—Emily and Katherine, especially. Even Zeke might be considered a friend.

A silver curtain of water fell from the red grist mill. Crimson leaves fluttered and shifted over the dark gray stones of the low wall. I walked the remainder of the way to the village, enjoying the pungent smell of woodsmoke in the crisp heady air.

Katherine answered the door herself with the comment that the maid, Janet, was washing windows at the back of the house. "And Heather is out somewhere—painting, I imagine. She does like to wander off with her box and canvas. There are days when I don't see her from morning until nightfall. Still, that's one of the good things about living here. A woman can roam around by herself and be perfectly safe."

"Except in the case of Julia Blaize," I said.

She frowned. "Yes. That was one of the things that was so strange about the whole affair. You never would have thought that anyone raised on Thunder Island would come to any harm here. People who live on an island—they know its moods and the moods of the sea. They very rarely do anything foolhardy or dangerous."

"Nicholas said she was rather ignorant of those things."

"Perhaps, but she was a determined sensible girl, the

308

sort who was very conscious of her position in life, her responsibilities. Not the sort who would do anything foolish to put her life in jeopardy. She always behaved correctly in every situation. She was very sure of herself; she gave a great care to what she said and did." Katherine smiled. "She was rather different from Nicholas and Emily that way. Not that I mean Nicholas was ever foolhardy or negligent. Nothing like that. It's just that if he feels a decision to be the right one, he often acts on it instantly. Emily too."

"But Julia wasn't impetuous like that, I understand."

"No, she was ruled more by her head than her heart. Her introduction to Boston society was an event which had been most carefully contemplated and prepared for, for years. Even in her piano lessons with me, she was not so much concerned with a love of the music but with a desire to become as accomplished a musician as she could be. She practiced the piano more motivated by that than by any sheer enjoyment of playing. Heather now, she paints because she loves it and is always wanting to improve — for the sake of the art, not herself. But here I am talking and we should be proceeding with your lesson."

We worked for the next hour and then I stayed to drink a cup of tea. She talked about her husband, how well loved he had been by the people of Nansett, how good and kind he had been to her and Heather.

"He was afraid in the early years that I was not happy in Nansett. He knew Lavinia Blaize was not and he was worried that I didn't like the local people either. But I was secure in the love of a good man, in my own personal happiness."

"Are you saying that Roger Blaize did not love Lavinia?" I asked.

"Well, no, I did not mean to imply that. The story was that he had gone to Boston on business and fallen in love with her at their first meeting. But later after they had been married awhile, I believe he was hurt by her obvious dislike of Thunder Island, her unconcealed boredom with her life here. She had been used to a very different life, you

309

know. I don't know what she expected, what her husband did or did not prepare her for when they married. I know that Roger tried hard to please her. He built the Folly in the south woods for her. Bruce was here when they were first married. It was later that he and I met in Camden and began to correspond, and months after that when I came to Thunder Island to live. Bruce had known Roger all their lives, and before we married he used to go up to Thunder House with a fair amount of frequency. He saw the way Lavinia was developing an aversion to the island and he felt compelled to warn me about life here so that I would not be under any false impressions when we wed. As if I had been used to any sort of fashionable life!"

"Did Lavinia ever go to Boston to visit?"

"Oh yes, Roger took her once a year without fail before she became ill the last few years of his life. But I suppose that even those visits could not compensate for what she imagined she had given up."

"What do you know about Sarah Thatcher? She's . . . a rather unusual person."

"Little except that she accompanied Lavinia back after one of her early visits to Boston. Apparently Roger had decided his wife needed a companion and I believe they had been girlhood friends although Sarah's family had since fallen on hard times. When Sarah came, Roger and Lavinia stopped giving occasional dinner parties and we saw no more of them socially in the formal sense. Heather used to be invited to Thunder House at times because she was between Nicholas and Julia in age, and Roger was fond of her. But I had not seen Lavinia in years until Roger's funeral, and since then I have not seen her. She never comes to Nansett."

"There are days when I don't see her myself and I live in the same house."

"Well, perhaps it's just as well, my dear. From what I know of Lavinia and Sarah, and I don't wish to sound uncharitable, I don't believe they make others feel very comfortable in their presence."

"Yet Lavinia doted on one person — Julia."

"She did indeed. I think she saw Julia as a means to live her life all over again. Julia had grown up on Thunder Island but Lavinia was convinced she was made for better things. She was determined her daughter would make the sort of marriage and lead the sort of life that Lavinia herself had not after coming to Thunder Island. And through Julia she would be able to live it again. She is a person given to instant likes and dislikes, even of her children. At an early age, I'm afraid, she rather washed her hands of Nicholas and Emily. But Julia was the favored one, the one in whom Lavinia could see herself."

"What was Nicholas's father like?"

"Oh, Roger Blaize was a kind, even-tempered man, the word *mild* comes to mind — he was eager to placate, eager to please. A very different sort of person than Nicholas, really. But he must have had a great inner strength which Lavinia depended on because her condition, both mental and physical, I understand, worsened after he died."

Shortly afterward I left her and went back to Thunder House. In the afternoon I went out again. The weather was so beautiful and I knew there were not many weeks left before it would be too cold to wander about the island so I wanted to make as much use of the good weather as I could. I enjoyed being out of doors alone — that was the time I was at my most content. I was continually awed by the beauty of Thunder Island; I found strength in the vistas around me.

Crossing the back lawn, I entered the woods on the south side of the house. I had not walked far before I came to the family cemetery. The gray granite mausoleum was unlike some of the other ornate, elaborately carved tombs I had seen before; it had a peaceful austere dignity. The letters B-L-A-I-Z-E had been carved into the stone above the entrance and there were small marble plaques secured to the wall. It was a fairly new building and I assumed that Nicholas's father had ordered it built at some point in his lifetime. His name was on one plaque and also the dates of his birth and death. The only other plaque listed the name Julia Blaize. Yet her body had not been interred inside the mausoleum—it had never been found. There was something eerie about seeing her name on the plaque when her remains were not inside.

Julia, what happened to you? I asked silently. Were you prepared for death at the moment it came or did it take you by surprise? Katherine had said that Julia was not the type to do foolish things, to put herself in a situation where there was likely to be danger. So that made it difficult to imagine her being lost in the fog. Wouldn't she have stayed where she was until the fog cleared? Or wouldn't she have stayed on Seal Island until the causeway cleared—if she had ever walked to Seal Island? I found such a thing hard to envision with what I had heard about her. That was not the sort of thing a sensible girl would do, perhaps.

Unless there had been something which had agitated her and made her take risks she might otherwise not have taken. But what could have upset a reasonable young woman like her that it had so affected her cool judgment, her rationality?

Her mind had been filled with plans for her upcoming Boston season. That was to have been the culmination of all her expectations, her careful grooming. She was eager to become the ideal society wife. With this brilliant future ahead of her, why had she allowed something to interfere with that, to threaten it? Yet death was not something we could avoid; it struck when we least expected it.

Just then I was startled by a sound nearby, the sound of dry leaves rustling. It was most likely a bird or an animal but nonetheless my head jerked toward the direction from which it had come and I peered into the woods. I saw nothing and the sound did not come again.

The afternoon breeze felt cold. I pulled my cloak more tightly about me, lifting the hood over my hair and fastening it. The falling leaves spun dizzily, tossed by the wind. Anxious to leave this morbid place, I walked away, following the trail deeper into the woods. The bright leaves littered the path; every step I took made that brittle rustling sound. Once I heard a noise directly behind me but it was only a squirrel searching for fallen acorns.

I had not gone much farther before I came upon the abandoned fairy-tale cottage, the Folly. And again I was reminded of stories where innocents, lost in the deep forest, came upon such cottages in search of warmth and nourishment. But instead something quite different always awaited them inside—a secret hidden evil, a witch that lured those innocents to their doom just as selkies were said to lure their female prey to the sea. . . .

Not that again, I admonished myself. This was nothing but a cottage Roger Blaize had built for his new bride's amusement, a perfect little house that he hoped would take her fancy. But it had not appealed to her for whatever reasons and so over the years it had been allowed to fall into decay. It was not evil but pathetic, a memorial to a spurned gesture of love and a wish to charm.

And to prove this to myself I opened the door and stepped inside.

The small dingy deep-set windows did not allow much light to come in. In the dim light I looked again at the delightful pieces of furniture which carried on the Germanic fairy-tale theme—the chairs with hearts carved out of their backs, the sturdy oak tables, the loveseat whose upholstery had first faded, then stained and rotted, the small cupboard also with hearts carved from its shelves, the painted dower chest with its design of lovebirds. Even inside, the Folly resembled what one imagined the gingerbread house had looked like. And just as Hansel and Gretal had been enchanted by its appearance, so was I with this Folly. It must have been so lovely, so charming when it was first built and furnished.

Yet I had to admit that I could not imagine Lavinia enjoying the cottage; I could not imagine her leaving luxurious Thunder House for this little place, no matter how delightful it seemed to me. *I* may have preferred it to the vast splendor of Thunder House, but then she was very different from me. Perhaps she had even considered it and the very idea of it to be vulgar—a love nest secreted deep in the woods for privacy, for intimacy. Roger Blaize must have been very disappointed by her dislike of his carefully constructed wedding gift.

And so he had done nothing to keep it up. It had been left to the elements of nature, to the scavenging birds and animals. Vines of ivy were clinging to it, choking it; the forest was encroaching around it like a protective shield, giving it its secluded slumbering look. A place which had once held much promise but was now pitiful and blighted.

I walked about the room wishing I had seen it when it was new. I wondered what colors the upholstery had been and how the wide-plank knotty-pine floors had looked when they gleamed with fresh polish.

There was a scratching on one side of the room and I guessed a mouse was running across the floor. And then I heard a somewhat louder sound, the sound of someone *outside* the cottage. Who could be outside in the enclosing forest where the sunlight was dwindling, where the chill of the afternoon had deepened? In the fairy story the evil had been *inside* the cottage—but here was I inside and it was outside that someone lurked.

I was being foolish, letting the mood of the place affect me. I would go out and see who it was. And Heather MacLeod stood there, a little away from the Folly. She was carrying her box of paints and a canvas under her arm. A brown and green paisley scarf was tied under her chin and she wore a brown cloak.

"Heather, it's you! I thought I heard someone."

"I'm sorry if I startled you, Miranda. I saw the cottage door opened slightly and I couldn't think who would be inside. No one ever comes here."

"I've been looking inside. What about you—what are you doing here?"

"Oh, I've been thinking I'd like to paint this place. I've always had a fascination for it. We used to play here once in a while as children though we weren't really supposed to. It has such a forlorn melancholy air, secretive almost, wouldn't you say so?"

Even though this was precisely what I had been thinking myself, I said, "I don't know why you would want to paint this old place. And I thought you only painted portraits."

314

"Yes, I usually do, but this fascinates me. It's nearly hidden in the woods — you don't realize it's there until suddenly it looms up before you. And then you have the feeling that it holds some hidden story, some history of its own. I'm really tempted to try and put that on canvas."

"It's just a delapidated cottage," I said abruptly.

She smiled. "Well, perhaps I see more in it than you do."

I looked at her sharply, wondering if there was some hidden meaning in that remark. "So you are really going to paint it?" I asked.

She nodded. "The good light is gone now, but another day I'll start when I've finished this one I've been doing of the Everett little boy."

"May I see?"

She held out the canvas. On it was a little boy with ash brown curls and a chubby face chasing a chicken. He was enjoying his riotous game and the chicken was running about alarmed, its feathers ruffled.

"It's very good."

She shrugged. "It's not finished yet."

"I'm surprised you don't go somewhere to study professionally."

"An art school, do you mean?"

"Yes, there must be several good ones in Boston."

"My mother doesn't have the money to pay for the tuition fees they charge. So I just keep on working and trying to improve on my own. Besides, I love Thunder Island. I have no wish to leave it."

Again I wondered whether there was a significance behind her casual words. Was she telling me her place was here with Nicholas? Was she subtly warning me that she would never leave? Suddenly I was conscious that we were alone here, perhaps miles from the nearest people.

"Well, I must be getting back to the house now. Nicholas will be home soon and will be looking for me. Good-bye, Heather."

"Good-bye, Miranda. Give Nicholas my best, won't you?" She smiled, the dimple in her chin quivering.

I hurried away. Before I had gone too far, I turned

around and could scarcely see her standing there amid the trees because of the brown and green attire she wore. Her corn-colored hair was hidden and she blended into the forest.

And it occurred to me that when I had heard something at the cemetery—the noise of leaves rustling—she might have stood close by, watching me. Shivering, I hurried on through the woods to the house.

Chapter Fourteen

When I reached Thunder House, I learned that Nicholas was staying to work late at the shipyard and would not return home to dinner. I wondered bleakly whether he was actually working or whether he had very different plans for the evening.

Sarah and Lavinia were again dining in the privacy of their rooms so I was compelled to eat alone in mine. I stayed awake for sometime reading, but when I finally blew out the candle, Nicholas had not come upstairs, if in fact he had returned to the house at all. I was in no position to object to this; I had no claim on him but a legal one. But I fell asleep wishing that matters were different between us, wishing that I could trust him as much as I had come to love him.

In the morning I went down to the kitchen to talk with Martha about the arrangements for the ball. As I had expected, she was delighted at the prospect of entertaining on such a grand scale.

"I'd like to have it in three weeks' time," I said, "if that's possible. Can we get all the supplies we'll need by then?"

"Ayeh. I don't think there'll be any trouble with that. The ships come often."

"What sorts of things do they bring, generally?"

"Oh, bolts of fabric, foods like sugar, flour, tea, coffee,

things we can't grow or make on Thunder Island, all sorts of things, ma'am. Folks order from Portsmouth, New Hampshire, from Boston, from the other parts of Maine."

"Do you think you and the girls can handle all the food preparation and decorating and such, or shall I arrange for some women from Nansett to help you?"

"We can do all right by ourselves, Mrs. Blaize," she said firmly.

"Very well, Martha, but if you later decide that you could use some extra help — after all, there will be well over a hundred people here — just let me know. All of you may be so occupied with the cooking that we will need to bring a few women in just to clean. Now, about the dishes. I think we ought to serve meats other than seafood since everyone has that so much. Venison, lamb, beef, goose, perhaps, or duck . . ."

Martha nodded, reaching for her cookbook. For the rest of the morning the two of us became pleasantly engrossed in discussing the menu and the ways we might decorate the ballroom. It was decided that Amos would recruit the musicians to play. Jenny and Mary kept making excuses to leave their work and come into the kitchen, where they listened avidly to their mother and me. They were nearly beside themselves with excitement and once began to dance about the room in each other's arms. Their eagerness brought to mind what a pity it was that such an event had never taken place before, and I said as much to Martha.

"It'll be the finest kind, Mrs. Blaize," she said. "If you don't mind me saying so, youh're lookin' a deal happier. And you and the captain never had a weddin' pahrty, did you?"

"This ball is for all of us on Thunder Island."

"And to brace ourselves for the comin' winter, could be. Ayeh, it's a grand idea, ma'am. And it'll be good to see this house full of people, with music and dancin.' " She paused and then asked, "Does the captain's mother know about it yet?"

"No, but I'm going to tell her tonight. If she chooses not to attend, that is certainly her right. But my husband and I

318

hope she will accept the idea. It will be something exciting for her to anticipate, and if she is well rested she should be able to attend. Miss Thatcher too, of course."

Martha nodded but her face revealed her uncertainty. "Well, I have a load of things to do in the meantime. Seth can be huntin' some deer. Don't worry, ma'am, everything'll be done proper."

"I know things are in the most capable of hands," I said before going up to my room.

The sound of the surf was a constant powerful rumble. In Thunder Cove the water was a glistening aquamarine wrinkled with white foam. The view from my window made me long to be outside.

After lunch I buttoned up my walking shoes and put on my new cloak of sapphire blue wool, fastening the attached hood at my throat. I went out, descending the stone steps in the woods which led to the cove below.

The tide was moving away from the shore, which naturally made my progress easier. I saw an eagle sitting proudly on a low branch of a spruce tree; he would be fishing soon. I stepped from rock to rock around the cove, carefully avoiding the dark slippery patches of Irish moss. There was a brisk wind blowing but my cloak was warm.

In a while I came to the Selkie's Throne, looking not in the least ominous on this sunny afternoon. I passed it without a qualm, sheepishly recalling my alarmed fancies about selkies on Seal Island, and continued on. I had decided to walk to Noah's lighthouse.

The boulders along this stretch of shore were large and peaked; it was hard going climbing or jumping from one to the next. I forced myself to go slowly, not wanting another turned ankle. Sometimes I had to bend down and grasp the rough surfaces in my gloved fingers before I could move on to the next rock. At high tide it would be dangerous indeed because one would have to climb the jagged ridges which were high above the shore. To my right were the black-green spruces, staunchly facing the ocean, and farther into the forest I saw glimmers of red, golds, and corals.

After I had rounded another bend in the island, the lighthouse came into view. It was constructed of whitewashed stone and there was an iron watch circling its tower light. A large bell hung above the red door. The lighthouse itself stood on a grassy knoll above a particularly jagged crop of rocks and boulders which lunged out to sea.

There was a wooden flight of stairs leading up to the lighthouse from the hazardous shoreline. They looked rather rickety but when I tentatively mounted the first step I saw that they were sturdy. But they would be perilous in a storm, I thought, swept by fierce gales and drenching rain.

When I reached the lighthouse, I knocked on the red door. Noah had asked that I come by to visit him and I needed a respite after all the climbing I had done. Before long he opened the door, blinking in the glaring sunlight. His sparse hair stuck out every which way and his clothes were even more rumpled than usual; it was evident that he had been asleep.

"Why 'tis Mrs. Nicholas," he said, grinning at me.

"Hello, Noah. This is a fine lighthouse you have. It's very charming."

"Ayeh. But not only that. To a ship at night 'tis a blessed wahrnin.' This is a wicked coast hereabouts, and the Thunder Island lighthouse is the only thing savin' ships from bein' ate alive by the rocks."

"I'm sorry if I disturbed you, Noah."

"Oh, no. I was just havin' a lie-down. I can't sleep, mustn't sleep. Must keep the lighthouse goin.' "

"I imagine that you nap during the day so you can be awake at night."

"Ayeh. There's truth in that, Mrs. Nicholas. Though if the light's on, there ain't much else for me to do."

I turned to hide a smile. I imagined that he spent most of his time here dozing. I had heard that he sometimes had a boy, a young man, to help him. And as long as the light shone in the fog or darkness, there was no harm in Noah's habits.

"Do you ever ring the bell?" I asked him.

"Ayeh. I ring it in the fog when it's hahrd to see the

light. Would you come inside?"

"Well . . ." I didn't especially care to but I couldn't think of an adequate excuse that wouldn't hurt his feelings.

"This way, Mrs. Nicholas. Watch your step, it's dahrk in here when you come in from the sun."

He was right. When he held open the door, I saw a narrow winding stairway of iron, but once we were inside, it was almost black and it took a while before my eyes adjusted to the gloom. Noah lit a kerosene lamp and I followed him up the long staircase, clutching the spindly iron bannister for support.

We reached a landing about halfway up, where Noah had his room. The sun filtered down from the tower onto the tattered chairs, the rag rug, the makeshift table, the sea trunk.

"I just made a pot of coffee. I'll fetch us some."

"Oh, that's all right, Noah, I really don't . . ." but he was already filling two tin cups.

Taking the one he handed to me, I tried not to speculate on when it had last been washed. He regarded me with such pleased expectation that I had not the heart to refuse it and took a hesitant sip. It was tepid—and very bitter. After taking another heroic sip or two, I set it down on the trunk.

"Do you cook for yourself, Noah?"

"Ayeh, mostly. Sometimes I get bahskits of food from Nansett folk. I keep fine," he said, a trifle defensively.

"I'm sure you do, Noah. And I've enjoyed seeing the lighthouse. But I really must get back to Thunder House now or I'll be late for dinner. Thank you for showing me about."

"Wait. I'll light ye down. Wouldn't do for ye to fall, would it?" He grinned. With the lamp shining from below, his face looked mischievous and elfin and it made me slightly uncomfortable. Suddenly I wanted to get out of this dark shabby place as fast as I could. But I waited for him to go down the precarious twisting stairway before me. When at last we reached the bottom, he pushed open

321

the door and said, "Mrs. Nicholas, I been wantin' to tell ye . . ."

"Yes?"

He rubbed his nose, squinting in the sunlight. "I heard what happened to you at the launchin.' How you was almost killed by them supports."

"Well, thank heaven I was able to jump out of way just in time. I suppose that accidents like that can happen to anyone."

"Somethin' like that's never happened before, Mrs. Nicholas. Strange that it was you and not no other . . ."

"I merely happened to be the one standing beneath the section that was not secure, that is all," I said but my voice trembled slightly.

"Ayeh — looks that way. Might 'a been meant to look that way."

"What exactly are you saying, Noah?" I asked tensely.

He shook his head. "Nothin'. I ain't sayin' nothin'. Only — look out, Mrs. Nicholas. Be careful. Accidents can always happen."

Relaxing slightly, I said, "I assure you, Noah, that I won't go near a ship's support structures again. I've learned my lesson. But I'll be careful just the same." He was a nice old man but definitely odd. People were always claiming he hadn't all his wits about him. "Well, good day to you, Noah," I said, relieved to enter the world of blue sky, green grass, and sunshine.

I was nearly to the flight of stairs when I realized that I had neglected to ask Noah to play his fiddle for the ball. Amos would officially round up the musicians but I thought it would be nice if I asked him personally.

I walked back to the red door and opened it, calling, "Noah? I wanted to ask you —" My voice faded when I saw with a shock that he lay in a crumpled heap on the bottom step of the iron staircase. He was weeping pitifully, like a child.

"Noah! What has happened? Did you fall? Are you hurt?" I bent down beside him.

He looked up and gave a loud sniff, rubbing his face

with his sleeve. "Oh, it's nothin'. I didn't fall—I ain't hurt."

"It can't be nothing. I can see that you're distressed about something. Can I help you?"

"I won't say nothin'! I never said nothin'! And I won't. They can't take this lighthouse from me."

"Of course no one is going to take it from you," I said soothingly. "Don't worry, Noah. This is your home. We need you to man the lighthouse. No one is going to make you leave. Now why don't you go upstairs and rest? You must not fret anymore."

I helped him to his feet and he said, "Ayeh. I'll do that. I'll go have a lie-down. G'day, missus."

"Can you make it up the stairs all right? I can help you."

"Ayeh. I'm fine."

"Very well," I said reluctantly, "if you're certain. Goodbye, Noah, and don't worry about the lighthouse."

Shutting the door behind me, I wondered what could have so upset him that he feared losing his post as lighthouse keeper. The poor man had been crying like a brokenhearted child. And the way he had warned me . . . could there be a real significance to his mutterings?

When Morwenna brought hot water for my bath, she told me that Nicholas had come in and was downstairs. Lavinia and Sarah would be joining us in the dining room later this evening. So tonight would be a good opportunity for me to tell them of my plans for the ball. I hoped that the announcement would not precipitate another scene, but I would not be belittled or bullied this time; I would not change my mind and cancel the affair no matter what they said. At least, that was what I told myself.

The door from the hall to Nicholas's room shut then and I assumed he had gone in to get ready for dinner. My heartbeat quickened; just knowing he was in the room next to mine filled me with the familiar fluttery feeling. I went over to the armoire and took time in selecting what I would wear.

I finally decided on a black satin gown, which gleamed and glinted in the candlelight. It was quite sophisticated

323

and had a low decolletage, lower than any I had ever worn. I chose this gown deliberately, my motives mixed and unclear. I told myself that surely in such a gown I would look older, feel older, more confident, and I wanted to create such a presence before Sarah and Lavinia. *That* was my reason for wearing it. The notion that Nicholas could not help but notice me — notice the way the bodice was scooped low and then fit tightly to my waist before dropping in a V in the front, accentuating my figure — well, such a notion was inconsequential.

I instructed Morwenna to coil my hair and pin it high on my head. This style contributed to my elegant self-assured look, I thought with satisfaction. I dismissed her and went to answer Nicholas's knock when it came.

At the sight of him, his broad tall frame dressed in deep blue with the white stock at his throat, his face darkly attractive, I could not keep my own face from becoming a trifle pink. "Good evening, Nicholas," I said as coolly as I was able.

His eyes raked over me but I discerned no admiration or even interest in his face. Perhaps my voice had sounded too cool. I tried again. "I'm glad you . . . that is, I'm glad we're dining together tonight. I confess I was rather lonely last evening."

His eyes narrowed. "Were you?" He turned to look out the window at the violet dusk settling over Thunder Cove. I wanted to reach up and touch the new-moon scar in his cheek.

Instead I said, "I went over the arrangements for the ball with Martha today. I haven't told your mother or Sarah about it yet, but I will at dinner."

He made some sound of assent, his gaze still fixed out to sea. I wished he would look at me; I wished I knew what he was thinking. His jaw was set hard.

Rather desperately I went on, "This afternoon I walked to the lighthouse. It took longer to get there than I had anticipated, the going was so rough over the rocks."

"Most people take the path through the woods."

"Oh." I should have realized there would be an easier

324

way to get there. "A rather peculiar thing happened there, Nicholas. Noah invited me inside and gave me some dreadful coffee. I didn't stay long with him. After I had said good-bye and was walking away, I realized I had forgotten to ask him to play for the ball. So I went back across the lawn and opened the door. And there he was, weeping his heart out."

That diverted his attention from the view. Swiftly he turned his head, his brow knit. "Noah? Weeping?"

At least now he was looking at me. "Yes, and when I asked him what the matter was, he began to say that he didn't want the lighthouse to be taken from his care."

"Hmmm. That's odd, certainly. But he's getting quite old, you know. He'll never see eighty again."

"I realize that, but something had genuinely distressed him. You have no plans to relieve him as lighthouse keeper, do you?"

"No, he'll have that post until he's bedridden. He may be old but he's a fine keeper."

"Well, that's a relief. I'll be sure to reassure him the next time I see him. Perhaps he's just afraid that people consider him too old now. Though he did say, 'I won't say nothing' . . ." I frowned. It was as though my visit had in some way triggered his behavior.

"Don't worry, Miranda. I'm the only one who could force him to retire, since the lighthouse is on my land and it is I who pay his wages."

"You do? Well, that is something else. They must be woefully inadequate wages. The state of his room was shameful."

He grinned. "I know. I've seen it many times. But that's not to my account. He gets good wages, which he keeps in a brass pot under his bed. And he uses them to buy a bottle now and then—a practice he thinks no one is aware of. Well, I think we should go downstairs. By my watch, it's past eight."

I moved ahead of him to the door. He opened it and then said, "Miranda, that gown . . . don't you need a wrap, a shawl or something? It is rather—bare, is it not?"

325

So he *had* noticed. "I'm perfectly fine, Nicholas."

"Well, they're your shoulders," he said, shrugging, his voice once again aloof. "If you catch cold, you have only yourself to blame."

Clenching my teeth, I whisked myself out the door. I did not look at him; I did not speak to him as we went downstairs. Sarah and Lavinia were awaiting us in the dining room. Holding my head high, I bade them a pleasant good evening while Nicholas held out my chair.

"A new gown, Miranda?" asked Lavinia, her brows raised.

My color heightened a little but I said, "Yes. Do you like it?"

"Well . . . I wouldn't have thought you suited to such a style, would you have, Sarah? You do look elegant, alarmingly elegant, I would say. Still, it's a wonder you aren't shivering. Myself, I've always been plagued terribly by the drafts coming off the sea in this house."

"I assure you that I am comfortable." I looked across at Nicholas and saw I was the subject of his gaze. But then he turned away.

"We heard about what happened to you — or what nearly happened to you at the shipyard, Miranda," Lavinia was saying. "It really seems as though you go in search of trouble, you know. First you are stranded on Seal Island with a turned ankle, then you're nearly killed by falling supports. What in the world will be next, I wonder?" A slight smile hovered about her mouth. I looked across at Sarah, who also appeared amused.

Well, they won't look so smug when I tell them about the ball, I thought spitefully. But I felt the faintest glimmer of fear, of uncertainty at the same time. And not about the ball. When Mary and Jenny were serving our roast and vegetables, I mentioned that I had walked to the lighthouse that afternoon and what a pretty place it was — at least on the outside.

Surprisingly it was Sarah who responded. "Pretty but practically useless with that doddering old fool Noah Todd manning it. He's not fit to run the lighthouse and well you know it, Nicholas. You should get rid of him. He drinks, too, so I've heard. And his mind is not all what it should be. It's fortunate that these waters are so little traveled except by ships who know the island or we'd have one tragedy after another laid at our door."

"Oh, Noah's all right," said Nicholas easily. "He knows what a responsibility he has. And Tom Cameron helps him often. He'll make a good keeper one day, though his father would prefer it if he worked at the lumber mill. But the boy's got to decide for himself what he wants to do and I told Luke Cameron so."

"Surely his father knows best," said Lavinia deliberately. "Just as your father did, Nicholas, when he didn't want you to go off whaling."

Holding my breath, I stole a glance at Nicholas. But to my surprise his expression remained bland and he said without a trace of bitterness, "It's up to every man to decide for himself what he wants to do with his life, Lavinia. And if afterward he finds that it was not the right decision—well, he has only himself to blame and again it's up to him to alter his course."

"But if by following such a reckless course, he has already caused misery and suffering, then any alteration he makes afterward is meaningless, is it not?" she asked shrilly. "Since it came too late?"

"It is never too late," I said, and they all looked at me. Now is the time, I thought, or else she may keep goading Nicholas. "Nicholas and I have a surprise for you," I said.

"A surprise?" Lavinia frowned. "What do you mean?" Her face stiffened. "Oh, I think I begin to see what is behind your strange manner this evening, Miranda. However, I do not think that this is either the place or time for such an announcement. In my day we were discreet about such things. And there is absolutely no need for a formal announcement—I find that vulgar in the extreme. There will be plenty of time for the . . . preparations."

I stared at her in consternation. "You mean you know about it?"

"One scarcely needs to be a detective to form a likely

327

conclusion," she said haughtily.

What on earth was she talking about? What did she mean about being discreet? Was she actually referring to the ball? Totally bewildered, I turned to Nicholas for elucidation.

There was laughter in his eyes, which surprised me, and his smile was broad. I was even more confused. "I assume that Lavinia is alluding to an announcement of the family nature, my love."

"Oh!" I cried, blushing scarlet. How in the world had she jumped to *that* particular conclusion? "No, no, that's not what I meant at all. It's something quite different, Mrs. Blaize."

"Well, thank heaven for that," said Lavinia briskly.

Her cold response quelled my embarrassment. "As a matter of fact we are going to have a ball at Thunder House."

I had shocked her. "A ball? Now you have taken leave of your senses! Who on earth would come to a ball here?" Her voice was disdainful.

"Everyone, I hope, on Thunder Island," I said firmly.

Lavinia set her fork down with a snap. "Just whom do you mean by 'everyone'?"

"I think the meaning is perfectly clear, Lavinia," said Nicholas. "Thunder House is hosting a ball for the people of Nansett, for all the islanders, our servants included."

"Was this your idea or Miranda's?" Lavinia spat out. "You must be mad — both of you — to even consider such a thing! And without my permission!"

"Your permission, Lavinia, is valueless. This is my house, if I remember the terms of my father's will correctly. And Miranda is my wife. She may plan whatever entertainments she pleases. And she can invite anyone she pleases to those entertainments."

"I hoped you and Sarah would like the notion once you became accustomed to it. After all, you are always reminding us that there is no social life on Thunder Island," I said mildly.

"By that I meant that there is no decent society! If you

think that I am going to stand by and do nothing while you permit, while you encourage, those ruffians to traipse through Thunder House, stomping about in those uncouth dances, playing those caterwauling fiddles, singing those indecent sea shanties—"

"I'm afraid that is precisely what you must do, Lavinia," said Nicholas curtly. "Because the ball will take place. I work with those men every day. And my sister lives in Nansett and counts the people there her friends."

"I discovered the ballroom," I said hastily, "and thought what a shame that it is never used."

Lavinia threw me a scornful glance. "And you think the way for it to be properly used is to be trampled in by cloddish lobstermen and farmers? I should hardly be surprised. You haven't the slightest notion of what it means to belong to a family of wealth and position, of how to be a great lady. You were nothing but a poor governess before my son married you. How we laughed at you, didn't we, Sarah? Naturally I cannot expect any evidence of pride or breeding from you!"

Nicholas brought the palm of his hand down on the table, making the wine in the glasses swirl. "Not one more word, Lavinia! Don't you ever speak to my wife again like that! Miranda is already a part of life here on Thunder Island whereas you've never been involved in it in the past thirty-odd years. Naturally you find her idea to entertain the villagers ridiculous, to add a little brightness and enjoyment to people's lives. You've never had such a notion in all your life!"

"Nicholas, you are addressing your mother!" shouted Sarah.

He laughed without humor. "Well, there is no need for that any longer, is there? Come, my love." He tossed down his napkin and came over to pull out my chair. "We won't trouble you with our presence any further, Lavinia. I know that you will never be anything but displeased and disappointed with either of us. But your feelings no longer concern me. I have stomached enough insults and bitter denunciations from you over the last couple of years, not

329

to mention ever since I was a child. And I have sat here and listened to you belittle Miranda for the last time. From now on, my wife and I will take our meals in my wife's sitting room. I've told Martha it is to be for her use. For once, I would like to eat my dinner without your stupid vicious reproaches and complaints."

"It's Julia's sitting room!" she cried, her face white as the tablecloth. "Julia's! No one else has the right to use it! We had it done over for her just a year before—"

"She died, Lavinia. And it's Miranda's room now. We will no longer have any shrines to the dead in this house," Nicholas said coldly.

"You unnatural boy—your own sister! Not that you've ever had any proper feelings! You've never caused me anything but grief! I wish you had never been born, do you hear me?"

Nicholas's face was as white as her own. "I should imagine that everyone in this house can hear you, Lavinia. But, God help them, it's nothing they haven't heard before. You've always made your feelings quite plain. Good night."

He swept me out of the room and up the stairs. I felt sick and unsteady but Nicholas seemed strangely calm. When we reached my room, I sat down and he poured himself a glass of sherry from the decanter.

"I apologize for my part in that, Miranda. You must wonder sometimes what particular hell you've been thrust into. But I had to say what I did; I should have said it long ago." He drained his glass at once and poured himself another.

"I knew she wouldn't be in favor of the idea, Nicholas, but I didn't think she would be so . . . enraged. Perhaps we should cancel the ball after all."

"You are not going to make one change in your arrangements, Miranda," he said firmly. "You are going to give that ball in a few weeks just as you've planned. To go back now, to let her bully you that way . . . you might never regain the ground you'd lose. I'm sorry it has to be this way, that we must always seem to be in direct opposition to her, but that is her fault entirely. My father gave in to her on everything, I'm afraid, but even that never made her happy. And I am not my father—someone she can dominate—and she's always resented me for that. I apologize for the way she spoke to you, for the way she has treated you since you entered this house. I can imagine how you must have felt time and again, subjected to that. You never complained, though, and I—well, I've had my mind on other things. But from now on, you don't have to see her if you don't wish. This house is large enough that we can live our lives quite separately from the two of them."

"She and Sarah really hate me," I said slowly. "It's . . . frightening to be the target of so much ill feeling."

"Well, try not to think about it," he said heavily. "There is absolutely nothing you or I can do about Lavinia's feelings. The only time she's happy is when she's living in the past, in her fantasies."

"I overheard her talking to Julia again, the day of the launching. I've heard her do it on two other occasions. Why does Sarah permit it? She doesn't seem to do anything to discourage her."

"I've asked myself on many occasions whether Sarah is, in fact, the right companion for her. I've even considered dismissing her. But they are so devoted to each other that I'm afraid if Sarah left—if I was the cause of her leaving—that Lavinia's grip on sanity would weaken even more. After losing Julia I think it would kill her to lose Sarah. And she needs someone to love her unconditionally—we all need that. Sarah would do anything for Lavinia, anything to make her life a little more bearable."

I felt suddenly cold but it had nothing to do with the bareness of my gown.

I moved closer to the fire. Nicholas went on, "I didn't allow you to finish your meal. Are you still hungry? Shall I ask one of the girls to bring something up?"

Wearily I shook my head. "I couldn't eat another bite tonight. In fact, I feel rather sick. My head's aching too." The weight of my hair was adding to my discomfort. I began to pull out the pins, shaking out the coils which fell down my back and over my shoulders.

"You look very beautiful, Miranda," said my husband quietly.

"Don't, Nicholas," I said shakily. "I know you don't care for this gown on me just as your mother didn't. I suppose someone like me does look rather ridiculous in it, trying to look like someone she's not, dressing up in her older sister's gown or something. If Miss Proctor made one mistake, it was designing this gown for me. I won't wear it again." I twitched a fold of it impatiently.

"Then you'll be doing me a great disservice, depriving me of such a sight. I've been thinking all evening how well it suits you."

I flushed and looked up at him. Setting down his glass he said, "Well, I'll leave you now. No doubt you wish to be alone after such an evening. Again, I'm sorry your ball had to be met with such a violent reaction, but on no account are you to give up the idea. I'll bid you good night."

He was opening the door to his room when the words were flung out of me, "Nicholas, don't go, please." Then I colored as he turned back to me.

"What is it, Miranda?" His tone was detached but in his eyes was a sudden keen smoldering. My heart began to thud in my breast. "I thought you said you felt poorly. Can I send for Morwenna?"

I began clenching and unclenching my hands. "No, I don't want Morwenna," I said in a small voice. "And I'm feeling better now."

"Well, what is it then?" When I did not answer he said, "What *do* you want, my love?"

"I . . ." We looked at one another across the distance that separated us and I thought that neither of us breathed. "I want you, Nicholas," I said simply.

"If I thought you really meant that—" He ruffled his hair with one hand, his eyes narrowing swiftly.

"But I do mean it, Nicholas. Do you want me to say it? Very well, please don't leave me. Don't let us sleep apart tonight."

There was a tinge of color in his cheeks; the scar was scarcely visible. There was still uncertainty in his face, and I knew why. So many times I had rejected his shows of affection or afterward I had shrunk from him, not seeking, not encouraging another ardent demonstration. Perhaps that was why he had left me to wake and sort out my feelings alone after the last time he had made love to me. And what had I done? I had acted as though the passion between us had never existed because I had learned that he had once been in love with Heather. I still had no answers to my doubts about her but just now that seemed irrelevant.

And my arrogant husband was unsure of how to proceed. I could tell he was wondering whether I was actually in earnest even after I had spoken and so I smiled, hoping he would realize that I meant what I had said in the most literal sense.

He seemed to relax suddenly, to loosen a hold on himself that had been self-inflicted. And then he came across to me and I stood up. When he took me in his arms, I could feel him trembling the way he had in the past when he had held me. I, too, was trembling and lifted my face to his and drew his head down. I gave a small sigh of contentment through parted lips and then his mouth was devouring mine, his tongue probing, demanding a response from me that needed no demanding. Through the folds of my gown I felt the urgent hardness of him; I was conscious of his desperate frustration, the longing he had kept tightly reined. He swept my hair aside, his kisses searing my neck and blazing a trail of fire down to my breasts. His fingers were undoing the buttons of my gown, and when it was off, he carried me to the bed, my body naked in his strong arms.

Nothing mattered now but this between us. Now was not a time for doubts or fears or questions. It was a time to revel in the wild torrent we aroused in one another until the delicious delirious torture had ceased its raging. Our all-consuming need for one another was more powerful than anything, greater than the two of us.

He covered my body with his own and moved his dark head over my skin, taking a nipple in his mouth. My fingers were buried in his thick black locks and I was straining against him, silently pleading with him to appease my frenzied longing, to possess me completely.

"Do you know you drive me wild, my prim little governess?" he said huskily, his breath warm on my bare skin. "Tonight I could scarcely trust myself to look at you, I wanted so to take you, to claim you as mine. In fact . . ." He was emphasizing every word or so with kisses. ". . . there are times . . . and many of them . . . when I cannot think . . . of anything else. I only have . . . to look at you . . . and then my blood . . . begins to boil."

I was beyond words. I could only see and touch and respond, my fingers running down his back to his hard buttocks, my hair in my face, in his face, his hands kneading my breasts, his body driving into mine until the heart-stopping moments when the world—our world, our only world—burst inside us in a white-hot explosion of ecstasy so intense, so violent, that we were both crying out, our bodies branded together in victory.

Sometime in the night I dreamed that someone was screaming—long harsh agonizing screams. I tried to reach out to whomever it was but there was nothing but a vast blackness; I could not find the sufferer. Then my shoulders were being shaken and a dear voice was calling my name. I awoke to see that Nicholas had lit two candles by the bed and was pulling on his dressing gown.

"What is it?" I asked. "Where are you going?"

It was then that I realized that the screams had not stopped. I was no longer dreaming; I had never been dreaming.

"You stay here until I discover what has happened. I only woke you so you wouldn't be frightened to find me gone."

I sat up, rubbing my eyes. Abruptly the screaming stopped. "But what's happened, Nicholas?"

334

"God only knows." And he was out of the room.

Immediately I got out of bed and stood shivering in the cold room. The fire had died long ago. I wondered what time it was. Reaching for my dressing gown, I fastened it across the bodice and picked up the other candlestick.

There was no sound now in the house, nothing but an ominous chilling silence. Who in the world had been making those dreadful sounds? Could it have been Lavinia in another sort of fit? I went out in the hallway, thinking that this silence was even worse, following so suddenly after the screaming as it had. I was conscious of a peculiar icy emptiness and I felt the prickles rise on the back of my neck.

As tempted as I was to run back in my room and hide beneath the bedclothes, instead I made my way down the dark paneled hallway. My shadow loomed before me on the wall. I must find Nicholas, I kept saying over and over. I must find Nicholas.

When I reached the second-story landing, I hesitated. A door was open on the corridor where Lavinia and Sarah had their rooms, and a meager wavering light shone from it. I heard hushed voices then and I hurried toward the room, not caring that my candle had flickered and gone out.

"There you are, Nicholas," I said in relief, pushing my hair out of my face.

"I told you to stay in your room, Miranda."

"I know, but I was frightened up there all alone. I didn't know where you'd gone . . ."

Sarah was standing by Lavinia's bed looking down at her form. Lavinia's fine-boned profile was to the ceiling. She lay very still.

"What . . ." I began, the truth gradually dawning on me. "Lavinia . . . is she . . . ?"

"Yes, she's dead," Nicholas said grimly. "Sarah found her. Apparently she took an overdose of laudanum. The bottle is there on her night table."

"Oh no!"

Sarah looked across at him, her face ravaged with grief

335

and loathing. "This is your fault, Nicholas Blaize! Now you see where your words this evening led! Are you finally satisfied now, having destroyed most of the people at Thunder House? My God, I could kill you for what you've done to her! Poor, poor Lavinia—I've never seen her the way she was tonight. You cut her down like an animal. You're a devil, Nicholas Blaize!"

"That's enough, Sarah," I said heatedly. "You've no right to speak to my husband like that! Isn't this situation terrible enough—"

"I've no right! I'd like to know who has a better one! I helped to raise him and his sisters!"

"Without ever giving him the slightest amount of love and affection. You've no rights to anything concerning him! Lavinia's unhappy tortured life is over—but that cannot be laid on Nicholas's door. And if you continue to blame him for her suicide, you'll be off this island when the next ship comes."

"Not another word, either of you," said Nicholas. "What's done is done." His voice was bleak; he ruffled his hair with his fingers. "I'm almost surprised she didn't do something like this before now. Maybe at last she has found the peace and comfort which was so lacking in her life here. I hope so." He paused and then said to me, "I only hope that this will not have any ill effects on Emily's condition."

"Still thinking of yourself and your selfish sister! Lavinia is dead, do you realize that? What does it matter what effect the news has on Emily, so what if she loses the lobsterman's brat? I hope now she'll finally show some proper feeling for her poor neglected mother!"

Nicholas ignored her and took my arm. "She doesn't know what she's saying, Nicholas," I said as we went up the stairs.

"Whether she does or she doesn't, it makes no difference," he said wearily. "As I said, what's done is done. Lavinia calculated very well. It was her final act of viciousness. She hoped I would feel an even greater guilt than any she had inflicted on me in the past."

"She is at peace now, Nicholas, no matter what her intentions were when she took the laudanum. She no longer hates you."

Neither of us could think of going back to bed so he built a fire in my room and we sat together, speaking little. My mind kept playing over and over the picture of Lavinia lying on the bed, her face tinged with blue.

Later I asked him, "What happens now, Nicholas?"

"Well, obviously certain arrangements have to be made. At first light I'll ride to Nansett to see the Reverend Whitcomb. We'll have the funeral service here at Thunder House, a private one. Of course the story will have to be that she accidentally took too much of the drug, that she was overwrought. That way she will be assured a proper burial in the mausoleum. Also I must break the news to Emily. There won't be any work done today at the mill or shipyard out of respect for Lavinia's memory. And Ben can help Emily through the shock."

When dawn eventually came, he insisted that I go back to bed before he went downstairs to inform the servants. Being at the back of the house and on the floor below, they had not been roused by Sarah's screams. I did not see how anyone could have slept through them. Amos was to order a coffin.

I slept for a few hours until Morwenna brought in a pot of tea and some toast. She was wide-eyed and filled with a suppressed excitement; I could not blame her for that. Lavinia had not been one to inspire affection or admiration from the servants.

"How is Miss Thatcher this morning?" I asked her as she helped me into a black bombazine gown.

"Oh ma'am, it were terrible. She be in her room now. Mary gave her a draught to make her sleep. But they had to pull her away from the missus. I was in the hall with Mary and we heard her. . . . It gave me the shivers."

I knew that the servants must have heard the shouting from the dining room last night whether or not they had heard the actual content. I wondered whether they had guessed the truth about Lavinia's death.

337

Nicholas came back early in the afternoon bringing with him Emily and Ben, who were to stay at Thunder House until the funeral service in several days' time. Emily was very pale but composed. She requested to see her mother, and Ben took her upstairs. After that they retired to her old room.

I looked for Nicholas but could not find him. I felt very troubled and restless so I walked to Blackett's Glade and stayed for a while by that melancholy forsaken place. I could only guess at what thoughts haunted Nicholas just now; I supposed there were both regret and sadness in his heart. I only hoped there was no guilt. As for myself I was still obsessed by my last sight of Lavinia, limp and still and frail. And I fancied that a new gray wraith had taken its place with the others, emerging from the cheerless depths of the glade.

Chapter Fifteen

Emily took her mother's death very hard. The first night when we gathered in the dining room with some pretense of eating, she began to weep uncontrollably and Ben had to take her upstairs. Later that evening Ben confided to us that he feared she was blaming herself for the tragedy, for abandoning her mother and leaving Thunder House when she married. Nicholas went up to her room and stayed with her for a long while and Ben and I remained in the drawing room in a rather helpless guilty silence. Neither of us said it aloud but I believe we were both remembering that to Lavinia we were the social outcasts, the upstarts who had dared marry into her family, and her suicide had been directed as much at us and at our intrusion as anything else. It had been her final shattering protest against life—hers and all of ours.

I learned from Martha that the memorial service for Julia had also been held at the house but in her case the same reasoning—a desire for privacy—did not apply. It was because her body had never been found. Lavinia had been too ill to endure the ride into Nansett, her grief too devastating to expose to people she considered strangers.

But Nicholas had invited Katherine MacLeod and Heather to Lavinia's funeral. I wondered at this because Katherine herself had told me that she had had little or no contact with Lavinia. But Nicholas explained that as they were the other family on Thunder Island with a status near to that of the Blaizes, it was the correct thing to invite them. Roger Blaize himself had been a friend of the Reverend Bruce and Mrs. MacLeod, no matter how much Lavinia had held herself aloof.

Nicholas did not add that in previous years Heather had occasionally dined at Thunder House with him, his mother, Sarah, Julia, and Emily—but he did not need to mention this. The image of her sitting regally (for how could she sit any other way?), never a prey to the anxiety which would overwhelm me at the dining room table, had strongly impressed itself on my mind since Sarah had gloatingly told me of my husband's interest and attachment to Heather.

Despite what had passed between Nicholas and myself on the night of his mother's death, I was not certain he had put Heather completely behind him. I knew little about men; it was not incomprehensible to me that Nicholas could take his pleasure with his wife and then also turn elsewhere. It was anguishing, unbearable to me—but not incomprehensible.

So I dreaded the day of the funeral for more reasons than merely succumbing to the morbid somberness of the occasion which afflicts all of us when we put the dead to rest. I dreaded it because Heather MacLeod would be present, and I might find a painful significance behind every word she spoke, every gesture she made.

Once again Nicholas was remote, silent, his face stony during those days following his mother's death. Yet I did not attempt to reach him, not this time. From Ben I learned that he had suspended work at the shipyard in respect to the wife of the former owner, but he himself went there and much of his time at Thunder House was spent closeted in his library. Ben and Emily spent long hours in her room and I was left to myself, wandering about outdoors despite the weather, which had turned sharply cold. The vivid leaves were muting, turning brittle, their luster dimming. Some had dropped to the forest floor, where they formed dense piles, making hissing and rushing sounds with every gust of wind, crunching beneath every step. They gave off a pungent smell, which seemed

340

the smell of decay and death.

The day of the funeral was inevitably a cold dreary day with the feel and scent of rain which refused to fall. Early that morning I went downstairs and knocked on Sarah's door. Since the first morning she had not left her room. Her meals had been left on a tray outside her door but Martha confided to me that they were scarcely touched. We had left her to her solitude, to her grief, perhaps cravenly, but we had done it. It was certainly less distressing than seeing her vengeful face before us. Emily had once tried to speak with her, but Sarah had tenaciously kept her own counsel. As for myself, I was shamelessly relieved that I did not have to see her ravaged countenance and listen to her ugly accusations.

But that morning I stood outside in the corridor, saying, "Sarah, it's Miranda. Are you there? Can you hear me?"

No answer.

"Lavinia's funeral will be held at eleven o'clock this morning in the drawing room. Will you come down?"

And still there was nothing but that unyielding malignant silence.

Before eleven o'clock we were assembled in the drawing room for the ceremony, Nicholas, grim and forbidding in his customary black; Emily, looking wan but calm, her hands folded over her rounded stomach in a touching protective gesture; Ben, a trifle ill at ease in his formal clothes, his face in its solemnity reminding me of Zeke; and myself, feeling a bit sick, longing for the ordeal to be over.

Amos ushered in Katherine and Heather. Katherine immediately went over to Emily and for a few moments Emily rested her head on the older woman's shoulder. Nicholas had gone to greet Heather and I stood there watching while she pressed his hand with her slim gloved fingers, her tilted violet-blue eyes expressing sympathy. Naturally she had known of the relationship between Nicholas and his mother; she had had years to observe and understand. She said something to him in a low voice which I could not catch and he bent his head toward her, nodding slightly. Then Katherine was taking Nicholas's hands in hers and Heather had moved across to speak to Emily and Ben.

I felt alien then, a distant stranger outside the bonds of years which linked the rest of them. Years they had lived through together, years I had missed. Now Ben was not an outcast; now it was only I who was not a part of their collective experience on Thunder Island. Even Sarah, who had entered and was standing at the back of the room, her eyes cast down, her face as tight and unyielding as always, even Sarah was a part of the dramas they had all played out on Thunder Island, whereas I was the latecomer, the interloper, bewildered, forlorn, uncertain of my role, of the part I was to play.

The Reverend Whitcomb arrived then. He was a young man rather pompously filled with the solemnity of his office, bent on striking the proper note of gravity for such an occasion. I wondered whether any of them, those not of the family, had guessed the truth that Lavinia's death had not been an accident. The servants undoubtedly had; for years they had been privy to the dark complex emotions festering in Thunder House from the anguish and bitterness unleashed in Lavinia by Julia's death to the seething outrage in Nicholas evoked by the ambush of the *Eagle* by great brutal mounds of ice.

The Reverend Whitcomb read the service for the dead and then the Twenty-Third Psalm. He spoke of Lavinia Blaize in almost saintly terms. When no doubt he had paid his infrequent visits to her, she had impressed him with the gracious condescending air she could assume. I found it all uncomfortably ironic and wondered what the others were thinking. At one point the minister paused and looked diffidently at Nicholas as though he expected him to say something, but Nicholas did not respond, his face as hard as granite, his eyes like gray flint.

Nicholas, Ben, Amos, and Seth carried the coffin from the house across the south lawn and into the woods. We waited, hushed, expectant, while the coffin was lowered into the ground and Mr. Whitcomb commended the soul of Lavinia Blaize to God. From the shore came the forlorn cries of sea gulls. The wind was raw, the sky a dark streaked gray. The odor of the crumpled leaves was very strong. I watched as Emily tossed a spray of yellow chrysanthemums onto the grave but I did not watch as the first clumps of soil struck the coffin with their conclusive thuds.

We made our way back to Thunder House, a somber procession of black-garbed figures. The Reverend Whitcomb was walking with Katherine and Heather; ahead of Nicholas and myself Emily was leaning on Ben's arm. Sarah did not follow us. When I looked back over my shoulder, I saw her standing rigidly by the grave as Amos and Seth filled it with earth.

Martha had prepared an elaborate funeral luncheon for us and our guests. After we sat desultorily in the drawing room over glasses of sherry, we went into the dining room to take our places. I was ready to sit down at what had been my usual place on Nicholas's right, but Nicholas was pulling out that chair for Heather. This struck me like a blow until I realized almost giddily that I was now truly the mistress of Thunder House and my rightful place was at the other head of the table. No longer could Lavinia withhold it from me.

But still I was disconcerted, pausing uncertainly before sitting down, until Nicholas frowned at me. The others had been waiting to take their cue from me. Flushing, I sat down and the rest of them followed suit. On either side of me were the Reverend Whitcomb and Ben; Katherine was on Nicholas's left; Emily was next to the young minister. A place had been set for Sarah between Heather and Ben but she did not appear. The empty chair and the glass of water were hostile reproaches.

Nicholas sat at the head of the table, his black brows drawn together. I watched him nod in response to something Heather had said and I wished desperately that I could also have heard what she had said. She was looking quietly radiant in black taffeta, a large cameo brooch at her throat. I wondered whether my own black gown with

343

its puffed sleeves and tucked bodice was too elaborate, whether I was possibly overdressed for such a solemn occasion. Her flaxen hair was parted and drawn back over her ears in a simple chignon; were my own ordered curls which fell to my shoulders too frivolous?

I knew I should be talking to our guests, drawing Ben and the minister into conversation, doing my best to dispense grace and charm, but I could not. I felt frozen inside, brittle, as though at one odd word or glance I would shatter into a thousand pieces. The food I found unappetizing. I looked at the rare rib roast swimming in a pool of redolent seasoned sauce and I had to press my hand to my mouth and look away. My head was aching again the way it had lately; it felt heavy, too heavy.

Gradually the mood of the funeral dinner was altering, improving. Ben was asking Nicholas something about the plans for the new ship. I overheard Katherine asking Emily what things she needed for the baby. She offered to sew some dresses. Heather also offered her services, "Though I'm not the seamstress Mother is." I wondered whether Katherine sewed their gowns, which were always beautifully cut and had an unassuming elegance. She might not be able to live as well as Lavinia had but she and Heather each looked the part of a great lady.

" . . . the week of the ball. We should have enough lumber from the mill by then." It was Nicholas talking and his startling words broke into my musings.

"The ball?" I asked incredulously. "You mean we are still to give it?"

All heads turned to me. "Of course," Nicholas said shortly.

"But . . . I assumed that now . . . that after . . . don't you think we ought to cancel our plans, or at least postpone them?"

"Most assuredly not. Granted, it may not be in the best of taste but this situation is unique. I believe that with all things considered, the ball must take place as scheduled."

"But Lavinia was so opposed to the notion," I pointed out.

"That is precisely why." Nicholas's voice was cold. "Lavinia spoiled enough pleasure for people when she was alive. She will not continue to do so in death."

Now everyone had turned to look at him. The Reverend Whitcomb stiffened. Katherine leaned over and put her hand on Nicholas's arm, her face warm and understanding.

"There has been talk of little else in Nansett besides the ball," said Heather. "The people here need such an event, Miranda. Nicholas knows what he is doing."

She spoke quietly without malice, but I felt hot anger welling up inside me. How dare she defend, explain, *my husband* to *me*? As though I were unable to comprehend or appreciate his reasonings! Again I was being shown that I was the intruder, the one who didn't belong, the one who could not understand all the complexities of life on Thunder Island. I felt my face growing warm; inside I was boiling with rage. I sat stiff as a board, staring down at my plate, wanting to scream, wanting to get up and shake Heather, wanting to run from the room, wanting to sob my heart out. I had not felt this towering anger since I had chased a boy in India who had stolen a coin from another boy.

Finally we got up from the table and returned to the drawing room for tea. Katherine came up to me and put an arm around my shoulders. "You look very tired, my dear. Why don't you go upstairs and rest? And I think Emily should do the same. This has been a prolonged ordeal for all of you. Don't worry about us; Heather and I will be leaving shortly. Mr. Whitcomb is graciously escorting us."

I did not demur; I was grateful for her suggestion. I wanted nothing more than to be alone. And a debilitating weariness was creeping over me. I longed to lie down. "I think I will, Katherine. Thank you for coming." I went across to thank the Reverend Whitcomb also, bidding him good-bye.

I went upstairs, scarcely caring that Nicholas was downstairs with Heather and I was no longer able to scrutinize

345

them together, to strain to catch their words. Utter exhaustion washed over me and I dropped on my bed, fully clothed, and gave myself up to sleep.

When I awoke, the dusk had already fallen. Morwenna had not drawn the curtains; the tall windows framed a purple blackness pricked with tiny stars. I wondered what was happening in the house, where everyone was, but I was too listless, too lethargic to consider leaving my room.

Groggily I sat up, unfastened the front hooks of the black gown, and took it off. Then I took off my undergarments, which felt unbearably confining, and trod unsteadily across the carpet to fetch my nightgown from the armoire. My last thought before I fell asleep again was of Sarah. What would she do now?

Emily and Ben returned to Nansett on the following day. She was looking much improved and she confessed to me it would be a relief to get back to her own house. "Ben doesn't feel comfortable in these surroundings and I find I prefer my own cottage, too."

Nicholas had ridden over to the shipyard before I was up, and after seeing Ben and Emily off, I had the day ahead of me. I went upstairs and as I was crossing the second-story landing I was surprised to see the doors opened to the corridor where Julia had lived. One of the girls must be cleaning her room, I thought, and Emily's room too.

The door to Julia's bedroom was open. When I entered, I was amazed to see that Jenny and Mary were there emptying the clothes from the wardrobe and chest of drawers. There were boxes lying about and gowns and things covered the bed, some folded, some tossed haphazardly.

"What are you doing?" I asked them.

"The captain's orders, Mrs. Blaize," said Jenny. "All of Miss Julia's things are to be packed up and sent to the village to the church bazaar. Mother's in *her* room packing her things, too."

"Do you mean Mrs. Blaize's things?"

Mary nodded. "Captain Nicholas told Miss Thatcher in

346

the kitchen this mornin' that she could have any of the old mistress's things, but whatever she didn't want was going to the church. Miss Thatcher—she was mad as a hornet though she didn't say nothin'. But her face—it went almost purple, didn't it, Jen?"

"You say that Martha is in Mrs. Blaize's room? Do you know where Miss Thatcher is now?"

"She's there, too. She said nobody was to go through the mistress's things without her there."

Nicholas wasn't wasting any time, I thought. And even though a part of me applauded his actions, I was conscious of a chill seeping through me. For Sarah this would be the last betrayal.

I went down the hall to Julia's sitting room. It was my room now, I realized, truly mine, but just now I got no comfort from that thought. I pulled the bellrope, and when Seth came, I asked him to build a fire. When he had done so, the room began to look more cheerful. I sat down at the piano. Now I would not have to practice anymore at the church; now I no longer had to feel confined in my bedroom because it was the only room in the house in which I felt at ease. This was my house now, and my piano. No longer must I furtively creep about Thunder House. I was the only Mrs. Blaize now; I was the only mistress.

I practiced for the rest of the morning and then at noon I went down the hall to Julia's room. I told the maids that I would take my luncheon in my sitting room.

That afternoon I put on my blue pelisse and poke bonnet with rutching across the top and went outside. A wan yellow light sifted through the rippled clouds but no warmth accompanied it. For some reason I headed across the lawn and entered the south woods, making my way to the cemetery. I felt drawn to that melancholy spot; I moved forward with an unholy fascination.

But when I reached it, I saw that someone was there before me. Sarah was hunched over the freshly dug grave, her shoulders heaving. I froze in my tracks but it was too late; she had already seen me. She had heard my crunching steps on the leaves and was now looking up, her face a mottled red, her eyes swollen and swimming with tears.

"What do you want here, Miranda?" she spat out. "Have you come to gloat over the way you and your husband rid yourselves of Lavinia? You think you've won, don't you? You had this in mind since first coming to Thunder House—you couldn't bear that she stood in your place as mistress."

"You're wrong, Sarah," I said, twisting my wedding ring round my finger. "I never wished to displace her. It was she who felt threatened by me. That was why she took every opportunity to try and convince me of my inferiority."

"She had no need to convince you! She *was* superior, innately superior. And you couldn't bear that, could you? She saw you for what you were—a scheming adventuress of no background who wanted desperately to improve her situation in life. Somehow you saw to it that Nicholas took pity on you. Lavinia and I wondered how you manipulated a man like Nicholas into marriage, but Nicholas is a fool in the way that every man is a fool. He was never impervious to a pretty face, and who knows what other wiles you used to tempt him into marriage?"

"How dare you, Sarah, how dare you suggest such a thing?" I asked in a trembling voice. "Of all the vile—"

"You and Nicholas tormented poor Lavinia until she took her own life! And now he wants to wipe every trace of her from the house, *her* house, sending her beautiful things, and Julia's too, to the fisherfolk in Nansett!"

"Lavinia and Julia no longer have need of their clothes. Why shouldn't others be able to enjoy them?"

"You and Nicholas, you revolt me! And now you're going to have your ball with his mother scarcely cold in her grave! I know that you both are pleased that she's dead, but must you show your feelings so blatantly? Can't you show the slightest bit of respect due to her, even if it's all pretense?" Her face had become skull-white; her eyes burned into mine.

"You are determined to see the worst in Nicholas and

me. It's not that way at all, Sarah. Nicholas, I think, feels that this is a special event for everyone that we should not cancel. If it's put off much longer, the weather will make it impossible for the people to get to Thunder House easily. Nicholas and Emily both grieve for their mother, but we all must look ahead. And even you can't pretend that Lavinia ever gave Nicholas the slightest bit of love that was due *him*."

"And so he wants to oust her from his memory, from his house? He knows she loathed the idea of opening the ballroom to the people of Nansett — Noah Todd and those other oafs! I'm almost happy that Lavinia won't be here to see it. It's a disgrace, Nicholas is a disgrace! He's a thoroughly bad sort — he always has been."

"And you and Lavinia doubtless lost no opportunities over the years to tell him so! And when he returned from the Arctic that last time, he believed it!"

"Why shouldn't he believe the truth about himself? You're the fool who refuses to see him for what he is. You've been married to him a month. You know nothing of his past, of his character. It was only his father's poor health that prevented him from throwing aside responsibility and going off whaling, and as soon as his father was dead and buried, he abandoned his family, his home, his business, threw it back in his poor mother's face and rushed off to Nantucket to hire himself out as a common sailor, a greenhand. He with his background, his advantages! He's a rash arrogant man with no proper feelings. He does what he pleases and cares nothing about others. Well, he finally got his just deserts. The icebergs were the death of all his fine dreams!"

"I'm not going to stand here and listen any longer, Sarah. Nothing I can say will have any effect on you. But nothing you say can touch me anymore either." I turned away from her.

"Nothing? Not even that he met with Heather MacLeod in the Folly in the woods, the Folly Roger built for Lavinia? I saw her there myself one day through the window. And I saw him."

And then I was running away from the cold graveyard but her face followed me, gloating, malevolent, speaking those words in a strange exalted voice which cut through me like a knife. She hates Nicholas, I said over and over. She'll say anything against him. But I myself had seen Heather at the Folly. Had she seen me in the woods and followed me there, deriving a twisted pleasure out of talking to me in the place where she had been intimate with my husband?

Dusk was falling. I hurried into the house, past Mary, who was lighting the sconces in the hall, and up to my room. Untying the strings of my bonnet with shaking fingers, I tossed it on the floor. After shrugging off my pelisse, I reached for the decanter of sherry on the low-bow, hoping a glass of wine would restore my composure.

I poured out a glass and was lifting it to my lips when the door opened behind me and a voice said, "So there you are."

The glass slipped from my fingers. Detachedly I watched it fall to the floor, spilling its contents and rolling to one side without breaking. Then I turned around to see Nicholas standing there, still in his work clothes, which were streaked and smudged, his hands black with soot, his hair disordered, his eyes gleaming like pewter.

"You've come for the final burning," he said. He looked triumphant, larger than life. He took my hand and drew me into his bedroom, where I was startled to see the hearth piled high with objects which were blazing fiercely.

"What . . . what are you doing, Nicholas?" I asked weakly.

"Burning everything from the *Eagle* that will burn. These nameboards are the last." He picked one up and tossed it into the fire, where the flames licked at the gold leafing and blackened the wood's varnish.

The candles had not been lit. There was no light in the room except that from the meager twilight and the brilliant dancing flames. Shadows flickered across his face. He was filled with a strange tense excitement. Dazedly I tried to make sense out of what was happening.

350

"Tomorrow I'll take the rest of these things to outfit the new bark at the shipyard. The captain can have them at no expense."

"Why are you doing this now?" My head felt fuzzy, thick.

"You told me to get rid of everything in here, didn't you, Miranda? Everything that reminded me of that last voyage."

I nodded dumbly, my gaze fixed on the *Eagle's* funeral pyre.

"Well, haven't you anything at all to say?" His gaze was intent; his face was taut, expectant.

The heat of the flames were dancing before my eyes; they whirled and twisted just as Sarah's last words whirled and twisted in my head with the same ferocity. I was becoming dizzy; I felt scalded by the flames.

"I have to get out of here—it's too close," I murmured, putting a hand to my hot cheek.

I saw through a thickening veil of discomfort that he was angry. His black brows were drawn together in a scowl. "Is that all you can say, Miranda?" he cried. "I confess I expected more of you. I thought you would be—" He broke off, clenching his jaw. "But I often seem to be wrong where you're concerned!"

"I'm sorry, Nicholas. I can't stay . . . I feel ill . . ." I stumbled from his room and into my own. There came then the deafening sound of splitting wood followed by a violent crash. He must have broken the other nameboard and savagely thrown it into the fire.

My room was permeated with the cloying nauseating odor of sweet sherry. I looked at the brown stain on the carpet and knew I could control myself no longer. With a great effort I reached under the bed for the chamber pot before succumbing to the needs of my heaving outraged stomach. I was repeatedly ill before I realized that Nicholas had come into the room. He held my shoulders and drew my hair back from my damp face. When the spasms had finally ceased, he wiped my face with a wet cloth and drew my head to his chest. We sat there on the floor.

"God, Miranda, I thought you just wanted to get away from me. I had no idea that you were going to be sick! What in the world has made you so ill?"

For a few moments I could not answer. Then I said haltingly, "I think . . . I think I must be going to have a baby."

There was a breathless silence. Opening my eyes, I sat up and looked bleakly at him. He was regarding me with something akin to awe on his face.

"My dearest girl, do you really think so?" he asked softly.

"I'm . . . I'm almost certain of it. I see now why I've felt the way I have. Are you . . . are you pleased?"

"Pleased? I—I hardly know what to say. It's wonderful! I don't know why but the idea hadn't really occurred to me before. I must admit I'm surprised—it's not as though we . . . We haven't been married that long yet; it must have been that first night, on board ship . . ." I said nothing in reply and his face tensed. "What about you, Miranda? How do you feel about it? Aside from the obvious physical discomfort, that is."

"I don't know." I pushed my hair back from my face. "I hadn't really thought about it either."

"So you mind, then?" he asked, his voice suddenly crisp.

"No, of course not. It's just rather . . . unexpected, I suppose. Coming so soon after your mother and after— everything."

"Perhaps it's providential," he said. "But I realize you don't feel much like talking now. I'll ring for Morwenna and she can help you." He lifted me in his arms and lay me down on the bed.

"No, don't call her, Nicholas. Don't . . . don't leave me. I think perhaps I can fall asleep if you'll just stay with me."

"Of course I'll stay with you, my love. I won't leave you." He unfastened my gown and gently removed my clothes before helping me into my nightgown. Then he made me drink a glass of water. I lay back on the pillow

352

which felt pleasantly cool.

Again the sweeping exhaustion was overtaking me and I could not keep my eyes open. "Good night, Nicholas," I murmured.

"Good night, sweet," he said and I felt his tender kiss on my brow. Then he said something else, which barely sifted through the veils of sleep. "I wonder if you know just how happy you have made me."

And I wanted to ask him to repeat his words, but I was asleep before I could form the question.

The next morning he was gone when I awoke but I realized when I saw his clothes from the night before lying in a heap by my bed that he had stayed the night with me. I felt a little better than I had in several days but I told Morwenna when she brought my hot water that I would just have tea and toast.

"Miss Thatcher be gone," she said, big with the news.

"Gone? What do you mean?"

"She's left Thunder House, Mrs. Blaize. She packed her things and was gone without a word to no one when we got up this morning."

"Does Captain Nicholas know?"

"Aye. Martha told him afore he had his breakfast in the kitchen. He said it be a good thing for all of us, especially you, ma'am. The old mistress left her some money, the master said she had plenty to live on for the rest of her life."

"But where did she go?"

"To the village, I reckon, to wait for a ship to take her away. One be due in soon, carrying the supplies for the ball."

"Poor woman. I wonder where she'll go. But I can't say I'm sorry she's left Thunder House."

"Aye, she were right cruel, she and —" She broke off, coloring. "Well, I be goin' to fetch 'ee tea and toast. The master said we was to take extra good care of 'ee now."

I smiled. "He said that, did he?"

She nodded, grinning. "He said 'ee be a frail little thing and we was to see 'ee took proper care."

353

"I'm feeling stronger today, really I am. And I'm not at all frail. I'd like to go to Nansett and tell Mrs. Somes. I want to tell her the news myself."

She looked doubtful. "I don't think 'ee ought to do that. The master did say 'ee was to stay in bed all day."

"Well, I can't stay in bed for the next eight months! I've got to get used to it. And I feel well enough to walk to Nansett. You can lay out the lavender cashmere gown and my plum pelisse and bonnet."

Outside the air was bracing. The bare branches of the trees were spiderlike and splintery. A few of the trees still were clad in their autumn leaves but the colors had dulled considerably. I had to pause several times to catch my breath on the trek to the village and I was relieved when I saw the white cottages nestled above the harbor.

I rapped on Emily's door but received no answer. I waited a few minutes and then went around to the back but there was no sign of her. Disappointedly I trudged up the winding street, dismayed at the prospect of the long walk home. And then it occurred to me that I could visit Katherine; I could tell her my news. She would be thrilled for me. Hadn't she herself said that a child would be good for our marriage? I would go and tell Katherine. And if Heather was there to also hear the news, well, so much the better. If there was anything between her and Nicholas, if Sarah's words had not been spiteful lies, her last vicious act to hurt me, perhaps whatever it was would be finally ended now. I felt almost smug as I went up the porch steps; it was an unaccustomed sensation.

"Is Miss Heather at home now?" I asked the maid casually.

"No, Mrs. Blaize. She's off somewhere paintin'. She's happy as a clam when she goes off some days with them paints o' hers."

I could not help the thought enter my head that perhaps painting was not all she did when she set off "happy as a clam," but I deliberately brushed it aside.

Katherine came in then. "Hello, Miranda. Did we have a lesson today — I must have forgotten it."

"No, I just wanted to call."

"I'm so pleased you did." She requested Janet to bring us some tea and muffins before saying, "Now tell me how things are up at the house. I haven't seen Nicholas since the funeral but Heather saw him yesterday at the shipyard and said he was looking better, more relaxed."

"Heather went to the shipyard yesterday?"

"Yes, she took lunch to one of the men because his wife is flat on her back after a bad fall."

"That was considerate of her," I said, thinking just the opposite.

"I know a little of the trouble between Nicholas and his mother, Miranda. I have been very concerned about him lately."

"So you can imagine some of what must have been passing through his mind at the time of her death and at the funeral. Yesterday he ordered Martha to pack up his mother's things for the church's Christmas bazaar."

"Well, that sounds like a very sensible thing," she said, nodding. "I donated many of my husband's clothes and things to the church after he died, and a number of his books I gave to Mr. Whitcomb."

"Mary and Jenny were also asked to pack Julia's clothes. Mrs. Blaize had wanted everything left just as it was during her lifetime. You got the impression the room was only waiting for her to return. It was . . . uncanny."

Katherine shook her head. "Poor Lavinia. How dreadful for her to lose her daughter like that. I don't know what would happen to me, what I would do if anything happened to Heather. She's all I have—and all I have left of her father whom I loved very much. But tell me, are you feeling all right? I could tell that the funeral was difficult for you, also."

"Yes, that's true, but partly due to the way I've been feeling lately. You see, I'm going to have a baby."

Her face turned pink with pleasure. "Why, Miranda, how wonderful! It's just what Nicholas and you need."

"You did tell me that," I said, smiling.

"I hope you've forgiven me for being such a busybody.

But I have known Nicholas for over thirty years. I think this is the best thing that could happen to both of you. I've been praying for Nicholas to at last be able to break away from his past, and this event couldn't be better timed. However, I do recall how poorly I often felt in the first few months of carrying Heather. Some Sundays I couldn't even play the piano in church."

"Were you extremely tired some of the time?"

"Yes, but it didn't last too long. In another month or so you'll be feeling perfectly well again."

"Oh, I'm glad to hear that. I . . . well, I haven't anyone to talk to about it — another woman, I mean. There's Emily, of course. I was going to tell her today but she wasn't home, so I came here. Not that you're a poor second! I wanted to tell you also because you've always been so kind to me. I think Heather is very fortunate to have a mother like you."

"That's very sweet of you, Miranda. I hope that if you have any questions or concerns about your condition, you'll come to me."

"I will, Katherine. Thank you."

"You must rest all day on the day of the ball so you will feel up to dancing that evening."

"Is there much excitement in Nansett over it?"

"Indeed there is. Many of the women have asked my advice on what to wear — a number of them are making new gowns for the occasion. None of them have ever been inside Thunder House and they cannot wait to see it. It was a lovely idea you had, Miranda."

"Perhaps we'll make it an annual autumn event," I said.

"That would be the 'finest kind,' as they say around here. I confess I'm as excited as anyone else. I'm sewing gowns for Heather and myself."

"Do you make all of your gowns?"

"Yes. My mother taught me to sew when I was a young girl. My parents couldn't afford to hire dressmakers except on rare occasions and so I learned how to fashion my own clothes as my mother had. When I got married and moved to Nansett, I was very glad I had learned because there are

356

no dressmakers on Thunder Island! Lavinia Blaize always ordered her gowns from Boston, and Emily's and Julia's too. But Heather and I have to make do with my efforts, I'm afraid."

"I think you sew beautifully," I said warmly. "Your gowns, and Heather's too, are wonderfully fashioned."

"Why, thank you, my dear. When I was young I used to order fine fabrics, but since my husband's death I can't always order what I'd like."

I thought then of giving her some bolts of fabric as a Christmas present, the finest I could order from Miss Proctor. My own mother had not cared about material possessions but Katherine appreciated fine things, as I did. I would definitely give her enough fabric to make several gowns.

We drank tea and ate freshly baked apple muffins glazed with cinnamon sugar. They tasted very good to me after the past week of inconstant appetite. Heather never came.

"You must take extra special care of yourself from now on," Katherine said. "But remember that exercise is very important. Don't let anyone tell you it isn't. When I was carrying Heather, I took long walks over the island on every day I was able."

"I enjoy walking too much to stop," I said. "Thunder Island is so beautiful—I love to roam the woods and the shore, I suppose as Heather does."

"Yes, you either love this place or you hate it the way Lavinia Blaize did. It was too bad for her husband. Roger loved the island and I think it saddened him that she never took a fancy to it. She used to sit and complain at the dinner parties . . . I'm so sorry, Miranda, that was a tactless thing for me to say in light of recent events. I shouldn't speak that way about her now. But we who love Thunder Island and take pride in it cannot understand those that do not."

"Well, I assure you that I'm not one of those. I think Nicholas was concerned at first that I might not like it, but that has not been the case at all. I think it's very beautiful."

"I'm so glad to hear you say that. When do you expect the child to be born?"

"Well, I believe in June sometime."

"Do you wish to stop your lessons for the time being, my dear? You won't feel like walking to Nansett as much as you have been. We could hold off for a few weeks, perhaps, while you're not feeling quite yourself."

"That sounds like a very good idea," I said. "Until after the ball, perhaps. In the meantime I will practice as often as I can."

"All right, that's settled then." She kissed my cheek and I began the walk back to Thunder House. It was a gruelling effort; I hoped sincerely that Katherine was right, that this debilitating weariness would not continue for long. I paused to lean against a tree trunk along the way. The island stretched before me to the gray foam-flecked sea, the bare trees looked spindly and vulnerable. And the mighty spruces spread their sweeping green branches haughtily in the face of their barren neighbors.

Chapter Sixteen

The ball was fast approaching and there was much to be done. Martha and I took pains with the menu. The same ship which had carried the supplies we would need had then sailed away with a passenger, one Sarah Thatcher. And I believe we all breathed a huge collective sigh of relief that she was gone from our lives.

I was still feeling poorly and spent a good portion of some days in bed. I knew I should be up and about as Katherine had urged, but on those especially hard days I would tell myself, tomorrow will be better; tomorrow I will go out.

One day Emily walked over to see me. She was overjoyed at the prospect of our having children near to the same age. "And Nicholas is so proud, you know," she said.

He was also patient and gentle; if I wearied him these days, he did not show it. In the evenings we were together, I felt little like talking. Often he took his dinner in my room or, if the smell of food was particularly nauseating to me on that day, he would eat in the library and then come to me afterward, sleeping at my side all the night.

Sometimes he would talk about how work was proceeding at the shipyard, at the lumber mill; sometimes we just sat together quietly by the hearth. This was a new side of him I had seen but little — a comfortable leisurely side, untroubled. But I did not dwell on his tenderness or the way he seemed to want to cosset me. I felt too ill to spend time in careful rumination over his manner toward me. He was the way he was and that was that. I was grateful, but I did not expect it to last. As for myself I often lived just from moment to moment, trying to keep my unruly stomach from rebelling.

The day of the ball was a brilliant November day. The sun glared yellow in a frosty blue sky. The air was cold but not bitterly so. But to this I did not give more than a passing thought. I could feel no thrill, no excitement, no sense of pleasurable anticipation at my carefully planned event. Just then I could not imagine myself dressing for the ball, much less welcoming guests, chatting, dancing, and — worst of all — eating. The realization that many women over the centuries had endured what I suffered did nothing to alleviate my discomfort. At that time I was convinced that no one could feel as ill as I did.

" 'Tis the same with most, ma'am," said Morwenna as she bathed my face with a cold wet cloth. "But 'twill pass later and 'ee'll be feelin' better before long." She had been saying the same thing for weeks now and her words were meaningless.

She continued to chatter to distract me. "The ballroom be lookin' lovely. Jenny and Mary be puttin' up bunches of colored corn, all yellow and red and brown and purple. And the tables are a pretty sight with those pumpkins and squash and apples and such. 'Tis a shame all the flowers be dead now but the fruit looks well enough. By tonight 'ee can see it for yourself. Just think on that, Mrs. Blaize. And 'ee will be wearin' your red gown and the captain'll be ever so proud of you."

"Yes," I murmured, trying valiantly to picture the scene she described. "Oh, Morwenna, I can't bear being like this. What if I can't go to the ball tonight?" I asked, my hand covering my mouth.

"Soon, by afternoon, 'ee will be feelin' better, I promise. And by evenin' your strength will come back. Ain't it been so these last few days?"

It was as she predicted. Gradually, ever so gradually, my stomach ceased its churning and my head stopped feeling heavy as a stone. By early afternoon I was able to eat the toast and drink the tea which Morwenna brought me. Afterward I dressed and went down to the kitchen. Martha was taking a turkey out of the oven.

"That looks delicious," I told her.

"If you can say that, I don't have to ask how you're feelin', Mrs. Blaize," she said, smiling. "It was the same with me only mine came on toward evenin'. Made it very hard to cook dinner, I can tell you."

I screwed up my face in empathy. "How awful for you. I'm very grateful to you for handling everything these days. I had hoped to do a lot more myself. Morwenna tells me the girls have already decorated the ballroom."

"The captain left instructions we were to go ahead, ma'am. He wanted you to be able to rest all day so you could enjoy yourself tonight. He was very worried about you, but I told him it's a natural thing and nothing to be alarmed about. But then men don't like to see their women sick, they never do."

"Well, I do feel better now and I want to help. What can I do?"

"Let's see. Oh, you can read out the ingredients while I mix up this batch of punch. And then you can slice some of the cranberry loaves I baked this morning. Nothing like the first cranberry bread of the season, is there? Amos been botherin' me all mawnin' for a taste but I shooed him out. He's roasting the venison now."

For a couple of hours I worked with her in the kitchen until I began to flag. She was quick to notice and sent me back to my room, assuring me that they would have everything ready by tonight.

"Captain Nicholas will be angry with me and with you, too, ma'am, if you don't rest some more," she said.

"Very well, Martha." I went upstairs and fell asleep almost immediately.

When Morwenna woke me, it was already dark. She brought a plate of small sandwiches, which she urged me to eat since the ball was still a few hours away. "Must keep your strength up, ma'am. The captain'll be wantin' to dance with 'ee tonight."

361

"I feel almost normal, Morwenna, I really do. And suddenly I can't wait for tonight. It will be fun, won't it? Is everything going smoothly?"

"Aye, Mrs. Blaize. Wonderful smells be comin' from the kitchen and there be so much food I don't see how we'll ever eat it all."

"Remember, Morwenna, you and the others are not to work tonight, except to refill the punch bowls. You're to put out all the food and then no more duties. Does Martha understand that? I don't want her fussing in the kitchen when she should be enjoying herself like everyone else."

"Aye, Mrs. Blaize."

"And after you help me dress, you must get ready yourself."

She fixed my bath and laid out the red silk ball gown. It had a bell skirt, leg-of-mutton sleeves, and a high, ruffled neckline.

"Soon we'll have to be letting out all my gowns," I said.

"Likely in another month or so, though now no one would know."

Nicholas came in. "How are you feeling, my love?" he asked.

"Well enough. I'm determined to enjoy myself tonight."

"You mustn't tire yourself out, Miranda. You must take care for both your sakes." He poured out a glass of wine for himself. "I would have been home sooner but there were some hitches at the last moment. Things seem to be ready for your ball, though."

"Oh Nicholas, I don't feel as though I've been much help at all. I really wanted to manage everything and then . . ."

"Martha and the others are quite capable, my love. And you did work with her on the details. So don't give that another thought. I'm just relieved you're feeling well enough tonight. I don't mind telling you there were times when I thought you wouldn't be able to go down at all."

He left me to get ready. Morwenna helped me dress and then arranged my hair, sweeping some of the curls back from my face and securing them with pearl-studded clasps. I pinched my cheeks ruthlessly to force some color into them and applied perfume to my temples.

Nicholas came in soon after, wearing one of his severely elegant dark suits and a silver waistcoat. At the sight of him my pulses started their fluttering; his eyes were warm on my face.

"Every time I see you I'm amazed at how beautiful you are, Miranda," he said simply, and I flushed. He walked over to where I stood and took me in his arms. I raised my mouth for his kiss and the wild clamor began in my body as I could tell it did in his. "Do you have any idea how much I want you?" he asked huskily. "Do you have any notion of how difficult it's been for me to sleep next to you these last weeks and not be able to take you?"

"Everyone says these spells should cease soon and I should feel back to normal again," I said shyly.

"That time can't come soon enough for me," he breathed into my ear, his kiss warm and wet on my neck.

Then he released me and drew a small velvet box from his coat pocket. "These are for you."

Lifting the lid, I saw inside a pair of teardrop ruby earbobs circled in diamonds. "Oh Nicholas—they're so beautiful! And just right for my gown."

"I confess I asked Morwenna what you would be wearing and she told me a red silk gown. And these are your very own, not family jewels belonging to Julia or anyone else."

I fastened each one on my earlobes and watched in the mirror the way they jiggled with every little movement of my head. "Just like Amelia Sears' did," I said laughing. "Thank you, Nicholas. I love them."

"Do you? I'm glad."

"What time is it?"

"After seven. Our guests will be arriving shortly but we have time to drink a glass of champagne. Sit down, my love. You'll be standing enough tonight." He went across to his room and came back with a bottle and two glasses.

"I really don't feel much like drinking champagne," I said.

"Just a small sip then. We have a great deal to celebrate tonight as you said some time ago. A ship sailed unexpectedly into Nansett's harbor this afternoon," he went on after he had raised his glass to me. "Apparently the captain needed his crew to make some repairs on her before they went out to sea again."

"They'll find the village deserted tonight."

He shrugged. "The tavern will be open. Jock won't miss an opportunity to make money off thirsty sailors."

Very soon after I went downstairs on Nicholas's arm. The musicians had come early to set up, and their merry tunes already filled the air. The ballroom sparkled with festive light; the harvest table groaned with an abundance of foods. There were sliced meats of all sorts, cheeses, breads, pies, tarts, fruits, and vegetables. Martha had outdone herself. She wore a gray gown with a circlet of pearls at her throat and Amos stood beside her looking slightly sheepish in his Sunday suit. Mary and Jenny and Morwenna stood together, giggling and whispering happily.

When Nicholas and I entered, the musicians stopped playing. He said, "Mrs. Blaize and I wish to thank all of you for the splendid job you've done on our first ball. It's high time Thunder House welcomed guests in this way. You are all to enjoy yourselves in the next hours and let the guests look to themselves."

He gave a sign for the music to begin again and the two of us went back into the front hall to greet the first arriving guests. I was proud and happy to be standing there with him while the people, excited and clad in their best, flocked through the doors. There were many people from Nansett that I had not met; Nicholas introduced them all to me, not missing a single name.

Emily and Ben arrived in the early part of the evening. She was radiant in a high-waisted gown of russet velvet. "The place looks amazingly well," she exclaimed, her hand pressing my arm. "I never liked the ballroom because it always seemed so dreary and useless. I hardly recognize it tonight."

"Martha and the girls are to be highly commended for it. I'm afraid I didn't do much, not as much as I had wanted."

"You look as though you're feeling better tonight — and what a beautiful gown."

"Thank you."

She went into the ballroom with Ben. A little later Katherine and Heather arrived. The gowns Katherine had made for them were highly becoming; I watched Heather remove her bonnet and cloak to reveal a rose-colored taffeta with a daringly low decolletage. She made me feel my own high-necked gown with its ruffled collar was a bit girlish. She wore no jewels, but then her beauty was the sort that needed no adornment. All heads could not help to turn and look at her, to admire. When she spoke to Nicholas and me, I thought her manner somewhat subdued, almost melancholy. Could she actually be jealous of me, I wondered, jealous of the child I would give to Nicholas? But I had no time to meditate on it.

Katherine herself was resplendent in purple taffeta and it struck me again what a handsome woman she was and how in her youth she must have been as beautiful as Heather. No wonder her husband had adored her.

"You look very lovely tonight, Miranda," she said. "And not nearly as pale as when I last saw you. I hope you are taking good care of her, Nicholas."

He looked down at me uncertainly, a tinge of color in his cheeks. I smiled. "He is," I said.

After we had been receiving guests for more than an hour, Nicholas said, "I think we can join the others now, Miranda. Those who are late will find their own way in. I think it's time you sat down for a while and rested."

"But . . . won't you dance with me first?" He looked so handsome I did not wish to leave his side.

"Nothing would give me greater pleasure, my sweet, if you are certain you feel up to it."

"Of course I do, Nicholas. Stop coddling me."

I was rather nervous to dance with him because I had never waltzed at a ball in my life. What if I were to step on his feet and make a fool of myself? But I needn't have worried; he was a good partner and made it easy for me to follow his lead as he swept me about the room. When we were finished, I was laughing and happy and light-headed all at once and he held my hands tightly, not letting go, smiling down into my flushed face.

Then I was being claimed by someone else and Nicholas himself went off to dance with different partners. Everyone was in the highest of spirits; the vast room was vast no longer as it pulsed with laughter, chatter, and frivolity. The punch, ale, and rum flowed freely; the musicians played merrily or plaintively; the chandeliers glowed; the dancers flurried; the plates were filled with food from the heaping platters and bowls. I caught sight of Nicholas dancing with Martha, then later with Morwenna. And I did a country jig with Amos, who did his best to explain the steps to me while I fumbled my way through it hilariously.

About midway through the evening I felt a hand on my elbow and I turned to see Zeke Somes. "Hello! I didn't see you come in, Zeke."

"No, I was late. I didn't know if I ought to come at all." He looked about the room, tugging slightly at his neckcloth. His fair hair was brushed neatly; he looked very attractive, his tall lean frame clothed in dark blue. I noticed several of the young women casting eyes in his direction.

"Nonsense, of course you should have come," I said.

"Place looks somethin' fine. I heard this room hadn't been opened in years."

"That's true. But we hope to change that. Have you had any supper? No, of course you haven't — you've only just arrived."

His solemn gaze was on me. "You look somethin' fine, too, Miranda."

"Thank you," I said, coloring.

"Why don't I get us both a plate and we'll eat together?" he said. "You sit over there and I'll bring some supper to you."

"Well . . ." I looked around for Nicholas but did not see

366

him anywhere. Zeke saw my hesitation and his face tightened. "All right, Zeke, I'd like to. Thank you." What harm could it do in a room full of people? Surely Nicholas wouldn't object. And Zeke was a guest in our home tonight.

He went to fill our plates and I sat down in a chair against the wall, feeling grateful to him. My head had begun to throb a little and I thought eating something would probably help. I was not exactly used to dancing. I caught sight of Heather dancing with the Reverend Whitcomb; he was looking at her as though he admired her very much. And well he might, I thought. She was the most beautiful woman in the room.

Zeke was back soon with two full plates and then he brought a glass of punch for me and one of rum for himself. Now I was relieved to be on the outskirts of the frenzied gaiety. The room was crowded, noisy, and very warm. Watching the dancers spin around, I suddenly felt weak. I put aside my half-eaten plate, unable even to look at the food any longer.

"Not hungry anymore?" asked Zeke.

"No, I've had enough. But you keep eating—don't let me stop you."

I leaned back, my head against the wall, watching the dancers. Emily was sitting across the room with Katherine; they were also eating. Morwenna was dancing with a young man with long side whiskers; she looked relieved when another young man broke in and claimed her as his partner. How pretty she was in her green gown. Ben had been dancing with Martha and now I could tell he was asking Katherine to partner him. Emily urged her to accept and then caught sight of me across the room and waved.

Nicholas's dark head came into view then but his partner was hidden from me. Then the crowd parted a little and I saw that he was dancing with Heather. She was saying something and looking up at him with a sort of entreaty; he looked grim. What on earth could they be talking about so seriously tonight? What were they saying?

Stop it, Miranda, stop it. If I was going to begin that game of watching and speculating again, my evening would be ruined. I began to babble to Zeke about different things just to divert myself. He had finished his meal and was nursing his second glass of rum. I did notice that his blue eyes were rather warm on my face, that the interest with which he regarded me could be construed as a bit unseemly, but I was so determined not to think about Nicholas and Heather that I did not pause to wonder about it. We talked about lobstering, about what the winters were like on Thunder Island, about whatever popped into my head.

Finally I said, "Zeke, I mustn't keep you with me any longer. You should go off and dance with some of the girls here. And I've noticed a number of them giving me annoyed looks. Go and enjoy yourself. You needn't sit here with me any longer."

"I'd rather stay here with you than dance with any other, Miranda. I only wish I could see more of you. Every time I check my traps off Seal Island, I — think of you," he said in a low voice. Then his mouth narrowed and he looked away almost angrily.

"You know how grateful I am to you for that, Zeke," I said, "but you mustn't . . . that is . . ." I broke off in confusion.

"I know," he replied roughly. "You're Nicholas's *wife*. I can't have any notions about you. I can never have notions about them I'd like to. I just hope he knows how lucky he is." He spoke gratingly with a hard piercing look at Nicholas across the room, who, I noticed again with mild anxiety, was dancing once more with Heather. "He doesn't seem to, though."

I had been puzzled by his earlier words concerning "them I'd like to" but now I stiffened. "It is the duty of the host to dance with all his female guests."

Just then Katherine came up to us. "It's a wonderful party, Miranda," she said. "Everyone is having a splendid time. Emily and I were just saying that you and Nicholas should do this again sometime."

"I'm certain we will, Katherine."

"It's good for Heather to have something like this to enjoy. She can be rather moody, you know, and spends so much time going off by herself." She looked across to where Heather was dancing with Nicholas and smiled. It was clear she doted on her lovely daughter and wanted her to be happy. She said something to Zeke and then moved away.

"If I was him, I'd much rather dance with you than Heather MacLeod," Zeke said, looking surly. "She's got no warmth in her, no feelings. But Nicholas and her are a pair that way, I reckon."

"Zeke Somes, I won't listen to this!" I cried. "If you are implying that—that—"

"I'm not sayin' anything, Miranda. But it was common knowledge that she and Nicholas were more than fond of each other."

"That was before, Zeke, long before." I was speaking as much to convince him as to convince myself.

"Some things have a way of never endin', some feelings don't die," he said. "Like the way I feel about *Captain* Nicholas."

I know Nicholas cares for me, I thought. I know he is fond of me now. But were his feelings strong enough to last a lifetime? I knew the love was strong enough on my side but I could not speak for him. He might be only expressing a fleeting interest in me that could burn itself out before long.

"Care to dance, Miranda?" asked Zeke.

"Why not?" I asked rather flippantly. It was another country dance where we dashed back and forth and whirled about. At the end I had to lean on Zeke for support. I was feeling uncomfortably warm and the room tilted ever so often.

"Are you ill?" he asked in quick concern.

"No, just a bit dizzy. I suppose I shouldn't have danced so soon after eating. I'll be all right in a minute." *I hope,* I added to myself. I mustn't get sick at my ball.

"You look like you could use a bit of air. It's close in

here. Come on," he said, leading me around the edge of the crowd to the doors. We went into the corridor and through the house to the rear door.

"The front door was much closer," I said faintly.

"Ayeh. But those out there are drunk as can be. It's no place for you just now, Miranda."

I made no reply. When he opened the door, I stepped out into the cold air and took several deep breaths. The air soothed my hot cheeks and braced my swimming head. "You're right, Zeke. I feel a little better already."

"You don't want to take cold. Better step back inside. Quite a breeze blowin' tonight."

"Yes, I will in just a minute. But I was so hot and it feels lovely out here. I'm not at all cold yet."

We stood there for a few moments without talking and then there came a sound from close by. The sound of a woman weeping, I realized with a slight shock. "Zeke, someone is out there," I whispered. "Perhaps we should see what is wrong."

I walked ahead of him a few yards to the corner of the house. What stopped me was not Zeke grasping my arm. It was the voice of my husband.

"Haven't I told you to trust me, Heather, to rely on me? Just give me some time to see what I can do."

"What can you do, Nicholas?" cried Heather on a despairing note. "I can't let my mother learn the truth. She'll be so disappointed in me. I don't know what to do. I really think I should go away."

"No," Nicholas told her firmly. "You must let me try and help you. Leave things to me for the present. I will do what I can and it will be our secret. The child was conceived out of love—that's what you must remember."

There was the sound of more muffled weeping and then Nicholas's voice again, low and tender. I did not stay to hear anymore. I stumbled away from Zeke, away from the two voices in the night. I could not breathe. Zeke's hand touched my arm and he was saying something but I couldn't hear him, I couldn't understand him. Why had I thought I was hot? Icy tremors were racing through my

370

shivering body.

Heather pregnant—like myself. And Nicholas—could he also be the father of her child? The way he had spoken to her, the way he had promised to help her. What did it all mean?

"That damn bahstard, damn his black soul," Zeke was saying over and over until I cried out for him to stop, clenching my fists and driving my nails into the palms of my hands.

"I must think, I must think," I said, and then, before he could stop me, I was running down the hall and up the staircase as quickly as I could. The waves of cold washed over me until I was shuddering with every breath I took. In the far distance came the sounds of music and merrymaking. The sounds of a successful ball. My ball.

In my room I was ill again and again but this time there was a kind of relief in it, a remedy for the tortured feelings inside me. Later when it was over I was numb, numb and possessed with a cold clearheadedness.

People might begin to wonder where I was. They would ask themselves why I had disappeared; some might have noticed the way I had raced headlong down the hall and up the stairs as though the devil were at my tail. I must not give them further reason to gossip or speculate. Horror of horrors—perhaps some of them knew about Nicholas and Heather. Zeke had seemed to; Sarah had claimed she did; but I had tried to dismiss their words because they hated Nicholas and would take any opportunity to slander him.

I had dismissed Sarah's warnings about Nicholas, but now they rose again to taunt me. She had told me of his relationship with Heather of some years ago, that everyone had assumed they would marry when he was ready to. And then she had claimed to have seen them through the Folly window in a stolen clandestine meeting. Was that the explanation for Heather's habit of roaming Thunder Island of late, disappearing for hours on some days with her box of paints and canvas? But surely the men who worked with Nicholas would notice if he were gone in the afternoons on occasion. Perhaps they knew the reason; perhaps everyone knew. Had she gone to the Folly that afternoon when I was there to relive in her mind her reconciliation with Nicholas? I myself has seen them together in the woods – had they been planning a meeting at the old Folly?

I could not have been mistaken in what I had heard, that Heather was to have a child and she was overwrought and ashamed at the thought of her mother learning the truth. Katherine would doubtless be horrified to learn that her adored daughter had been having an affair with a married man. And as Heather was the daughter of the former minister, and a lady, it was even more of a disgrace. It would make life very difficult for them both if the truth were known. I could imagine the Reverend Whitcomb saying in his pompous voice, "In the light of recent developments I consider it inadvisable for you to continue to play for our Sunday services, Mrs. MacLeod. I am certain your late husband would agree were he here to witness his daughter's dishonor so exposed." The Reverend Whitcomb's fondness for Heather would make him even more severe.

Poor Katherine, I thought, she who was so careful of putting her best foot forward, so mindful of having been the ideal minister's wife. Such a thing as this would hurt her very deeply. No wonder Heather had wanted to leave Thunder Island rather than so shame her mother. But Nicholas would not let her. He was going to do what he could to help her; she was to leave things in his capable hands.

I knew that I was not a woman to inspire love, devotion, the way Heather MacLeod was. I recalled how diffident I often was with Nicholas, how tongue-tied and awkward and ill at ease in his presence. Sarah and Lavinia had scorned and despised me when I had first come to Thunder House – how could Nicholas have possibly cared for me the way I was?

But Heather with her solemn poise, her gently humorous air, her confidence and grace, her cleverness – naturally he would be drawn again and again to such a woman.

And what of Zeke? My face was scarlet when I thought about what we had overheard together. How could I face him now, especially after having reproached him, after defending my husband to him? The whole thing was humiliatingly hideous enough without him being a party to it. If only he had not gone outside with me—if only I had not gone outside myself, for that matter! But wasn't it better that I realize the truth about my husband instead of conveniently deluding myself that his new attitude toward me meant his feelings had deepened, something I had half hoped had or was happening?

Standing up, I walked across the room and splashed water on my face. Automatically I smoothed my hair, noting in the glass that I was flushed and my eyes glittered like two hard sapphires. My face did not reveal the turmoil inside me. And I was determined to return to the ball and act the way a hostess should—graciously, light-spiritedly. People would not have the opportunity to wonder about me, to laugh at me behind my back the way Lavinia and Sarah had. I would return to the ball as though I had merely gone up to my room for a few moments' privacy. Not as though I had retreated in a distraught state. I must go back down now.

Nicholas was standing in the hall talking to several men when I descended the stairs. When he saw me, he disengaged himself from the group and came to my side. "Where have you been, Miranda? I've been looking for you everywhere. I was about to go upstairs and see if you were feeling poorly."

"No, I'm well enough," I said, relieved that my voice sounded normal. "I went up to have a few moments to myself, that is all." I would not accuse him; I could not. Besides, I had no claim on his affections. He had married me and provided me with a home and security. He had promised me nothing else.

"Are you feeling able to rejoin the festivities once again?" he asked, putting a hand on my arm.

"Quite, thank you." How could I have thought my voice sounded normal? It wasn't my voice at all. It was light, high, brittle.

"Well, then, would you give me the next dance?"

"If you like." His hand folded around my waist and his other entwined in my fingers. I did not look at him. I looked about the room as we danced, smiling at the other faces which were a blur to me. I did not see Heather. I did not wonder where she was.

"I've scarcely danced with you all evening," he said.

"We've both been busy," I acknowledged coolly.

"I saw you with Zeke Somes—I had hoped we could have supper together."

"Is it not the duty of the host and hostess to circulate among the guests?"

"I suppose so. Are you enjoying yourself? Your ball is a great success, you know. You should be very proud."

"Is it? Yes, I suppose it is. Certainly I'm proud; I'm very proud."

"You look ravishing, Miranda. Doubtless Somes thinks so, too."

"Well, we have no control over what people think, do we?"

"I don't want him having any thoughts about you," he said curtly.

I almost laughed in his face. How dare he act jealous of Zeke when he himself—but I wouldn't think of that now. "You have nothing to worry about, Nicholas. He is well aware of your feelings. I don't think he'll risk being knocked down, not tonight at least."

He grinned. "Tonight even Somes can't get under my skin. I've been wanting to tell you, Miranda, not that this is the proper place, but these last weeks we've spent together, the nights I've stroked your face, watched you sleep—well, they've meant every—"

"Oh, there's Ben!" I exclaimed. "Ben, you haven't danced with me all evening. Nicholas, you don't mind, do you?" I asked gaily, almost throwing myself into Ben's arms and whirling away from my deceitful husband.

The next hour I danced energetically with different men. To all appearances I was radiantly happy. I laughed when

374

Amos and I again stumbled our way through another country jig. The Reverend Whitcomb complimented me on the success of the ball. "What a pity Mrs. Blaize could not be here to enjoy herself on this night."

"Yes, isn't it?"

"I understand Miss Thatcher has gone."

"She had no desire to stay here after Mrs. Blaize was dead."

"I understand, naturally. But she did seem to leave in undue haste." His look was probing, speculating.

"She and my husband have always had their differences," I said shortly.

"Yes, so I gathered from Mrs. MacLeod. She kindly had me to dinner recently. She and Miss MacLeod have been most gracious to me since I came here some months ago. Nansett had not had a minister since the death of the Reverend MacLeod three years ago — just traveling pastors who would visit briefly to perform necessary services. Naturally the villagers were most pleased to have the post filled by me."

"I understand people were very fond of Mrs. MacLeod's husband," I said, and noticed that his gaze was fixed on something across the room. I followed it to see Nicholas and Heather dancing together again.

"Just as it should be, the flock should be fond of their shepherd," he murmured, and I thought again what a pompous bore he was. No wonder Heather displayed no real interest in him. No wonder she coveted my husband.

The dance was over and there was a short period of silence before one of the musicians, a young man with a pleasant tenor voice, began to sing. The crowd was hushed, but soon after he had begun the shanty, they began to sing, clap, stamp their feet to the rollicking music. Noah was playing his violin and nodding his head up and down while the other musicians played on their guitars and concertina.

Hey, hey laddio! Swing the capstan round, round, round!

When the money's all gone it's the same old song—
Get up Jack, John sit down!

The ships will come, the ships will go
As long as the waves do roll, roll, roll
And the sailor lad much like his dad
He loves the flowing' bowl, bowl, bowl!

Singing, hey, hey laddio! Swing the capstan round,
    round, round!
When the money's all gone it's the same old song—
Get up Jack, John sit down!

I'll take me a trip on a man o' war
To China or Japan—an—an
Where in Asia there are ladies fair
Who love the sailor man, man, man!

Singing, hey, hey laddio! Swing the capstan round,
    round, round!
When the money's all gone it's the same old song—
Get up Jack, John sit down!

After that rousing song the musicians began to play a
hornpipe. A few of the men who had been, or still were,
sailors folded their arms over their chests and began to do
that dance which required a very little space, nimble feet,
and no partner—an ideal dance for sailors who spent
much of their time clambering about the rigging, who had
no women to dance with them and little space in the
forecastle in which to dance.

Zeke came and stood beside me in the middle of this but
I pretended to be so absorbed in the men's dancing that I
did not notice him.

"I was lookin' for you, Miranda," he said softly afterward.

"Oh Zeke, there you are. Would you bring me a glass of
punch, please? All this dancing has made me
thirsty."

He frowned slightly but went to do as I asked, and the Reverend Whitcomb moved over to the dessert table, where others were now gathering.

Again I lost myself in the crowd before bumping into Seth and on impulse asking him to dance with me. I was careful not to let my eyes roam the room lest I should see Nicholas or Zeke. I had no desire to be near either of them, much less to engage in conversation. At one point I looked up and saw Nicholas coming toward me. The music had stopped momentarily, and as I was just in front of the musicians' dais, I stepped up to speak to Noah.

"Your music is wonderful tonight," I said to all of them. "But Noah, I've been hoping you would ask me to dance."

"I been fiddlin', ain't I? And I ain't much of a dancer," he said, his face screwing up.

"Come now, Noah. I insist you dance with me." And I took his hands in mine and led him across the floor as the men began to play again. I could not stop the way I was acting; another person had taken me over.

"Are you enjoying yourself, Noah? The music has been perfect. We're very grateful to all of you."

"Ayeh. 'Tis a fine evenin', Mrs. Nicholas."

"No dire predictions tonight?"

His forehead wrinkled. "Eh?"

"I mean, no warnings for me to be careful, to beware of selkies and other mysterious things?"

"I didn't mean no harm, I only wanted to . . . I like ye, Mrs. Nicholas. I want ye to be safe and happy."

"Can't you see I'm ecstatic?"

"What's that?"

"That I'm very happy?"

He nodded. "Ayeh. Looks like way. But Miss Julia—she was happy too."

"Miss Julia? What do you mean, Noah? What has she to do with—with anything?"

"She didn't take care, Mrs. Nicholas. She didn't know about the evil luhrkin' to take her without wawnin'."

"Oh, Noah, not all over again. You're obsessed with

377

selkies! Not tonight of all nights—I don't want to hear anything more!"

"Is he worrying you, Miranda?" asked Katherine, dancing with an older man just beside us. "Really, Noah, you shouldn't go on about such things. You know my husband disapproved greatly of those old superstitions and I am certain the Reverend Whitcomb would be similarly displeased if he knew you were trying to frighten Mrs. Blaize." Her voice was rather stern and Noah ducked his head.

"Oh, he may be trying to frighten me but he won't succeed tonight. After all, I was stranded on Seal Island in the mist and saw no sign of the Great Selkie then. I suppose I'm not the sort he steals for his brides." I laughed and she laughed with me. Bright artificial laughter. It jarred my head. The dance was over, and Noah had stepped back onto the dais to pick up his violin.

"I think Noah is not the only one with selkie creatures on his mind tonight," said Katherine. "So we will forgive him this time."

"What do you mean?"

"Listen. They are beginning the old ballad from the Shetland Islands off Scotland, "The Great Selkie of Sule Skerrie.""

The same young man who had led the other shanty was now starting a plaintive haunting song which everyone hushed to hear. It was totally unlike the jaunty music they had played until now. I bit my lip as the melancholy melody and words pierced my brittle gaiety.

An earthly nurse sits and sings
And aye she sings by lily wean,
And little ken I my bairn's father
Far less the land where he dwells in.

For he came one night to her bed feet
And a grumbly guest I'm sure was he,
Saying, "Here am I, they bairn's father,
Although I be not comely."

378

"I am a man upon the land
I am a selkie on the sea
And when I'm far and far frae land,
My home is in Sule Skerrie."

And he had ta'en a purse of gold
And he had placed it upon her knee,
Saying, "Give to me my little young son,
And take thee up they nurses' fee."

"And it shall come to pass on a summer's day,
When the sun shines bright on every stane,
I'll come and fetch my little young son
And teach him how to swim the faem."

"And ye shall marry a gunner good,
And a right fine gunner I'm sure he'll be,
And the very first shot that e'er he shoots
Will kill both my young son and me."

By the time he had finished singing, I had been stripped
of all my affected frivolity. I was reduced to a shaken
drooping creature with an aching heart. The song I found
strange and obscure; it did not describe the tale of the evil
soulless sealman coming ashore to lure a hapless girl to a
doomed fate. In this ballad the Great Selkie was a pitiable
unloved creature who only wanted to take his son with him
back to the sea before they were eventually shot to death.
That wrenching melody and the mournful foretelling of
death were almost more than I could bear. Even the selkie
could be vulnerable, it seemed. None of us was immune to
pain and woe. There was no mention in the ballad of the
child's mother—what had become of her, I wondered. As
in so many ballads the betrayed lover lamented of the one
who had proved false.

"What a strange song," I said to Katherine. "I don't
understand it."

"It's very old and doubtless some of the verses have been

forgotten. But it's always been a great favorite on Thunder Island since the first Scottish settlers came."

"I've always been fond of it," said Heather dreamily. I had not seen her come to stand beside us. "You get the impression the bairn's mother fell in love with someone she shouldn't have—and that she must be dead."

"Why do you say that?" I asked sharply.

"Because she is not there with the child. Why would a nurse have care of a child before the Great Selkie comes to claim it? It's so tragic, really."

"She had no business loving that creature," I said deliberately. And she smiled, a little sadly, I thought.

The ballad must have been a swan song for the musicians and a sign to the guests that the ball was at its close. They began to leave in small groups and gradually the crowd thinned and quieted. I waved and smiled as people thanked me, as they said good night.

"Finest kind, ma'am."

"Yes."

"You ought to have another someday, Mrs. Blaize."

"Yes."

"Good night to ye."

"Yes."

"Thank you, Mrs. Blaize."

"Yes." Could I say nothing else? Were there no other words in my head?

Zeke was beside me. "We must talk, Miranda. I have to see you. . . . I want to help you. Meet me at Blackett's Glade tomorrow at midday."

I looked at him, puzzled. Why did he look so intently at me? Why did he speak so compellingly? Blackett's Glade? I turned away from him nodding and smiling at the departing throngs.

Emily kissed my cheek; Ben did also. I smiled broadly at them, at them all, a frozen stupid smile. Heather and Katherine said their good nights and left. I felt numb, dazed, wooden. And then Nicholas and I were left standing alone in the front hall, still with that foolish smile on my face.

380

"Come, Miranda, you must get to bed," said Nicholas. "You look ready to drop. Shall I carry you?"

I looked at him. "Carry me? No . . . no, of course not. But you are right, Nicholas. I'm dreadfully tired."

"You must rest tomorrow," he said as we climbed the stairs. When we reached my room, he put his arms around me. "I've been wanting to have you to myself all evening," he said, his voice deepening.

"You could not bear sharing me with our guests for a few hours?"

"It was hard, damnably hard," he breathed into my ear, and his lips moved to my neck.

Pushing against his broad chest, I turned my head away. "Nicholas, please, I am very tired as you said. And due to the child, I have not been sleeping too well." I paused, biting my lip. He was frowning.

"I wonder if you would return to your own bed tonight. I think I will sleep better if I am alone."

He abruptly let me go, ruffling his hair with one hand. His gaze was searching, uncertain. "I had no idea I was preventing you from resting well, Miranda. After all, you have seemed to want me with you and I thought —"

"Yes, I know, Nicholas," I said heavily.

"What's wrong, Miranda? What's happened?"

"Nothing is wrong. It's just with the child coming I feel . . . I want to be left alone."

He did not say another word. His face darkened, the scar paling, before he turned and left the room.

Chapter Seventeen

The morning after the ball I lay in bed. Morwenna had come in earlier but I sent her away and did not even allow her to draw aside the curtains. I lay in the darkened room with no inclination to rise, feeling ill, considering myself the most ill-used creature alive. But after several hours the bilious feeling subsided and with that my spirits began to rally.

Nicholas had not looked in this morning—he could hardly have been expected to after our cold parting last night—and I assumed he was at work at the shipyard.

As Morwenna drew my bath, she talked animatedly about the ball. "I'm so glad you all enjoyed yourselves," I said. "Didn't I see you dancing with the same young man several times?"

She nodded, coloring. " 'Twas only Matt Soady. He do fair admire me, I reckon," she said airily.

"And how do you feel about him?"

"Well, he be a rare man," she acknowledged.

"He ought to be. You deserve someone special. Only I hope . . . I hope you won't leave me now, Morwenna."

"I won't be leavin' 'ee, ma'am, don't 'ee fret on that."

"You'll stay until the baby is born?"

"Aye, and longer besides. Now, ma'am, don't 'ee cry.

'Tis only your condition makes 'ee weepy."

"Oh, Morwenna, if you only knew!"

"T'aint nothing to know. 'Ee's just feelin' low after the ball last night. 'Twas a bit too much for 'ee, I reckon."

"Too much for me . . . yes," I murmured. I recalled my show of bravado, my silly frivolity—I had even forced old Noah Todd to dance with me! Anything to avoid Nicholas and Zeke.

Zeke. With a jolt I remembered his last words to me as he left Thunder House, that he would await me at Blackett's Glade at noon today. But what on earth had we to say to one another? Perhaps Zeke knew something that I didn't. Perhaps he could shed some light on this murky muddle I was in. Nicholas had said to Heather, "Just give me some time to see what I can do." What did that mean? What could he do? What did it all mean?

I told Morwenna to lay out my fur-trimmed pelisse, the red bonnet with imitation cherries, and my white fur muff. "I'm going out for a while," I told her.

"Goin' out! But 'ee's not well enough. 'Tis cold and windy out, besides."

"I'll be all right. Perhaps a walk will improve the way I feel," I said shortly.

"But 'ee hasn't eaten, Mrs. Blaize. Would 'ee like some toast first?"

"No, I'll have something later. I had those cups of tea and that's all I want now." I knew that if I saw or smelled food, I might be ill again.

When I left the house, the cold air hit me with a blast. I hurried across the back lawn, the wind at my back, and into the grove of birches. In the forest the wind swirled and tossed the dead leaves like waves in the ocean. Wading through them, I walked the way to Blackett's Glade. Today the dark clouds hung low in the sky, reflected in the sheenless swamp. A thin mist had settled on the surface in places, wreathing the feet of the tall gray wraiths of trees.

"Miranda."

383

I looked over in the direction of the voice and saw Zeke sitting on a massive log at the edge of the water. He got up and walked over to me.

"I doubted you'd come."

"I honestly don't know why I did. I just had to get away from the house."

"We have to talk."

"Well, what do you have to say?" I snapped. "Is there something you know you've not told me, something about . . . Nicholas and Heather?"

"Well, folks, the lads around here, they've wondered from time to time if she was meeting some man. She's never given any of them a second glance . . ."

"And they have suspected that it was Nicholas that she was meeting?" I asked bleakly.

He scowled. "Daow!" He kicked at a rock with his muddy boot, sending it into a pile of leaves. A squirrel ran up a tree in alarm. "When we came back from the Arctic, Nicholas took no notice of her. And she didn't seem to mind. Everybody reckoned they'd outgrown each other and were just friends after that. But with what we heard last night — well, it looks like she and the captain've lately taken up where they left off."

"You believe her lover to be my husband." I could say it aloud. My voice had not betrayed me; it was normal, even cool. I could say it as though the two of them were nothing to me, as though they were characters in a book. Her lover is my husband. I could say it.

"I know what we heard last night," Zeke said. "Her with child and him consolin' her. He said he'd take care of her."

"He said he would try to help her, not that he would take care of her," I said sharply. His gaze was pitying; I looked away.

"I wanted you to meet me here, Miranda, because I wanted to tell you that I'd . . . look after you, take you away, if you like. There's nothing keepin' me here. And you don't have to stay with that bahstad one day longer. I'd look after you, I'd take care of you. I know I can't give

384

you what Nicholas can, but I promise I wouldn't make you unhappy the way he does."

I licked my dry lips. "Perhaps he has broken it off with her since our marriage. Perhaps they met once . . . or twice . . . before, more for old time's sake than for anything else, and it's just now that she is with child that she has come to him for help. It might not mean that they are still lovers."

Zeke's blue eyes were as cold as a clear winter sky. "Damn him! What he wants with her when he's got you! I should've killed him that day on the *Eagle*—but then I wouldn't've known you."

"Zeke, don't say that, about killing him! Don't even think it! And you shouldn't talk to me this way, you shouldn't be suggesting such things! I can't think . . . I can't think . . ."

He took both my arms and drew me close to him. I stiffened and tried to pull away but he did not release me. "Miranda, I meant what I said. Nicholas doesn't deserve you. He never did. When I heard he'd married and brought a bride here, I wished he'd be miserable for the rest of his life, that his wife would suffer along with him. I hated you before I met you just because you'd married him. But then, since meeting you, knowing you—you must know the way I feel about you. I've made it plain as day."

"I don't think you love me more than you hate Nicholas, Zeke. I think the love you think you have for me is all bound up in your hatred for him. And I don't think that can be called real love. If you did have me, if we did go away together, I think your interest in me would fade because it was no longer fed by the fire of your contempt for my husband."

His face hardened but he still did not release me; his grip tightened. "Don't talk that way, Miranda. Don't think about Nicholas anymore. He's shown he's no fit husband for you. We can go away and never think about him again. No one would ever know we weren't man and wife—we could go where Nicholas'd never find us, assuming he'd

385

try."

"Heather is not the only one carrying his child," I said softly.

He caught his breath and abruptly let me go. "That devil."

Horse's hooves came thundering near, startling us, and we turned to see who approached. It was Nicholas, and from the look of black rage on his face, I realized with dismay that he had seen Zeke holding me through the bare trees. He did not dismount. He rode up to us and pulled on the reins while his horse snorted and stomped at the edge of the glade.

"It might be wise if you waited until spring for your assignations, my love, when the trees will shield you," he said sardonically, his mouth curved in a sneer as he looked down at us.

"Damn you, Nicholas—" Zeke began, but I said quickly, "Be quiet, Zeke. Nicholas, you have no right to speak to me like that. There is no reason for . . . what you are supposing."

He ignored me. "How's the lobstering at Blackett's Glade, Somes?" he asked. "Trap many here, do you?" Zeke said nothing, glowering at him. His fists were clenched. "It appears I must teach you a lesson again," said Nicholas. "And this time I shall make bloody sure you don't forget it—if I don't kill you, that is." He dismounted and I caught his arm.

"Nicholas, stop it! I mean it! This is absurd. Zeke and I were only talking."

"Does he ordinarily take a woman in his arms when he talks to her? And you, my girl, you seem to again need reminding that you are *my wife!*"

"Yes, I am your wife. I am not the only one who needs reminding of that fact, am I?" I put a hand to my cheek and swayed a little. "But I'm not feeling up to this sort of thing right now."

He said in icy tones, "Perhaps you're right, my dear. This is neither the time nor the place in light of your

386

condition. We can't have you upset, can we? We can't have you disturbed in any way. Last night you made that most apparent!"

"Nicholas, please," I begged, red with mortification, "just take me home."

"Oh, I will, my love. And I'm tempted to lock you in your room if this is the sort of thing you get up to behind my back! And to think I wouldn't have come across the two of you like this if it weren't for poor Noah Todd."

"Noah Todd?" I asked dazedly.

"Yes, he's dead." Nicholas's voice was curt.

My hand flew to my throat. "Noah — dead? When . . . how?"

"Last night. And he was stabbed. Not a pretty tale. Tom Cameron found him this morning and rushed to the yard to tell me. I've just come from the lighthouse. His money's gone, too."

"You mean he was murdered . . . for his money! But surely . . . surely no one on Thunder Island would do such a vile thing!"

"The ship, the *Marianne* . . ." said Zeke.

Nicholas nodded but his scowl was still fierce. "There was a ship that stopped here for minor repairs last night, Miranda. It cast off this morning for southern waters. It looks as though one or more of those sailors did it. I'll have to make inquiries."

"But how would one of those sailors know about Noah's money?"

It was Zeke who answered. "Noah's a well-known character. He's been wohrkin' the Thunder Island lighthouse for years and years. Someone might'a heard about his hoahrdin' money there."

"The room where he lived was ransacked and the money stolen. There's no other plausible solution. But a few men have questioned whether in fact he had that much money at all. Some of them didn't think he had an amount worth killing for."

"Any amount's wohrth killin' for to some," said Zeke

grimly.

"Oh, poor Noah," I said. "He was so proud of his lighthouse. And just last night he was playing for us." And I had danced with him, danced with him to avoid Nicholas.

"Come, Miranda, I'll take you home. You must be cold—you look pale," said my husband.

Zeke watched, his face shuttered, as Nicholas set me on the horse and climbed up behind me. I did not say good-bye to him. Nicholas spurred on the animal and we were riding through the woods away from the glade.

We rode for a while in silence and then Nicholas slowed the horse to a walk, saying, "What were you doing there with Zeke Somes, Miranda? And don't tell me you were just out walking! Zeke had no reason to be at Blackett's Glade."

"You seem determined to think the worst," I said wearily.

"I told you to stay away from him." Again his voice was like steel.

"If I told you to stay away from someone, would you do it?"

"I don't understand you. Last night you sent me away in no uncertain terms and today I come upon you there with another man. Damn it, Miranda, he was holding you!"

"A shock, wasn't it? I know how that can be."

He drew sharply on the reins. "I'm fighting a strong inclination to shake you until the teeth rattle in your head, my girl! Now answer me! *Why were you with Zeke Somes?*"

I wanted to hurt him, if that were possible. Why not let him think the worst? "Am I not allowed to have friends? Am I not allowed to meet people where I wish? You do, Nicholas, don't you? I've never asked you to give up your friends, have I? We've never made such claims on one another. It's not as though we have any sort of—ordinary marriage. I have friends; you have friends."

"You don't need a man like Zeke Somes for a friend!

388

There's only one thing he wants from you, damn it, and you can no longer be so blind or so stupid that you don't know it!"

"I didn't say I didn't know it, Nicholas," I said deliberately. For an instant I thought he was going to strike me. I did not flinch. But then a wave of such acute nausea and dizziness came over me that I fell forward into a whirling red-and-black void.

When I came to, I was in my room lying on my bed. Morwenna was looking down at me worriedly. I shook off the wet cloth that lay across my forehead. "Oh, I feel awful. What . . . what happened? Did Nicholas . . . bring me here?"

"Aye, ma'am. The captain brought 'ee in and carried 'ee upstairs. He was terrible upset. He said 'ee'd fainted in the woods. 'Ee oughtn't to have gone out, Mrs. Blaize. And with hearin' the news about Noah . . ."

Noah. I had forgotten all about him.

He had been murdered, and all for the sake of a few coins he kept under his bed in a brass pot. He had played his fiddle at the ball and then trudged home, unknowing that every step led him closer to death. Had his murderer or murderers known he was not at the lighthouse, and had he returned to surprise them in an act of thievery? His very age, his infirmity, had made him no threat to anyone. Or had they stolen in while he lay asleep and then stabbed him when he woke to see them? I thought of how vulnerable Noah had been, alone on the southeastern tip of the island when Tom Cameron was not with him—and he had not been with him last night. I wondered how the people of Nansett were taking his death. They would all be saddened and appalled, I was certain. And just last night he had danced with me.

I had not expected to sleep at all that night but instead I slept well and heavily. The next day I awoke, sitting up tentatively, waiting for the crippling nausea to overtake me but it did not come. And this morning my head did not feel as though it weighed a ton. I walked over to the window and drew aside the curtains. I stood there, shivering slightly, but pleasantly conscious of a sensation which had occurred but rarely in the last month. I was hungry, very hungry.

The sun sparkled on the water in a scaly sheath of dazzling white-gold which made me blink. There was scarcely a ripple on the sea's surface and no sound as it glided over the rose-colored rocks in Thunder Cove. I touched the window; the glass was cold despite the illusion of shimmering warmth.

I rang for Morwenna, and when she brought my hot water, I ordered a rather substantial breakfast such as I had not eaten in weeks. She was delighted and hurried off to tell Martha to prepare a tray. I took a bath and washed my hair and then sat in my dressing gown by the cheerful fire eating my breakfast and drinking several cups of tea while my hair dried. I felt even better after I had eaten. I put on the cherry-red cashmere gown, which brought out the color in my cheeks, and even tied a perky bow of the same color in my curls.

I would not stand by mute and helpless while Nicholas carried on behind my back with Heather MacLeod. Perhaps if I tried very hard, I could win him from her. When he had learned that we were going to have a child, he had been happy with the news. He had married me, after all, not her, and that was what I must remember. Perhaps I should tell him tonight that I had heard them talking on the night of the ball and ask him directly if he was the father of her child. I should ask to know the exact nature of his feelings for her. I could even seek out Heather and demand that she end their affair. I could threaten to tell Katherine if she continued to meet with my husband. Katherine would be devastated if she learned her daughter had been meeting a married man. And I had no doubt that she would be doubly grieved because she cared about me. I did not think Heather would wish her to learn the truth, and that was my weapon.

I did not know what was to be done about Heather's

child; first I would have to talk to Nicholas and learn precisely what she meant to him. Only then, by approaching him and admitting what I knew, could we begin to sort our way through the tangled events. I was his wife, after all, and I was carrying the child which, if it was a boy, would inherit Thunder House and much of the island. My child, not Heather's. I could plead with him to send her away, to give her a sum of money so that she could settle elsewhere respectably as Sarah had done after Lavinia's death. Just as my pregnancy could make me vulnerable, so could it make me powerful, strong, confident, a woman to be reckoned with. I had the upper hand, that was what I must remember. I was the woman Nicholas had married. I would not sit by any longer worrying that my husband had resumed an old love affair yet doing nothing about it. I would demand that he end it.

With this resolve firm in my mind, I decided to fill some of the long hours before Nicholas returned from the shipyard by practicing the piano in my sitting room. I might decide later down the road that I would not want to continue my lessons with Katherine, but it would not hurt to practice and it would help to pass the time. I asked Morwenna to see that the fire was lit in the sitting room, and a short time later I went downstairs.

The music I had most recently played was open on the stand. I worked on my scales for a time and then began to practice the music in the book Katherine had given me. When I had played for an hour or so, I was tired of those pieces. I played some things from memory and then opened the piano bench in search of something different to play, something to challenge and absorb me further. Sifting through the books, my eye was caught by a small book with a red leather cover. I picked it up, realizing it could not be a music book.

Opening it, I read on the first page, written in a precise feminine hand, "This book belongs to Julia Blaize, Age 13 years." Probably a book of poetry, I thought, or devotions. Turning the page, I was surprised to see paragraphs in that same copperplate. A journal, I thought, with rising excitement and curiosity. This was Julia's journal. And she was dead. So what harm could there be in my reading it?

August 1845

This journal was a birthday gift from my dear mother. Two days ago I turned thirteen. We had a lovely party. Martha prepared all my favorite foods—I was allowed to choose the menu—and Father permitted me to drink one glass of champagne. I didn't like it very much, the bubbles were too tingly, but I didn't let on. Later I got a rather nasty headache but by then it was time to go to bed so I didn't mind much. Mother looked beautiful all dressed up for my party. Her hair is all white now but it suits her, and she wore the tiara of diamonds in it which Father had given her several Christmases ago. We dined late and Emily was allowed to stay up. She is only eleven but she acts even younger than that because she is always running about outside with the village boys like some ragamuffin. She trails after Ben Somes who is fifteen, and acts like a puppy dog, hanging on his every word and trying to get his attention. I'm certain he thinks her no more than a silly child, which she is. Mother says she had better mind her ways by the time she is my age or she will never acquire any of the graces and arts so essential to a young lady of good breeding. Mother says they are instilled in me quite naturally and for that I am grateful.

I am not going to spend all my life on Thunder Island. I'm going to meet someone very special who will take me away from here. I said as much to Emily recently and she was shocked. "Leave Thunder Island? Why would you want to do that?" she asked. I tried to explain about the other places Mother has told me about, the fine cities where there is much excitement and all sort of elegant cultured people, but she only looked at me like a dolt and said, "I never want to leave here." Well, she may feel like that now, she may even feel like that in ten years, but by then I will be gone, long gone.

Mother has spoken often to me of her life growing up in Boston, of her introduction to society before she met Father and came to live at Thunder House. She is eager for me to experience the same sort of life for myself. "There is a great deal more to the world than Thunder Island," she always says. Poor Mother; she is happiest when she and Father go to Boston every year for a visit. She always brings Emily and me lots of presents and her eyes shine when she talks about all the things they did, the people they saw. Father always smiles and says nothing, letting her talk, listening to her. She is always happy just after she returns from a trip because she says she missed me even though she had such a wonderful time. She has promised to take me on a trip to Boston when I am grown up. She says I must practice my deportment so that I will make just the right impression on the people there, the sort of people she wants me to impress.

She wants me to practice the piano every day so that I will be accomplished and can play for groups of fashionable people. Sometimes I have to walk with a book on my head and sometimes I must stand with my shoulders against the wall so that I do not stoop. These things are difficult and often uncomfortable but Mother insists that they are crucial to my future. She is right, of course, she did the same things as a girl in Boston. In fact she told me once that her governess used to strap her shoulders and chest to the back of a chair for hours to improve her posture, and I should be glad that she does not do that to me.

But I suppose it is all worthwhile in the end because no one is more elegant, more graceful, more poised than Mother. I adore her. I want to be just like her some day. I try to do everything she says. I don't mind practicing the piano but I'm not fond of Mrs. MacLeod, my teacher. She is a very good pianist — brilliant, even, I heard Father say once — but I do not like her. It's not because she is unkind to me or anything like that. Quite to the contrary. She says

393

I have a natural gift and play very well.

But once, many years ago when I was just five or six, I was playing in the south woods, looking for fairies and elves which Martha used to tell me lived in the forest. It was Midsummer's Eve when Martha said the fairies danced in a clearing. When she said that I thought of the clearing by the Folly Father built for Mother. I always liked it there even if Mother didn't. It was like a cottage out of a fairy tale and I thought what a perfect place for fairies to come and dance. Perhaps they even lived there though we were unable to see them, I used to think. So I waited in the woods at the edge of the clearing, just a ways from the Folly, waited to see if any fairies would come out and dance as it was Midsummer's Eve. The wildflowers were blooming in the clearing and the cottage was looking very pretty and quaint — not shabby the way it does today.

I waited for what seemed to be a very long while before I began to grow bored and disappointed that the fairies weren't going to come. (I was a very silly child then, believing in fairies.) Then I began to think that perhaps they might not come out until nightfall in the hours before Midsummer's Day and I knew I would not be allowed to stay here after dark. I had just decided to leave since Mother and Sarah would be looking for me — Mother never did like me wandering far from Thunder House although she never cared when Nicholas and Emily did it. And then the door of the cottage slowly opened and I thought excitedly, "Oh! Here they come! They were in the cottage after all!"

But instead of an enchanting tiny creature with gossamer wings and flower petals for clothes, I saw a tall woman come out of the cottage. It was Mrs. MacLeod, the minister's wife. I had seen her many times in church playing the piano. She did not see me as I was standing behind a trunk. I was going to run up and speak to her but just then someone else came out of the cottage. It was Father. And I knew even then that there was something odd about the way they whispered and looked about. I knew I mustn't let them see me. So I stayed behind the trunk and watched them set off on different paths through the forest behind the Folly. I never forgot about it though I never said anything.

When a year or so later Mother insisted I begin lessons with Mrs. MacLeod, even then I said nothing although I didn't want to go to her house. But I knew that Mother wanted me to learn to play the piano and Mrs. MacLeod is the only person on Thunder Island who plays well. Father always says I'm fortunate to have her for a teacher. When he talks like that I become very angry inside and I wish I had not seen them that day acting so strangely.

Mr. MacLeod is a very nice man and has always invited Nicholas, Emily and me to a party at the manse on Christmas Eve. He and Mrs. MacLeod have a daughter named Heather. She is older than I — last year, or was it the year before, she had her sixteenth birthday. Nicholas and I were invited to the manse for her party. Mother didn't go but the two of us went. At least, I went. I was allowed to wear my new blue organdy dress and Sarah walked with me to Nansett. Nicholas and Father were supposed to come over from the shipyard and take me back after it was over.

But Nicholas wasn't at the manse and neither was Heather. They had gone to gather bittersweet, Mrs. MacLeod said, hours before and were not back — and it was Heather's own party! I would never have been so rude. Many people from Nansett were there already. Mrs. Mac-Leod served me a plate of food and told me to have a seat in the parlor. I did but I hardly said a word to the people there — "fisherfolk" Sarah calls them. Mrs. MacLeod seemed rather excited; she was nervous about Heather being away so long. Everyone was whispering about it, about Heather and Nicholas, though they stopped when they saw me looking at them. I can look at people quite sternly if I try.

Nicholas is my brother, as I've said, and a great deal older than I. I think he's twenty-four but I can't be sure because Mother doesn't have birthday parties for him the way she does for Father, Emily and me. A long time ago I asked him if he minded not having birthday parties and he gave a kind of laugh and said, "Daow!" which is that down-eastern way of saying, "No!" Nicholas doesn't really talk like that though, not the way Martha, Seth and Amos do. He does it sometimes just to annoy Mother. Father thinks it's funny.

I ate all the food Mrs. MacLeod had given me and Father came over to sit with me. Finally Nicholas and Heather came. They had been caught by the tide on Seal Island! Father thought it a great joke but I saw some elbow-nudging and head-nodding among some of the people. Mrs. MacLeod scolded Heather at first but then she kissed her and brought out her birthday cake. It was a spice cake which I don't like at all so I didn't have any. Afterwards there was dancing and Zeke Somes wanted me to dance with him but I refused. His fingernails were dirty and I told him so. He wouldn't call me "Miss Julia" and that made me angry. I asked Father to take me home and he did after kissing Heather and wishing her a happy birthday. Nicholas stayed to dance with her. Everyone says what a beautiful girl she is but I think her hair's too yellow and that mark in her chin is rather ugly. Nicholas seems to like her though.

She came to my birthday party the other evening. I heard Martha say to Amos when she didn't know I was listening that Nicholas would marry Heather some day. That means she would come to live here. I don't think I like that idea. She never says much but she makes me uncomfortable. Mother says for being a girl unused to society she does very well. When she does talk she does seem to always say the right thing and Mother likes that. I don't think she would mind if Nicholas married her (Mother, I mean) and Father would probably be glad. But I don't like to think about that because it reminds me of him and Mrs. MacLeod coming out of the Folly.

May 1849

I found this journal under my old piano music. I had forgotten all about it. I suppose I'm not the sort of person who enjoys keeping a journal, writing in it week after week. I read over what I had written — rather silly, but then it was four years ago and I was only thirteen. There have been some changes at Thunder House since then.

Father is gone now. He had a heart attack at the shipyard and was dead before he could be brought home to Mother. She was devastated and went up and down the halls wringing her hands and wailing all that afternoon until Sarah gave her a sedative. It was horrible.

I was a little sad, but not too sad. I couldn't stop thinking about Father and Katherine MacLeod (now I understand more than I did four years ago) and I realized they must have been lovers at one time. Why else meet at the Folly? Why leave together and act as though they didn't want to be seen, the two of them hurrying off in different directions the way they did?

I hate Father for that. How could he do such a thing to Mother who is so good, so beautiful, so perfect in every way? How could he betray her with that woman? What on earth did he see in her that would have made him betray his wife and his friend, the Reverend MacLeod. I would say that if Father had had a best friend it was the Reverend MacLeod. And both of them with families even! I wonder how long they continued their disgusting disgraceful affair. Poor Mother — I hope she never learns the truth.

And she must never know. She is not well these days. Sarah says we must be patient and hope that she will fully recover from the shock of Father's death soon. She was never strong. She has always had days when she would stay in bed. Sometimes I would hear her crying. Sometimes she would make herself ill, her spirits were so low. She has always missed her old life in Boston. Often Father would take her there after one of those spells but sometimes he wasn't able to leave the shipyard then. He knew Mother was often unhappy on Thunder Island but he couldn't take her to Boston as often as she would have liked. I think he felt very guilty about this. He should have felt guilty, about this and the other thing. I'm ashamed to call him my father.

This has made me distrust men. If you can't trust your own father to be faithful to your mother then who can you trust? How does a woman know that if the man who marries her and professes to love her will not then turn around and dally with someone else? That is why I am going to do my utmost to make a brilliant marriage to a very rich Bostonian. I have been preparing for this for a good part of my life. I will have a fashionable life, security and a social position and these will do very well for me. I will not expect love; I will not seek it. Emily dreams those types of foolish dreams — and always about Ben Somes — but I do not. If my own lovely mother could not inspire fidelity then perhaps it is not possible.

Even Nicholas. We used to think he would marry Heather but instead he left soon after Father's death on a sort of apprentice whaling voyage. He is obsessed with whaling; he has always wanted to be a whaler but it was understood he would go into the business with Father and some day take it over. Mother says he has betrayed Father's memory in the most selfish reprehensible manner. And she's surprised that he should go off and leave Heather, too. Emily used to stand up for him when Mother would begin complaining but Mother would get very angry with her so now she just sits and says nothing.

If the truth be told, Nicholas seems to be doing very well. He has his own vessel, the *Eagle,* and he is hunting bowhead whales in the Arctic. Heather came to see Mother recently; she brought her a basket of fruit. Mother seemed pleased to see her. I had to sit politely when all the while I was thinking, "your mother was my father's mistress!" I hope that Heather does not marry Nicholas. I do not want her coming here and taking my mother's place, the daughter of the woman who entered into an adulterous

398

relationship with my father.

I wonder if Father was so fond of Heather because of what he felt for her mother, and whether he hoped Nicholas and she would marry as a sort of poetic justice. That makes me very angry. I do not want them to ever be married but I do not see how I can prevent it without the truth coming out and reaching my poor mother's ears. She must never know. Sarah says that anything, any other shock, could make her very ill indeed. But Nicholas is away for months and months at a time and Heather is here and so nothing permanent can happen in the near future.

I am still taking piano lessons from Katherine MacLeod. I begged to stop after Father's death but Mother and Sarah both insisted I continue so that when Mother is well enough she will take me to Boston and introduce me to society. She says that not only should I be beautiful and graceful but also as accomplished as I can be. Sometimes I play for her in my sitting room when she is feeling up to it. She says I am very good and must not stop my lessons. So I go twice a week to Nansett to the manse which is also a house of mourning as the minister passed away three months ago. And I look at Katherine in her black gowns, her face so kind and composed, and I think, "You cared nothing for your husband since you were meeting my father in the Folly many years ago." But of course I say nothing. I practice dilligently and then I play for Katherine twice a week. I get a strange sense of pleasure in the fact that I can go there week after week and apply myself to my music and never reveal the contempt I have for that woman. People have always said that she has made the ideal minister's wife. Ha! If they only suspected what I do.

Sometimes on fine days I go to the Folly. I seem to be drawn there again and again almost against my will. Sometimes I go inside and look around. But it's rotten in there now — filthy and smelly. It ought to be torn down. Perhaps one day I shall ask Mother but I doubt if she would agree because even though she never wanted to go there it was still a gift from Father. A gift which he then sullied in the most disgusting way possible. She looks back on their life together in a rather unrealistic light now. She talks about how happy they were, how much he adored her and it takes all my fortitude to not shout out, "He may have adored you but he was sleeping with the minister's wife!"

One day last week I went to the Folly and stepped inside. I had left the door open so that some light could come in and suddenly there was a darkening and I knew someone was standing in the doorway. I looked around to see Zeke Somes. He was staring at me and he said, "Good afternoon, Miss Julia," with an insolent emphasis on the "Miss." I was vastly annoyed to see him there and told him to leave at once. "You followed me here," I said and he did not deny it. Whenever I go into Nansett it seems he turns up and contrives to speak with me on any pretext. I mistrust him. He knows I dislike him but this seems only to amuse him.

Instead of leaving the Folly as I asked, he came inside and stood close beside me. Then he took an odious and unfair advantage of me. He took me in his arms — I was most relieved that his clothes did not smell of fish — and kissed me on the lips! I managed to slap his silly grinning face and then I ran out of the cottage and into the woods. He did not follow me, I am thankful to say. What an insufferable cad he is! Haven't I shown him in as many ways as possible that he is beneath me, a boor, a rude fisherman? Just because Emily makes a fool of herself with his younger brother Ben doesn't mean I have any interest in Zeke. Ben is not a bad sort and, I trust, would not take advantage of Emily's youth and innocence. Once she took out his lobster boat and rowed it halfway round the island. He was furious but that didn't seem to bother her since she had his attention.

I can only suppose that Emily's familiar behavior with those yokels has put ideas into Zeke's mind, ideas concerning me. Instead of outgrowing her fondness for those fisherfolk she becomes more intimate with them every day. Mother is too ill to pay much attention to her and Sarah is preoccupied with her. Emily will not listen when I tell her she should not associate so easily with them. And Zeke Somes thinks he can look my way! It will be a very different man than he whom I will marry. Oh, Mother must get well soon so she can take me away from here!

July 1850

Here I am again finding this journal and making another entry. But I am so excited — we are going to Boston in two months! Mother is much improved these days and is determined that I shall make my appearance in Boston society this season. We will stay with a cousin of hers and order new wardrobes when we arrive. None of our present things will do; everything must be new and in the most up-to-date fashions. She has given me a sapphire necklace which is part of the Blaize family jewels.

I had my last lesson with Katherine MacLeod the other day and I longed to tell her what I truly think of her and accuse her of being my father's plaything. But I did not; I thanked her for all her years of devoted teaching. I hide my feelings very well, as I have said.

Nicholas is due home soon. He sent us news of a very profitable expedition to the Arctic. He will be home before we go to Boston and then he will leave on another expedition in the spring. This winter he will oversee the shipyard business. There is talk that some of the Nansett men will sign on the next journey with him since he has proved so successful a whaler. I saw Zeke Somes in the village recently and he told me he was thinking of signing on the *Eagle*'s next voyage. "Will you miss me?" he asked insolently. I told him I would doubtless be married and living in Boston by then and I could see that took him aback. I don't know why he would consider going to sea with Nicholas. They have never liked each other. As boys they were in constant competition with one another. Each had to be the one to climb the highest tree or remain under water the longest when they were bathing in the ocean, things of that nature which boys do. I believe Zeke has always been jealous of Nicholas and discontented with his lot. But whether Zeke goes with Nicholas or not, I will be far away by then.

Something so terrible, so shocking has occurred to me that I can scarcely write it. But I must write it. I must allow it a release or I shall go mad. Perhaps then I will know what course to take. Though it seems there is only one course. Nicholas is due home very soon and I shudder to think what I must tell him. I cannot keep silent about what I have learned. Such silence on my part would make me as much a part of this evil and heinous thing as Heather and Nicholas have been all unknowingly.

This morning I took a walk along the shore to the lighthouse. It was a beautiful warm day and the sea was like a mirror. I decided to return to Thunder House by way of the south woods. As I drew near to the Folly I again felt compelled to go inside. It was looking worse and worse and again I wished it would be torn down. I looked with disgust at the frayed and stained upholstery, the wooden furniture with its coats of animal droppings and grime. It was filthy, foul. I opened the doors of the cupboard and then pulled up the cover of the little writing desk. There were many dusty pigeon holes inside and two little drawers with brass holdings that had long since tarnished. I opened one of the drawers and then the other. And in the second was a yellowed piece of paper pushed far to the back. I picked it up very carefully so as not to damage it and drew it out. What on earth could it be, I wondered.

I recognized my father's handwriting and assumed it was some sort of instructions about the furniture when he ordered it long ago. But it was not that at all. It was a letter, a letter which began, "My dearest Katherine." It was a letter he had written to that woman! "Every time we are apart I don't believe I can endure the separation from you. I think about being with you, about when we were last together. Heaven help me, I loathe myself for the terrible deception we are playing on my friend Bruce and on Lavinia. But I don't know whether I can stop seeing you. The thought of life without you is unbearable. Lavinia is my wife but you know the way things are between us. She has never been happy with me from almost the first; she will never be contented. Though I feel sorry for her and still esteem her, the passion I once felt for her (which as you know she never returned) is all at an end. You are the one I love now, God help me, the one I long to see sitting across from me at the table, the one I wish could bear my children. If only we had met before I married Lavinia, before you married Bruce. For now we are betraying those two people in the worst way imaginable. I cannot bear that I have brought you to this. Every day I tell myself I should end it but then again I am weak. I only live for the moment when we can meet again. Yours, Roger."

The letter was dated July 1826. I was about to tear it up in a hundred pieces when the phrase "bear my children" jumped before my eyes. And that was when my heart gave a sickening lurch. Was it possible that Heather was my father's child, that she was the fruit of their illicit union? I recalled his affection for her. But no, he couldn't have been aware of their relationship, not the way he approved of Nicholas' interest in her.

Nicholas and Heather—half-brother and half-sister! Katherine had never told him. But perhaps Katherine didn't know herself, not if she were playing the part of a normal wife to her own husband. Perhaps she only suspected but was not certain. I did not believe that she would condone an incestuous relationship between her daughter and the son of her lover. It wasn't as though the two of them were affianced so perhaps she saw no need to admit the possible truth to Heather.

But I see the need. Heather must know what her mother was, who her father might have been. At least I can now

403

release the knowledge I have held inside me for so long. I will go to Heather and tell her that she is probably my brother's half-sister, *my* half-sister. It was providential they have not married by now as they might have done. I know Nicholas would not take advantage of a lady and then not marry her, not a minister's daughter, and so I am certain there is no fear that they have consummated this unholy union. But now Heather will have to realize that there is no chance of her ever marrying Nicholas because I am going to tell him of their relationship on his return. Whether he truly loves her or not, what I have to tell him will kill *those* sorts of feelings he may have for her.

Heather was born, I know, in June of 1827, less than a year after this letter was written. The letter had been written in July and Heather must have been conceived in September, just two month later. One of the next meetings my father had had with Katherine MacLeod could have been the fateful one.

It is fate that I have discovered this vile letter of my father and I know what I must do. I have always hated Katherine for stealing my father's love. Now I can go to Heather and spoil her love for Nicholas the way her mother spoiled my father's love for my mother.

It is my duty. And I have never been one to shirk my duty.

Chapter Eighteen

Very carefully, very slowly I stood up, lifted the top of the piano bench, and slid the small leather book underneath layers of music books, where it had lain undisturbed for more than two years. And I wished with all my heart that it had still sat there undiscovered, its pages unturned since Julia had last written in it.

I walked across the room to the window and put my hot face to the cold glass. The sun's rays glared through the grove of birches; the delicate white trunks were sooty, spotted with smut. I turned away from the window.

And then Katherine's words came to me, words she had spoken weeks ago which I had scarcely taken notice of: "Heather is all I have left of her father." "All I have left of her father." "Her father." Roger. Roger Blaize was Heather's father. Katherine MacLeod, that gracious kind handsome woman had been Roger Blaize's mistress while she was married to another man and he to another woman. They had committed adultery again and again, and one of those times they had conceived a child. A child accepted as his own by the Reverend MacLeod, a child who did not realize her own father was the same father of the man she loved.

How could Katherine, I thought with a lurch of sick horror, how could she have permitted an intimacy to grow between two people who were half-brother and half-sister? What kind of woman was she that she had allowed this under her nose? Unless Julia had been right, unless Katherine did not know for certain which man had fathered her daughter. Still, just the possibility that Heather and Nicholas might be related by blood, wouldn't that have been enough for her to prevent Heather from becoming too fond of Nicholas? Perhaps she had had no intention of disclosing the truth to Heather until the two of them had declared their wish to marry. Then she would have had no choice but to come forward with the truth.

She had kept her silence until that moment, and that moment had never come. For I had married Nicholas, and Katherine must have breathed a huge sigh of relief when he brought a bride to Thunder Island and her daughter was no longer in danger of marrying her own brother. Such relief must have prompted her growing fondness for me—no wonder she had been so sincerely welcoming, so kind. I had spared her daughter from committing a heinous sin.

But, I thought, my chest very tight, I suspected something of which she was not aware. The saga of Nicholas and Heather had not seemed to stop when he married me. True, it had stopped after his return from the Arctic when he had closed himself off from others, but sometime since our marriage they must have resumed their love for one another. And now Heather was carrying her *half-brother's child*.

I sat down on the sofa before my legs gave way. Images of Nicholas and Heather flitted in and out of my head, clamoring for space. The two of them talking so seriously in the woods that day, the two of them sitting together at the funeral dinner, their disembodied voices in the darkness of the night at the ball. But I had not needed to see them to imagine the scene as she wept in his arms and he promised to help her. "Remember, the child was conceived out of love." Oh Nicholas, I thought with a wretchedness beyond description, what have you done? What have you and Heather unknowingly done? You have committed incest—innocently, but still you have done it.

So, Katherine, this is where your silence all these years has led them, led all of us. Your sin has created a much worse one. You could not admit to Heather that you, the minister's wife, had been unfaithful to your husband and with his closest friend. The guilt which had overwhelmed Roger must also have consumed Katherine that she could act as though it had never happened, and close her eyes to the relationship between her daughter and the man who was now my husband. And now there was to be a child of that — union.

Shaking now, unbearably so, I left the room and hurried upstairs. I poured water from the pitcher into the basin and sluiced my face and neck again and again. I took a bar of soap and smeared it over my skin, my hands, the bubbles getting in my eyes, stinging me, my mouth tasting the soap, the dryness of it on my tongue, my face stiff with it, taut, my eyes streaming. Then the water was splashing all over, wetting my gown, dripping on the carpet as I put my whole face into the basin again and again. Then I took a towel and scoured my face until it was raw, chafed, terribly tight. My eyes still burned from the soap bubbles, the whites of them red, outraged. I yanked the red ribbon from my hair.

I wanted to run away. I wanted to run as far away from Nicholas as I could. I didn't want to see him; I couldn't look at him; I couldn't speak one word to him. His infidelity had been bad enough but now nothing seemed as bad as this. I climbed into bed fully clothed and covered myself with the bedclothes. And I willed my mind to grow dark, blank, vacuous, to separate from my trembling body, be apart, at peace. Later I would think of what I should do. But not now. Now I could only block out the horrific thing I had discovered.

I must have fallen asleep because the next thing I remembered was a knock on the door. I looked over and saw Nicholas entering the room.

With a supreme effort of will I forced my face to remain expressionless, even though I was choking with disgust and horror. It's not his fault, I kept telling myself. He does not know. Katherine, it's Katherine's fault.

"How are you feeling, Miranda?" he asked softly, his

face unreadable in the dusk-filled room.

"Not well."

"Morwenna told me just now you were much improved today."

"I did feel better this morning."

"Did I wake you? I'm sorry."

"It doesn't matter."

He paused, frowning. "I came to tell you that I have to go away for a while."

"Go away? You're leaving?"

"Yes, tomorrow morning when the ship sails. I have to inform the authorities of Noah's murder and find out what information I can about the crew of the *Marianne*."

"How long will you be away?" I asked listlessly.

"I don't know. Several weeks perhaps. That news awards you some gratification no doubt." His voice had hardened.

I looked away from him and out the window at the violet twilight.

"Miranda, we cannot continue in this way. When I return, we are going to have to talk very seriously about our future. I know you have felt poorly so I did not press you to talk last night. But there are some things I must tell you and some questions I must ask. While I'm gone, I hope you will continue to improve in health so that when I return, we can discuss what has been uppermost in my mind for weeks now, and which for one reason or another I have refrained from telling you."

He was talking about his feelings for Heather. Do not think. Your mind is a gray void, a cloud of mist.

"Well, have you nothing to say?" His tone was now abrasive.

"Nothing . . . except — good-bye, Nicholas."

"Good-bye, Miranda," he said coldly. And then, after a pause, "God keep you." He turned and strode from the room.

The next day he was gone. I awoke realizing this and the tremors did not come. I rose and ate breakfast, then bathed and dressed all in a state of calm. He was not here; there was no fear of my seeing him. Now I could think and decide what I must do.

There was only one course of action, surely. I must go to Heather and tell her, tell her that I had discovered evidence that she was Nicholas's half-sister. She would confront Katherine and Katherine would be forced to admit the truth at last. Heather must realize she and Nicholas could not have a future, no matter what he planned to tell me on his return. She would have to be the one to tell him and beyond that I could not think.

Once I had told Heather, the rest would be up to her. Whether or not she would tell Nicholas I did not know. Perhaps she would leave Thunder Island, leave while Nicholas was away so he would have no way of tracing her. Perhaps Katherine would also leave; they could go together to make a new life. Or it might be that Heather would want nothing to do with her mother when she learned the truth about her birth. But that had nothing to do with me.

I set off through the woods to Nansett. While I walked, I imagined what I would say to Heather. I saw myself knocking on the door, asking to see her. She would come into the parlor and I would say, "Heather, I know you are in love with my husband, that you never stopped loving him." She might deny it or she might not. I would continue, "I overheard the two of you outside on the night of the ball. I know you are carrying his child." My voice would be steady, cool. "But this is not why I have come to speak with you. I have come to tell you that I have learned that your lover, my husband, is your half-brother. Yes, it's true. I have Julia's journal to prove it. Ask your mother. Or perhaps she is not certain, but the mere possibility is enough—I'm sure you realize that. Your affair with him must end."

But what if Katherine were there? What if she, too, came into the parlor? Should I accuse her of hiding the truth, of jeopardizing her own daughter's immortal soul? Or should I insist on speaking to Heather alone and then leave the two of them to face each other with the harsh reckoning? After all, it was not really my business the way Katherine had deceived everyone, deceived herself perhaps. That was between her and her daughter. My concern was for my husband, whom in spite of my shock and repulsion I was realizing I still loved deeply. I could not alter my feelings for him; they were bound up with all that I had become, all that I now held dear. I would love him for the rest of my life.

I remembered Heather's studio and the portrait of Nicholas she had painted years ago. "That man is your half-brother, Heather," I could say.

By the time I reached the manse, I was breathless and my heart was pounding. I curled my trembling fingers into a hard fist and rapped on the door. When the maid answered the door, I said, "I've come to see Miss Heather."

"I'm sorry, ma'am, but that ain't possible today."

"Why not?" I asked sharply.

"Because Miss Heather is very sick, Mrs. Blaize."

"What is wrong with her?"

"Oh, terrible pains in the belly last night, the missus said. I've been told not to disturb her so she can sleep. The missus were up with her all night, and looks pretty poorly herself because of it."

"Is Mrs. MacLeod home?"

"No, ma'am she went out for a while."

"Do you know where she went?"

She shook her head.

"If I could just see Miss Heather for a very short time—"

"Oh no, ma'am, I'm sorry, but Mrs. MacLeod told me not to let anyone in today. She said Miss Heather was took sick in the night and has to stay in bed for the next few days. She's nursing Heather herself, wouldn't even let me take up her tea this morning. Could be it's something the sailors brought."

"The sailors? What sailors?"

"The ones that stop here from time to time—they sometimes bring disease. When my mother was a girl, there was a terrible spread of measles."

I was not interested in an outbreak of measles which had

410

occurred years ago. "All right, Janet. I'll come back another time. Tell Mrs. MacLeod and Miss Heather I called. Good day."

She closed the door and I walked off the porch and down the steps. The need to tell Heather what I knew was bursting inside me; the truth screamed to be let out; my mind longed to be salved and relieved.

What if Heather was not truly sick at all but was only experiencing similar side effects of her condition as had I? Perhaps Katherine had guessed the truth or Heather had broken down and told her. If Katherine knew her to be pregnant, and by her half-brother, then perhaps she had confided her secret to Heather. Unless Heather had not revealed the identity of the child's father to her mother. Katherine was shrewd enough; I felt certain she would not mistake pregnancy for a bout of real illness.

Then a thought occurred to me which made me stop in my tracks. What if—what if Katherine's description of "terrible pains in the belly" had been actually a miscarriage? Wasn't that possible? Many pregnancies were ended by nature before their time and in a painful way—couldn't such a thing have happened to Heather? Heather could have suffered a miscarriage in the night and Katherine had nursed her through it. But there was no way I could know for certain unless I forced my way into the old manse and waited for Katherine, accusing her of what I knew and asking her directly about Heather's condition. Or I could rush past the maid to Heather's bedroom and ask her myself.

But I could not do either of those things. I could not go into a sickroom and badger a sick weak woman. If what I supposed were true, Heather doubtless knew by now about her mother and Roger Blaize and whether she was his daughter or not. She did not need me storming in like some fury, accusing her of an incestuous relationship. I couldn't go to her now. And somehow I did not think it was my place to go to Katherine. I had too much affection for her to face her with what I had learned.

Perhaps in a few days I could talk to Heather, when she

411

was recovered. I would have to bide my time before confronting her with what I had learned from Julia's journal. I might not even have to do such a thing now. Perhaps now the bond between her and Nicholas was severed, if she had indeed lost the child she was carrying. If she now knew the truth, that they were related by blood, then their affair would be over.

For the next few days I stayed in the house because I had no inclination to go anywhere or see anyone. I took some relief in the monotony of those days, which slipped by so slowly and placidly after the staggering events of the previous week.

One morning before I awoke, I dreamed of Nicholas, that his powerful body was hard against mine, that his dark tousled head lay on my pillow. But it was only a dream; I was conscious of a deep stab of disappointment, of despair. Nicholas would come home but he would tell me of his love for Heather. Perhaps he had been planning to take her away somewhere. That, of course, would now prove impossible, but would he ever learn to love me, to seek from me what he had from her? Or would he, when he learned of their blood relationship, turn from both of us and enter for good that dim caged world he had inhabited after the Arctic disaster? I knew he had greatly desired me on occasion, but would that desire be permitted to surge into love, or had my discovery not only damned Nicholas and Heather but also myself? Was I now doomed to an empty futile existence?

Perhaps I could say nothing; I could wait and observe what happened between them. When they parted (for how could Heather not end it knowing what she must know?), I could act as though I knew nothing. Perhaps Heather would never disclose the whole truth to Nicholas and he would be in blessed ignorance of the terrible thing they had done. Perhaps we could begin life anew together. After all, he was looking forward to our child's being born and I believed he cared for me a little.

After breakfast I dressed and decided to go for a walk; I was feeling in better spirits than I had had in some time.

Outside, the gulls dove and cried out above my head; the waves were the color of bayberries, the gales whipping them into flurries and peaks. I knew how they felt. It was cold and blustery but I went across the south lawn, now ash yellow, and into the woods.

I purposely took a path which veered away from the cemetery, having no wish to intrude on its gloominess today, and walked swiftly through the woods, the wind piercing my cloak and blowing bitterly in my face. It was a relief to be out of the house, to be away from Morwenna's concerned watchful eyes.

I wondered if tomorrow I should go to Nansett and see Heather. I was eager to learn if her sickness was indeed what I suspected, but I was also reluctant to face up to it all again. These past days had lulled me to a peaceful dull existence wherein I had withdrawn to a pleasant world of myself and my child. I had no wish to puncture my new equinamity. Perhaps I was deluding myself, but I wanted to believe that Heather had lost her baby and things would now be at an end between her and Nicholas.

My mind conjured up comforting scenes of myself, Nicholas, and our child, of him regarding us with joyful loving lights in his eyes. I imagined Heather boarding a ship and sailing far away, never to be seen again by either of us. That made me think of Sarah Thatcher and wonder what she was doing now. She had been my enemy but now she was gone and could never intimidate me again. If there had been any substance at all to my momentary wild suspicion, that it was she who had hurled the structures from the deck of the ship, nearly to crush me — well, she was gone from Thunder Island now and could not threaten me again.

When I saw the outline of the thatched-roof Folly through the trees, I was surprised. I had not realized that this path would lead me there as did the one which passed through the cemetery. But it was logical that they both converged at the same clearing in the south woods.

Again as I drew near the Folly, I was enthralled with its charming fairy-tale appearance — even knowing what it had been used for, and by whom. Julia had also been drawn to it again and again as I was. She had learned that it had been the meeting place for Katherine MacLeod and her father, and Sarah had claimed it was also where Nicholas and Heather had their trysts. It was ironic that the cottage that Roger Blaize had erected for his wife's amusement had ultimately become the place where he practiced his infidelity to her. And if Roger Blaize, in love with Lavinia but gradually disappointed in her, could have been unfaithful with another woman, then so very well could his son, who had never professed to love his wife, me, in the first place.

As I stood there, I became filled with the same fascinated loathing that Julia had experienced when she used to look on the Folly. Now I also longed to see it destroyed. It held an allure for me as it had for Julia, but it was a baneful allure. And its unearthly appearance which had inspired images of elves and fairies in Julia as a child was the essence of its sorcery. Inside, it held a secret as depraved as did the gingerbread house, which had been a house where little children were roasted and eaten by the wicked witch. It enticed while it repelled; it suggested charm and delight while corruption and infamy were all it held. Just like the age-old tales in which the unwary travelers were always fooled. But I would not be deceived. I knew it for the evil place it was behind its innocuous appearance.

I opened the door and stood at the entrance. It was a bit warmer there out of the wind and I went inside, closing the door behind me to hold off the gale for a time. My breath rose before me in a vapor and I shivered in my heavy cloak. I moved forward a few feet, my eyes adjusting to the dimness. In here Katherine and Roger had met as often as they could steal away; in here Julia had discovered Roger's letter. Idly I wondered what she had done with it. She had never told Heather what she had discovered, what she believed the letter proved, because she had died before she was able. And so the secret had gone on, undetected.

What peculiar surroundings for lovemaking, I thought. But it had not looked this way when Katherine and Roger had begun to meet here. The upholstery had been clean and fresh, the colors vibrant. The large hooked rug had been neat, unblemished; the plank floors had doubtless gleamed with layers of varnish. The air had not been stale, musty, and indicating the periodic visits of animals and birds. I could not believe that Nicholas would bring Heather here. In these ugly surroundings, how could the act of love be anything but ugly? Perhaps that had made it somehow appropriate, but I couldn't see Nicholas and Heather punishing themselves in so subtle a way. That was for characters in a melodramatic novel.

I walked about the room noticing the desk which had held for so long a time the letter from Roger to Katherine. Why had it ever been left there, I wondered. I wondered if he had written any other letters to her and what had become of those. Perhaps Katherine had always made it a habit to destroy any letter he wrote her and somehow the one Julia had found had slipped her notice.

There was something draped on the arm of the tattered sofa. I went over to look at it. It was a paisley scarf in hues of brown and green. It had not been left here to rot over the years; it belonged to someone who had been here recently. And I had seen it before, a pretty soft scarf with the browns and greens of the trees.

It belonged to Heather. I had seen her wearing it herself, here at the Folly. That day she had come upon me here. She had worn a brown cloak and this scarf over her head and she had blended in with the trees.

I took the scarf in my hands and tore it as hard as I could, taking a vicious pleasure in the way the strands split, in the way the material shredded. When I had torn it beyond recognition, when the pieces lay on the floor in a spilled untidy heap, I turned away and moved toward the door.

And as I walked across the floor of the Folly, I suddenly smelled another odor mingling with the unpleasant ones in the Folly. It was the smell of smoke. Woodsmoke, as

415

though something was burning. Puzzled, I lifted the latch of the door and pushed but it did not open. It would not budge, it would not swing out the way it should have. I pushed as hard as I could but it was as though something was wedging the door shut, something was keeping me from opening the door and leaving the cottage.

The smell of smoke was stronger now. I wondered what was burning outside. With rising panic I pounded on the door, calling as though someone were within earshot and could help me out. Then I was conscious of a rushing roaring sound that seemed to be coming from above my head, from outside, from all around me. And I saw the smoke swirling in coils past the small, deep-set windows.

It was not something outside the Folly that was burning—it was the Folly itself. The thatched roof had somehow caught fire and the flames were this moment raging above my head. Aghast, I watched the rolls of black smoke twist past the window and up toward the sky.

I was trapped in this cottage and it was on fire. I would be killed if I did not get out very soon. The thatched roof would burn quickly, the fire gaining momentum, the flames consuming the walls, enclosing me in a frenzied inferno.

With renewed vigor I ran at the door, battered at it with my whole body, but it would not move. Looking around wildly, I saw the small chair with the heart cut out of it. I rushed over, picked it up, and slammed it against the door. A leg splintered off but the door was immovable. The smoke was now in my nostrils and I turned to see the back wall of the cottage a wall of rollicking flames. I began to scream harshly, brokenly, while the smoke filled my head, my throat. And then I was coughing and choking. The gusts of wind were causing the fire to spread even faster, I realized, to spread and consume. The other walls of the Folly were blackening with soot before they, too, would be a mass of flames. The thatched roof must have been burning brilliantly, going up like a dry pile of sticks.

Again and again I pounded on the door while the smell of the smoke singed my nose. I grabbed a remnant of

Heather's scarf and held it to my face. As I stood up, my eyes streaming, I caught sight of one of the two windows. Of course, why hadn't I thought of that before? I picked up the broken chair leg and heaved it at one of the windows, then at the other. They smashed; the cold fresh air rushed in and I gulped it avidly, gratefully. But it was soon swallowed up in the massing clouds of smoke. I put my face up to the smashed window and screamed as loud as I could. But the roaring of the fire was so loud in my ears that I could scarcely hear my own voice. And the windows were too tiny for me to crawl through.

My baby, I thought, my baby, it will never be born. I was losing strength and breath even with my face in the cold air of a golden midday. I threw off my cloak and raced to the door, beating on it with my fists, then rushing back to the nearest window for the fresh air my lungs craved. I shouted and screamed. The Folly was burning and I would burn along with it. I had wished for the Folly to be destroyed even as Julia had. And now I was getting my wish.

And then I saw a figure outside, a woman's figure. She was running toward the cottage with a man some distance behind her. Her form was vague and shadowy through the coils of black smoke. I began to sob with relief because whoever it was had reached the door and was now opening it. And then I was falling out the door and into Katherine MacLeod's arms.

"Oh Miranda, thank heaven, thank heaven. I thought I heard someone screaming and I saw the smoke through the trees. . . . Look, Amos! It was Mrs. Blaize in there. We have to get her away."

I was lifted and carried some distance beyond the clearing, the frigid air rushing in my lungs as I coughed and gasped. My eyes were closed against the smarting glare of the sun.

"She needs to be brought back to the house but we'll have to stop the fire before it spreads — with the ground so dry, the forest is in danger," said Amos.

"You go get Seth and some others to help you put it out.

I'll stay with Mrs. Blaize. Bring her maid and she can help me take her back to Thunder House."

"Ayeh, Mrs. MacLeod."

When my breathing was more normal and my eyes had stopped their stinging and tearing I said, "Thank you, Katherine. I never thought I would get out of there. The door was stuck—I couldn't move it at all."

There was a long pause before she said slowly, "There was a wedge of stone under the door, Miranda, preventing it from being opened. I couldn't pull it open myself. And then I looked down and saw that wedge."

"A wedge that someone had put there, someone who wanted to trap me inside . . ."

"There must be some explanation for its being there."

"There is. Someone meant to kill me."

"No, I don't believe that for an instant. And don't you think that way either, Miranda. Don't think that!" To my astonishment she had begun to cry, the tears running down her cheeks. She was holding my hands tightly clasped and her shoulders were shaking as she bent toward me. I watched, moved with a great pity, appalled. It was as though she knew that someone had indeed tried to murder me—and she knew who that person was. Someone dear to her; a person she could not admit would do such a terrible thing. Heather.

"It's all right, Katherine. I'm all right," I said.

"Oh Miranda, if anything had happened to you—" She put her arms around me and I patted her shoulder helplessly.

"But nothing did. You saved me. You and Amos. I owe you my life."

"I was out walking—I like to come here sometimes . . . I saw the smoke rising, the thatched roof was ablaze, the walls . . . I had seen Amos at the cemetery raking the leaves, so I hurried back to get him. But I never thought . . . I had no idea anyone was inside. I might not have come back in time—oh God!"

"But you did, Katherine, you did come back. And you saved me. I'm alive now because of you."

418

"Oh my dear, my dear child!"

Morwenna found us later and the three of us went back to Thunder House. Martha took charge of Katherine, who was as shattered by the experience as I, saying she would give her a strong drink. I went upstairs with Morwenna.

"Amos and Seth put out the fire," she told me a while later as I lay resting. "But that old cottage be gone."

"Yes, it's gone now," I answered. But its secrets were still alive, still potent, and they would continue. Katherine knew that and it terrified her. As it terrified me.

Someone had deliberately begun that fire, knowing I was inside. Someone had stalked me to the Folly and watched while I went inside and shut the door. Then someone had slipped a wedgelike stone under the door and set the thatched roof ablaze. It was someone who had been growing increasing impatient to see me dead, impatient enough to watch for me to leave Thunder House and follow me as I walked to the Folly. When I went inside, the person must then have seen her chance. The Folly was isolated, miles from Nansett and even Thunder House, and setting it on fire must have seemed the perfect way to end my life.

And why was this person so impatient, desperate even, for me to die? Because this person had tried to kill me twice before. Two attempts to kill me had been made—yet I had not been killed either time. The first had been the boulder which had tumbled down the slope of Bald Mountain, missing me by inches. Someone had sent that boulder toppling down, someone who surmised I might come along the path that afternoon. If it had been successful, it would have been viewed by all as a freak accident, as no doubt the murderer had planned.

My death had to look like an accident so no suspicion would fall on anyone. The second attempt had come at the shipyard on launching day. What had struck my mind with a dizzying impact just after the structure had missed crushing me—the notion that someone had tried to kill me—I realized now beyond a doubt was true.

Now there could be no doubt. The fire couldn't have

419

started on its own; I knew that whether Amos and Seth did or not, and it had not been an accident that the wedge of stone had been placed under the door preventing my escape. And I had found Heather's scarf on the sofa.

From now on, I told myself, I must be very watchful, very wary. I must be constantly on the lookout for another possible attempt. I could not walk distances without furtively looking over my shoulder, without hurrying to my destination, without considering that *that* day might be my last on earth.

When Nicholas returned, I would tell him everything. I would confess that I knew about his involvement with Heather, about the child I believed she had lost, and I would tell him I believed that she had tried three times to kill me so that she could have him to herself.

But what if it was Nicholas himself who was trying to kill me? What if he wanted to rid himself of an encumbrance — a wife — so he could marry the woman he had decided he loved after all? What if he had not gone away as he had said but instead was hiding somewhere on Thunder Island, waiting for the opportunity to kill me? He and Heather working together toward that one resolve.

But what of the first attempt, the boulder? We had only been married a short time. Had he realized so soon that he had made a grave mistake in marrying me and was already trying to kill me? Or could the first attempt have been made by Heather on her own? And in light of what I had learned about Nicholas and Heather's blood relationship, the irony of one of them trying to kill me so that they could be together was incredible in the extreme. I had assumed that Heather knew nothing of this — what woman would knowingly marry her half-brother? She would have to be a kind of monster, totally devoid of what was right and good and moral. But if she was someone who had tried three times to take a human life, then who knew what else she was capable of? Julia had believed that Heather had not known of her mother's affair. Julia had planned to tell Heather of it and end the love between them with her announcement that they were half-brother and half-sister.

Julia had planned to tell Heather. Each word split my skull like a bolt of lightning. Julia had written that she would disclose to Heather the identity of her true father, not Bruce MacLeod but Roger Blaize. I had assumed that she had never done so, that she had disappeared before she was able to meet with Heather. I had been stupidly, unbelievably blind to the sinister implications in the course of events.

Julia had discovered the letter from Roger to Katherine. She had drawn her own conclusions and planned to reveal all to Heather, and when Nicholas returned, she had also planned to tell him. Yet she had not had the opportunity to tell Nicholas because she had disapppeared without a trace. What if, in fact, she had been killed, silenced, so that no one would know the truth about Roger's fathering Heather? What if her death was no mysterious accident but a deliberate murder?

Now I knew what I had been too blind to see before. It had been too much of a coincidence that she had died or disappeared just after discovering the truth about Heather's birth. She had been killed for possessing that knowledge so she would never be able to admit to Nicholas what she knew. It was so obvious to me now, yet without knowing what Julia had written in her journal, it could never have been figured out. I had the key; I had figured it out.

But that was not why my life was threatened. Heather did not realize that I also had learned that she was Roger's child. She was trying to kill me simply because I was Nicholas's wife and I stood in her way. I filled the position that she herself wanted to fill, must have always wanted to fill.

Chapter Nineteen

Desperately I longed for another person to confide in, now, that moment. I felt I should go mad, so anxious was I to reconstruct what had happened, to delve into the mystery of Julia's disappearance. She had gone out one warm summer day and never returned. I longed to know all the answers but at the same time I was very frightened. Not only had three attempts been made on my life in the past months, but just recently I had stumbled across certain knowledge—that Heather was Nicholas's half-sister and Julia had been killed for knowing exactly that—that was very dangerous for me to possess.

Julia had lost her life because she had gone to Heather and confronted her. Whether or not Heather had had any idea of her parentage before Julia's revelation I had no way of knowing, but it now looked as though she had killed Julia to prevent her from telling Nicholas they were related. The level of depravity of which she was capable was astounding. No one but a fiend would consider marrying her own half-brother, and kill someone to prevent his finding out that they were in fact bound by blood ties. I believe that Heather wanted Nicholas so intensely that discovering that he was her half-brother had made no difference. She had been determined to have him at all costs.

For years Heather had played a patient waiting game, waiting for Nicholas to ask her to be his wife. She had waited while he tried his hand at whaling, while he was gone on voyages for months, even years, at a time. And then Julia, just before he was due to return from the second expedition to the Arctic, had found Roger's letter to Katherine. She had gone to Heather and accused Katherine of being Roger's mistress and bearing his child. She must have wanted Nicholas with a hunger so powerful, so evil, that finding out they were bound by blood did not dissuade her. She had disposed of her only threat, Julia, and then had sat back to wait again for the day when Nicholas would ask her to marry him.

But he had not. He had stayed a few weeks, coming home soon after Julia's disappearance, before sailing off again to Nova Scotia to spend the winter. Lavinia, tortured, had told him that his neglect was to blame for Julia's death. She had told him to leave Thunder House and never to return. And he had left — without ever proposing marriage to Heather. He had returned briefly in the spring to sign on some of the local men to round out his crew — Zeke included — and he had then sailed to the Arctic again. And in September of that year, last year, the ice fields had blocked the *Eagle*'s passage in an early freeze. He had come back to Thunder Island some months later, defeated, bitter, ridden with guilt. And he had avoided Heather as he had avoided everyone.

How she must have felt, tormented by all those feelings she could not express, knowing she had killed her own half-sister, only to have Nicholas turn from her! How difficult it must have been for her to again patiently bide her time and wait for Nicholas to come to terms with the Arctic tragedy and seek her out again. She must have comforted herself day after day with the reminder that he had loved her once and he would come to love her again. She must have told herself that eventually she would become Mrs. Nicholas Blaize, mistress of Thunder House.

But again fate had thwarted her. Nicholas had gone to New Bedford to sell his bark and had returned with a bride. I remembered coming across her that first day in Nansett—how friendly and natural she had seemed. But I now knew that that was a gift she had that she used to advantage. She had pretended to be pleased to meet me, to see Nicholas again, while inside she must have been raging with fury and despair.

But she had not given up her desire to have Nicholas for her own. She had begun a plan to do away with his new bride. First she had pushed the boulder down the slope; a tall strong girl such as she would not have too much difficulty in toppling over a boulder already unsteady and loosened from rain. That attempt had not succeeded and so she had cut loose the support structures from the side of the ship and sent them crashing to the ground where I stood. With all the people milling around on deck involved in various duties, her presence would not have been noticed, and she had been careful not to remain on deck just after the supports had fallen. While attention had been focused on me and the narrow escape I had had, she had hurried away from the ship. And then a while later she had come to me to express her concern.

And weeks later had come the setting of the Folly on fire. Perhaps she figured that the best time to do away with me was while Nicholas was gone from the island. I would not believe that he was working with her to kill me. That just was not possible, I kept telling myself.

But Heather had not known her mother would be out walking and spot the smoke rising above the trees. When Katherine had seen the wedge under the door, she had realized that someone had purposely trapped me in the Folly and then set it afire. And as Heather's mother she would know, perhaps, of Heather's obsession, her love for Nicholas that refused to die even though he had taken a wife. Perhaps by inviting us to dinner that evening she had hoped Heather would come to terms with our marriage. But then the next day Heather had made her second attempt to kill me.

I was terrified and I did not wish to be in this alone. Yet in whom might I confide? I might talk to Emily. She was the most logical person. Yet I did not feel as though this was a good time to tell her that I suspected her sister had been murdered, nor that her father had been unfaithful to her mother and had fathered a child who was not afraid to commit incest! I could not go to her with such a story — it was too appalling and the shock might have had serious consequences on the child she was carrying. And she was suffering both grief and remorse over the loss of her mother. I could not involve her in another trauma just now, a couple of months away from her delivery. No, I could not tell Emily of my suspicions.

Ben? I liked and respected him but I couldn't tell him my most private thoughts and anxieties concerning Nicholas and Heather — and not of the secret blood tie between them. Perhaps I could just tell him about Julia's discovery of Heather's birth and the possible consequences — but if I confessed that to him, I feared the rest might come out. And it was too terrible a tale to confide to him, a man I didn't know well. He might even think I was mad for telling such a story with no real proof.

There was Katherine; she was the most likely one since she was Heather's mother. In fact, I was sure she suspected Heather of setting the fire. Yet if she knew of Heather's obsession with Nicholas, why had she not warned her away from him before Julia did? Perhaps she had; perhaps Heather could not be controlled. Even though I believed she had miscarried, she was still determined to kill me to free the way for her and Nicholas. His renewed interest in her would make her doubly desperate to have me out of the way.

The other person was Zeke. Nicholas didn't trust him but he had shown concern — and more — for me on a number of occasions. I was certain that he would try and help me. He knew about Nicholas and Heather, about the child she was or had been carrying. He might be the best person to tell, if I decided to tell someone. But what could the two of us do? What could we discover together? If we could find proof that Heather had murdered Julia, then it was likely that more matters would come to light than just

425

the solution to her disappearance.

The following day my fears had not subsided any. I was afraid to go out of the house. I contrived things to discuss with Martha in the kitchen, reluctant to be alone. I still wanted to confide in someone—whether Zeke or Katherine—but the idea of walking to Nansett filled me with terror. On that long lonely walk anything might happen; Heather might be lying in wait for me. When I thought of the way the path skirted Blackett's Glade, I realized how easy it would be for her to hide nearby and then come up behind me and attack me, even push me into the swamp. I could struggle, I could fight, but she would have the edge on me and my actions might prove ineffectual. I didn't want to do anything to harm my child, to put it or myself in any unnecessary jeopardy.

After lunch I was in the sitting room leafing through a book when there was a knock at the door. Even then I could not prevent the sudden lurch my stomach gave me or the way my heartbeat quickened. "Who is there?" I asked, a quake in my voice.

"Miranda, it's I, Emily."

"Emily!" I jumped up and went over to the door, opening it. "How good of you to call."

"I was concerned about you when I heard about the fire at the Folly yesterday, and the way you happened to be inside when it caught. I had to come over today and see how you were."

I nodded, pressing my lips together. It was such an effort not to cry out, "Emily, help me. Heather MacLeod is trying to murder me. She set that fire and it was her third attempt to kill me. I believe she also murdered your sister Julia because Julia found out that Roger is not only your father and Nicholas's father, but Heather's as well. I believe she has committed incest with Nicholas and has recently lost his unborn baby." No, I couldn't say any of that. There was no way of convincing her I spoke the truth except to show her the journal and I could not do that. The shock might do her real harm.

She went on, "You must have been so terrified—how

426

horrible it must have been! Are you all right? In your condition . . ."

"I'm fine, Emily. I was shaken, but that's all. Katherine got me out just in time."

"How awful that Nicholas is away just now. Have you heard from him?"

I shook my head.

"Oh well, I didn't expect you would have. The mail is very slow in coming to Thunder Island. And as busy as he undoubtedly is trying to learn information on the crew of the *Marianne,* it's likely he hasn't had time to write."

"I wonder how long he will be gone."

"He told Ben that it might take several weeks. But I'm certain he'll return before long. If you are lonely, you are welcome to come and stay with Ben and me."

With Heather MacLeod a short distance away? "Thank you, Emily. That's very kind of you. But I think I'll just stay here and wait for Nicholas to return. Perhaps he'll be back later this week."

She smiled. "Perhaps he will. I hope so. I wonder if he'll learn much about the men who killed Noah. The sailors responsible are most likely far out to sea now and cannot be reached, despite his efforts. The whole affair is queer, really."

"How do you mean?"

"Well, as I was saying to Ben several days ago, how could those men have heard about Noah's habit of storing money under his bed? He was a well-known character, but that seems a trifle much to swallow. And it doesn't seem that there was as much money as people have believed all along, because Jock has admitted that Noah used to come to the tavern quite often and buy bottles of scotch whiskey. It was suspected that Noah drank more than was good for him, especially in the last few years. That's why Nicholas was paying Tom to help him, though Noah didn't realize it. But no one would ever say such a thing to Noah. He was too proud and the people respected him for the work he had done at the lighthouse for years and years. He thought his drinking was a secret. With Tom there on foggy nights there wasn't anything to worry about—he could ring the bell and work the light if Noah wasn't able. So with Noah spending a good deal of his wages on scotch—well, it stands to reason that he couldn't have had as much money as people thought he did. What's more to the point, it is very difficult for me to imagine those sailors, strangers to Thunder Island, finding their way from Nansett in the dark halfway round the island to the lighthouse. Of course, there's no other explanation, is there? Ben told me to put the whole thing out of my head. No one in Nansett would have committed such a crime. Noah might have been considered a foolish old man, harping on old legends and superstitions, but he had no enemies."

"You mean his belief in selkies, don't you?" I asked, smiling wryly. "He tried his best to frighten me with all that nonsense the first time I met him, but after that I got used to him and stopped paying him any mind. Why, there were a number of occasions when he gave me vague mysterious warnings . . ." My voice trailed off. I looked into the fire, mesmerized by the dancing flames. Then shuddering, I had to look away from them.

"Well, he was just recalling things he had been told as a child. People who make their living on or by the sea are often superstitious. I remember the time Father telling us of one sailor who claimed he saw a mermaid swimming along the ship. Two other men had to restrain him or he would have jumped in after her."

I heard her voice coming from far away, as though a blanket of mist separated the two of us. With an effort I tried to comprehend what she had just said and answer her. "Noah did have his share of superstitions. But Emily, it seems from what you said before that robbery may not have been the motive behind his death."

"I shouldn't have come to you with all my wonderings," she said ruefully. "Ben says it's just the fancies I get from my condition. He would be annoyed if he knew I had gone through it again, upsetting you. I don't like mysteries, that's all. I like everything to be laid out and easily

428

explained, easily understood. But life can't always be like that, can it?"

"No," I agreed ironically. "It's very seldom like that."

She rose. "Well, it won't be a mystery for long. I daresay Nicholas will return very soon after informing the proper authorities, who will have the ship stopped at its next port of call. And I've got to be on my way if I'm to be home before dark. It gets dark so early these days, have you noticed?"

"Yes," I said, looking out the window at the edge of the forest, where the birches were pale and ghostly in the gray afternoon light.

"Well, I'm quite relieved that you suffered no ill effects from the fire yesterday; Katherine was very worried about you, too. She seemed very distressed about the whole thing."

And well she might be, I thought.

When Emily had gone, I stood by the window. Noah had warned me in an obscure way when I had visited him in the lighthouse. And then at the ball, on the night of his murder, he had warned me of a lurking danger. And I had impatiently assumed he was referring to those demon lovers of the sea, the selkies. He had said that there was an evil waiting to take me by surprise, an evil which had taken Julia. I had laughed off his words, convinced he was again talking about his favorite obsession. I had been so distraught by what I had overheard Nicholas saying to Heather that I had paid him no mind. I had not realized then that my life was in danger, deadly danger.

But what if on those two occasions he had not meant that the Great Selkie lurked nearby, threatening to take me off to a watery grave, but instead that someone quite human wished me ill? What if the danger he had referred to had been a danger from a human enemy? And wasn't it possible that he might have been murdered because Heather suspected he might warn me, that he knew something which linked her to Julia's death—something he had kept to himself in the past years out of fear? "I won't say nothin'. I never said nothin'."

My blood ran cold. What if Noah *hadn't* been killed by one or more of those sailors from the ship which had dropped anchor in Nansett harbor on the day of the ball? What if the murderer had seen that as a perfect opportunity to get rid of Noah, who was the only one who suspected that she had had something to do with Julia's disappearance?

It would not have been difficult for someone who knew the island very well to make her way through the woods to the lighthouse even in the dark. She would have carried a torch. Emily had questioned whether strangers to the island could have done so. I now saw the logic behind her doubts. Tom had not been at the lighthouse that night; he had been at the ball and then, I assumed, had returned to Nansett to sleep. Noah had walked from the ball at Thunder House to the lighthouse, where he had been alone and defenseless. Had Heather waited for her mother to go to sleep and then stolen out of the house and through the dark woods to the lighthouse?

Heather had killed Noah; I was certain of it. He had been afraid that he would lose his post as keeper—that must have been the threat which Heather had held over him. She had said she would tell Nicholas to dismiss him—and if he loved her, perhaps her request would have been adhered to—if Noah told anyone what he knew or suspected about Julia. Idly I wondered why she had merely threatened him—why had she just not killed him at first too? Human life seemed to mean so little to her.

If only I knew the manner of Julia's death. If only I knew what had happened after she had written the last entry in her diary. Had she indeed left the house with the intent of confronting Heather? But what had happened then? Where had they met? What had Heather done with Julia's body?

Outside it was dusk. The slender birches trembled in the wind as if they, too, were afraid. The sky was leaden, the lawn a dirty unhealthy yellow—a dead color. Even in this charming room fashioned like a rose garden of pinks and greens there was no comfort, no respite from fear. No

430

escape from the harsh brutal knowledge.

When had Nicholas and Heather conceived a child? What exactly did he feel about her? I wanted to believe that it had happened prior to our marriage, that somehow she had thrown herself at him and afterward they had parted. This was not supported by what Sarah had smugly told me, and I myself had seen her scarf in the Folly, where Sarah insisted they were meeting.

That night I had no appetite for dinner. I told Morwenna that I had had a return of my earlier queasiness and she believed me. She brought up some toast and I ate it to stop her from worrying about me.

I can't go on like this much longer, I thought as I lay in bed that night. I had asked Morwenna to sleep in the room with me because I was so frightened to be alone on the third floor of this vast house. I now wished desperately that Nicholas would come home so I could tell him what, or some of what, I suspected. I had to know the nature of his feelings for Heather and his feelings for me. I had to tell him what I believed had happened to Julia, to Noah, and then nearly to myself on three occasions. He must know what Heather was, what she was capable of. He also must know the truth about her parentage; I no longer thought he should be kept in the dark about that. And when he discovered that he and Heather were related, then their affair would end. My safety depended on his learning that Roger was also Heather's father. Julia had not had the opportunity to tell him and she had died. But once I told him, I believed I would be safe from Heather.

The next morning I was again tense and jittery and found myself repeatedly going to one of the long windows in my bedroom to gaze out to sea in hopes of spotting a ship. A ship bringing Nicholas home. But one wouldn't necessarily be seen on this side of the island, I told myself. It could dock in Nansett without passing Thunder House. Even now he could be on his way here.

That afternoon I said to Morwenna, "I need some fresh air but I'd rather not go out alone. I'd like you to walk with me." Surely together the two of us would be safe.

431

"Aye, ma'am, I be glad to," she said.

And so we bundled into warm clothes and went out in the frosty air, heading through the woods. It was a bright day, blue and golden, the air thin and piercing. We walked rather aimlessly, following one path, then another. I did not really care in what direction we went, though I was careful to steer clear of the Folly. It was good to stretch my legs; the ground felt hard as stone but the dirt crumbled as we walked upon it.

"Do you miss Cornwall, Morwenna?" I asked her at one point.

"Aye, but I be tryin' hard not to think on it much. And 'ee and the captain be good to me."

"I know what it's like to have lost one's family and be alone in the world. Even now I know it."

"Aye, I can tell 'ee be frettin'. But he'll be back soon, don't 'ee worry."

I nodded, trying to reassure myself that she spoke the truth. And for the present, as long as I stayed in Thunder House, I was safe.

Or was I? Julia had been in Thunder House the morning before she had disappeared. Yet she must have gone out. She must have arranged to meet Heather. Surely nothing could have happened *inside* the house. Heather wouldn't have come *here*, would she? And no one had glimpsed her entering or leaving the house.

Perhaps someone had. None of the servants, perhaps, for they would have mentioned it, but perhaps Noah had. Noah Todd, who had so feared losing his position that he had kept someone's secret. Had his talk of the Great Selkie carrying off Julia just been his way of whistling in the graveyard to cover up what he knew or suspected? Had he used the seal creature as an excuse to babble on about something, to not admit the truth to himself and to others?

I now wondered if there was any place where I was actually safe. Oh Nicholas, I prayed, come home soon.

When I arose the next day, there was a tiny row of scarcely visible clouds on the horizon lit up like tongues of flames. A bluish-lavender haze filled the rest of the sky and was reflected in the dull pewter hue of the sea. Morwenna said that Amos had warned that bad weather was on its way.

"What sort of bad weather?" I asked.

"A storm or even a blizzard, he said, from the mainland."

Just the sort of thing to prevent Nicholas from getting back, I thought with a rising panic. "Morwenna, do you know if a ship is expected in soon? Perhaps one of the men heard talk in the village?" I asked hopefully.

"No, ma'am," she began, but when she saw my face fall she quickly added, "but one could be on its way, all the same."

I nodded, sighing.

By noon, long low clouds spanned the length of a sky now gray with the merest hint of blue. The wind had picked up too, and its fierce whining and roaring could be heard distinctly in the house.

"Amos do say it don't snow the way it do on the mainland," said Morwenna, "but storms do bring sleet and snow and the sea be somethin' savage. Ships be blown off their course. 'Tis as though we be all alone in the world on Thunder Island, Amos do say."

Such a cheerless thought made me speak sharply to her. So we were to be marooned, I thought glumly. I went downstairs to the kitchen, where the two men, Martha, Jenny, and Mary were gathered, all discussing the weather. They looked slightly guilty when I entered.

"Do you really think it will be bad—I mean, lasting for several days and preventing ships from docking?" I asked.

"No way of knowin', ma'am," said Amos, scratching his long chin. "It might be blowed out by tomorrow—or it might not. But you're safe and snug here."

"Amos, Seth, have you both been locking up the house every night?" I asked.

"Ayeh, like always," answered Amos, and Seth nodded, puffing on his pipe.

"All the doors and all the windows?"

433

They exchanged glances. "The doors—ayeh. The windows were locked when it first got cold, a month or more ago."

"Will you check them today to make certain they are all locked? I—I just don't feel as safe with my husband away."

Their faces relaxed; I saw Jenny and Mary smile at each other. A young bride, they were all thinking, with child and missing her husband. Everyone knew that carrying a child made one fanciful. And I was not native to the island as they were.

I did not care what they thought. I went back upstairs and into my sitting room. The wind sounded even louder on this side of the house since it was blowing from across Thunder Island instead of from the cove. I went to the windows and drew the heavy drapes, which muffled some of the sound. I asked Morwenna to light all the candles and bank up the fire, apologizing to her for my shortness earlier.

"That be all right, ma'am. I know you'm frettin' 'bout the master returnin'. But he's bound to soon."

"Yes," I agreed, but derived no comfort from her words. It was what I had heard many times lately.

Well, I thought, Heather would surely not leave the old manse with a storm coming and I certainly am not going out. So I should be in no danger for the present. I sat down to play the piano for a while and then Morwenna came in, announcing that I had a visitor and where would I like to receive him?

"Him? Who is it?"

"Zeke Somes, ma'am, come to call."

"Zeke!" Zeke, coming here to my husband's house to see me? What on earth about? "Show him into the drawing room, Morwenna."

When I went down, he was standing by the fire in the sea-colored drawing room. I came in and closed the door behind me.

"Hello, Zeke," I said a bit warily.

He turned to face me; his cheeks were red from the wind and cold, his blue eyes keen and penetrating. He was holding his navy knit cap in his hand. "Hello, Miranda. Or should I say Mrs. Blaize? Nicholas hates when I call you by your first name."

"Oh, that's all right, Zeke. What did you want to see me about? You know Nicholas is away or you wouldn't have come here."

"I wanted to make sure youh're all right. Your fool of a husband went off on some wild goose chase, leavin' you alone here. I hearhrd you'd been in the old Folly when it caught fire. You might've been killed."

"I know. Believe me, I've thought of little else since then."

"Miranda, I want you to tell me just how it happened, don't leave anything out. You took a walk to the Folly and decided to go inside?"

"Why are you asking me this, Zeke?" I was twisting my wedding ring around and around my finger.

"Because I don't think it was just an accident, that cottage flarin' up the way it did."

"You think someone set the fire deliberately?"

"Ayeh."

"With me inside. You think someone wanted to kill me."

"That's what I think, Miranda," he said evenly.

"Oh God, Zeke, I think so too!" The relief of having another person to talk to was overwhelming. "You see, what no one knows, except Katherine, was that there was a wedge of stone put under the cottage door after I had closed it behind me. When I smelled burning and saw the smoke, I ran to the door but it wouldn't open. I did everything I could to move it, to force it open, but it wouldn't budge. Because it had been deliberately wedged shut. Someone had trapped me in there and then set the roof on fire!"

"That's what I thought myself, that somehow you couldn't get out because someone didn't want you to. Folks thought you must've fainted and that's why you didn't get out yourself. But I came today because I'm afraid for you. I'm afraid someone will try again."

435

"The same person has already tried twice before that. I don't think he or she will give up either." I told him about the boulder and the launching day accident.

"Ayeh, I thought at the time that was somethin' strange. But I didn't figure—" He shook his head. "Who do you think it is, Miranda? Who do you think wants you dead?"

I took a deep breath. "Heather. Heather MacLeod. I'm convinced she's tried to kill me three times so she can have Nicholas."

"Because they're lovers. Because she's carryin' his child."

"Oh Zeke, there's so much you don't know! It's so complicated, it's much uglier than we even thought on the night we overheard them at the ball. For one thing, I think she's lost the child . . ."

He whistled between his teeth. "Lost it?"

I nodded. "Yes, I visited her last week with some idea of forcing a confrontation between us. There was something I felt I had to tell her. Instead I learned that she had been taken very ill in the night with stomach pains and couldn't have visitors. I can't tell you exactly what alerted me, Zeke, but I just had the very strong feeling then that she wasn't pregnant any longer. And that is even more of a miracle than you realize."

"Why do you say that?"

"Because I've learned something that is rather horrible considering what we know about Nicholas and Heather. I don't know how to tell you . . . but Heather is much much worse, much more evil than even you'd believe. You see, I found a journal that Julia Blaize kept. And in it she wrote of a discovery she had made concerning Nicholas and Heather . . ."

"Discovery? Not that they were lovers, that's not much of a discovery."

I shook my head, feeling sick. "No, not that. But something that makes that fact even worse. You see, Julia had reason to believe . . . that is, she thought that—that Heather is Nicholas's half-sister."

"What?" he said after a long pause.

"That . . . that's what I said. Julia found a letter in the

436

Folly just before she died, a letter Roger Blaize wrote to Katherine MacLeod . . . a love letter. A letter where he admitted in no uncertain terms that they were . . . that they had been intimate."

"So?"

"So Julia did some calculating and deduced that Katherine had Roger's child less than a year after the letter was written. And she believed Heather was the result of— of their affair."

"She'd no proof of it?"

"No . . ."

He shook his head. "What did the letter she found say, exactly? Did Roger mention that Katherine was . . . in the family way? And that he could be the father?"

"No, he just said that he knew it was wrong but he didn't want to stop meeting her, that sort of thing. But Julia suspected that Heather might be her and Nicholas's half-sister and she wrote in her journal that she was going to tell her so. She also said she would tell Nicholas when he returned from his voyage so that he would not marry her unknowingly. But, Zeke, she didn't write in the journal again—she disappeared before she had the chance, before Nicholas returned, before she was able to tell him what she knew. Heather must have killed her to prevent Nicholas from knowing, don't you see?"

"But that would mean that Heather knew—and that it didn't matter. That she would willingly . . . with her own flesh and blood!"

"I know. But if she loved Nicholas that much, if she was so obsessed with him to begin with, perhaps she couldn't turn her feelings off like that. She—she can't be normal, Zeke, she must be very sick, mad really. To knowingly take her half-brother as her lover! Naturally Nicholas knows nothing, but I hate to think what will happen when he learns the truth about their relationship. I don't want to tell him, but how can I not? It's so unbelievably *sordid*."

"Good God."

"And that's not all, Zeke. I believe Heather killed Julia to stop her from telling Nicholas. I also think she killed

Noah Todd because he knew something, and she was afraid he wouldn't keep silent much longer."

"Noah?"

"Yes, I don't think his death was caused by sailors who sought to rob him after all. I've wondered if Heather killed him."

"That girl? How?"

"If she took him by surprise or waited until he was asleep, it would have been easy for her. What else could have happened, now that we know what we do? It's just too coincidental that Julia disappeared after she had made that discovery about Nicholas and Heather, and I think it's too coincidental that Noah was killed since he began giving me these obscure warnings. Two years ago Heather must have come to the house, or she met Julia somewhere."

"But why wasn't her body found, then?"

"I admit that puzzles me, too. Perhaps it did wash out to sea as people assumed. Two things are certain, though. Julia wasn't carried off by any selkie! And she didn't disappear by accident."

"Ayeh. It'd seem so. But . . ." He shook his head.

"I know. There's no proof. I don't know what happened to the letter Roger wrote. Julia most likely destroyed it."

"Just why would Heather kill Noah? He can't've known anything 'bout Heather bein' Nicholas's sister."

"No, but he may have known something about Julia's death. He told me once that Julia didn't 'take care' and that I should. Heather may have realized that she couldn't trust him to keep quiet much longer. She had apparently threatened him with the loss of the lighthouse and for two years that ensured his silence. But when I came to Thunder Island, he decided he liked me and thought I might be in danger. He began to drop hints, but I was too dim to interpret them. Until now."

Zeke laced his hands together, flexing them. "If we can find some proof of Julia's murder, then it should be easy to stop Heather. I don't like that youh're alone here, Miranda. I don't want anything to happen to you. I know

I don't have the right to speak to you like this but your husband don't deserve it either. And how do you know he's truly gone óff? How can you be sure he's not helpin' Heather?"

I put my hand to my cheek. "I can't be certain. But I don't believe he is. I know you hate Nicholas, Zeke, and you think . . . you care for me. The two of you have been competing for things all your lives. I'm glad and grateful for your friendship, but you mustn't make anything more of it than that. I think you regard me as another of Nicholas's possessions which you would like to have for yourself. Just as, if you'll forgive me for speaking frankly, you wanted command of the *Eagle.*" I looked into the fire as I spoke; I could not look at Zeke even though I knew it was essential that I said what I did. I knew he found me attractive and that he had felt protective toward me ever since rescuing me from Seal Island. I was the wife of the man he hated and envied, and he longed to take me from Nicholas in the same way a boy would take a toy or pet from another—simply because he didn't want the other boy to have it.

There was a long tense pause. Then he said, "Those are hard wohrds."

"I'm sorry." And I looked over at him.

He had shoved his hands in his pockets; a muscle jerked in his cheek. "Don't be. Maybe youh're right. Maybe not. But it doesn't matter, does it? Youh're Nicholas's wife and that's what you'll be for the rest of your life. Still, I don't want to see you huhrt, Miranda. And so I think we ought to look for proof that Heather killed Julia. Since Nicholas ain't here to help you, I will."

"Thank you, Zeke. I do need your help. Do you think we'll be able to find any proof now, two and a half years later?"

He shrugged. "No tellin'. But we ought to think of what could've happened that day and try to figure things out."

"All right. Where do we start?"

"Well, we know that Julia wrote in the journal about her father and Katherine MacLeod. We know she planned to

439

tell Heather. Either that same day or the next she went to see Heather or asked to meet her someplace — maybe even here in the house, with no one the wiser. Maybe Julia wanted Heather to come here so she wouldn't have to face Heather's mother. We know that Julia went out that day and wasn't seen to come back. But that doesn't mean she was killed then. What if she told Heather what she knew, threatened that she would tell Nicholas, and then came back to the house? Heather could've slipped in and gone up to Julia's room and struck her down, maybe stabbed her like Noah was stabbed. No, then there'd be all that blood to clean up."

I shuddered. "But what would she have done with the body? And wouldn't they have found a trace of something, evidence of some sort that a struggle had gone on?"

"You'd think so. But who knows? Maybe they weren't lookin' for the right thing. Nobody's thought Julia might've been murdered."

"All right, but what on earth would she have done with Julia's body if she killed her in Thunder House?"

"The only thing is that she must've hid it somewhere. Carried it off somewhere else in the house where no one goes and hid it away. She couldn't take the chance of taking it from the house."

"You mean, she might have put it in a trunk or something?"

"Could be."

"In the attics, perhaps," I said. "I've never been up to the attics. But they are just a floor above mine. She could have dragged Julia's body up there and hidden it. But wouldn't they have searched the attics when they searched the house?"

"A search don't always mean something turns up. If she hid her well . . ."

I grimaced. "It does seem possible. But I still don't see why Heather would have taken the chance to come to Thunder House instead of killing Julia somewhere outside. But they did search the island and found no trace. And Heather could easily have slipped in the house, I

440

suppose, since she knew her way about, knew all the entrances and staircases. She probably knew where the people in the house were at the time and she was careful to avoid them. How horrible to think Julia may have been in the house all this time. We should look for her, I suppose . . ."

"There's no need for you to be doin' any lookin', Miranda. I can do it," he said quickly.

"Well, perhaps. I admit I'm not exactly looking forward to finding a—a decomposed body. But we can't do anything about it now. It's nearly dark and you would have an awful time trying to search up there now. And with this storm approaching, you had better go back to Nansett while you can. Perhaps tomorrow you can come back if the storm is not too severe, or the day after. Heather won't be able to try anything in this weather. I was fearing the storm, but now I'm beginning to see it might be providential. Heather won't be hovering nearby with a sinister purpose in mind. And Nicholas should be home soon."

His mouth tightened. "All right. I'll try to be back tomorrow then." He got up.

"Thank you for coming, Zeke. I'm glad I could confide in you. I've been sick with worry, keeping it all to myself."

He took my hand. "You know you can tell me anything, Miranda. I—well, good night then."

"Good night."

After having dinner alone in the dining room, I went up to my sitting room. Morwenna had built up the fire, and the corners of the room glowed with candlelight. But the ferocious gale outside had not diminished; it spun around the house like a mad creature. Amos had predicted snow or freezing rain—and a good bit of it—by dawn.

It had helped me to talk things over with Zeke and know that he was an ally. But I still had many unanswered questions, too many to indulge in any real feeling of relief. And over dinner I had begun to be troubled by something. Something was niggling at the back of my mind, something that Zeke's visit had triggered, something that I had

441

overlooked. Something in Julia's journal. I decided to read it again carefully.

Feeling slightly repelled by her personality, I nevertheless was determined to reread every word she had written. Only that way could I bring to the fore and examine that which was bothering me, that which I could not identify.

I was rereading the section where she talked about visiting the Folly and being surprised by Zeke's appearance in the doorway. "I was vastly annoyed to see him there and told him to leave at once. 'You followed me here,' I said and he did not deny it. . . . he took an odious and unfair advantage of me. He took me in his arms . . . and kissed me on the lips. . . . I told him that I would doubtless be married and living in Boston . . . I could see that took him aback. . . . It will be a very different man than he whom I will marry. . . . I believe Zeke has always been jealous of Nicholas . . . they were in constant competition with one another . . ."

That was it. It was that section which she had written about Zeke which had been softly rapping at my memory. I had scarcely paid it attention before, so stunned was I by the revelation about Nicholas and Heather which had followed. Yet what about it disturbed me? Julia had described a case where a man had shown interest in a girl who wanted nothing to do with him. It was a common occurrence. Julia had been a very lovely girl. It would have been natural for Zeke to have found her appealing even though their stations in life were different. Yet somehow I felt uneasy. There had to be a significance which I could not fathom. Zeke had admired Julia, had paid her unwanted attention. He must have been referring to her at the ball when he had implied that he seem to fall in love with women who were not for him. She had looked forward to ridding herself of his attentions when she left for Boston. But she had never gone to Boston. Instead she had disappeared.

And then I knew.

I knew what significance there was in all this. Heather . . . I had suspected Heather of Julia's death because Julia had discovered it was highly likely that Heather and Nicholas had the same father, and Heather had wanted that speculation kept secret. But what if Heather had never met with Julia at all? What if Heather still knew nothing of her parentage? *What if Julia's death had nothing whatsoever to do with Heather?*

What if Zeke had come to Thunder House that afternoon—or, more likely, what if Julia had gone out after writing in the journal and then somewhere come upon Zeke? What if he had again tried to kiss her and again had been coldly rebuffed? Had he then attacked her out of frustration—and killed her? Was it possible?

And I was seized with a wave of fear so intense that it made me weak and faint. Zeke had wanted Julia, who had spurned him. And Julia had disappeared. Zeke had shown an interest in me, a deep interest that I believed was further complicated and escalated by the hatred and jealousy he felt toward my husband. What if now Zeke wanted to kill me? I had implied that day at Blackett's Glade before Nicholas came upon us that I loved my husband and was carrying his child. So he knew then, if he had refused to believe it before, that there was no hope for anything between himself and me. And then this afternoon I had again intimated that he wanted me only because I belonged to Nicholas; I had angered and humiliated him with my perception. And I had told him about Julia's journal. He knew that no one else knew of it. He might be wondering right now whether it contained anything about him which could link him to her disappearance.

In the hearth a log fell off the others with a loud crackling sound and I jumped. A cold sick terror possessed me, creeping over my flesh and through my blood. I looked over my shoulder at the closed door of the sitting room.

Zeke hated Nicholas. He had relentlessly competed with him over the years. He had attempted to take command of the *Eagle* during the Arctic whaling expedition. Just now Zeke might be reasoning that if he couldn't have me, then

443

Nicholas wouldn't have me either. He knew Nicholas had some affection for me, despite his involvement with Heather; Nicholas's outraged jealousy evinced that. And so by killing me, Zeke might feel he had avenged himself on Nicholas. Especially now since I was carrying his child. But what of the first two attempts on my life? Had Zeke been planning to kill me all along, to take me from Nicholas as he had not been able to take his ship? He had admitted hating me before meeting me just because I was Nicholas's wife. He had not met me when the boulder had nearly crushed me—had he lain in wait for me anyway, his sole purpose to hurt Nicholas by killing me? Then when he rescued me from Seal Island—why had he not pushed me out of his boat and had done with it? Was it possible he had begun to grow fond of me on that night and changed his plans, deciding that instead of killing me he would try to take me away from Nicholas, hoping I would fall in love with *him?* He had seen on that night in his cottage how jealous and enraged Nicholas had been—perhaps he had considered the second plan a better one.

But what of the support structures? Had their falling, in fact, been an accident, pure and simple? I was so confused at that point that I could not think clearly.

All this time I had been blaming Heather for Julia's death, assuming that she wished me dead so that she could have Nicholas. But if she had been pregnant with his child, then in a sense she did have him. Perhaps she was content to be his occasional mistress. Perhaps she was as ignorant of their blood tie as he.

Zeke could have followed me to the cottage, knowing after our last meeting at Blackett's Glade that I had no more feeling for him than friendship and I never would have. He might have realized then that he had to revert back to his original plan of killing me to get back at Nicholas. He had realized that I would not run away with him, that I would not allow him to take me away from Nicholas. And so now he was going to do it by force, and in no uncertain terms . . . but in a final one. He had lain in wait for me to go outside the house and then he had

444

followed me to the Folly, looking for an opportunity to murder me. It still had to look like an accident. And when I had entered the old run-down Folly with its dry thatched roof, what a perfect opportunity that must have seemed.

But what about today, why had he come today and pretended to be concerned for me? What could have been his reasoning for that? Was he just using his concern as an excuse to get into Thunder House, to see the lay of the land, before coming back to get rid of me for good? Had he come today because he was tired of trying to create accidents that might kill me and inste ' was attempting to think of a more reliable way? Had his real motive in coming to see me been to figure out a way he could get into Thunder House on another occasion when the servants were in bed, or occupied elsewhere with their duties?

And what of Noah? Was it possible that Noah might have been warning me away from Zeke? Noah could have been hinting all along that Julia had been killed by a scorned suitor. Again, nothing whatsoever to do with Heather. And Noah had heard of Zeke rescuing me from Seal Island as all of Nansett had; he might have been warning me to have nothing further to do with him. Yet because he had been frightened of what Zeke might do to him, he couldn't tell me outright but could only drop vague mysterious warnings about demon lovers! Noah might have seen Zeke with Julia that day and then Zeke might have threatened him to keep silent. What if Zeke knew of something against Noah — his drinking, perhaps — that Noah feared would cause him to lose his position as keeper? Noah had thought his drinking a secret and perhaps Zeke had played on that, threatening to go to Nicholas and tell him that Noah was a drunkard. And so Noah had promised to keep his own counsel until recently when he began to worry that I, too, might become another one of Zeke's victims. And so Zeke had silenced him permanently. Nicholas sometimes roamed the woods at night — why not Zeke? It would have been very simple for him to go to the lighthouse after the ball and stab Noah to death.

445

Zeke had been here a few hours ago. What if, in fact, he were still lurking about, waiting until the household was asleep before breaking in the house to search for the journal or seek me out and kill me? What if — oh God — what if he had not left the house at all but was hiding somewhere? What if he had resolved to kill me tonight, the night of the storm, before Nicholas returned?

Chapter Twenty

I had to know.

I rushed downstairs calling, "Morwenna! Morwenna, where are you?"

She met me in the first floor hallway, her eyes wide with fear.

"What is it, ma'am? Be it the baby?"

"No, no," I gasped, my heart pounding, "nothing like that. I just want to know . . . I want you to find out if anyone saw Zeke Somes leave this afternoon. If anyone showed him out."

"If he be gone from the house?" she asked, puzzled.

"Yes, I want to know if he was shown out, or if he left by the kitchen door, or what. Go and ask."

She hurried away while I sat down on the bottom step of the staircase and waited, catching my breath. Images were passing through my mind: Zeke kissing Julia; Zeke and myself in his cottage; Nicholas dashing in, enraged; Zeke in an echoing rage; Nicholas knocking Zeke down; Zeke saying he should have killed Nicholas in the Arctic; Zeke holding me too tightly as we danced at the ball, as we stood together at Blackett's Glade; Zeke saying, "He doesn't deserve you."

Morwenna came back then and said, "Martha gave him

some coffee and a bite to eat and then he left by the kitchen door. He be gone, ma'am. He be gone for hours. Did 'ee want him back for something?"

"No! No, I just wanted to assure myself. . . . Martha is certain that he's gone?"

"Aye, ma'am," she said, regarding me with bewildered concern.

Feeling relieved and also a bit foolish, I told her to ask Amos and Seth to check every lock on the doors and windows on the first floor before they retired and then for her to come up to my room. "Is there plenty of firewood up there? I feel so cold."

"Aye, Mrs. Blaize. Seth took a great load up this afternoon."

"Good." And I went back upstairs.

For tonight then I was safe. Tonight Morwenna would be with me and the house locked tight as a drum against the storm. And against whatever—whomever—else was outside. Again I thought of the storm as a blessing. No man could be lurking about in that—he would freeze to death. Zeke must have returned to Nansett—for now. Naturally he would not have been able to harm me this afternoon when the servants knew us to be together in the drawing room.

But he was planning to return to Thunder House tomorrow, and at my request! He was going to come back as soon as the storm abated to help me search the attics for Julia's body! He might be plotting to take me up to the attics and kill me there and then hide my body as he had hidden Julia's! I could insist the Morwenna accompany us and even Amos or Seth, but even with the two of them there, I didn't want to face Zeke again. It would be impossible for me to treat him with normal friendliness. And seeing that, he would wonder whether I suspected him of Julia's death. He knew I had read the journal and he might fear that there was something in it that made him a suspect in her disappearance. He would sense my fear of him . . . and that would make him desperate. I could not allow him in the house again. If he came back tomorrow, I would have Morwenna tell him I was indisposed. But that wasn't good enough. He would come again, and again I would refuse to receive him. And he would wonder why.

No, I could not wait for him to stalk me. Something had to be done tonight. Tonight I had to find proof that he was Julia's murderer. I could not wait until tomorrow or the day after—or until Nicholas returned. By the time he returned, I might be dead. If Zeke had his way; if I weren't very, very careful.

The servants would think I had taken leave of my senses but I no longer cared what they thought. It seemed years ago that I had been afraid of them and cared what they thought of me. Besides, if we succeeded in discovering something, the circumstances would speak for themselves.

I went back downstairs and saw Amos coming from Nicholas's library.

"Amos," I said, "I want you and Seth to get some oil lamps and come with me up to the attics."

The mild taciturn man was startled into saying with disbelief, "You want to go to the attics now, Mrs. Blaize? Tonight?"

I looked straight into his face. "That's what I said, Amos. It's very important. I can't tell you why now, but if we find what I believe we will, then I'll explain everything."

He was frowning stubbornly. "Don't you think you oughta go to bed, ma'am? We can go up there tomorrow, in daylight."

I nearly stamped my foot. "No! It must be tonight. Please do not argue with me any further. I'm not being fanciful. I haven't lost my wits. I have a very good reason for this request."

He regarded me somberly for a few more moments and then gave a slight nod. "I'll fetch Seth and the lamps."

"I'll wait for you both here."

I had no way of knowing if Julia's body had been hidden in the house but just now anything and everything seemed possible. I had considered so many conflicting assumptions that I felt it was time to stop thinking, to stop considering, and take action. Whether searching the attics on a stormy night was mad or not—well, that didn't matter when the whole world had gone mad. The fact that Zeke himself had mentioned her body might be stashed away somewhere did not reassure me. If she weren't hidden somewhere in the house, then surely the search of the island would have turned up a freshly dug grave, or some trace of her clothing washed up on the shore, *something.*

I waited impatiently, pacing up and down, until the two men came, each armed with an oil lamp and wearing a heavy jacket. They did not meet my gaze although Amos said as we ascended the staircase, "Ye'll be needin' a cloak or something, Mrs. Blaize. Colder than a backhouse, it'll be up there."

"Yes, I'll fetch one."

The men waited outside my room while I took my warmest cloak from its peg in the armoire and donned it. Then we walked to the end of the corridor to the door which led to the attics.

"Is this the only way to the attics?" I asked.

"No, ma'am, there's a staircase off the kitchen that goes to the top of the house."

Seth opened the door to reveal a shadowed narrow flight of stairs which wound its way up in darkness. A blast of cold air hit us as we began to ascend. I braced myself, buried my hands in my pockets, and followed the two men upstairs.

"Watch your step, ma'am. It's easy to miss your footin' and fall," said Seth just in front of me.

The wind was thunderous up there under the eaves. And suddenly there came a sound of pellets dropping, tapping, brisk and hard, from all directions.

"Sleet, that is," said Amos, and Seth nodded grimly.

"Better not snow," he said.

They held up their lamps and we surveyed the attic room. It was vast and cavernlike and very cold. Above our heads the eaves were shadowed, and beyond the light of the lamps was a yawning blackness.

I could make out shapes of trunks, boxes, furniture, tools, a jumble of large and small objects littering the wooden floor. I was filled with despair at the seeming hopelessness of the task. Where would we begin to look? It would take us hours to plunder this enormous storehouse. I was beginning to think I was being very foolish, maybe a little deranged, to insist on coming up here in the dead of night while the storm raged all around us and the frigid darkness sapped the energy and feeling from our limbs.

"If ye cud tell us what youh're lookin' fohr, ma'am," began Amos. "Somethin' of the captain's, is it?"

"No, no, it's nothing like that. But I can tell you it's something large which may have been hidden in a trunk or an old wardrobe. It *must* be here. I don't know where else to look . . . what else to do . . ." With difficulty I got a hold on myself. "Let's begin so we can get out of here as soon as possible."

The three of us started at a corner and moved outward. It was not as overwhelming a task as I had first assumed. We moved fairly rapidly as there were only several things here and there large enough to contain a body.

I felt sick at what we were doing but at least it helped to keep the stark terror somewhat at bay. I was safe with the two menservants. If we did find Julia's body, then such a discovery would lead to the proof of her murder and hopefully the identity of her murderer. That person would be brought to justice and could threaten me no longer. So even though I shivered from the fierce raw cold and cringed at the howling of the wind, I was at least taking action in my defense instead of cowering in my room. And waiting.

Still, it was a long bone-chilling job. The attics stretched the full length of the house though fortunately not the width. We covered ground as quickly as we could but the search went on a very long time. Both men wore gloves and mufflers; I kept my hands in the folds of my cloak. It

451

was just my fear and nervous energy that kept me from calling off the search. Our breath rose in shreds of vapor before us. The wind screamed like a banshee and the noise of the sleet on the roof sounded as though hundreds of them were dancing and leaping.

We opened trunks of old clothing, papers, ships' accounts, maps, ledgers, crockery. Each time they went to open a trunk or something similar, I'd steel myself for the gruesome discovery. But no hideous skeleton was revealed.

After a very long while—I had no way of knowing just how long we had been up there—Amos said firmly, "I think we oughta continue in the mawnin', ma'am. We've opened all the lahrge things we can. And it's just too dahrn cold to be up here any longer."

I sighed heavily. "You're right, Amos. I'm sorry I've kept the two of you up here for so long. Let's go down."

"It's not good for you either. The captain'd have a fit if he knew."

Dejectedly I went with them downstairs to the kitchen. Martha was still up and had mulled cider spiked with brandy for us simmering on the stove. We drank the hot soothing drink in silence and I could tell they were all wondering what had possessed me to insist on such a futile foolish expedition. And that was exactly what it had been.

I did not believe that continuing the search once daylight returned would do any good. Amos and Seth had opened trunk after trunk, wardrobe after wardrobe, cupboard after cupboard. It was clear, even in the semidarkness, that nothing in the attic had been disturbed in longer than the two and a half years since Julia's disappearance. We had covered the length of the attic and turned up nothing. I no longer knew what to think; no longer were my thoughts running on any sort of course the way they had in the past week or so. I could not see any pattern, any method in Julia's death, in the three attempts on my life; it was all a great horrible blur which I had ceased trying to interpret. I sat huddled in my cloak, sapped of the fearful excitement which had gripped me earlier.

Finally I rose and said, "Good night, all of you. And thank you."

"Will ye be wantin' to go up there tomorrow, ma'am?" asked Amos, willing but dubious.

"No, that won't be necessary. What I was looking for was apparently not up there. I just wish I knew where else to look. Where is Morwenna?"

"In your room, Mrs. Blaize," said Martha.

"Thank you. Good night." I trudged up the third floor to my bedroom. Morwenna was already asleep in the cot she had set up for herself but she awoke when I moved about the room.

"There 'ee be! What 'ee be doin' in that attic in the dead o' night?" she scolded sharply. " 'Ee could be sick and feverish from this night's work, don't 'ee know that?"

I just shook my head, tears stinging my eyes.

"Well, 'ee won't be doin' no more o' that, I do tell 'ee. I don't care what 'ee say next time. The master, he'd have my head if he knew I let 'ee go up there — and in this weather. I don't care what Amos do say the next time about you bein' the missus and we havin' to do as 'ee say. 'Ee don't know what's good for 'ee and that's a fact."

"Go to bed, Morwenna. We both need sleep."

"Aye, ma'am, we do that."

And before long I was warmed under the bedclothes and able to fall asleep. When I awoke in the morning, I could still hear the sleet striking the windowpanes but the wind had died down to a low murmur. I could tell it was late in the morning; I hoped that the servants had also slept longer than usual since I had kept most of them up until very late.

When Morwenna came in with my breakfast tray, I asked her, "Is the storm letting up any?"

"Amos did say he think it be passin' over, out to sea. But it still be bad. There be ice on all the branches and ground, like everything be covered with glass. I ain't seen nothin' like it afore."

"Morwenna, if Zeke Somes comes to the house today, he

453

is not to be admitted. And tell the men to make certain the house is still locked up.

Her eyes dropped. "Aye, ma'am."

"I know what you're thinking, Morwenna. You're thinking I've gone mad or something."

"Did that Zeke Somes bother 'ee in any way yesterday?"

"Let's just say that I don't trust him and I want to make certain he doesn't return to Thunder House while the captain is away."

"Don't 'ee worry your head on that account, Mrs. Blaize." My fear of Zeke making nefarious advances to me she could comprehend. Still she was faintly puzzled; that did not explain my visit to the attics last night.

"I'd like a bath now, Morwenna. And I'll wear the peacock blue gown with the organdy shawl collar. You can help me wash my hair too."

For over an hour we were occupied with my toilette and I found the mundane tasks comforting. That afternoon I sat by the fire in my bedroom reading one of Julia's books. Morwenna remained with me as I had asked her to do and did some mending.

I had reached the conclusion that there was nothing for me to do until Nicholas returned. As long as I was not alone for long periods, I felt safe. Morwenna reported that the air was freezing and the ground icy outside. Surely no one would make the trek from Nansett to Thunder House in this weather. I was secure for the time being and Nicholas would come back soon, perhaps at the storm's end. And then I could tell him everything and put the entire affair in his hands. The time had come for me to share all my questions and suspicions with him. Beyond that I did not think. I had no idea what would happen when he learned that he and Heather had shared the same father, but the time for concealing the truth was over. It had been kept secret too long.

And with his answers, whatever they were, with his awareness of the dark discovery I had made would come a release from the speculations which tormented and terrorized me. Perhaps together we could unravel the tangled strands from the past which lingered to envelop us while we groped in muddled attempts to make our way to the light.

The next day a pale watery sun rose above a tranquil blue sea which had no touch of green. The clouds had blown over the ocean; the sky was a hazy blue. On Thunder Island the ice was melting, the air was warming, the ground was thawing.

It was now difficult to imagine the way the sky had looked two days ago, darkly ominous, sullen, and the way the wind had sought to blow Thunder Island into the cove below. Yesterday a veneer of crystal had coated the outside world, even to the tiny needles of the spruce trees, but that was dissolving in the morning sun.

Still I was a raw bundle of nerves. The dramatic change in weather could only mean that Zeke would come to Thunder House today and expect me to admit him. And I could not see him. I could not speak to him calmly, rationally, all the while knowing it was he who had killed Julia and had been trying to kill me. Even if we met in the presence of one of the servants and I was perfectly safe, I would not be able to keep him from realizing that I suspected him. If only Nicholas would come home!

I was working on some of the mending I had put aside for Morwenna when she herself came to my room. When I saw her face, I knew instantly that something had happened. She looked worried and hesitant at the same time, as though there was something she knew she had to tell me but was reluctant to all the same.

"What is it, Morwenna?" Holding my breath, I winced as the point of the needle went into my thumb.

"I just came to tell 'ee, ma'am—"

"Yes?"

"Zeke Somes was here earlier this morning, asking for 'ee."

Oh God. "Did you speak to him?"

"Aye, Amos let him in and asked me to fetch 'ee but I

455

told them both 'ee was feelin' very poorly—too poorly to see anyone."

"What—what did he say?"

"Amos?"

"No! Zeke—what did Zeke say?"

"He said he be sorry and he be goin' to check his traps and 'd come back afore too long." ·

"Today? He said he would come back today?" I was almost shrieking. "Why didn't you tell me this before?"

She twisted her hands together. "I didn't want to worry 'ee, but I feared one of the others might say somethin' so I reckoned I better tell 'ee myself."

"He is not to be admitted to this house, Morwenna. I thought I had made that clear."

"Aye, ma'am." She was not looking at me, and her voice was subdued. "Martha asked me to ask 'ee where 'ee'd care to have your lunch."

I started to say that I didn't want any lunch, that at this point I didn't care whether I ever ate again. But that was foolish; I had to eat if only for the child's sake. "Well, on second thought I'm rather tired of trays in my room or eating alone in the dining room. I'd like to eat in the kitchen with the rest of you, if I may." I also would feel safer. ·

She smiled at that and we went downstairs together. When we reached the kitchen, the others were gathered around the table, the men hastily rising at my appearance.

"I want to thank you, Amos, and you, Seth, for accompanying me to the attics the other night. I know it seemed a very odd thing to ask of you, but I promise that when the captain returns, you'll understand why I requested you both to go up there with me."

They looked uncomfortable. "Weren't nothin', ma'am," said Seth.

"I hope you won't mind if I eat in here with all of you."

"Of course not, Mrs. Blaize," said Martha. "The captain does it from time to time." Amos pulled out a chair for me and Martha set down a bowl of steaming oyster stew at my place. "Amos was just sayin' the storm did damage to the stable roof, blowin' off shingles and such."

Amos nodded. "Left two good-sized holes in the roof. Yesterday the place was all puddles when I went in to feed the horses. We'll be needin' to fix them leaks after lunch, Seth."

I felt better sitting with them at the pine harvest table, eating the creamy stew and corn muffins. When we had finished, Martha cleared our plates and covered her mouth to stifle a yawn. "I oughta know better than to eat so heavy at noon," she said. "It always makes me sleepy."

I knew she wasn't sleepy from the meal but because I had kept her up so late the other night. "Why don't you have a nice long rest in your room this afternoon?" I suggested rather guiltily. "You, too, Morwenna." I was anxious to make amends for my shortness with her earlier.

They exchanged glances. "Well, I won't say no to that," said Martha. "Mary, Jenny, you girls can pluck those chickens for supper."

I was feeling rather weary myself and went up to my room. Locking my door, I lay down on the bed and before long had fallen asleep. What awakened me was a soft rapping at the door. Groggily I sat up, then my heart leaped. Could it be Nicholas? Not Zeke, I thought, terrified. Oh God, please not Zeke! I got up, smoothing my hair, and moved quickly to the door.

"Who is it?" I called softly. I was thinking that if it was Zeke, I could scream fit to bring the house down.

I was startled to hear a voice say, "It's only I, Miranda. Katherine."

"Oh, Katherine!" Hugely relieved, I hastily unlocked the door. She wore her black cloak and bonnet; her cheeks were rosy and her breathing rapid as though she had been hurrying. "Miranda, thank heaven," she said. "You're here and safe. For a moment I was afraid . . . I need to talk with you, my dear. I came as soon as I was able after the storm. Before that I had not put it all together in my mind. Or perhaps I've always known and refused to see the truth."

"What are you talking about, Katherine? Forgive me, I'm still a bit groggy." I shook my head.

"Oh my dear child, I'm so sorry to have to come to you like this. To think my own daughter, my own flesh and blood — but I mustn't shrink from the truth any longer. Miranda, I believe you are in very grave danger."

An icy cloak was wrapping itself about me. "What — what sort of danger?"

"Danger for your life, Miranda. You must put on your warmest cloak and come with me at once."

"Come with you — where?"

"To the place I've been earlier today. The very same place where I found her this morning."

"Found her? Do you mean Heather?"

She shook her head, her violet-blue eyes full of pain. "No, not Heather. Julia. Julia Blaize."

"Julia? Do you mean you've found her? Is she . . . she's not *alive?*"

Her lips trembled; she pressed them together. "No, I'm afraid she's not alive. She is dead, as everyone assumed."

"Where did you find her . . . her body?"

"In a cave on the far side of the island. A cave just above the place where the ocean shoots up from the chasm — do you know where I mean? There's a cave in the cliff across from Seal Island."

"I know where you are describing. Though I did not know of the existence of a cave."

"It's very difficult to find if you don't realize that it's there. It's a place that — that Heather has been fond of all her life. I used to beg her not to go there when she was younger; I was afraid that she might slip and fall from the cliff. But she never paid me any heed."

"Are you saying that Heather killed Julia and put her body there?"

"Yes, yes, that's what I'm saying. I can't believe it. But now I know that's exactly what happened. For this morning I found things of hers in that cave near Julia's . . .

458

remains . . . the tortoiseshell comb I gave her last Christmas; there was even a set of her paints there."

"So you believe she killed Julia in there or put her body in there once she was dead . . . and then she goes there from time to time to look at her handiwork?"

Katherine's face contorted; she turned away from me, her hand pressed to her mouth.

"What made you go to the cave today?" I asked.

"It was a wild notion I had. I hoped and prayed I wouldn't find — anything, but I knew I had to look."

"So Heather did kill Julia and she has been trying to kill me," I said softly. It had not been Zeke after all.

She began weeping in earnest into her handkerchief. "Oh Miranda, if only I was wrong about it all. But when you were trapped in the Folly, when I saw that that wedge had been placed under the door, I knew. Heather had gone out that day. She — she hadn't been out in some time; she had not been feeling well. But that day she left the manse. She must have hidden in the woods near Thunder House, hoping you would come out. And when you did, she followed you to the Folly and set the fire."

"It wasn't just the fire, Katherine. There were other times. You were there the second time, at the launching."

She looked up at me, startled. "The support structures. Oh my God. I never thought — but I suppose she could have done that. If only Nicholas were back!"

"Why do you say that?"

"Because he would know just what to do. I could leave everything . . . the arrangements . . . up to him. Something will have to be done with Heather. She knows I found the body today; she knows I know now. I'm afraid she will do something to conceal the body before anyone else has a chance to see it. I thought of going to the Reverend Whitcomb — but I can't, I just can't face anyone like that yet. I was hoping Nicholas would come back today so I could show him the body and then there would be proof that she had done it."

"But what about Amos or Seth? We could get one of

them to go with you and see it."

She shook her head. "No, not yet. I know the gossiping will start soon enough but I don't want it to begin yet. I need you to come with me, to see for yourself. And it's safer if you are with me—she may come to the house even today. She's very clever, she could easily find a way to slip in without anyone seeing her and come up here to your room."

"But if she tried to harm me, if she killed me even, everyone would know it was not an accident. She couldn't possibly get away with it!"

"She's not thinking clearly these days. I've watched her slip more and more into a—a fantasy world lately. The best thing for you to do is to come with me to the cave so there is another witness to her . . . to what she's done. And then after that I suppose we must go to the Reverend Whitcomb. Later then if the body is missing, he at least will not think I've taken leave of my senses. If both of us go to him and tell him how dangerous she is . . ."

"Of course I'll go with you, Katherine. And then we'll go to Nansett—perhaps Nicholas will come later today. Just let me get my things."

I took my cloak and bonnet from the armoire and put them on. Katherine was calmer now but her eyes were red from weeping.

"Let me just go through the kitchen and tell Jenny or Mary that's I'm going out."

"Oh Miranda, please, let's not. They'll all know soon enough—and I can't face anyone just now, not yet."

"But one of them must have let you in," I pointed out.

She shook her head. "No, I saw them go over to the stables and then I went in the kitchen door. I could not let them see me like this, in this state. My own maid Janet is already wondering what on earth is afflicting me—I don't want them gossiping about me too."

She did look totally unlike her normal poised self. I had never seen her so distraught. She gave a sound between a laugh and a sob. "I didn't even know which room was yours. I've knocked on most of the doors on this corridor."

We went into the hall and I turned to the left but she laid a hand on my arm. "Not the central staircase. There must be another we can use."

"Well, yes, there's another at the end of this hall."

"Let's take that." She took my arm and we went down the narrow stairway and then left the house by the door on the south side. "Come, we must hurry," she said, and we went into the woods, her hand clutching my arm.

We walked rapidly through the forest. The mud was deep in places and my shoes became quickly coated with it and dead leaves. It was cold. Several times I had to pause to catch my breath.

"How are you feeling, Miranda? It was very bad of me to bring you out like this but with Nicholas gone there wasn't anyone else I felt I could share—all of this—with yet. But I wasn't thinking. I'd almost forgotten about the baby. I'd never forgive myself if something happened to it."

"As something happened to Heather's?" I asked quietly.

She jerked her face to me, her eyes widening. "You knew about that? You knew Heather was carrying a child? And that she lost it . . . how?"

"I overheard her telling Nicholas at the ball that she was pregnant. I also realized he had to be the father," I said bleakly.

We were walking again but not as quickly now. She had realized I could not keep up her pace.

"How did you know she had lost it? I didn't think anyone knew."

"I came to your house that day . . . didn't your maid tell you? From what she said about Heather's illness, I just assumed that's what had happened. It was only a guess, though. And that is not all I know, Katherine. I know enough to know that it was a blessing that she lost that baby."

"What—what do you mean?" she asked distractedly.

"Do you know *why* Heather killed Julia Blaize? Because

461

Julia had learned whose daughter Heather really was. And she told her and that's when Heather must have killed her. You see, I read Julia's journal. She knew all about . . . about you and Roger Blaize."

"Miranda, what are you saying? Yes, Roger Blaize and I were lovers. But he was not Heather's father. I swear to you. If Roger were alive today, he could confirm what I say. The times Roger and I—met—were few and far between. There is no doubt in my mind that Bruce was Heather's father."

"But Julia found a letter from Roger to you. She thought—she calculated that Heather was conceived soon after—"

"I thought I had destroyed all of Roger's letters! Where did she find it, do you know?"

"In the Folly, at the back of a drawer in the desk."

"That was where we used to leave messages for one another. I don't see how I could have left it there, unless I never found it, unless it was the last one he wrote. We decided we could not go on—he hated deceiving Bruce and Lavinia. He was very fond of my husband, and Lavinia he had loved when they were first married. He told me he could not see me any longer . . . in that way. And it was sometime later that I became pregnant with Heather. There was no chance in the world that Roger could have been Heather's father. I cannot possibly be mistaken about that. Do you think for an instant that I could have permitted any sort of special fondness to grow between Heather and Nicholas if there were the slightest chance, even the slightest, that they were half-brother and sister? I did a terrible thing in my youth, deceiving my husband in the worst way possible, but there is no way I could condone anything so monstrous!"

"But then—why did Heather kill Julia, if not to stop her from telling Nicholas, if it wasn't true?"

"The only reason I can imagine is that she feared that Nicholas wouldn't believe her—or me—if it became known we had been lovers, no matter much I swore she was

462

Bruce's child. She had to stop Julia from telling him because the knowledge might have—tainted his feelings for her. My poor girl, it's not as though she's normal. Her mind does not work like other people's. She has always loved Nicholas, loved him to obsession. It began years ago. That time on Seal Island when they were stranded—I believed even then that she had seen to that deliberately, hoping to trap him into marriage or something. I thought later, when he returned from the Arctic last year, I thought she had accepted that he was no longer interested in her. And then when he married you, I was greatly relieved. God help me, I assumed she would finally put those feelings behind her."

"But sometime recently they began seeing each other again."

"I hoped you didn't know, Miranda, although I suspected something. And then when I discovered that she was with child, she broke down and confessed it was Nicholas's."

I closed my eyes as the pain of her words shot through me. I felt weighted down with it, consumed, leaden.

"You love him too," she said sadly.

I nodded. "I hoped . . . but I suppose it's always been Heather—he just didn't realize it fully before."

"If only I could spare you all this, but it must come out somehow. And perhaps it's better hearing it first from me. But we must hurry." She secured my arm in her own and we continued on the path until we reached Blackett's Glade. There we took another trail leading away from the swamp and followed that to the lake, which glinted in the afternoon sun.

Finally I broke the long silence between us. "So Heather has been trying to murder me since I came. Why, did she think Nicholas would marry her?"

"I don't know what goes on in that mind of hers. She doesn't confide in me at all. So much of this I'm just deducing. But I daresay when he came back with you she couldn't contain her jealousy. The man she loved had

463

married another, the man she had killed Julia for because she saw Julia as a threat to their relationship."

"But you realized none of this until the fire the other day?"

"No, I blame myself entirely. If I had seen . . . if I had only realized . . . perhaps I even could have saved Julia. That is why I am determined that you shall come to no harm." She was quietly weeping again.

We were traversing the long meadow, no longer green and lush, but ash yellow and soggy from the thawed sleet. I could hear the sound of gulls; we were nearing the island's edge. The sun slanted through the trees. I squinted, hating its harsh naked light.

"So Noah must have suspected something . . . he must have seen Heather the day Julia disappeared. She must have first threatened him to keep silence but then when she was no longer sure of him she must have gone to the lighthouse and stabbed him."

"No! I can't believe she would . . ." Her voice drained away. "But I daresay that's as likely as all the rest. I had forgotten about Noah."

The wind was blowing in our faces, salty and brisk. Up ahead I caught glimpses of the blue horizon of ocean. The thundering sound grew as we neared the cliff above the chasm where the surf surged fifty feet into the air. Soon we would creep into the cave beneath the cliff's summit and I would have to view what was left of Julia. I pressed my hand to my mouth.

But surely now I had nothing to fear. Katherine would protect me from Heather, and together we would tell Nicholas about her when he returned. At least I now knew their relationship, whatever it had been, was not an incestuous one.

"I've been so frightened," I said, "and never certain of whom to trust. Yesterday and the day before I had convinced myself that Zeke had killed Julia and sought to kill me."

"I can imagine what you have been going through,

Miranda. I'm sorry I couldn't—or wouldn't—realize any of this sooner. I would have warned you, I would have told Nicholas what I suspected. They say a husband or wife is always the last to know. In this case it was the mother who was blind. But what you must have felt all this time . . . ever since the boulder nearly struck you down."

"At first I didn't see that as an attempt on my life. I even convinced myself that the ship's support structure toppling over that way had been an accident. It wasn't until I was almost killed in the Folly that I realized someone all along had wished me harm." I caught my breath, tensing. The wind was blowing in frigid waves over me. I was turning to ice, to stone.

The boulder. I had not mentioned the episode of the boulder to Katherine; I had only referred to the ship's structures, not the boulder tumbling down the slope of Bald Mountain. Then how had she learned of it? By her own words Heather had not confided in her. How on earth did she know about the boulder almost striking me?

The only way she could have known was if she had been there herself. If she herself had dislodged the huge stone and sent it rolling down and into my path. She had been there, just as she had been near the Folly at the time of the fire. She had been the one to wedge the door shut; she had been the one to set the fire. She had admitted seeing Amos working at the graveyard; she must also have been seen by him and knew she would be suspected in the aftermath. So, in the guise of a rescuer, she had hurried to tell him the Folly was on fire. Together they had raced through the woods to the old cottage, Katherine just a little ways ahead so she would have time to remove the wedge from under the door and let me out. She had saved me so she could not seriously be suspected of my death should it occur at a later time.

"We're nearly there, Miranda. I know you're tired; I know this was a great deal to ask of you but we're nearly there now. And then you will see for yourself." Her voice came from far off, muffled in the swarming fears inside

465

me. "Why are you stopping? Come on, Miranda, before Heather returns."

"It is not Heather I am afraid of, Katherine," I said, my voice strangely steady. I had to keep her talking while I looked for my chance of escape. Because soon we would reach the cliff's edge and she would send me over, falling into that torrent of water which would then toss my body like a piece of driftwood into the embrace of the sea.

"Julia came to see you, didn't she, Katherine? She never saw Heather at all. She went to the manse and Heather was not there, so instead she told you what she had discovered, what she supposed was the truth about Heather's birth."

Katherine's expression did not undergo any change. Her eyes were still full of pity; her lips still trembled. "I told her the truth. I told her they were not related. I did everything I could to convince her. I even took Bruce's family Bible and swore on it. But I could see she still didn't believe me. She didn't want to believe me. She hated me because she knew I had helped her father betray her mother and so she was determined to hurt me. She was still going to tell Nicholas that she believed Heather was possibly Roger's child. And then no matter what my protestations were, he might have harbored doubts which would have turned him from Heather. He was never really in love with her, you know. But she was beautiful and they had always been fond of one another; even his parents condoned a match between them. Roger told me once, years after our affair was over, that his fondest wish was that they should be married, that they could have the life together that we never had. The life I had always wanted to have with Roger.

"It was my curse that we met after we were both married. I knew I could never have all that Lavinia had. I would think of her as mistress of Thunder House, surrounded by all that was beautiful and splendid, never wanting for anything, while I counted the pennies Bruce's salary provided, trying to stretch them as far as I could, having to make all my clothes myself instead of ordering gowns the way Lavinia did, having to be content with jewelry made of jet and mother-of-pearl while Lavinia wore diamonds and rubies and sapphires. We would dine with them in the early days, in that magnificent house with all those priceless things and I would sit in the simple gown I had made listening to her talk about her shopping spree in Boston, her crystal that came from Ireland, the trouble she had with servants with a house as large as that to take care of. And the irony of it was that she wasn't happy—none of it made her happy. I would have given anything to be in her place, to live in that house, to call all those precious possessions mine. But I had grown up a poor minister's daughter and it was my lot to marry an impoverished minister when I've always wanted to have beautiful things and the life that went with them."

Her hand was pressing into my arm. The surf boomed nearby, shaking the ground with its intensity.

"And since you weren't able to have that life for yourself, you wanted Heather to," I said. "You wanted Heather to marry Nicholas so she could live in Thunder House as its mistress, so you could have lived there too if you chose."

"It would have worked out so well, so beautifully, don't you see that? It was what I had planned all the years of Heather's life after Roger and I had stopped meeting the way we had. It was the only thing which got me through. But Julia would have ruined it. There would have been no hope of Nicholas marrying Heather if she told him about Roger and me—even though Heather was Bruce's child."

"But then when he returned he made no proposal of marriage," I said deliberately.

"I did not give up hope. He was sewing his wild oats, like many young men. He was in love with the sea, fascinated with whaling. But I knew eventually he would return and marry her. I had imagined it so many times, and such a thing had to make it so."

"Yet when he did return from his last voyage, I understand he had nothing to do with her, he did not seek her out."

"That was a temporary thing, I was certain. How could he not turn to Heather? She was so beautiful, so lovely, what man could resist her? Just the way I used to be when Roger could not resist me, until the guilt became too much for him."

"But Nicholas married me instead, didn't he?"

Her eyes narrowed. "I had never considered Nicholas a fool until then. But when I heard he had come back with a wife, a girl taking my Heather's rightful place, I could quite easily have killed him. Though that would have defeated my purpose, wouldn't it?" Her smile was wry; it invited me to smile with her. It was horrible.

"Do you think that when I'm gone, Nicholas will marry Heather?" I asked.

"Of course. She nearly spoiled everything with that sailor, that common sailor, but thank heaven she lost his baby."

"What sailor? Are you saying that her child was not Nicholas's?"

"Her child was Jack Bourne's," Katherine replied with disgust. "She confessed she had been meeting him whenever his ship docked at Thunder Island to pick up lumber. They would meet in the Folly, she said, just as Roger and I used to. I slapped her face when she said that. It was never like Roger and me. A common scoundrel like that—how could it be the same?—what sort of life could he give her? An even worse one than Bruce had given me."

I was suddenly light-headed with joy. Nicholas was not the father of Heather's baby; he was not the man Sarah had claimed to see her with at the Folly. But I had to keep her talking. "Tell me about Noah, Katherine."

"Noah?"

"Yes. You went to the lighthouse after the ball, didn't you?"

"Heather went back to Nansett with Mr. Whitcomb and some other young people. I had told her I would walk

468

back with another of the women. I had heard Noah talking to you when you were dancing with him. He was beginning to hint at what he suspected about Julia Blaize."

"Just what did he suspect?"

"He had taken the path from the lighthouse along the shore, under the cliff. He had looked up and seen us together. I couldn't be certain if he recognized us but I could not take that chance. Julia didn't see him; her back was to the shore. He went around the cove and disappeared from view, but he had seen us together whether he had identified us then or not.

"After Julia was dead I went to his lighthouse on the pretext of bringing him a basket of food and I told him that perhaps Nicholas, when he returned, should consider replacing him. I sounded sympathetic, caring. I said, 'I think it's become too much for you, Noah. I could speak to Captain Nicholas and recommend that you be dismissed for your own good, for your health.' And tears sprang to his eyes and he took my hand, wringing it, begging me not to say anything to Nicholas. We understood one another very well, I saw immediately. He knew that if he mentioned he had seen me with Julia on the day she disappeared, I would see that he lost his position as keeper. He had more to lose than did I. So what if I had met her? There was no proof that I had had anything to do with her death. He knew that he had better keep quiet if he wanted to keep his job. Of course, I couldn't have persuaded Nicholas to make him retire, but I made him believe that I could."

"And then when I came, you began to worry that he wouldn't keep quiet much longer."

"I didn't want to kill Noah, Miranda, truly I didn't," she said sadly, her eyes pleading that I understand. "But what other choice did I have? He might have come forward with what he had seen despite his fear of being dismissed. And I knew he suspected that the support structures had not collapsed on their own. It wouldn't have been much longer before he confided to you what he knew and you told

469

Nicholas and perhaps linked me with the first two attempts on your life. The night of the ball gave me a perfect opportunity. I stole his money so everyone would assume one or more of the sailors had done it."

"All those lessons you gave me, Katherine! How difficult it must have been for you, hating me the way you must have."

"Oh, I never hated you, Miranda. How could I? You were the daughter of a minister just as I was. But you had been fortunate—you had married a wealthy man and left that sort of life. Still you should never have married Nicholas. Nicholas has always been meant for Heather."

"What exactly happened to Julia, Katherine?"

Her hold on my arm grew stronger; her face was close to mine. "I pushed her off that cliff just there. It would have looked as though she had fallen whether they found her body or not. I had begged her to meet with Heather, to tell her what she had learned. She agreed readily. She *wanted* to see Heather, to slander me to my daughter. She wanted to tell her that she planned to tell Nicholas on his return that Roger and I had had an affair. So she agreed to meet Heather here the following day. But it was not Heather who came. I pushed her off before she even suspected that I would do such a thing. It took her totally by surprise; she had thought she was in control of everything, that everyone danced to her tune. That was why she didn't scream . . . and the surge would have drowned out her screams anyway, the way it will drown out yours."

This was what I had been waiting for all along. I had talked, I had encouraged her to talk so that I could gather my strength, the strength I had lost on that long hurried trek across Thunder Island. And learning that Nicholas was not Heather's lover, had never been Heather's lover, had swept away the leaden depression. I would not let her push me over the cliff; I would not be taken by surprise the way Julia had; I would fight her with every nerve and muscle and bone and sinew inside me.

I wrenched out of her grasp but she quickly caught me

470

again and I struggled to free myself as she edged us closer to the cliff. The sound of the surf was deafening yet I heard her desperate ragged breathing. She was taller than I, and stronger, but I was invigorated with the knowledge that my husband had never wished me dead, that he did not love Heather nor she him. My heart was pounding, my body was coldly sweating, but somehow the terror that had consumed me in the burning Folly was held at bay. I was fighting for my life, for my love, for my child, and this pathetic demented woman was not going to take them from me.

We were at the edge now and I caught sight of the massive surges which towered up the wall of the cliff; I felt the drops of spray on my face. Digging in my heels, I gave a sudden twist with all my energy. But her hold on me did not weaken. Her arm came around my neck and she was forcing my head down. I saw the torrents of water reaching up to me; I tasted the salt on my lips. With an effort I closed my eyes from the sight and kicked backward with the heel of my boot. It took her unawares and she cried out so that I was able to wrench away from her. But as I was moving away from the shore, she caught my cloak and was now dragging me back, pulling on the hood of it so that it was choking me, urging me backward to the cliff's edge. I was going to fall; she was going to yank me back until I lost my balance and tumbled to the water and rocks below.

"Miranda!" came a voice, a voice I knew and loved, and I heard Katherine gasp and start. With everything I had, I caught my cloak under my chin with both my hands and then jerked forward, away from her, away from the cliff. And the sky was split with a cry more terrifying, more horrible, than anything I had ever heard. Over my shoulder I saw Katherine stumble backward, teeter on the cliff's edge, her arms flailing, flapping, her cloak billowing out around her. And then she was gone.

Nicholas's arms came around me and I thought I would be crushed by the force of them. "Oh Miranda, my dearest

471

love," he was saying, his lips pressing against my hair, his woolen cloak scratching my face. "I thought I was too late, I almost was too late. I couldn't get to the two of you fast enough—"

He had come on horseback; the horse was some feet away. "How did you know to come here, Nicholas? No one saw me leave the house with Katherine. She made certain of that, and I didn't even think . . . she had always been like a mother to me."

"I would have returned days earlier if it had not been for that storm. I had promised Heather that I would try and locate Jack Bourne for her to let him know she was carrying his child. She had given me a letter to give him when I left to make inquiries about the crew of the *Marianne*. I learned he is away on a voyage to the Caribbean. Then I went to Portland and obtained a list of the crew and was going to urge the authorities to order the ship stopped as soon as possible. But a feeling gradually came upon me that Noah's killer wasn't from that ship. It began to look as if someone had used their presence in Nansett that night for his or her own purposes. I wondered how strangers to Thunder Island could walk six or more miles through the dark forest from Nansett, not meeting anyone returning from the ball, which was very odd in itself, and go to the lighthouse where Noah kept some money hidden. It began to seem more and more unlikely to me that that was what had happened. And so I began to wonder if anyone in Nansett would have wanted Noah dead. God help me, it never occurred to me that you might be in danger from the same person."

I leaned against his broad chest. "Katherine had told him that he would lose his position as lighthouse keeper, that she would tell you he was too old and infirm to man the lighthouse if he told anyone that he had seen her with Julia on the day of her disappearance. She killed Julia, Nicholas, just as she tried several times to kill me."

"Yes, I know. Unbelievably enough, it was Zeke Somes who sent me here."

"Zeke?"

He nodded grimly. "I can't say that when I saw him coming toward me at the dock after I'd disembarked that I was happy to see him, or eager to listen to anything he might say. But the hard truth is if he had not drawn certain conclusions in his mind and come to me with them, then Katherine might very well have succeeded in sending you over that cliff."

"What did Zeke tell you?"

"It seems he came to Thunder House earlier today and then saw Katherine hovering near the house, in the woods. He couldn't understand why she'd be doing such a thing, just standing there looking—he watched her for a while without her noticing him. He said he was remembering how frightened you'd been lately and he knew about the attempts on your life. When Katherine finally left he decided to follow her, but more out of curiosity than actual suspicion. You and he had apparently suspected Heather."

"That's right, we had."

"Zeke followed Katherine to this spot and watched her climb to the cave just below."

"So there is a cave!"

He nodded, frowning. "And Zeke told me what he found inside the cave."

"Not Julia! Julia fell over the cliff."

"No, not Julia, but something he recognized which had belonged to Julia, a brooch which had obviously been torn off, probably as she fell. When Katherine left, Zeke himself looked into the cave and found the brooch. He assumed Katherine had gone back to Nansett so he went after her, taking the brooch with which to confront her. But she wasn't at the manse so he feared she had gone to Thunder House to seek you out. He was going to go after her when he saw the ship docking in the harbor and me coming ashore. When he told me about the Folly burning with you inside and showed me the brooch, I took Ben's horse and rode to the house as fast as I could. But you

473

weren't there and no one had seen you leave. I remembered the cliff, the cave, and I rode here, nearly out of my mind, wondering if I would find you, terrified that my hunch was wrong and she hadn't led you here or terrified that she had and I would be too late. When I saw the two of you struggling, I knew I might not reach you in time so I shouted, hoping to startle Katherine. It was my only chance."

"You did startle her," I said, shuddering.

"Don't think of it now, Miranda. Don't think of any of it any longer. You're safe now. Katherine is dead and can no longer try to hurt you. And I'll never let anything touch you again."

"Oh Nicholas, the terrible things I've thought about you! I thought you and Heather were lovers, Sarah had told me you were, you see, and I had seen the two of you in the woods talking one day. And she keeps a portrait of you in her studio. I thought it was your child she was carrying, I even wondered at times if you were working with her to try and murder me. I knew you didn't love me, you see, and so I—"

He took my shoulders in a hard grip and held me away from him, frowning down at me. "You knew I didn't love you? That's rich! I've loved you to distraction since first seeing you at the Bethel that day. You were the answer to a prayer although at first I refused to see that. And then you made it clear that you had only married me to save yourself from Sears and wanted nothing to do with me. I wanted so desperately to touch you, to make love to you, but more often than not I was rebuffed, rejected in no uncertain terms. Every time I hoped you were beginning to change toward me, every time you seemed to welcome any demonstration of the love I had for you, you would just as abruptly draw away again, hold yourself off from me. I've gone crazy pacing night after night in my room, or roaming about outside wondering if you would ever come to share my feelings, if you would ever come to welcome my embrace for more than a brief period here and there.

474

You blew hot and cold so I never knew what to think, what to expect. I convinced myself I hated you at times, hated your interference — the way you told me I should get rid of all the things from the *Eagle*, the way your lovely face could make me feel. I resented you while I was head over heels in love with you. And then when I did get rid of those things, then I didn't get the response I longed for. I resented you because you didn't feel the same way about me, you wouldn't allow me to love you and cherish you the way I wanted to, the way I tried to do on cursedly few occasions. I knew you were shy, uncertain of everything when we married, that you knew nothing of me. I had resolved not to touch you until you were ready for me to love you, but then that night on the ship when you had had too much to drink, you were so warm and sweet and not nearly so nervous when I held you and I couldn't stop myself from making you mine. The next morning I knew I'd made a mistake I might regret for a long time because you were ashamed of what we had done. But I was angry with you also — and hurt. I hoped you'd come around, that you'd grow to like me, that you'd stop looking at me as though you were terrified of me. I was afraid you feared me in the same way you'd feared that clod, Sears. So I tried to stay away from you as much as I could, hoping you'd get used to me gradually. Most of the time you were so distant, so diffident with me. I knew you weren't happy here; I knew my mother and Sarah were doing their best to make life hell for you. I felt very guilty for marrying you and bringing you to Thunder House the way it was. I thought it was another disastrous mistake I had made. It was obvious to me you weren't learning to love me, in spite of what I had thought on certain occasions. And then when you met Zeke Somes in the glade that day and it seemed to me you were growing fond of him — well, I wanted to strangle the both of you. I was afraid you regretted the child coming, you blamed me, you didn't want our baby. I was afraid to show you the intense joy I felt because I was afraid you would make it plain you felt very differently. I wanted to tell you how I felt, how much I had always loved you, how happy I was about the baby, how my life had changed so much after I married you, but I thought you wouldn't want to hear any of those things from me."

"Oh Nicholas," I said between tears and laughter, "you were so wrong, we were both so wrong. I thought you regretted your hasty impulse in marrying me, I thought you wished me at Jericho! Sarah told me you had always been in love with Heather and I believed her. I could not believe that you could have fallen in love with me. When I overheard the two of you together at the ball that night, I was convinced she was your mistress. Zeke was there, too, and that was why we met at the glade the next day. He was trying to comfort me—"

"Comfort you?" he said, scowling. "Heather means nothing to me in the way that you thought. She had painted that portrait of me years ago and I no longer wanted it. You have no need of his comfort! Still, though, I owe him more than I can ever repay. I told him so. It was—difficult—for both of us. We'll have to send word to him, and to Emily and Ben, that you're all right. The entire village is probably agog. I wish the truth could somehow be kept from Heather, but perhaps it's better this way. When Jack Bourne returns, she'll be able to marry him as she feared doing while her mother was alive. She knew Katherine never considered Jack good enough for her—she talked to me about it. But now she can go away with him, away from all of this here."

I shook my head, smiling. "And all this time I thought you were in love with her. But now that I know you love me I'll never need anything else, Nicholas. It's all I've always wanted—and what I always thought was beyond my grasp."

"Well, what about you?" he asked, his black brows drawn together.

"What about me?"

"I've been waiting for you to tell me what I've told you,

476

what I've hungered to hear from your lips for the last three months."

I flushed. "Oh Nicholas, I do love you. I was terribly nervous around you for a long time, but now I realize that was due to the effect you had on me, the feelings you aroused in me. I was afraid to trust you — and myself. I've been so miserable for such a long time, thinking you'd gone back to Heather and would never come to love me."

"Silly child," he murmured. And then his mouth came down on mine, ravenous, seeking the response which flowed from me to him, from him to me, like the powerful surge of spray mere yards away from us. Now there were no more barriers, no secrets, no doubts to come between us and torment us. And then he lifted me in his arms and carried me over to where the horse waited to take us home, to the only home I had ever wanted, to the only life I had ever wanted.

THE BEST IN REGENCIES FROM ZEBRA

PASSION'S LADY   (1545, $2.95)
by Sara Blayne
She was a charming rogue, an impish child—and a maddeningly alluring
woman. If the Earl of Shayle knew little else about her, he knew she was
going to marry him. As a bride, Marie found a temporary hiding place
from her past, but could not escape from the Earl's shrewd questions—or
the spark of passion in his eyes.

AN ELIGIBLE BRIDE   (2020, $3.95)
by Janice Bennett
The duke of Halliford was in the country for one reason—to fulfill a
promise to look after Captain Carstairs' children. This was as distasteful
as finding a suitable wife. But his problems were answered when he saw
the beautiful Helena Carstairs. The duke was not above resorting to some
very persuasive means to get what he wanted . . .

RECKLESS HEART   (1679, $2.50)
by Lois Arvin Walker
Rebecca had met her match in the notorious Earl of Compton. Not only
did he decline the invitation to her soiree, but he found it amusing when
her horse landed her in the middle of Compton Creek. If this was another
female scheme to lure him into marriage the Earl swore Rebecca would
soon learn she had the wrong man, a man with a blackened reputation.

BELOVED AVENGER   (2192, $3.95)
by Mary Brendan
Emily shivered at the sight of the thin scar on the sardonically handsome
features of Sir Clifford Moore. She knew then that he would never forget
what her family had done to him . . . and that he would take his revenge
any way he could. This time it was Moore that held the power—and Emily
was in no position to defy his wishes, whatever they might be . . .

SWEET TEMPEST   (2143, $3.95)
by Lauren Giddings
Despite his reputation as an unscrupulous rake, Amberson was not a man
likely to shoot a woman—even if she *was* dressed like a ragamuffin and
intent on robbing his coach. So his remorse was considerable when he discovered that the highwayman he'd wounded was actually a beauty named
Tempest. Letting her out of his sight would be unbearable, turning her
over to the authorities, unthinkable. So the cynical lord did the only thing
possible . . . he took her to his bed.

*Available wherever paperbacks are sold, or order direct from the
Publisher. Send cover price plus 50¢ per copy for mailing and
handling to Zebra Books, Dept. 2218, 475 Park Avenue South,
New York, N.Y. 10016. Residents of New York, New Jersey and
Pennsylvania must include sales tax. DO NOT SEND CASH.*